SONIC™ THE HEDGEHOG

URBAN WARFARE

SEGA®

IDW

@IDWpublishing
IDWpublishing.com

Cover Artist:
Aaron Hammerstrom

Series Editors:
Riley Farmer and David Mariotte

Collection Editor:
Alonzo Simon

Collection Group Editor:
Kris Simon

Collection Designer:
Amauri Osorio

ISBN: 979-88-87240-41-1 26 25 24 23 1 2 3 4

Originally published as SONIC THE HEDGEHOG issues #57–61.

Davidi Jonas, CEO
Amber Huerta, COO
Mark Doyle, Co-Publisher
Tara McCrillis, Co-Publisher
Jamie S. Rich, Editor-In-Chief
Scott Dunbier, VP Special Projects
Sean Brice, Sr. Director Sales & Marketing
Lauren LePera, Sr. Managing Editor
Shauna Monteforte, Sr. Director of Manufacturing Operations
Jamie Miller, Director Publishing Operations
Greg Foreman, Director DTC Sales & Operations
Nathan Widick, Director of Design
Neil Uyetake, Sr. Art Director, Design & Production

Ted Adams and Robbie Robbins, IDW Founders

Special thanks to Mai Kiyotaki, Afia Khan, Michael Cisneros, Sandra Jo, Sonic Team, and everyone at Sega for their invaluable assistance.

For international rights, contact licensing@idwpublishing.com

SEGA®

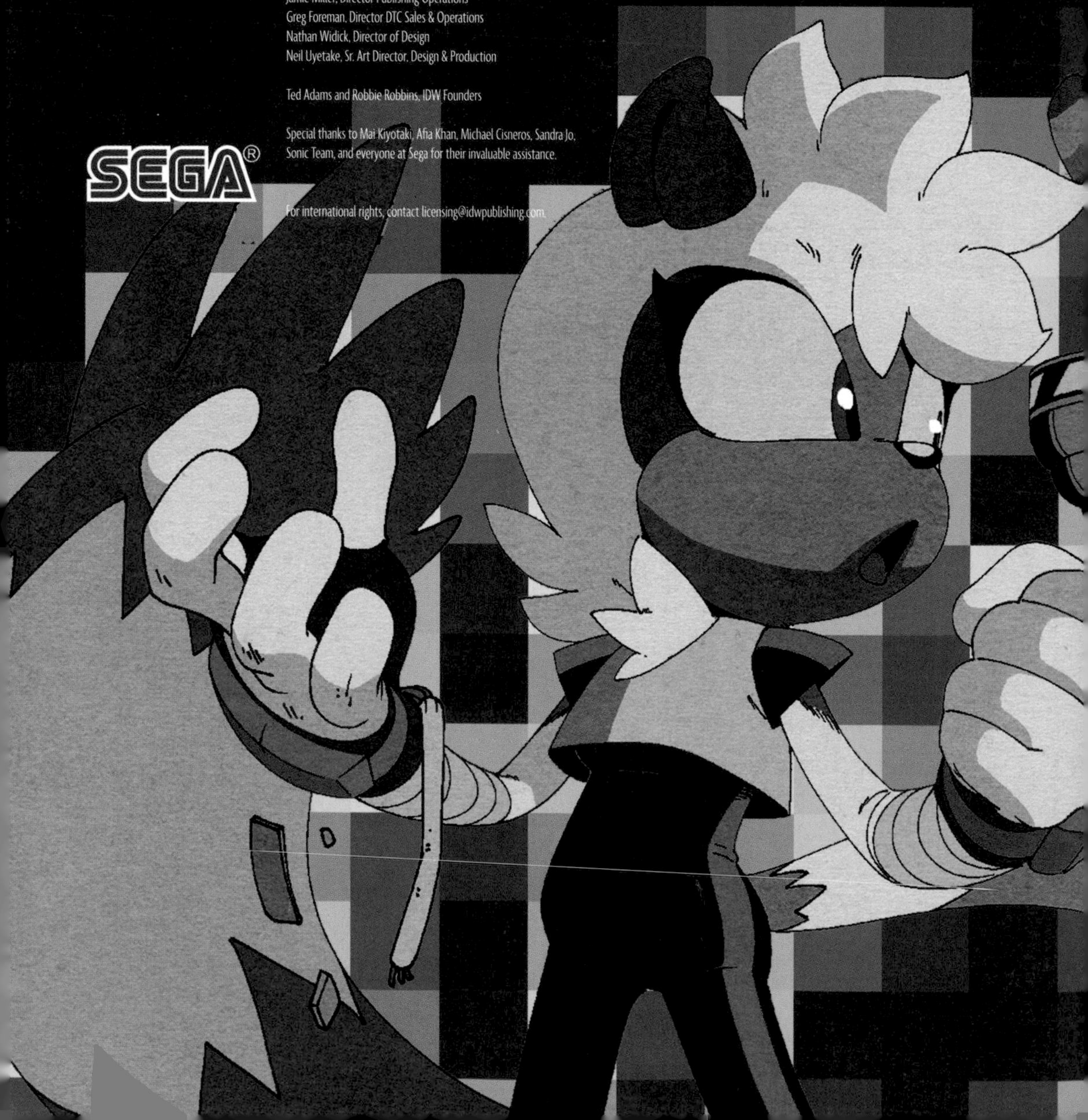

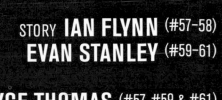

STORY **IAN FLYNN** (#57-58)
EVAN STANLEY (#59-61)

ART **ADAM BRYCE THOMAS** (#57, #59 & #61)
THOMAS ROTHLISBERGER (#58 & #60)

COLORS **MATT HERMS** (#57-58)
VALENTINA PINTO (#59 & #61)
JOHN-PAUL BOVE (#60)
RIK MACK (#61)
COLORS ASSISTS **ED PIRRIE** (#60)

LETTERS **SHAWN LEE**

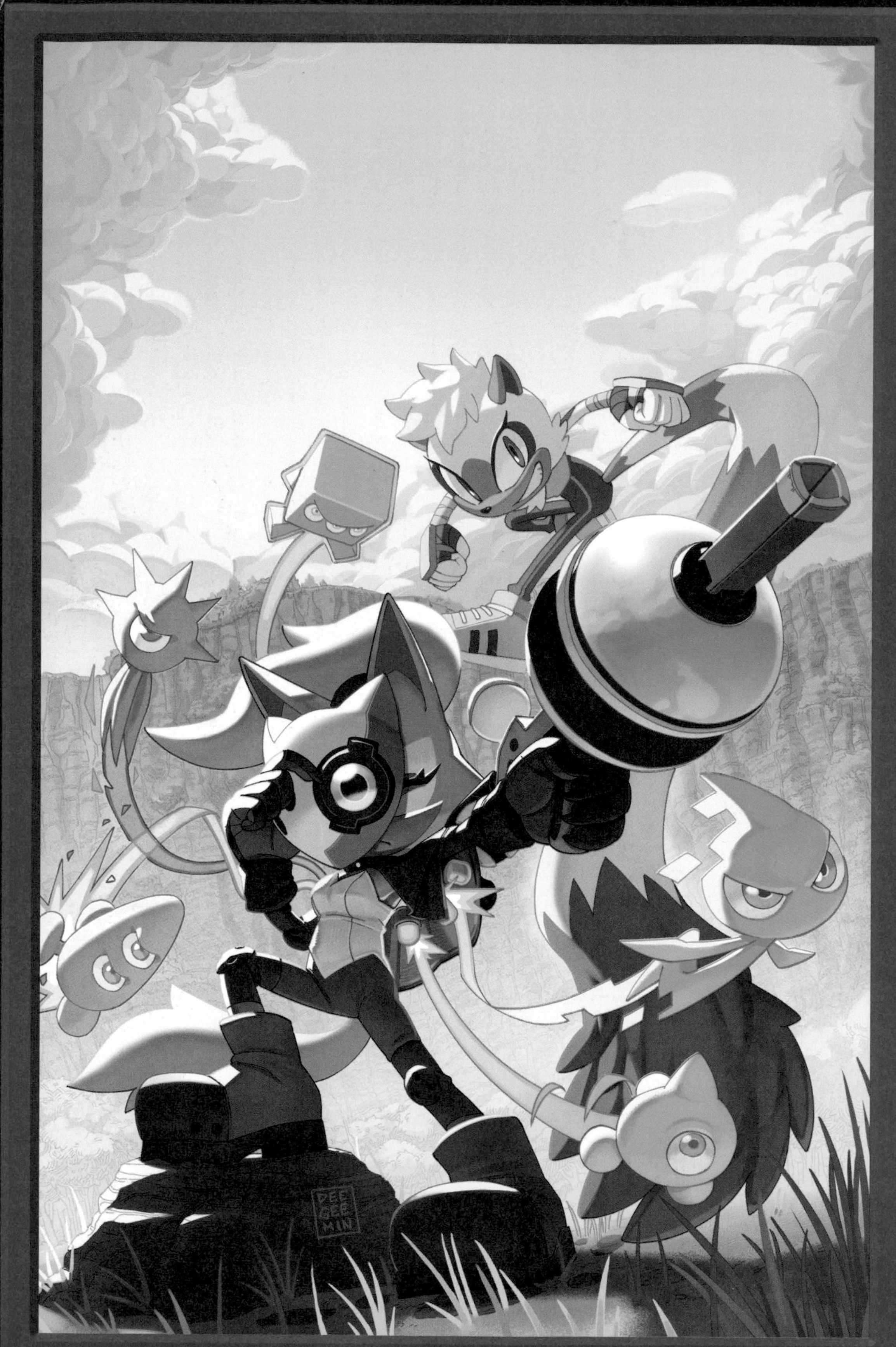
DEE GEE MIN

ART BY MIN HO KIM

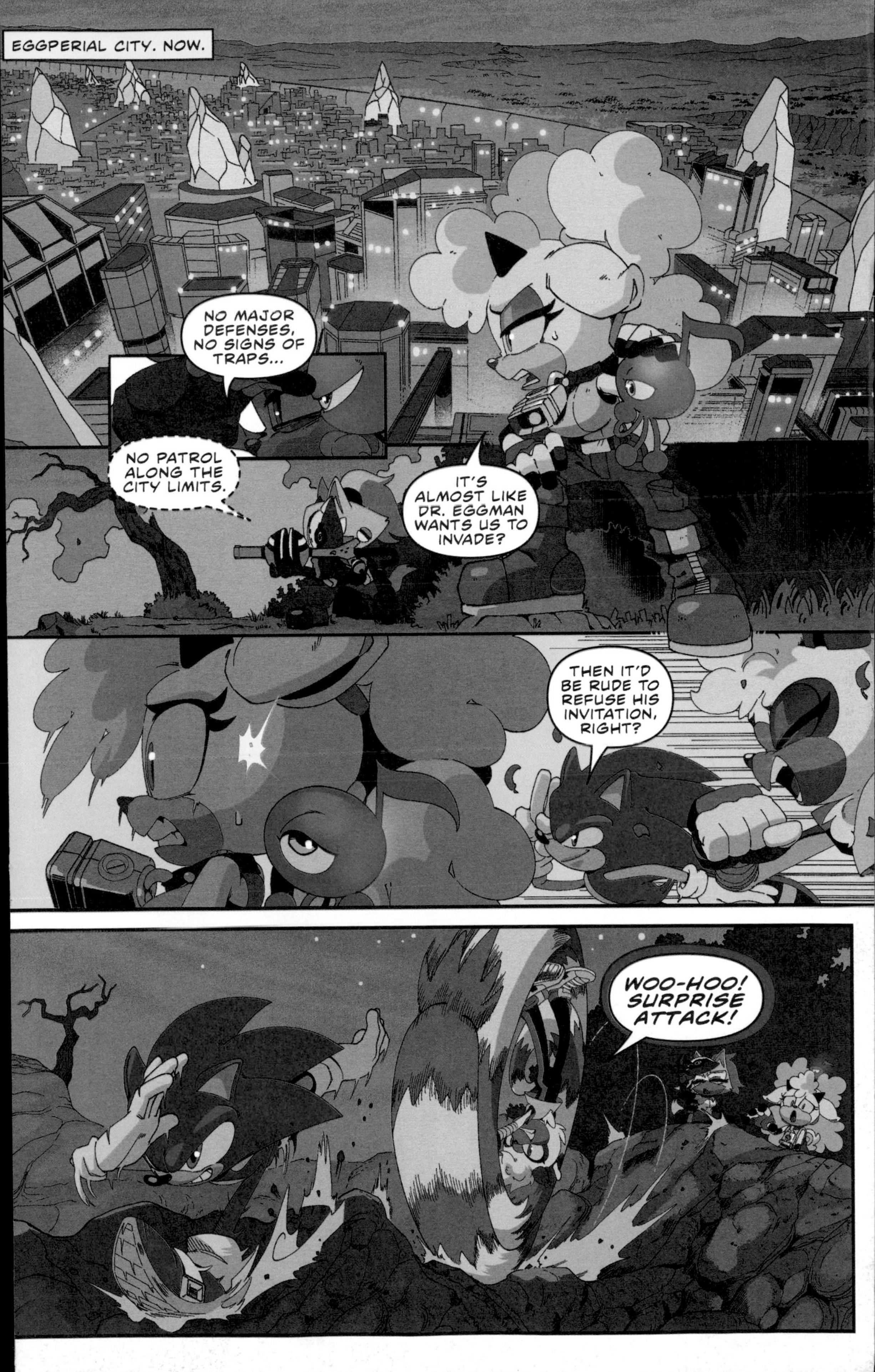
EGGPERIAL CITY. NOW.
NO MAJOR DEFENSES, NO SIGNS OF TRAPS...
NO PATROL ALONG THE CITY LIMITS.
IT'S ALMOST LIKE DR. EGGMAN WANTS US TO INVADE?
THEN IT'D BE RUDE TO REFUSE HIS INVITATION, RIGHT?
WOO-HOO! SURPRISE ATTACK!

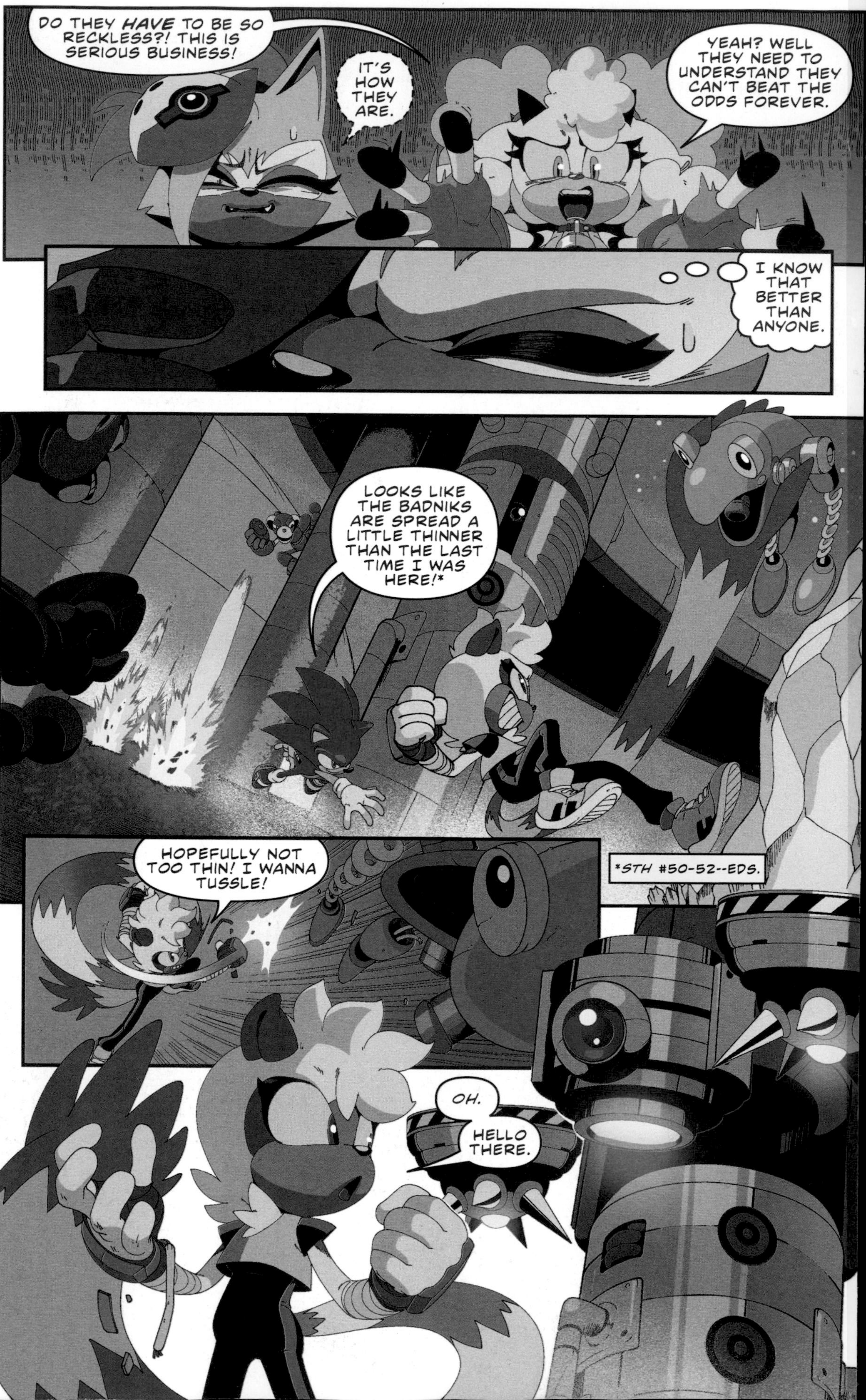
DO THEY *HAVE* TO BE SO RECKLESS?! THIS IS SERIOUS BUSINESS!
IT'S HOW THEY ARE.
YEAH? WELL THEY NEED TO UNDERSTAND THEY CAN'T BEAT THE ODDS FOREVER.
I KNOW THAT BETTER THAN ANYONE.
LOOKS LIKE THE BADNIKS ARE SPREAD A LITTLE THINNER THAN THE LAST TIME I WAS HERE!*
HOPEFULLY NOT TOO THIN! I WANNA TUSSLE!
*STH #50-52--EDS.
OH.
HELLO THERE.

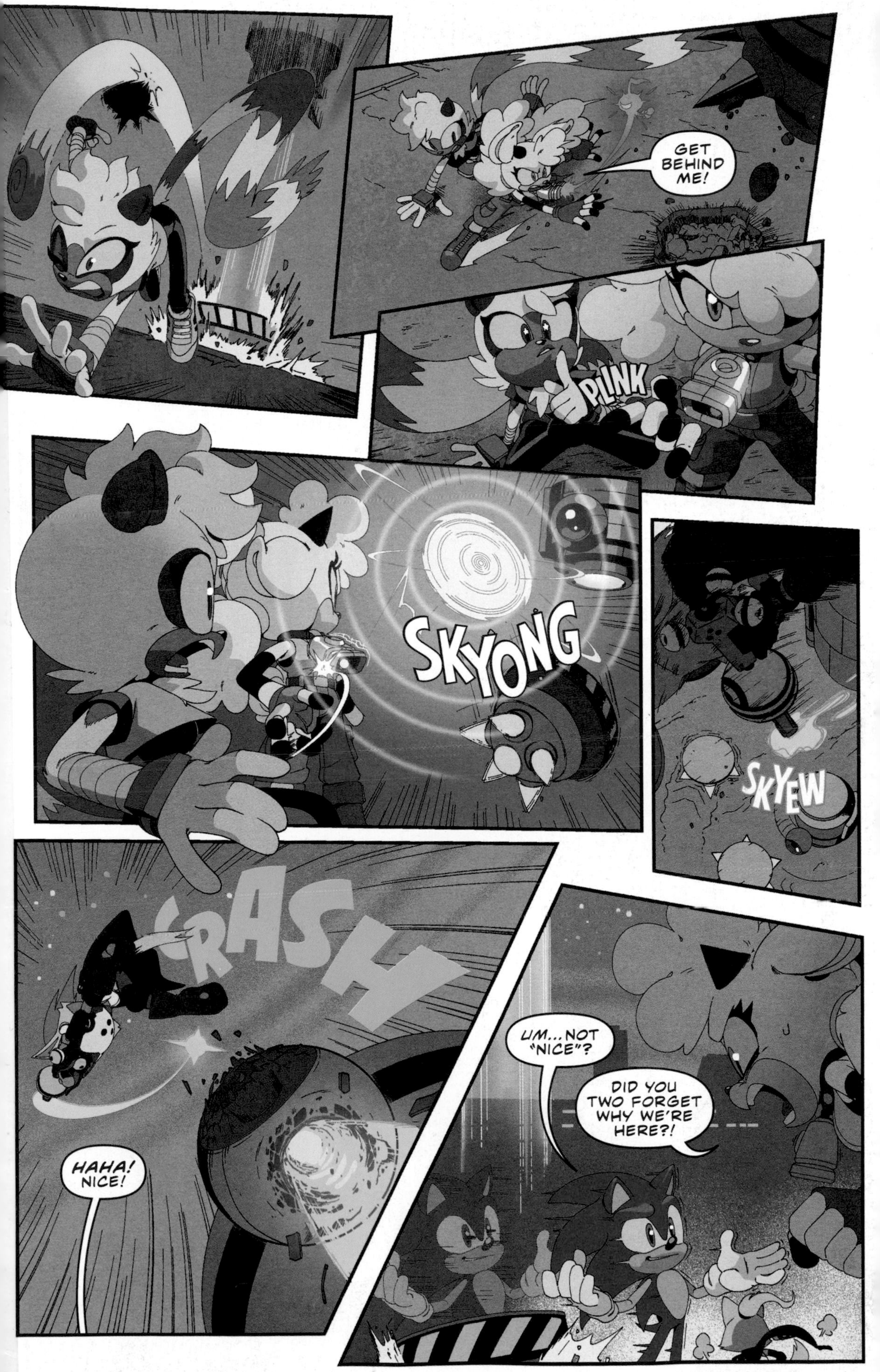
GET BEHIND ME!
PLINK
SKYONG
SKYEW
CRASH
HAHA! NICE!
UM... NOT "NICE"?
DID YOU TWO FORGET WHY WE'RE HERE?!

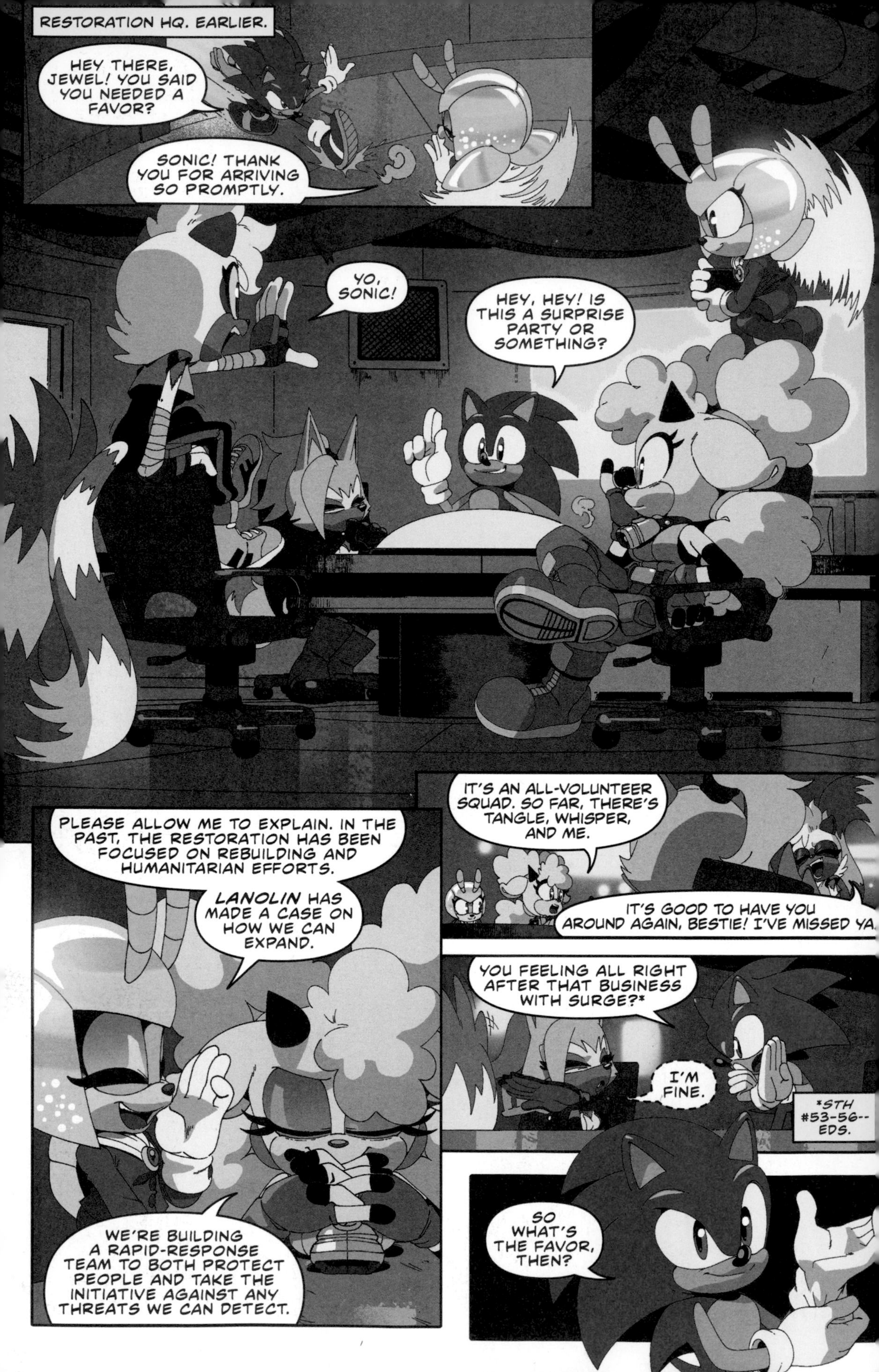
RESTORATION HQ. EARLIER.
HEY THERE, JEWEL! YOU SAID YOU NEEDED A FAVOR?
SONIC! THANK YOU FOR ARRIVING SO PROMPTLY.
YO, SONIC!
HEY, HEY! IS THIS A SURPRISE PARTY OR SOMETHING?
PLEASE ALLOW ME TO EXPLAIN. IN THE PAST, THE RESTORATION HAS BEEN FOCUSED ON REBUILDING AND HUMANITARIAN EFFORTS.
LANOLIN HAS MADE A CASE ON HOW WE CAN EXPAND.
WE'RE BUILDING A RAPID-RESPONSE TEAM TO BOTH PROTECT PEOPLE AND TAKE THE INITIATIVE AGAINST ANY THREATS WE CAN DETECT.
IT'S AN ALL-VOLUNTEER SQUAD. SO FAR, THERE'S TANGLE, WHISPER, AND ME.
IT'S GOOD TO HAVE YOU AROUND AGAIN, BESTIE! I'VE MISSED YA.
YOU FEELING ALL RIGHT AFTER THAT BUSINESS WITH SURGE?*
I'M FINE.
*STH #53-56--EDS.
SO WHAT'S THE FAVOR, THEN?

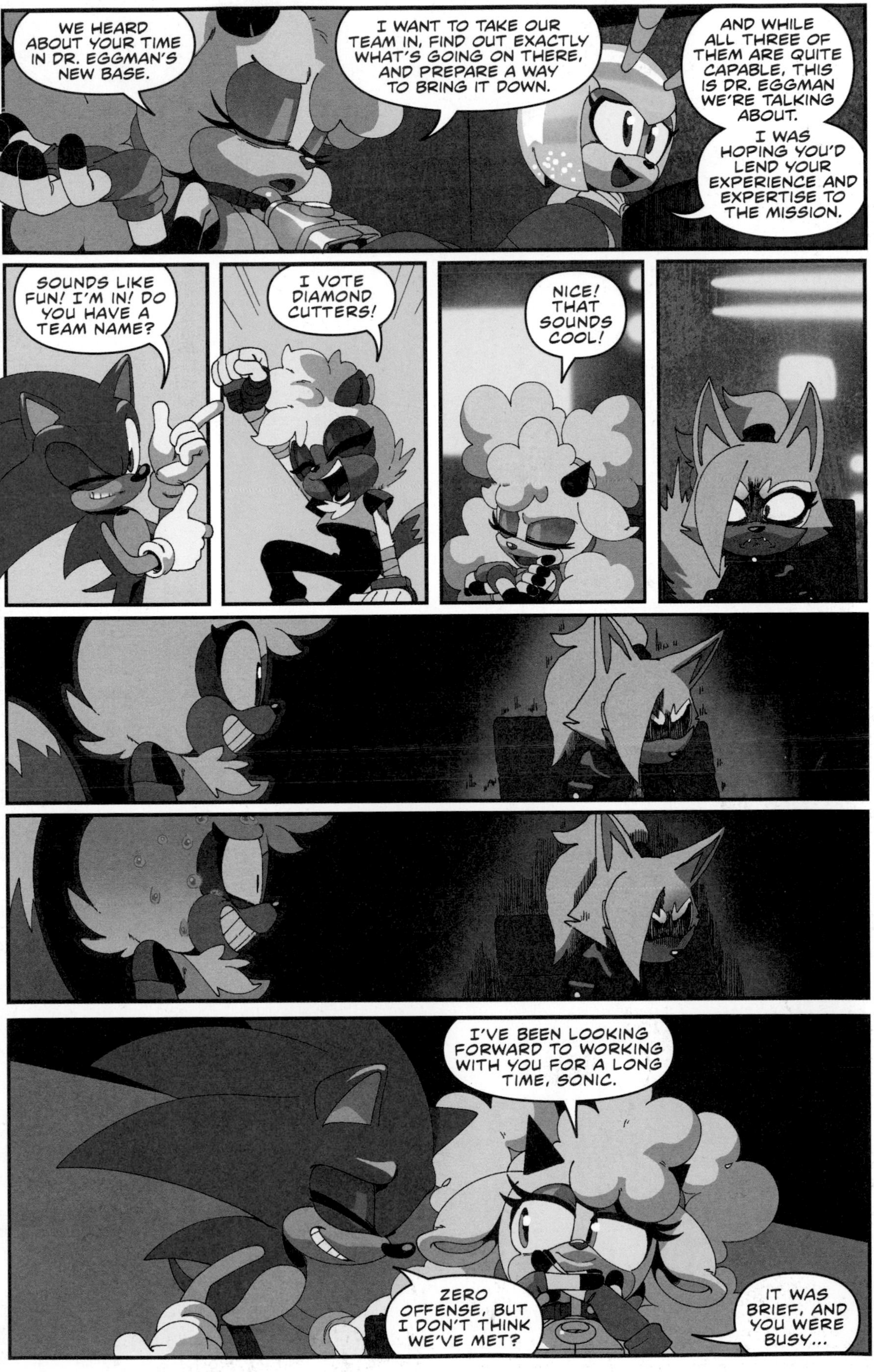
WE HEARD ABOUT YOUR TIME IN DR. EGGMAN'S NEW BASE.
I WANT TO TAKE OUR TEAM IN, FIND OUT EXACTLY WHAT'S GOING ON THERE, AND PREPARE A WAY TO BRING IT DOWN.
AND WHILE ALL THREE OF THEM ARE QUITE CAPABLE, THIS IS DR. EGGMAN WE'RE TALKING ABOUT.
I WAS HOPING YOU'D LEND YOUR EXPERIENCE AND EXPERTISE TO THE MISSION.
SOUNDS LIKE FUN! I'M IN! DO YOU HAVE A TEAM NAME?
I VOTE DIAMOND CUTTERS!
NICE! THAT SOUNDS COOL!
I'VE BEEN LOOKING FORWARD TO WORKING WITH YOU FOR A LONG TIME, SONIC.
ZERO OFFENSE, BUT I DON'T THINK WE'VE MET?
IT WAS BRIEF, AND YOU WERE BUSY...

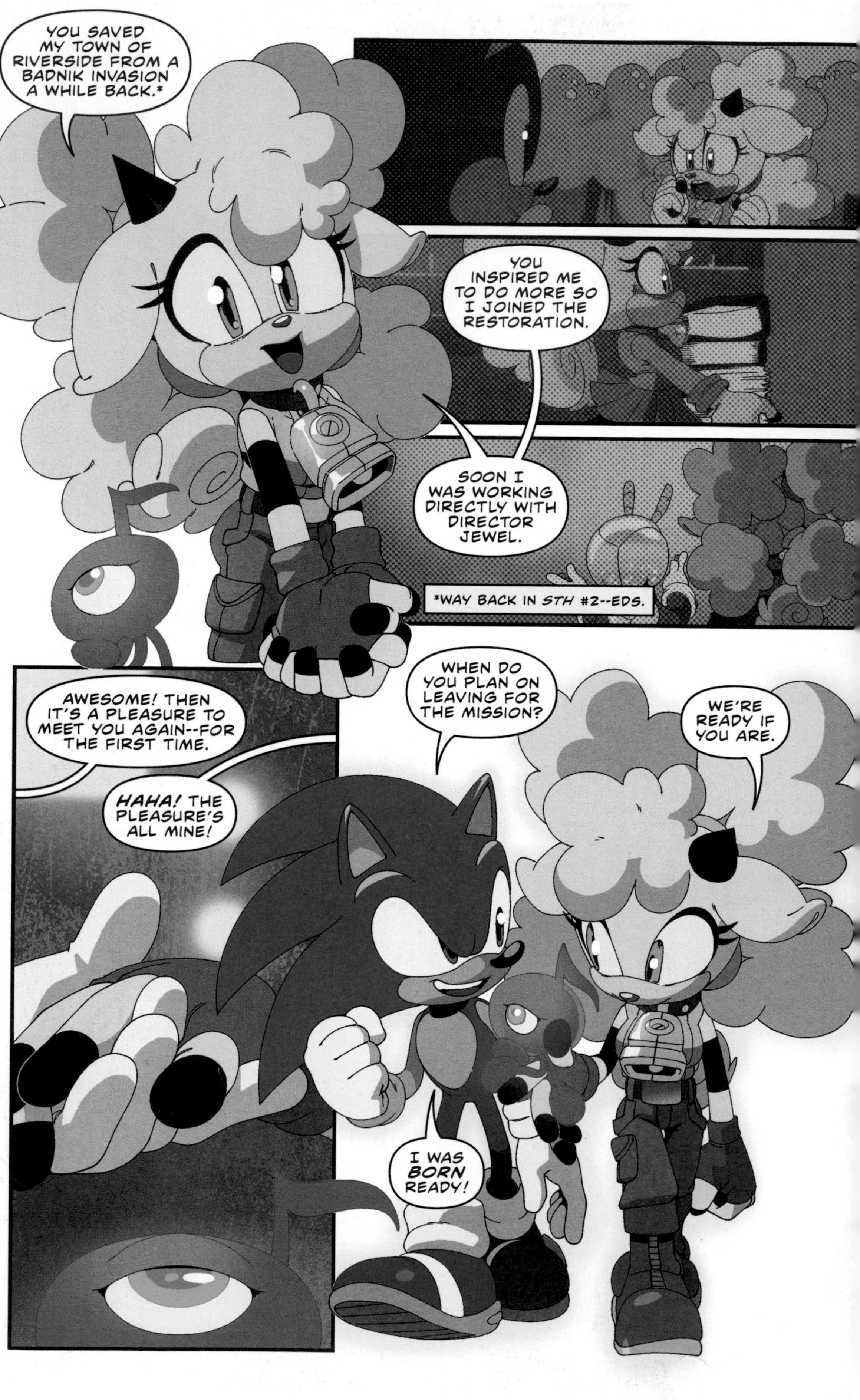

YOU SAVED MY TOWN OF RIVERSIDE FROM A BADNIK INVASION A WHILE BACK.*
YOU INSPIRED ME TO DO MORE SO I JOINED THE RESTORATION.
SOON I WAS WORKING DIRECTLY WITH DIRECTOR JEWEL.
*WAY BACK IN *STH* #2--EDS.
AWESOME! THEN IT'S A PLEASURE TO MEET YOU AGAIN--FOR THE FIRST TIME.
HAHA! THE PLEASURE'S ALL MINE!
WHEN DO YOU PLAN ON LEAVING FOR THE MISSION?
WE'RE READY IF YOU ARE.
I WAS *BORN* READY!

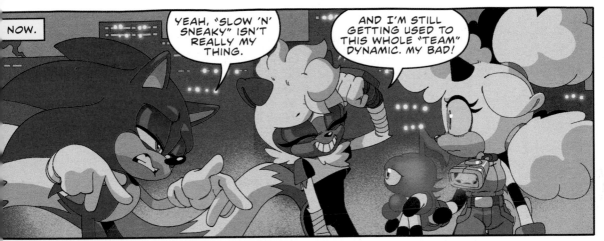

NOW.

YEAH, "SLOW 'N' SNEAKY" ISN'T REALLY MY THING.

AND I'M STILL GETTING USED TO THIS WHOLE "TEAM" DYNAMIC. MY BAD!

HONESTLY, HOW DO YOU HANDLE HER?

I DON'T.

WHISPER... IS THERE SOMETHING WE NEED TO TALK ABOUT?

NO.

SO...SHOULD WE KEEP HEADING INTO THE CITY, OR...

I'D LIKE TO ASSESS OUR SURROUNDINGS FIRST.

WHISPER, CAN YOU SEND THIS UP WITH YOUR HOVER WISP?

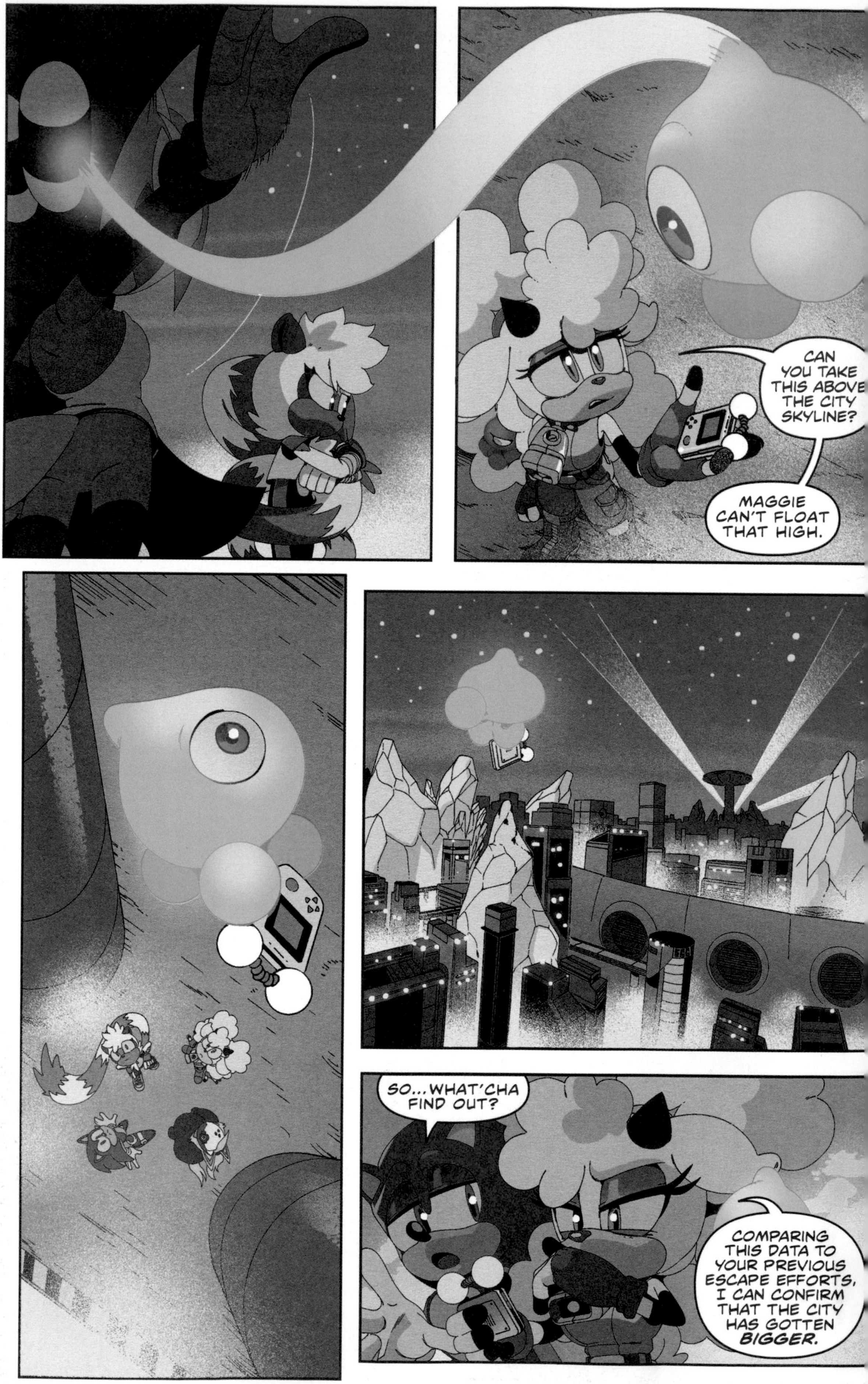
CAN YOU TAKE THIS ABOVE THE CITY SKYLINE?
MAGGIE CAN'T FLOAT THAT HIGH.
SO...WHAT'CHA FIND OUT?
COMPARING THIS DATA TO YOUR PREVIOUS ESCAPE EFFORTS, I CAN CONFIRM THAT THE CITY HAS GOTTEN *BIGGER*.

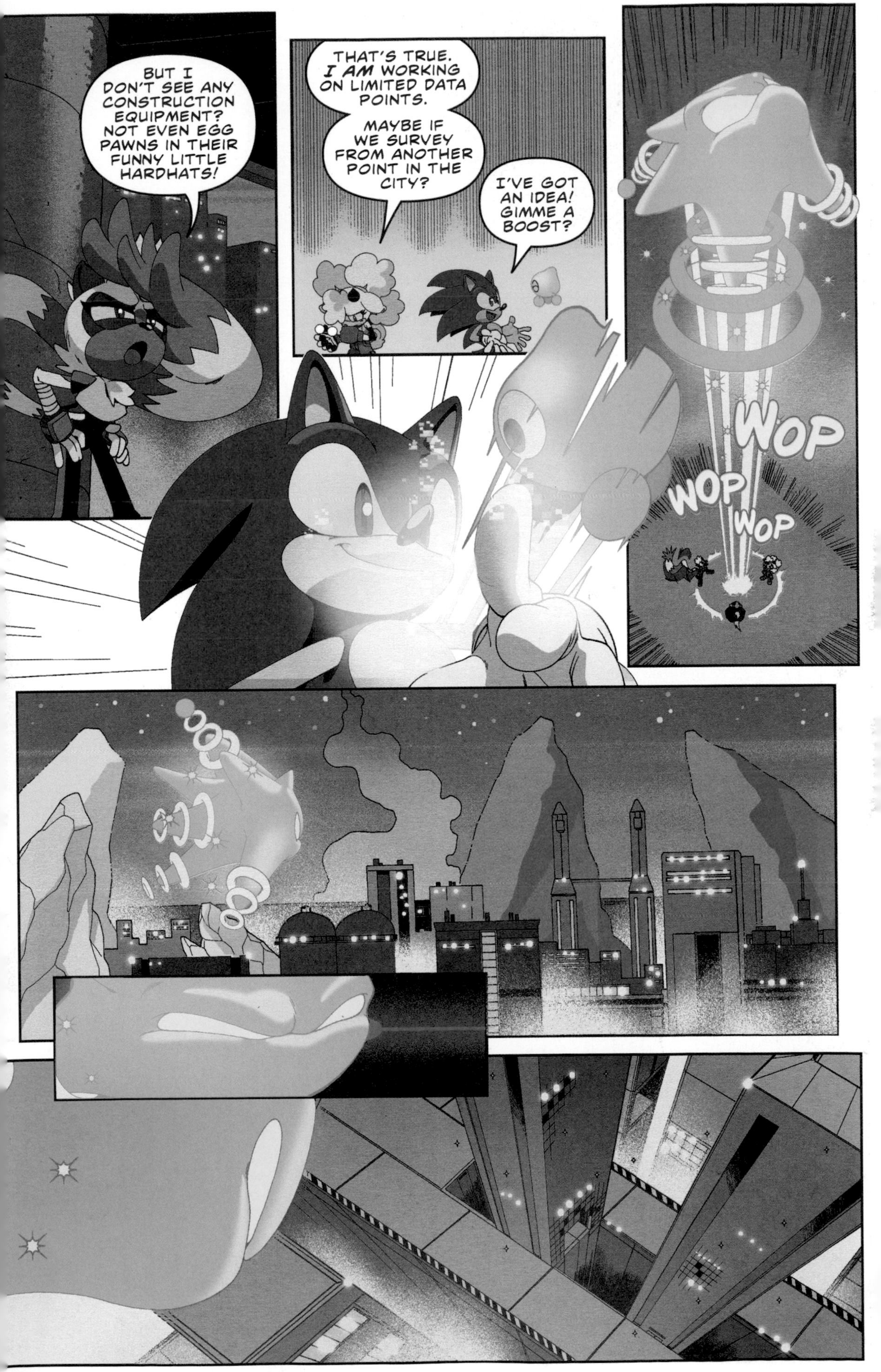
BUT I DON'T SEE ANY CONSTRUCTION EQUIPMENT? NOT EVEN EGG PAWNS IN THEIR FUNNY LITTLE HARDHATS!
THAT'S TRUE. I AM WORKING ON LIMITED DATA POINTS.
MAYBE IF WE SURVEY FROM ANOTHER POINT IN THE CITY?
I'VE GOT AN IDEA! GIMME A BOOST?
WOP
WOP
WOP

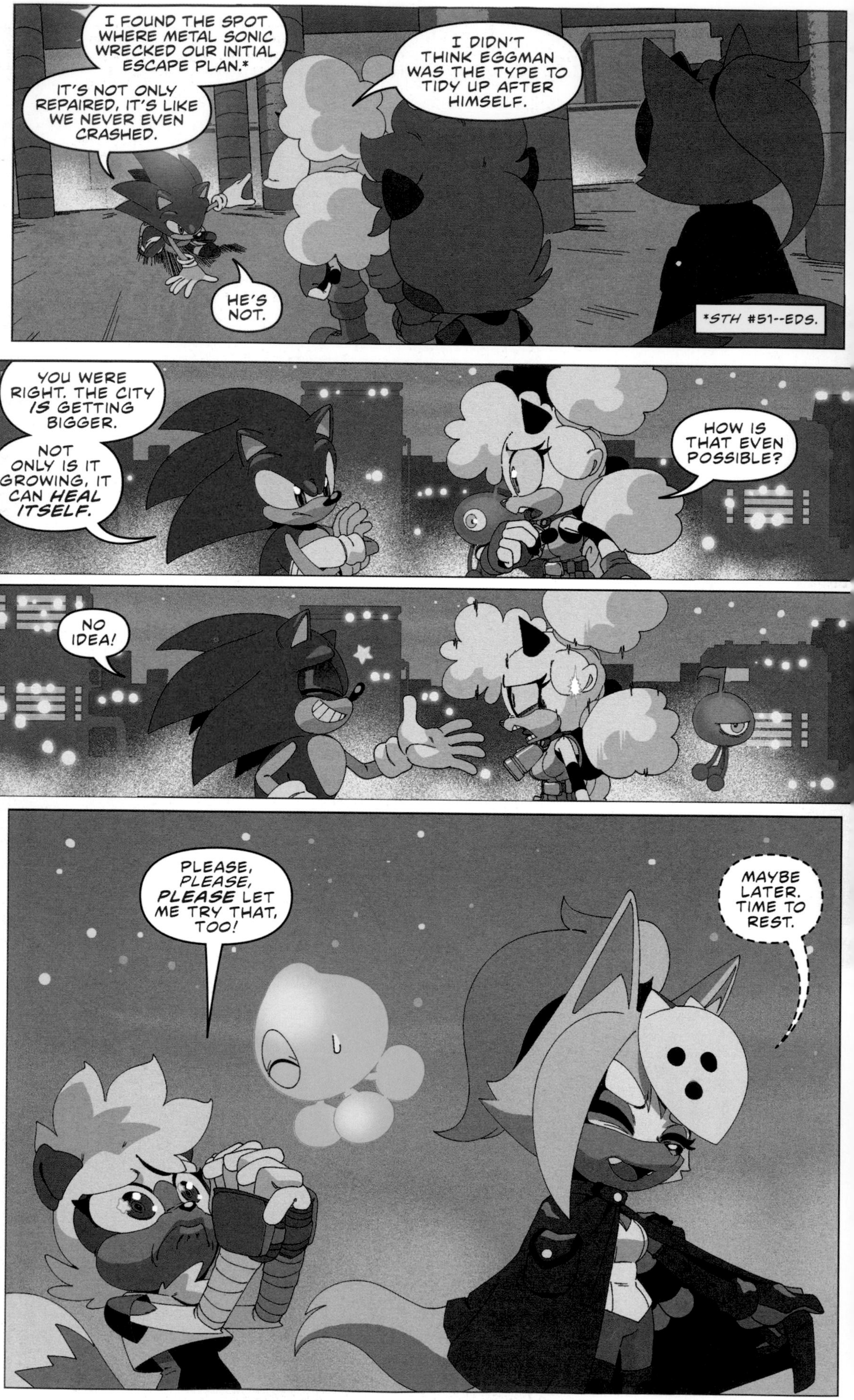
I FOUND THE SPOT WHERE METAL SONIC WRECKED OUR INITIAL ESCAPE PLAN.*
IT'S NOT ONLY REPAIRED, IT'S LIKE WE NEVER EVEN CRASHED.
I DIDN'T THINK EGGMAN WAS THE TYPE TO TIDY UP AFTER HIMSELF.
HE'S NOT.
*STH #51--EDS.
YOU WERE RIGHT. THE CITY *IS* GETTING BIGGER.
NOT ONLY IS IT GROWING, IT CAN ***HEAL ITSELF.***
HOW IS THAT EVEN POSSIBLE?
NO IDEA!
PLEASE, PLEASE, ***PLEASE*** LET ME TRY THAT, TOO!
MAYBE LATER. TIME TO REST.

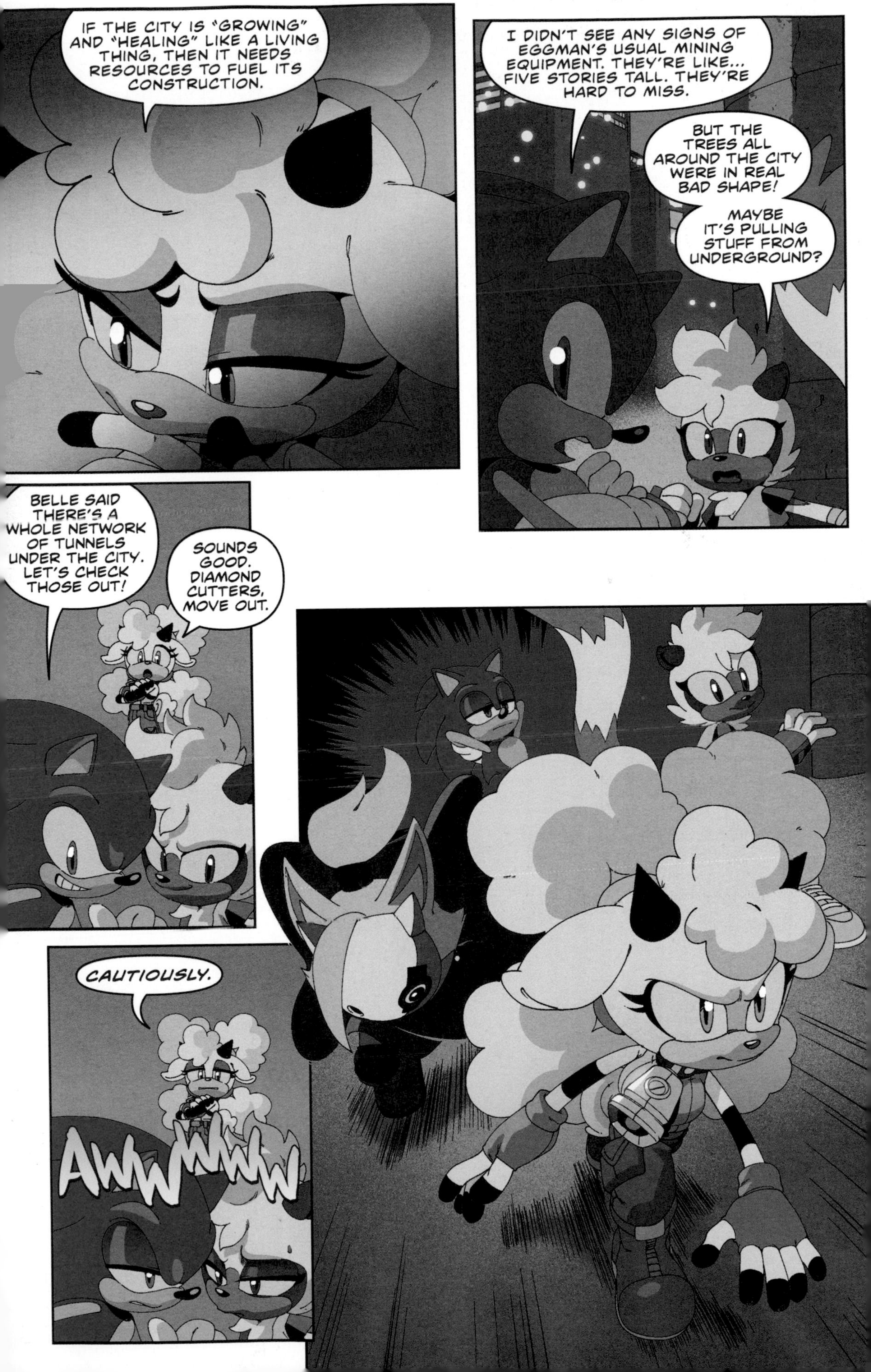
IF THE CITY IS "GROWING" AND "HEALING" LIKE A LIVING THING, THEN IT NEEDS RESOURCES TO FUEL ITS CONSTRUCTION.
I DIDN'T SEE ANY SIGNS OF EGGMAN'S USUAL MINING EQUIPMENT. THEY'RE LIKE... FIVE STORIES TALL. THEY'RE HARD TO MISS.
BUT THE TREES ALL AROUND THE CITY WERE IN REAL BAD SHAPE!
MAYBE IT'S PULLING STUFF FROM UNDERGROUND?
BELLE SAID THERE'S A WHOLE NETWORK OF TUNNELS UNDER THE CITY. LET'S CHECK THOSE OUT!
SOUNDS GOOD. DIAMOND CUTTERS, MOVE OUT.
CAUTIOUSLY.
AWWWWWW

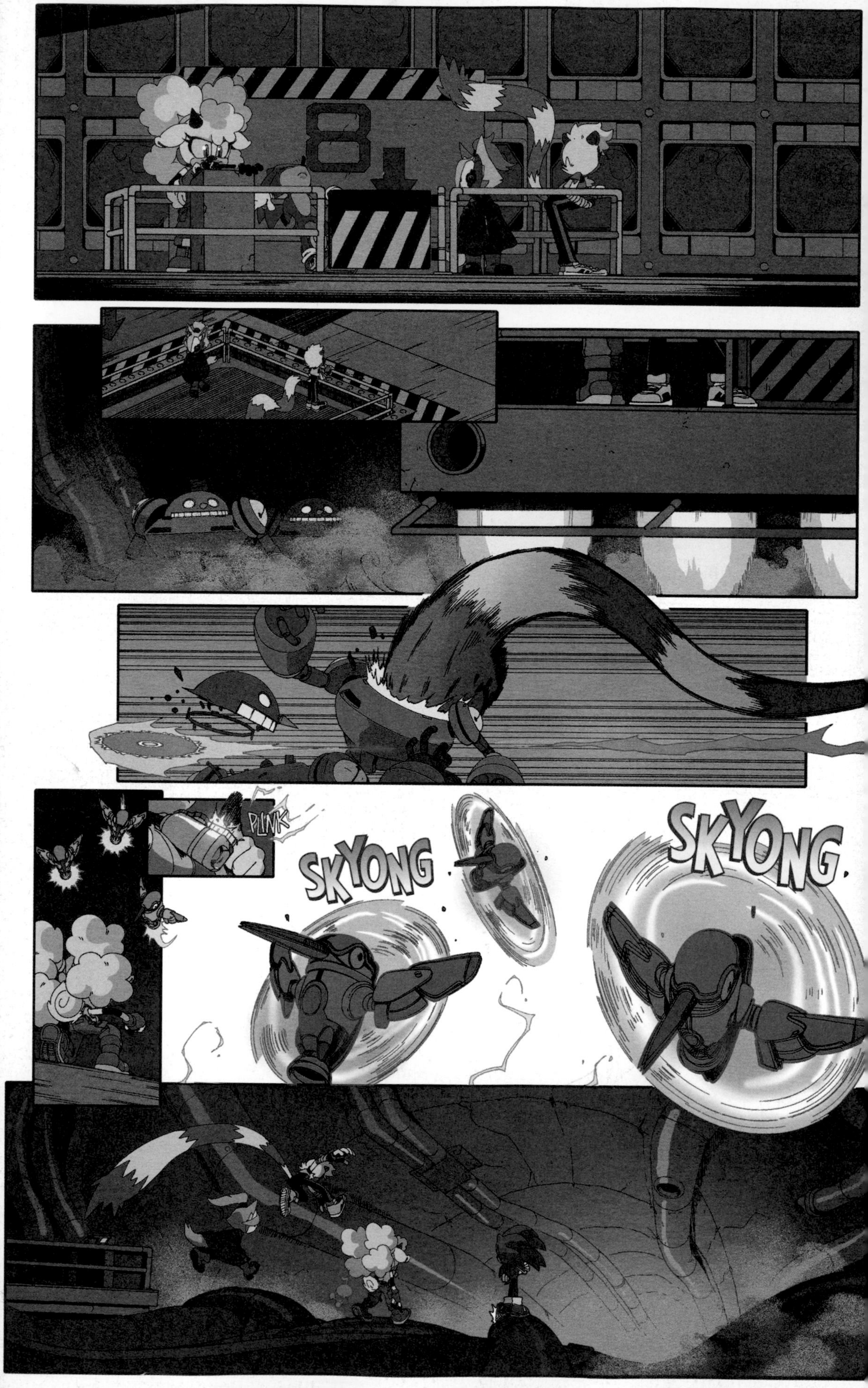
PLINK
SKYONG
SKYONG.

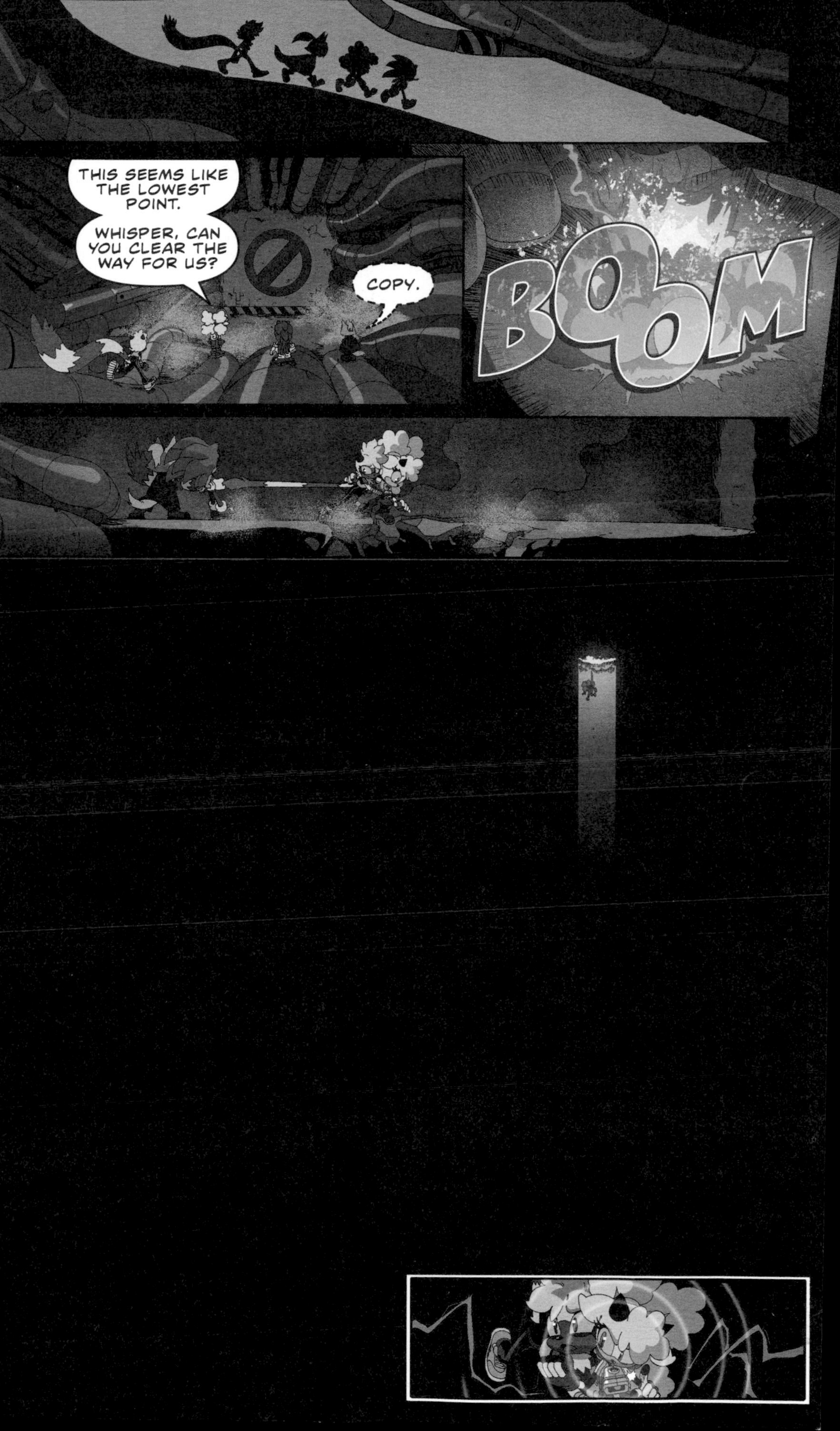
THIS SEEMS LIKE THE LOWEST POINT.
WHISPER, CAN YOU CLEAR THE WAY FOR US?
COPY.
BOOOM

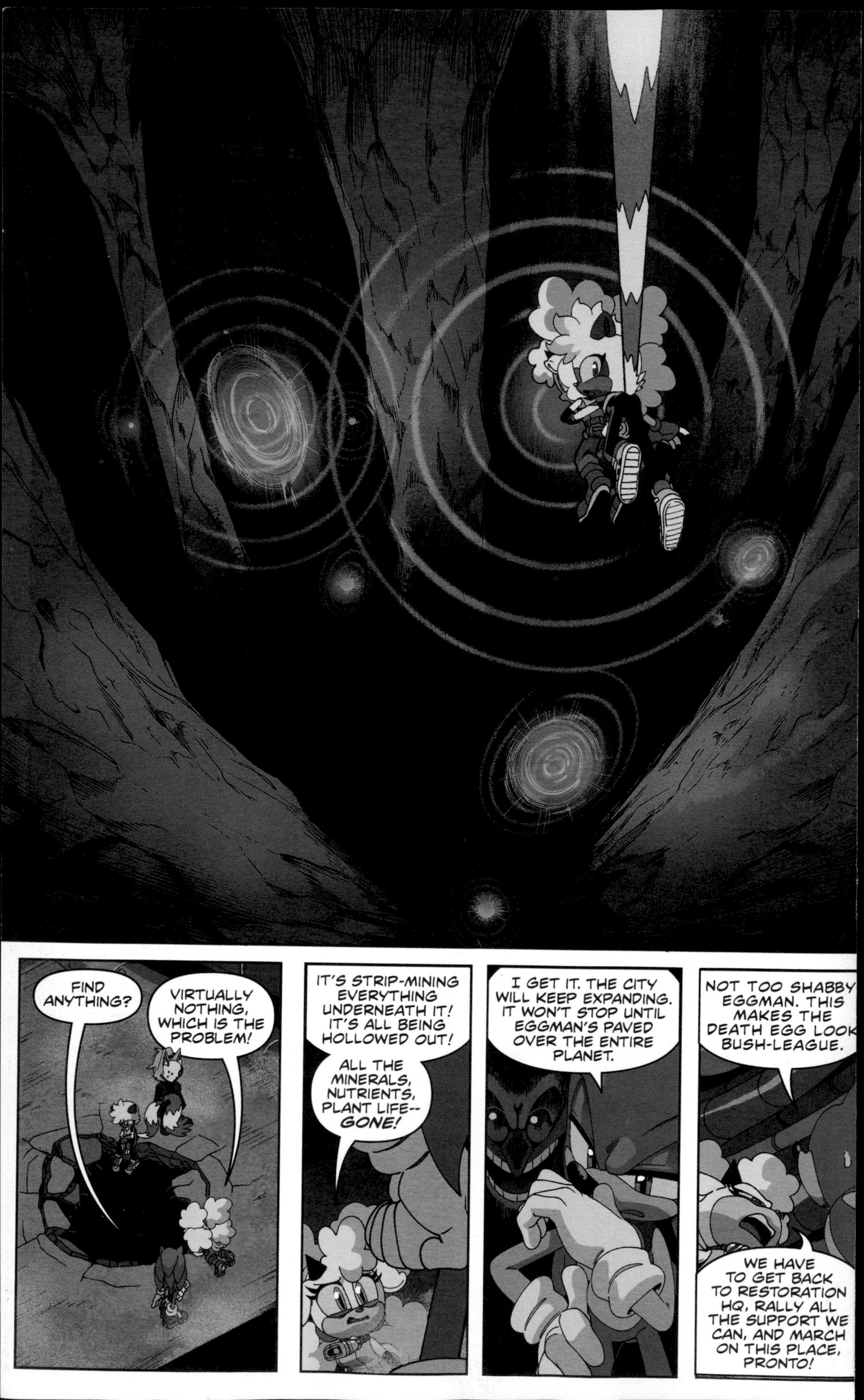
FIND ANYTHING?
VIRTUALLY NOTHING, WHICH IS THE PROBLEM!
IT'S STRIP-MINING EVERYTHING UNDERNEATH IT! IT'S ALL BEING HOLLOWED OUT!
ALL THE MINERALS, NUTRIENTS, PLANT LIFE-- GONE!
I GET IT. THE CITY WILL KEEP EXPANDING. IT WON'T STOP UNTIL EGGMAN'S PAVED OVER THE ENTIRE PLANET.
NOT TOO SHABBY EGGMAN. THIS MAKES THE DEATH EGG LOOK BUSH-LEAGUE.
WE HAVE TO GET BACK TO RESTORATION HQ, RALLY ALL THE SUPPORT WE CAN, AND MARCH ON THIS PLACE, PRONTO!

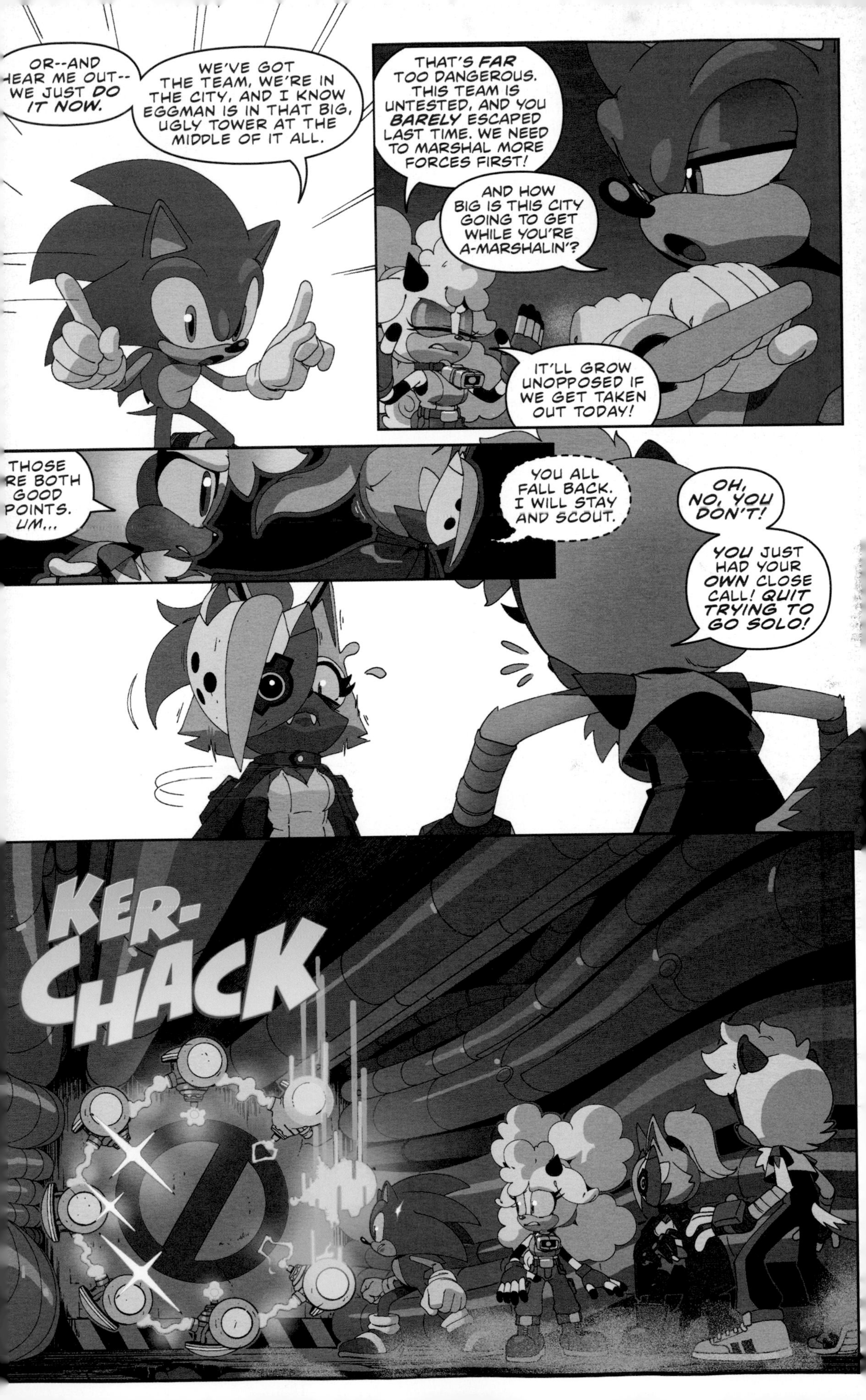

OR--AND HEAR ME OUT-- WE JUST DO IT NOW.
WE'VE GOT THE TEAM, WE'RE IN THE CITY, AND I KNOW EGGMAN IS IN THAT BIG, UGLY TOWER AT THE MIDDLE OF IT ALL.
THAT'S FAR TOO DANGEROUS. THIS TEAM IS UNTESTED, AND YOU BARELY ESCAPED LAST TIME. WE NEED TO MARSHAL MORE FORCES FIRST!
AND HOW BIG IS THIS CITY GOING TO GET WHILE YOU'RE A-MARSHALIN'?
IT'LL GROW UNOPPOSED IF WE GET TAKEN OUT TODAY!
THOSE RE BOTH GOOD POINTS. UM...
YOU ALL FALL BACK. I WILL STAY AND SCOUT.
OH, NO, YOU DON'T!
YOU JUST HAD YOUR OWN CLOSE CALL! QUIT TRYING TO GO SOLO!
KER-CHACK

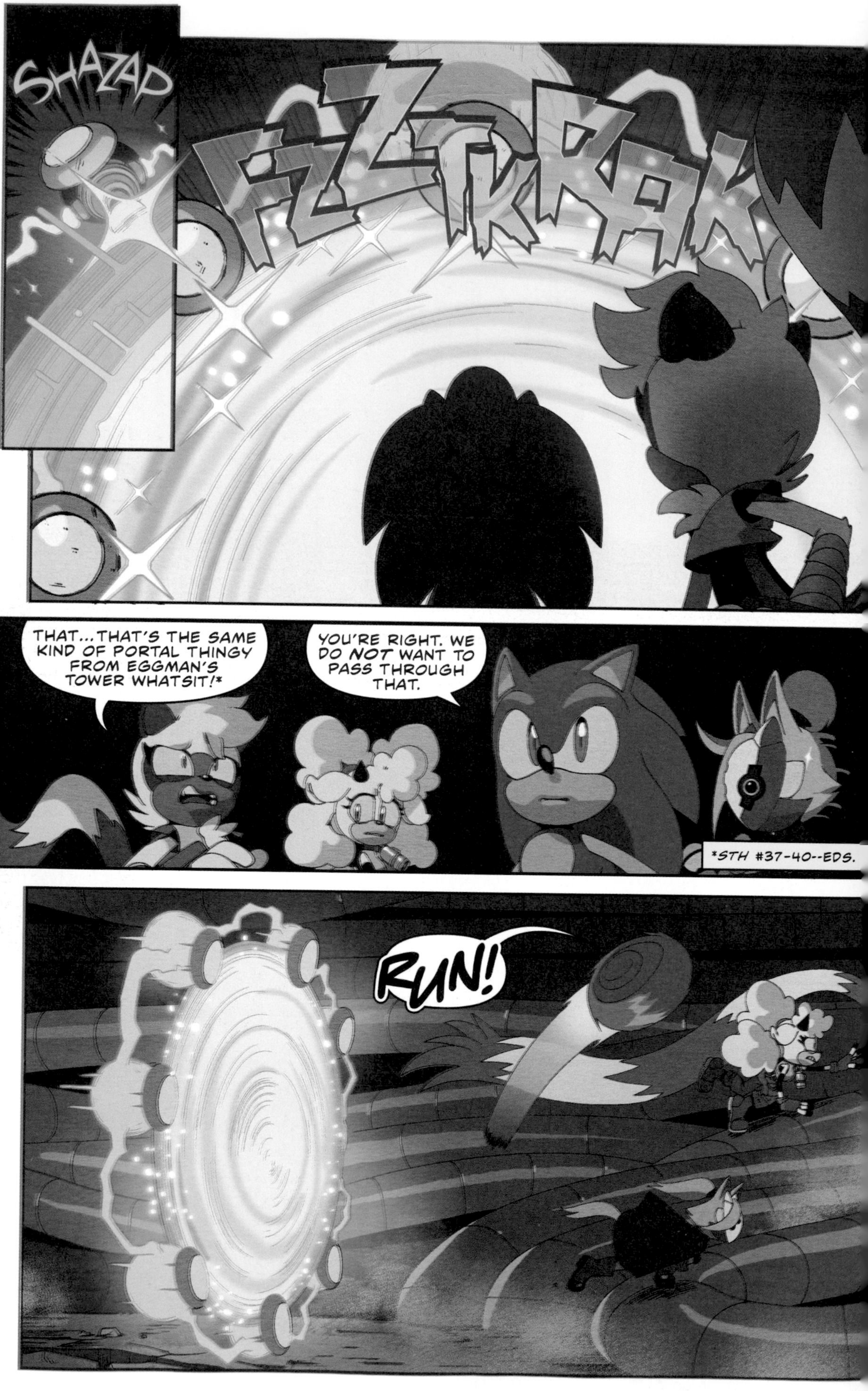
SHAZAD
FZZTKRAK
THAT...THAT'S THE SAME KIND OF PORTAL THINGY FROM EGGMAN'S TOWER WHATSIT!*
YOU'RE RIGHT. WE DO NOT WANT TO PASS THROUGH THAT.
*STH #37-40--EDS.
RUN!

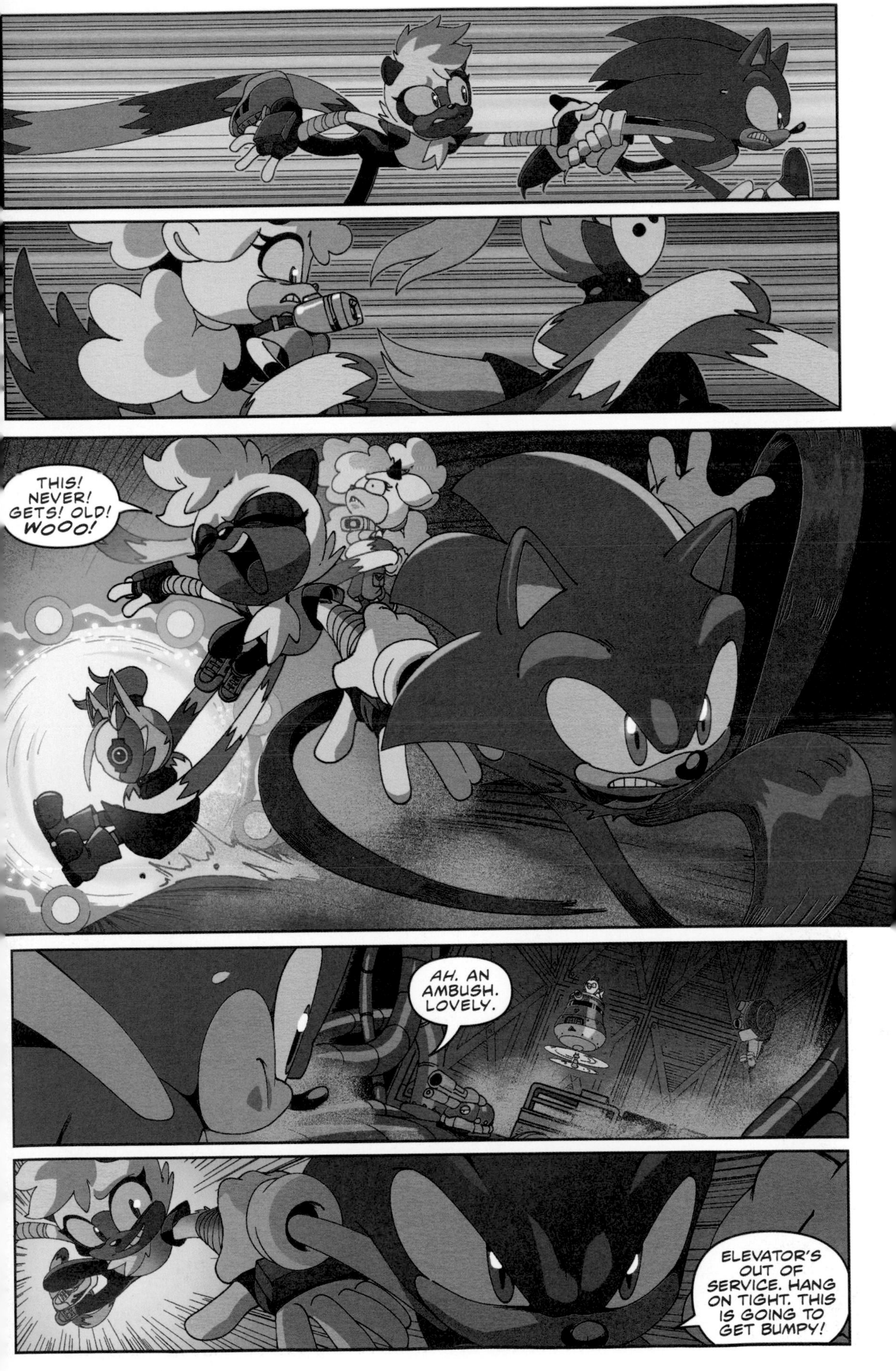
THIS! NEVER! GETS! OLD! WOOO!
AH. AN AMBUSH. LOVELY.
ELEVATOR'S OUT OF SERVICE. HANG ON TIGHT. THIS IS GOING TO GET BUMPY!

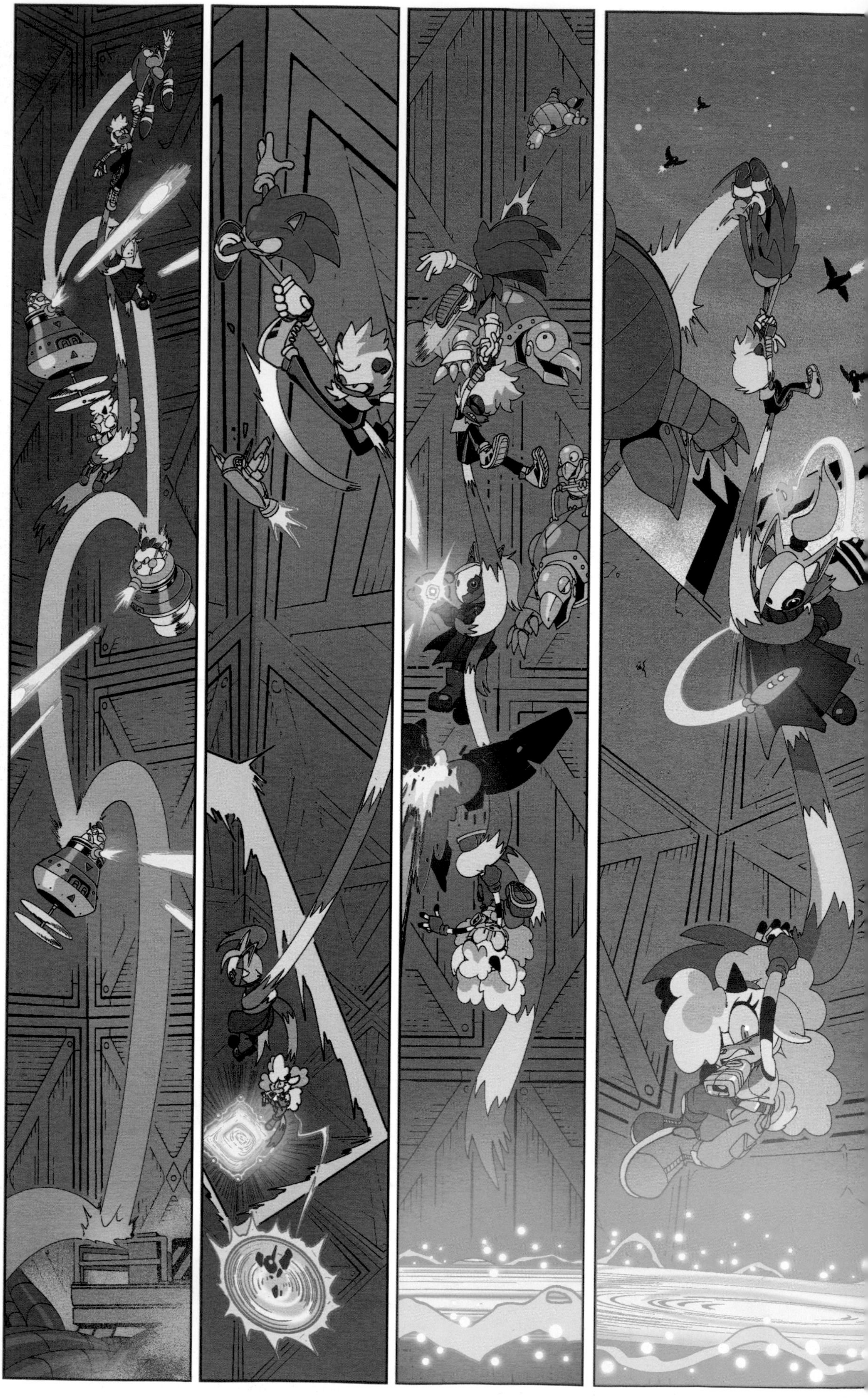

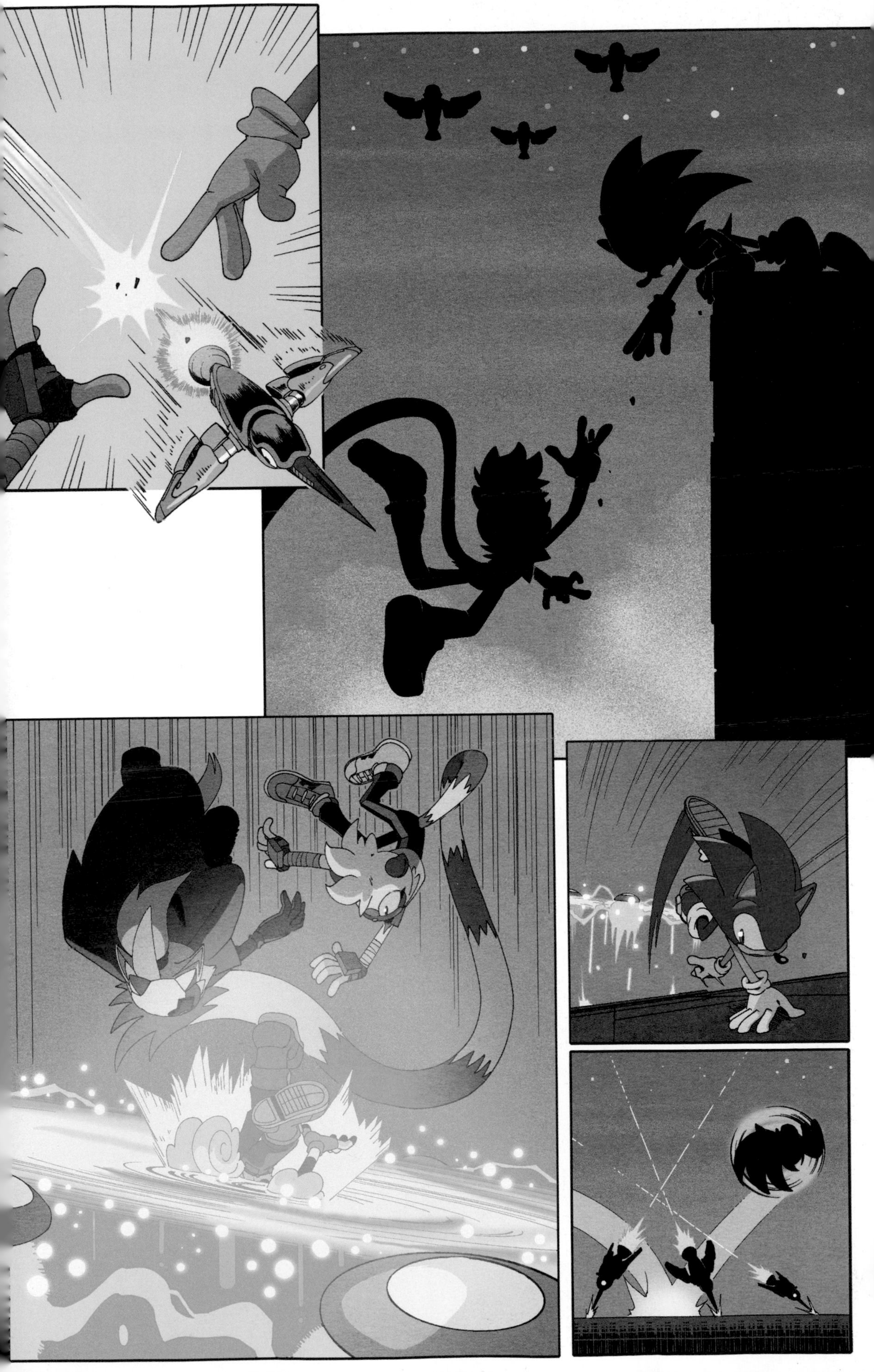

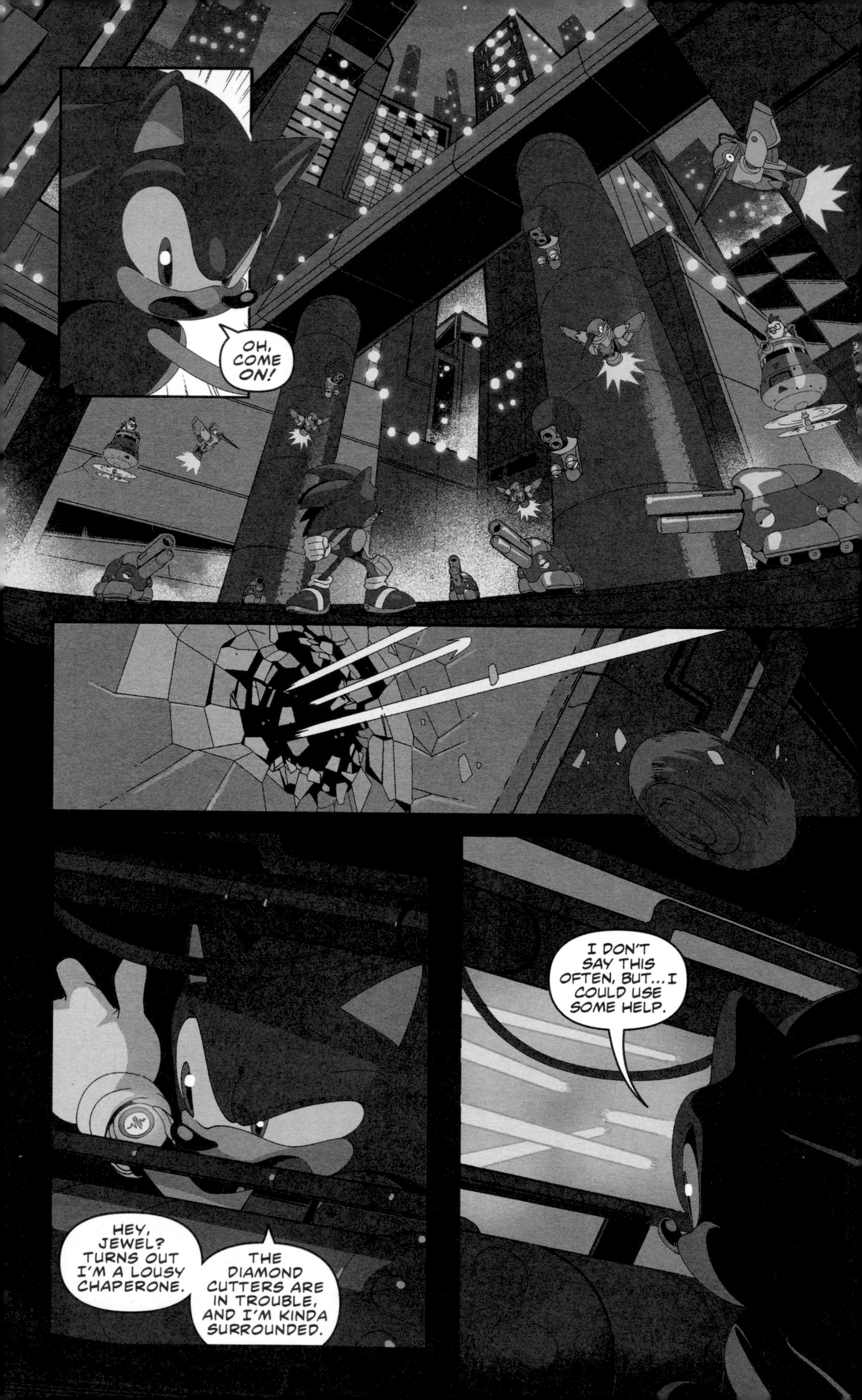
OH, COME ON!
HEY, JEWEL? TURNS OUT I'M A LOUSY CHAPERONE.
THE DIAMOND CUTTERS ARE IN TROUBLE, AND I'M KINDA SURROUNDED.
I DON'T SAY THIS OFTEN, BUT... I COULD USE SOME HELP.

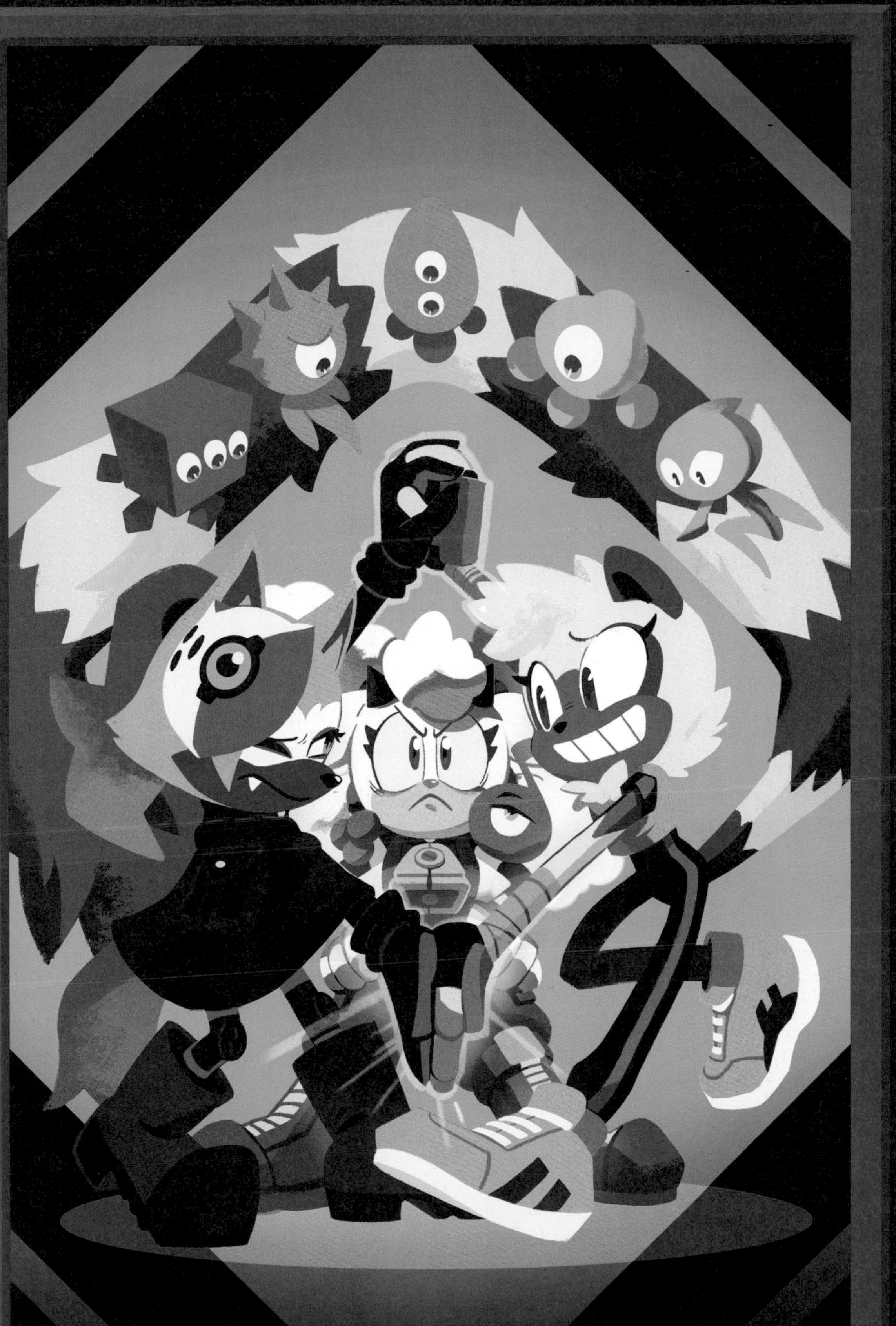

ART BY **NATHALIE FOURDRAINE**

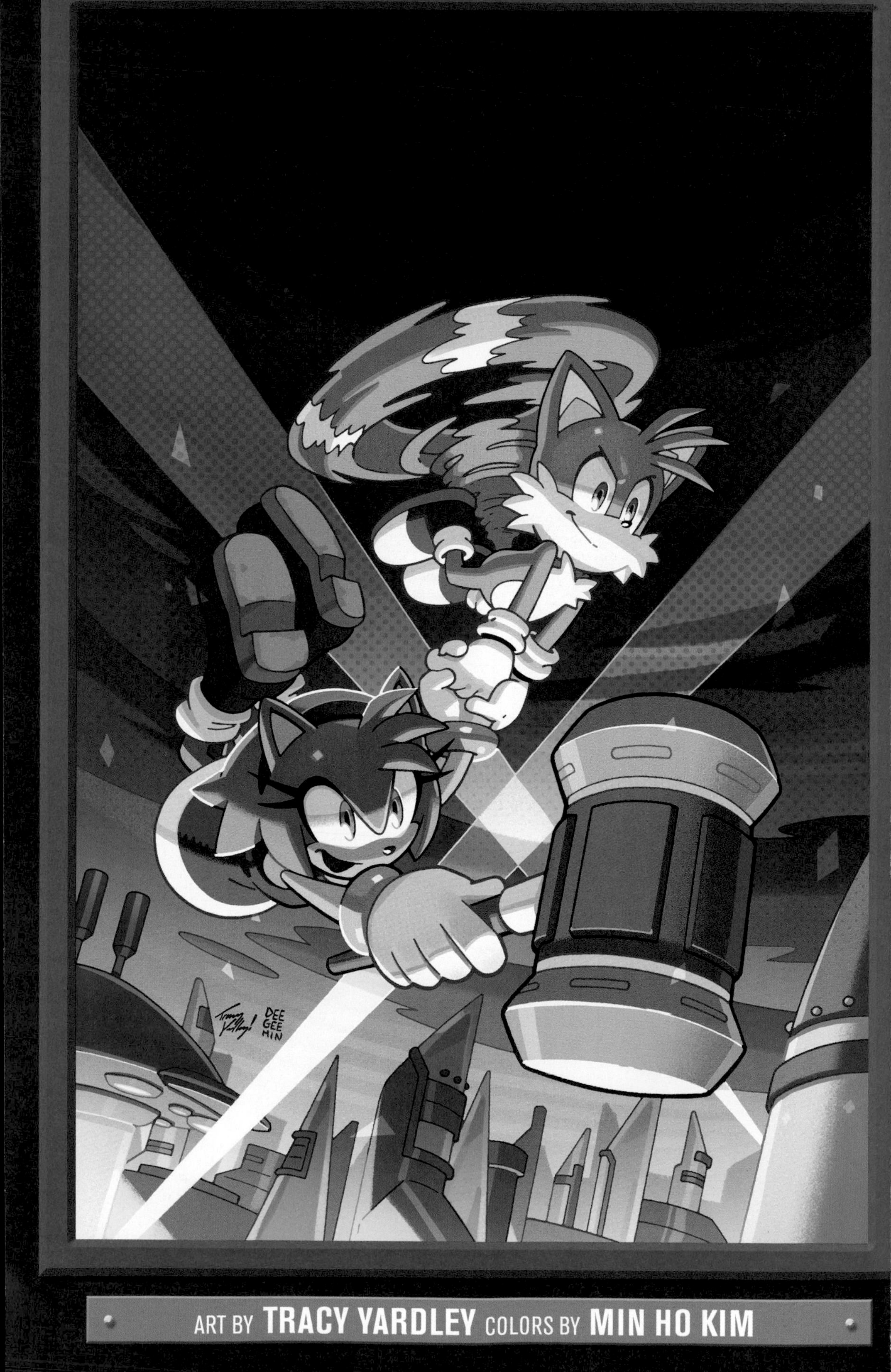
DEE
GEE
MIN

ART BY **TRACY YARDLEY** COLORS BY **MIN HO KIM**

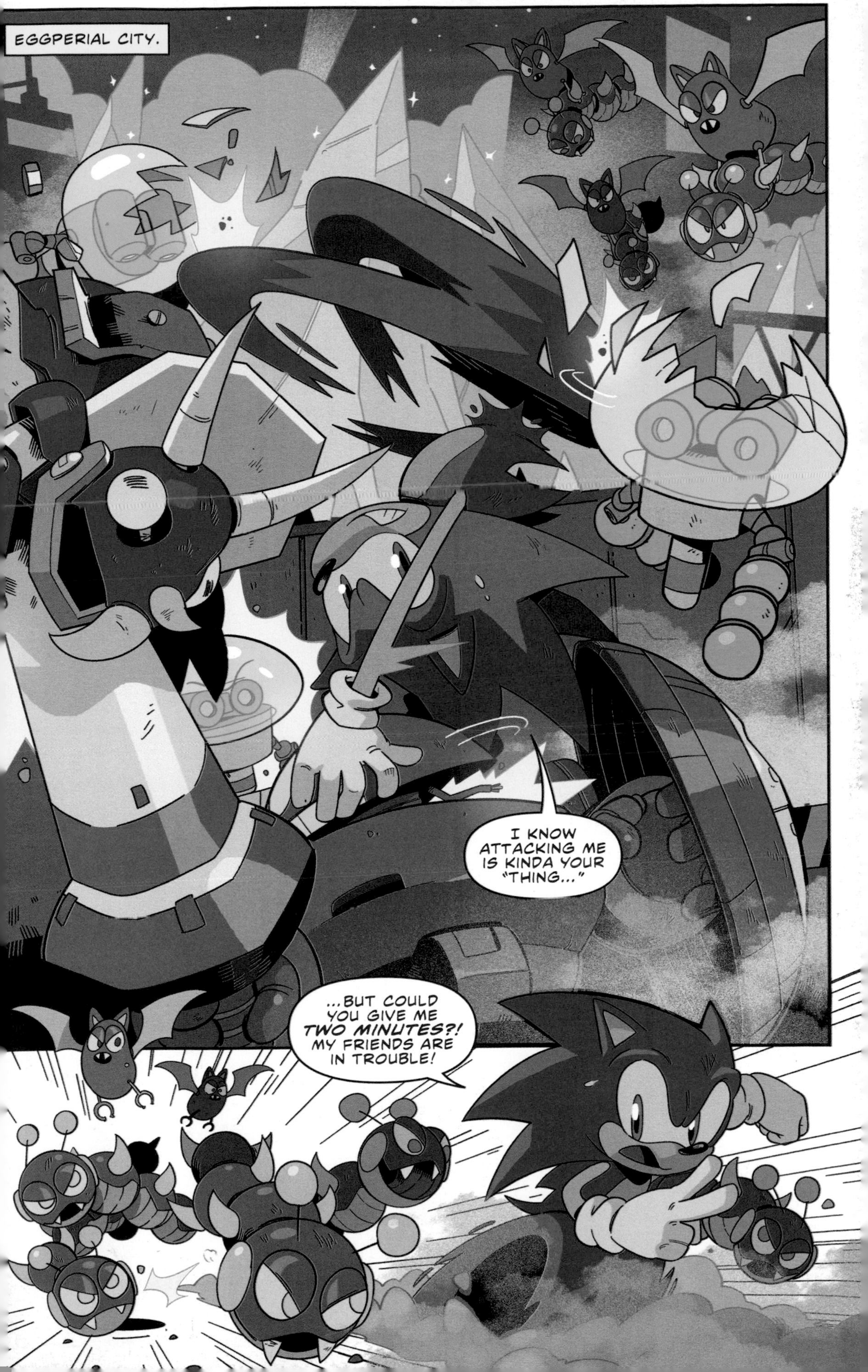
EGGPERIAL CITY.
I KNOW ATTACKING ME IS KINDA YOUR "THING..."
...BUT COULD YOU GIVE ME *TWO MINUTES?!* MY FRIENDS ARE IN TROUBLE!

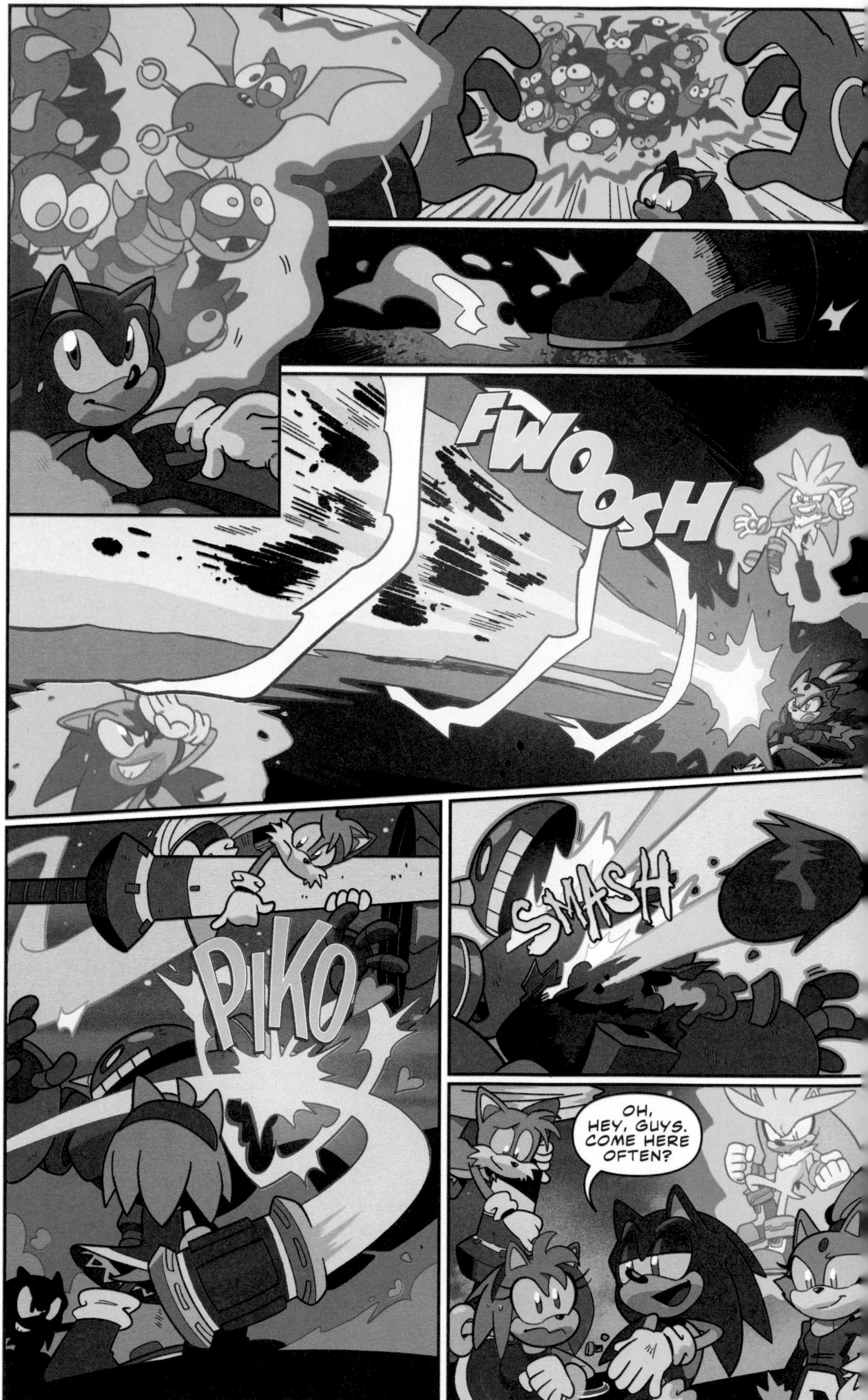
FWOOSH
PIKO
SMASH
OH, HEY, GUYS. COME HERE OFTEN?

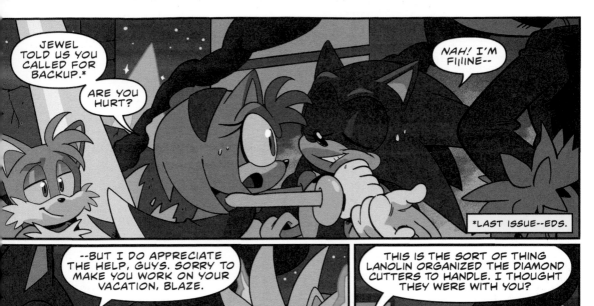

JEWEL TOLD US YOU CALLED FOR BACKUP.*

ARE YOU HURT?

NAH! I'M FIIIINE--

*LAST ISSUE--EDS.

--BUT I DO APPRECIATE THE HELP, GUYS. SORRY TO MAKE YOU WORK ON YOUR VACATION, BLAZE.

THINK NOTHING OF IT. I WOULD NEVER TURN A BLIND EYE TO VILLAINY.

AND I'M JUST HAPPY TO HAVE SOME DIRECTION!*

*SEE THE SONIC 2022 ANNUAL FOR MORE ON BLAZE & SILVER--EDS.

THIS IS THE SORT OF THING LANOLIN ORGANIZED THE DIAMOND CUTTERS TO HANDLE. I THOUGHT THEY WERE WITH YOU?

THEY WERE. LEMME GET YOU UP TO SPEED.

WE FOUND OUT EGGMAN'S CITY IS AUTO-BUILDING ITSELF BY STRIP-MINING THE EARTH BELOW.

WE GOT AMBUSHED, AND THE TEAM WAS CAUGHT IN THE SAME KIND OF TRAP AS THE ONES WE RAN INTO WITH EGGMAN'S TOWER BASE THINGY.*

*STH #37-40--EDS.

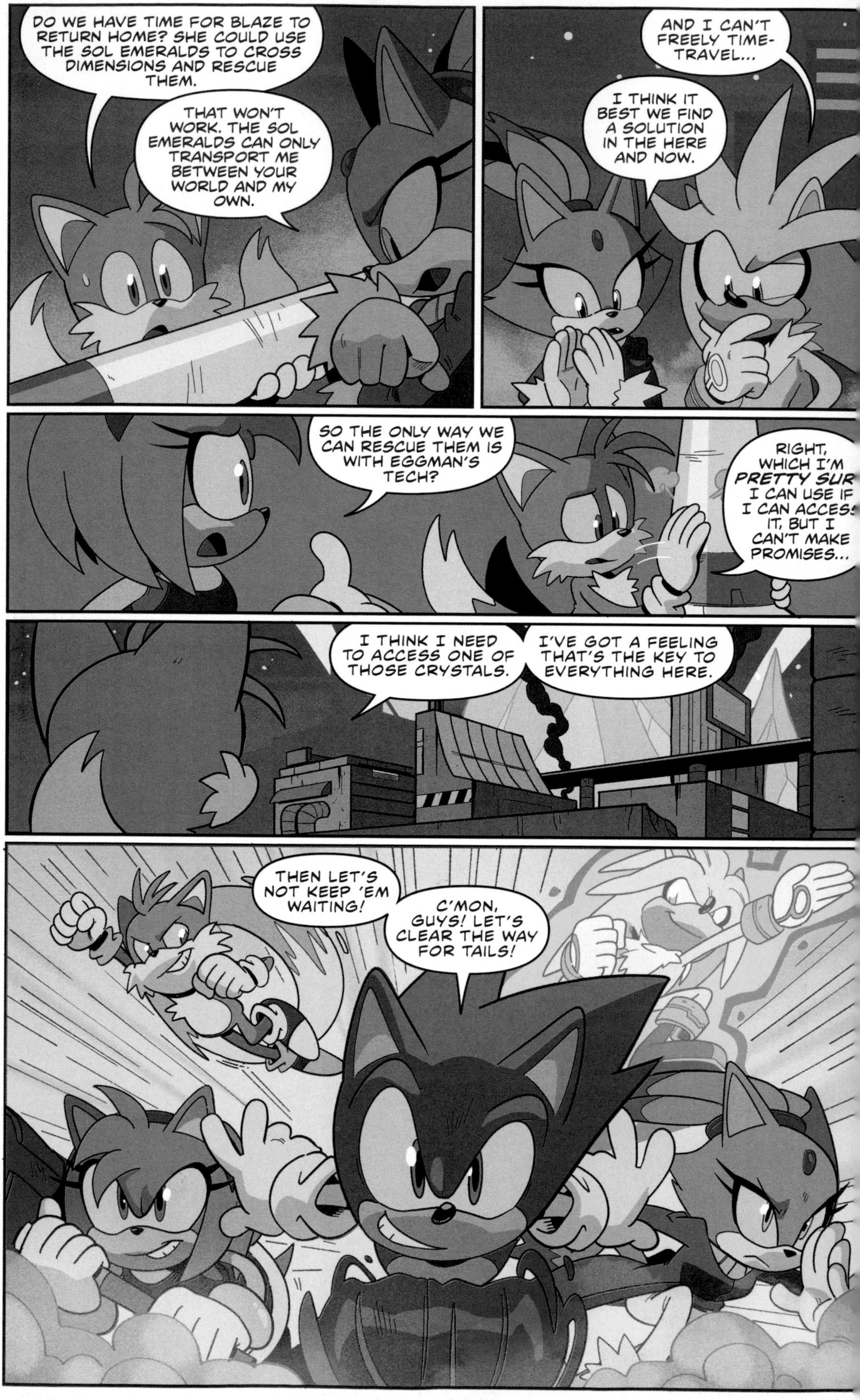

DO WE HAVE TIME FOR BLAZE TO RETURN HOME? SHE COULD USE THE SOL EMERALDS TO CROSS DIMENSIONS AND RESCUE THEM.
THAT WON'T WORK. THE SOL EMERALDS CAN ONLY TRANSPORT ME BETWEEN YOUR WORLD AND MY OWN.
AND I CAN'T FREELY TIME-TRAVEL...
I THINK IT BEST WE FIND A SOLUTION IN THE HERE AND NOW.
SO THE ONLY WAY WE CAN RESCUE THEM IS WITH EGGMAN'S TECH?
RIGHT, WHICH I'M *PRETTY SUR* I CAN USE IF I CAN ACCES IT, BUT I CAN'T MAKE PROMISES...
I THINK I NEED TO ACCESS ONE OF THOSE CRYSTALS.
I'VE GOT A FEELING THAT'S THE KEY TO EVERYTHING HERE.
THEN LET'S NOT KEEP 'EM WAITING!
C'MON, GUYS! LET'S CLEAR THE WAY FOR TAILS!

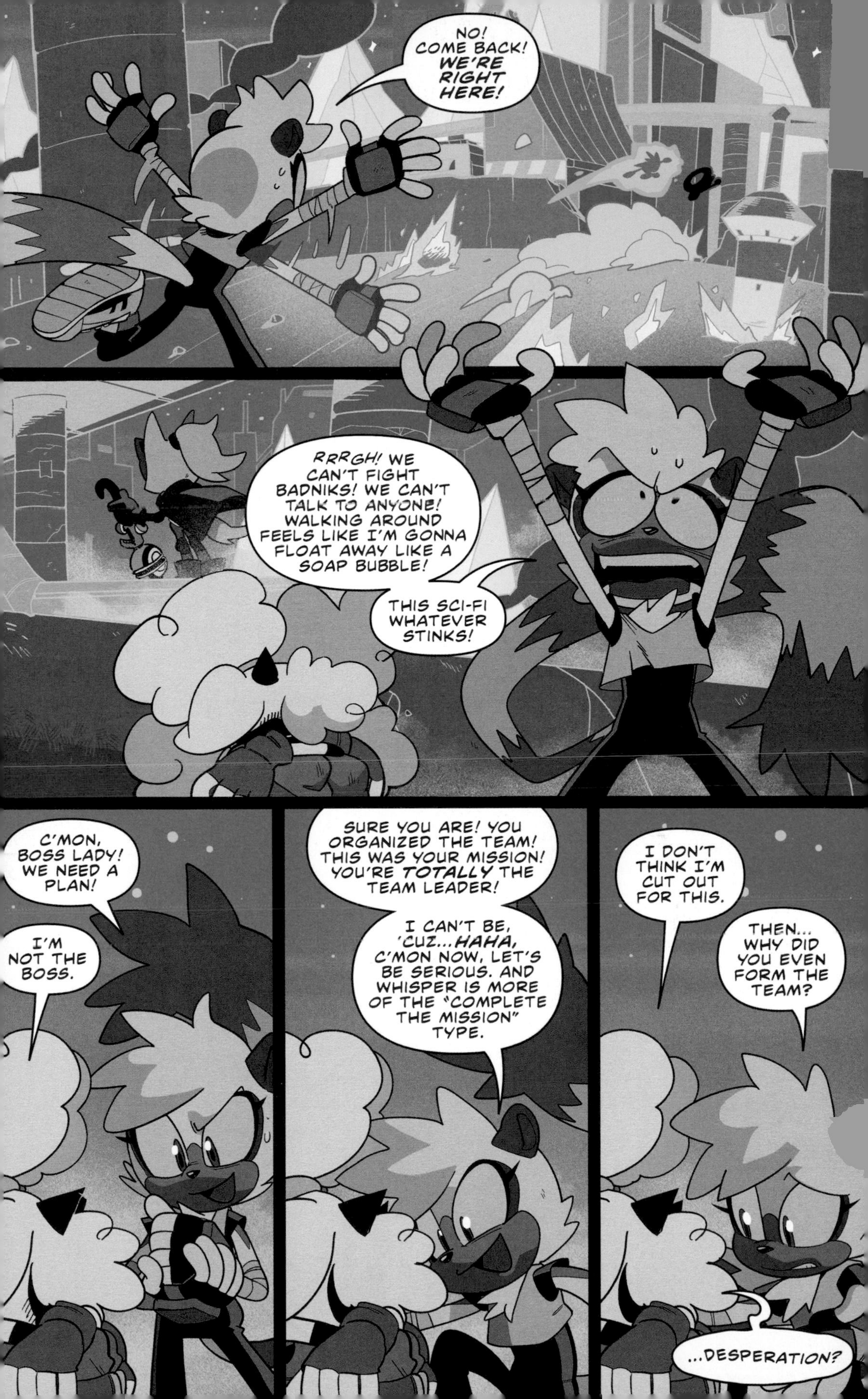
NO! COME BACK! WE'RE RIGHT HERE!
RRRGH! WE CAN'T FIGHT BADNIKS! WE CAN'T TALK TO ANYONE! WALKING AROUND FEELS LIKE I'M GONNA FLOAT AWAY LIKE A SOAP BUBBLE!
THIS SCI-FI WHATEVER STINKS!
C'MON, BOSS LADY! WE NEED A PLAN!
I'M NOT THE BOSS.
SURE YOU ARE! YOU ORGANIZED THE TEAM! THIS WAS YOUR MISSION! YOU'RE TOTALLY THE TEAM LEADER!
I CAN'T BE, 'CUZ... HAHA, C'MON NOW, LET'S BE SERIOUS. AND WHISPER IS MORE OF THE "COMPLETE THE MISSION" TYPE.
I DON'T THINK I'M CUT OUT FOR THIS.
THEN... WHY DID YOU EVEN FORM THE TEAM?
...DESPERATION?

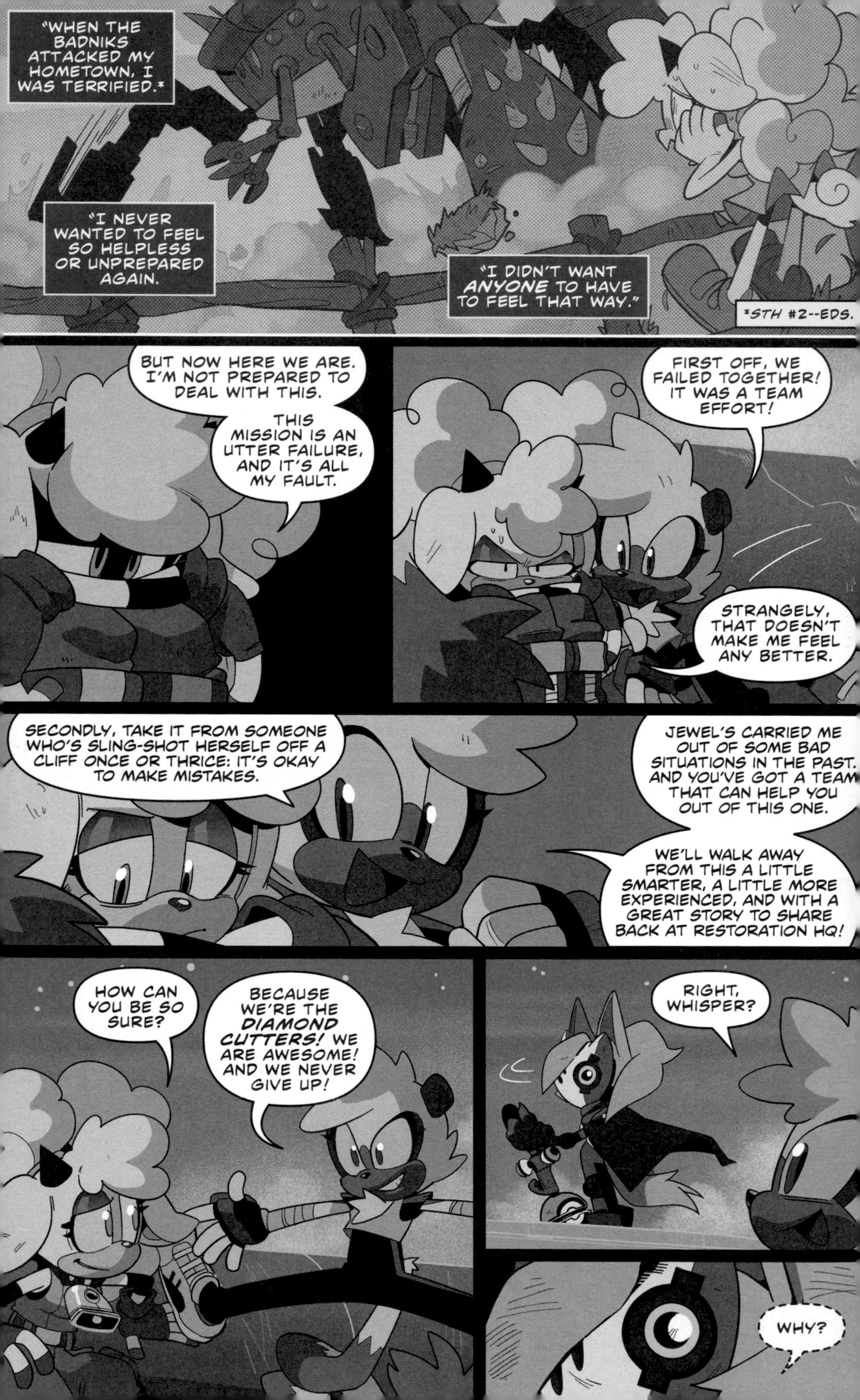
"WHEN THE BADNIKS ATTACKED MY HOMETOWN, I WAS TERRIFIED.*
"I NEVER WANTED TO FEEL SO HELPLESS OR UNPREPARED AGAIN.
"I DIDN'T WANT ANYONE TO HAVE TO FEEL THAT WAY."
*STH #2--EDS.
BUT NOW HERE WE ARE. I'M NOT PREPARED TO DEAL WITH THIS.
THIS MISSION IS AN UTTER FAILURE, AND IT'S ALL MY FAULT.
FIRST OFF, WE FAILED TOGETHER! IT WAS A TEAM EFFORT!
STRANGELY, THAT DOESN'T MAKE ME FEEL ANY BETTER.
SECONDLY, TAKE IT FROM SOMEONE WHO'S SLING-SHOT HERSELF OFF A CLIFF ONCE OR THRICE: IT'S OKAY TO MAKE MISTAKES.
JEWEL'S CARRIED ME OUT OF SOME BAD SITUATIONS IN THE PAST. AND YOU'VE GOT A TEAM THAT CAN HELP YOU OUT OF THIS ONE.
WE'LL WALK AWAY FROM THIS A LITTLE SMARTER, A LITTLE MORE EXPERIENCED, AND WITH A GREAT STORY TO SHARE BACK AT RESTORATION HQ!
HOW CAN YOU BE SO SURE?
BECAUSE WE'RE THE DIAMOND CUTTERS! WE ARE AWESOME! AND WE NEVER GIVE UP!
RIGHT, WHISPER?
WHY?

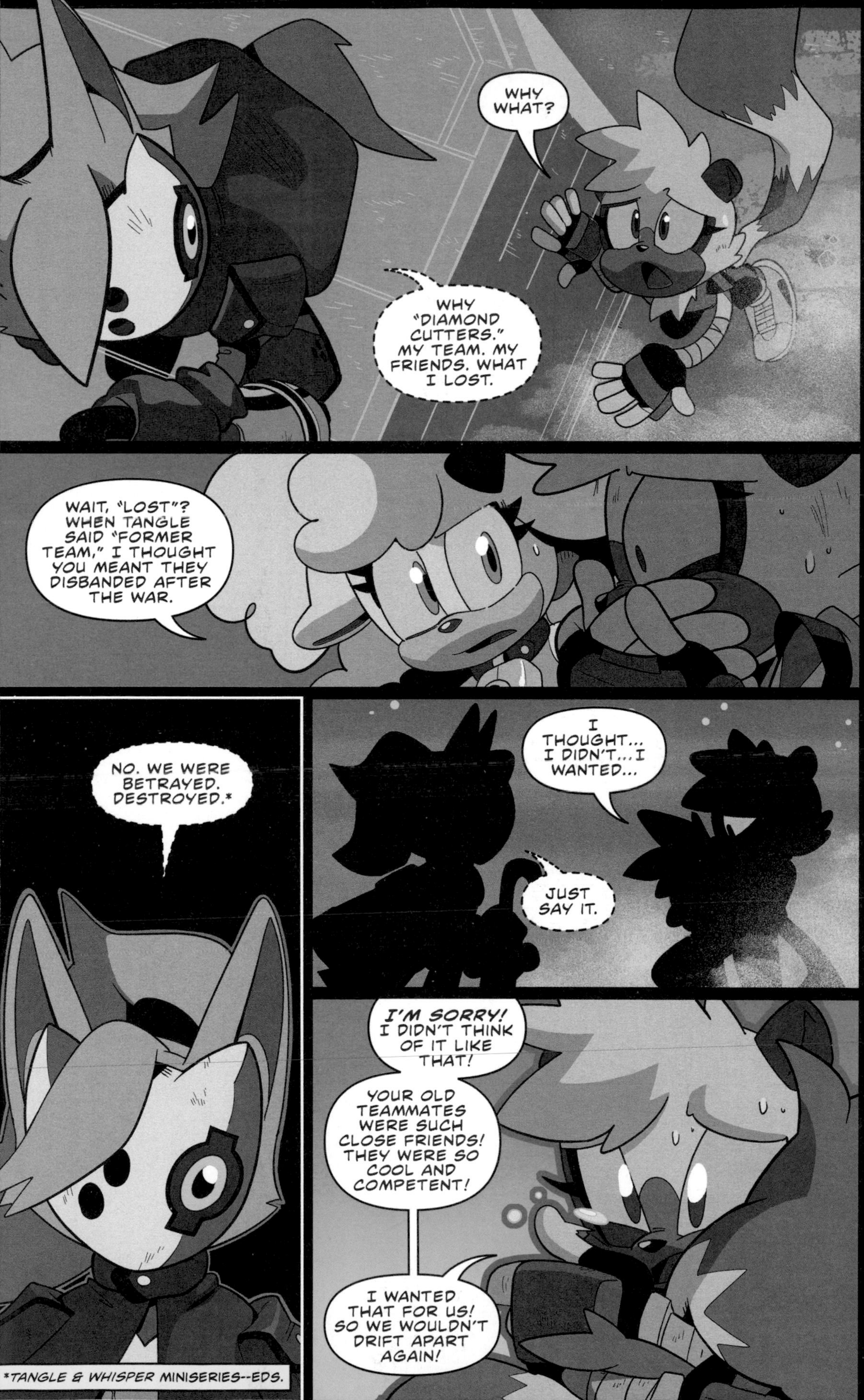
WHY WHAT?
WHY "DIAMOND CUTTERS." MY TEAM. MY FRIENDS. WHAT I LOST.
WAIT, "LOST"? WHEN TANGLE SAID "FORMER TEAM," I THOUGHT YOU MEANT THEY DISBANDED AFTER THE WAR.
NO. WE WERE BETRAYED. DESTROYED.*
I THOUGHT... I DIDN'T... I WANTED...
JUST SAY IT.
I'M SORRY! I DIDN'T THINK OF IT LIKE THAT!
YOUR OLD TEAMMATES WERE SUCH CLOSE FRIENDS! THEY WERE SO COOL AND COMPETENT!
I WANTED THAT FOR US! SO WE WOULDN'T DRIFT APART AGAIN!

**TANGLE & WHISPER* MINISERIES--EDS.

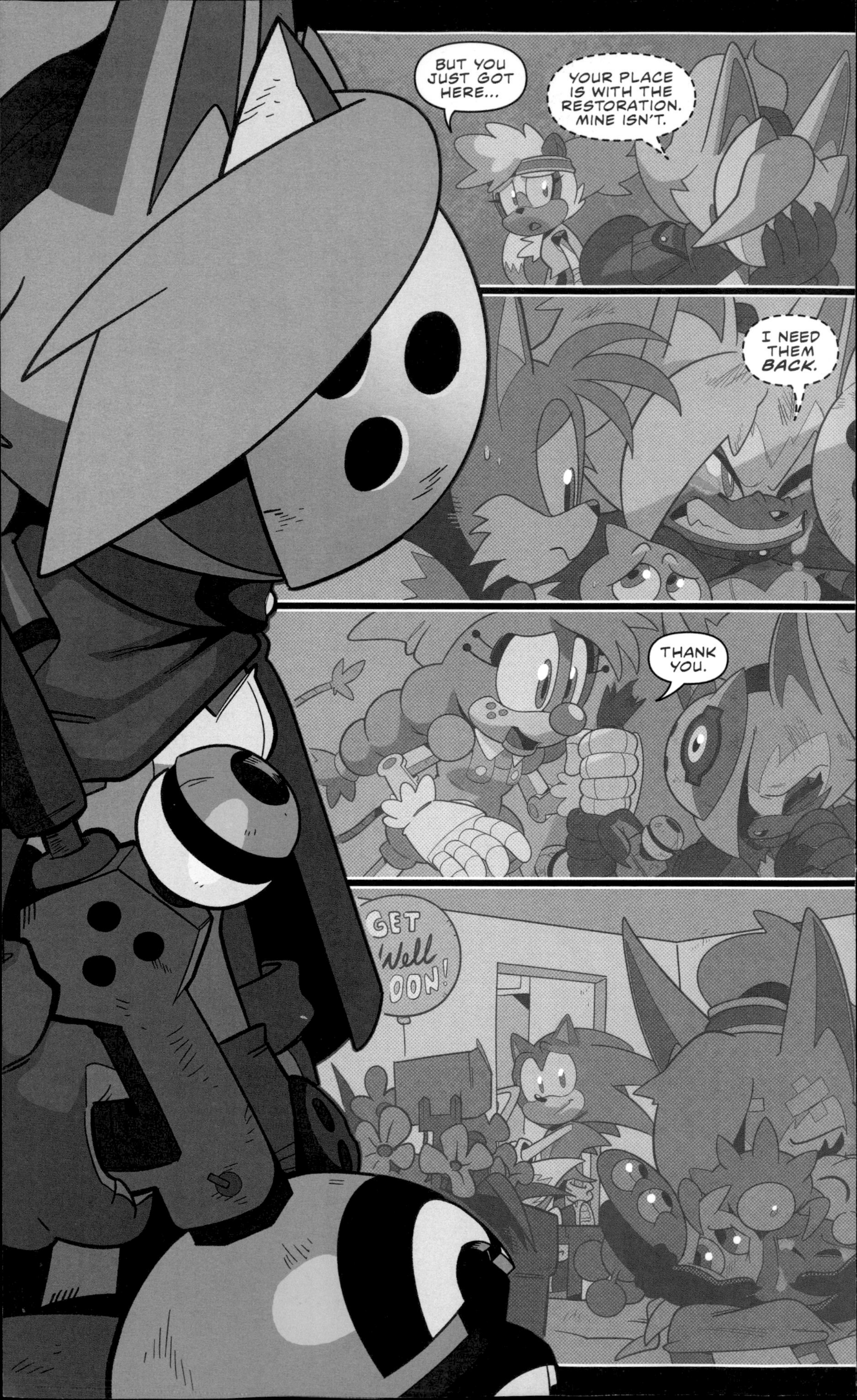
BUT YOU JUST GOT HERE...
YOUR PLACE IS WITH THE RESTORATION. MINE ISN'T.
I NEED THEM *BACK.*
THANK YOU.
GET Well SOON!

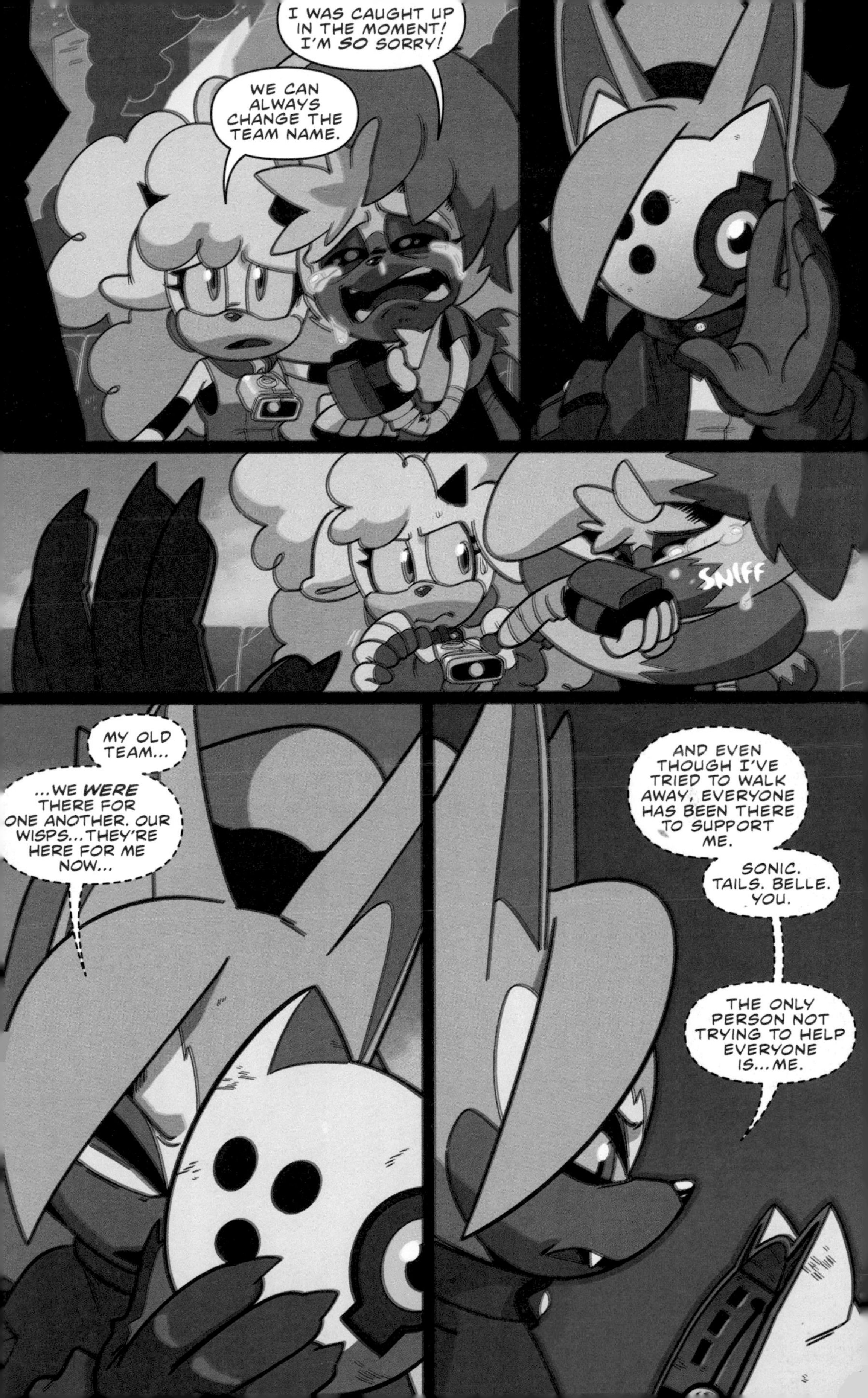
I WAS CAUGHT UP IN THE MOMENT! I'M *SO* SORRY!
WE CAN ALWAYS CHANGE THE TEAM NAME.
SNIFF
MY OLD TEAM...
...WE ***WERE*** THERE FOR ONE ANOTHER. OUR WISPS...THEY'RE HERE FOR ME NOW...
AND EVEN THOUGH I'VE TRIED TO WALK AWAY, EVERYONE HAS BEEN THERE TO SUPPORT ME.
SONIC. TAILS. BELLE. YOU.
THE ONLY PERSON NOT TRYING TO HELP EVERYONE IS...ME.

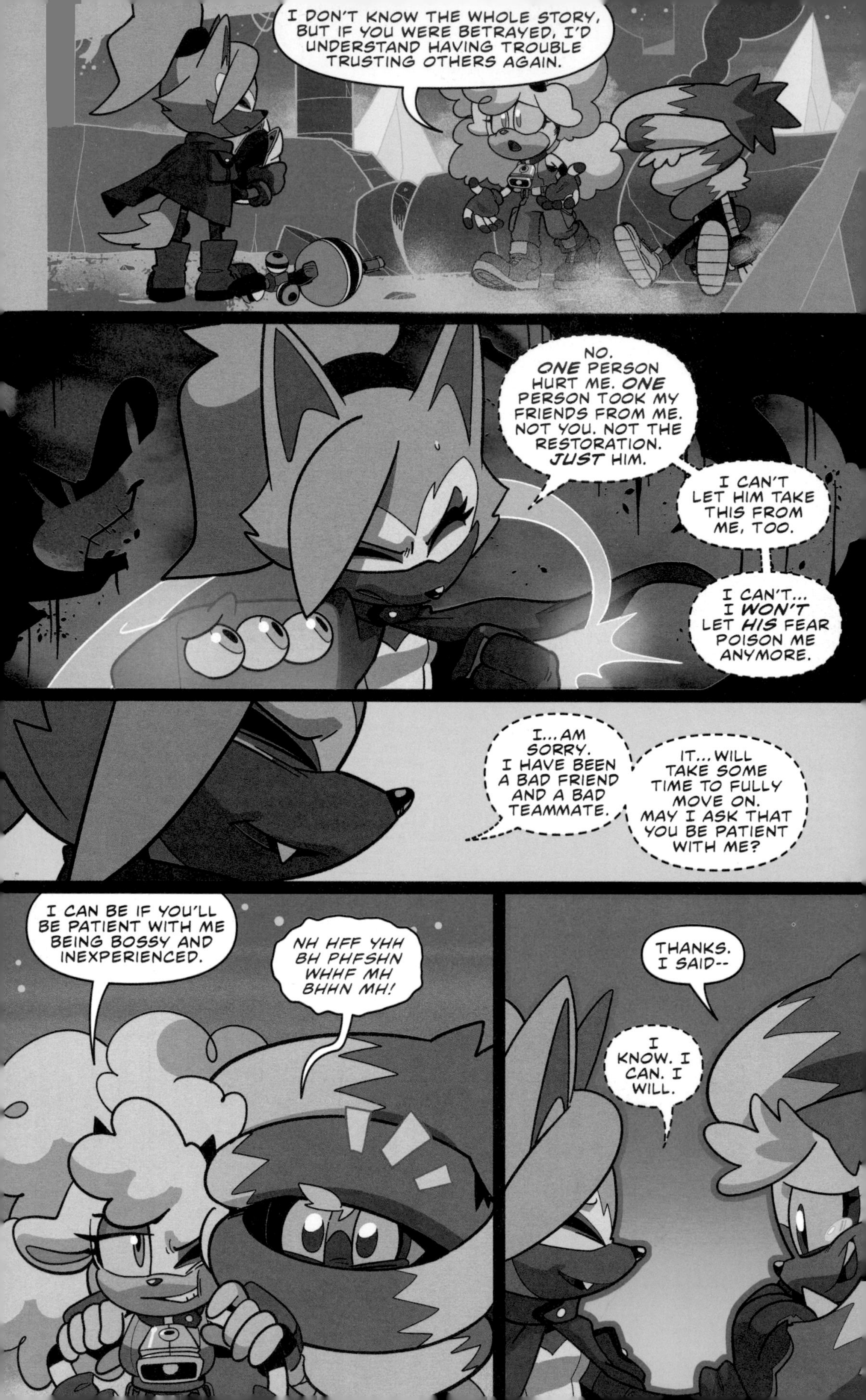
I DON'T KNOW THE WHOLE STORY, BUT IF YOU WERE BETRAYED, I'D UNDERSTAND HAVING TROUBLE TRUSTING OTHERS AGAIN.
NO. *ONE* PERSON HURT ME. *ONE* PERSON TOOK MY FRIENDS FROM ME. NOT YOU. NOT THE RESTORATION. *JUST* HIM.
I CAN'T LET HIM TAKE THIS FROM ME, TOO.
I CAN'T... I *WON'T* LET *HIS* FEAR POISON ME ANYMORE.
I... AM SORRY. I HAVE BEEN A BAD FRIEND AND A BAD TEAMMATE.
IT... WILL TAKE SOME TIME TO FULLY MOVE ON. MAY I ASK THAT YOU BE PATIENT WITH ME?
I CAN BE IF YOU'LL BE PATIENT WITH ME BEING BOSSY AND INEXPERIENCED.
NH HFF YHH BH PHFSHN WHHF MH BHHN MH!
THANKS. I SAID--
I KNOW. I CAN. I WILL.

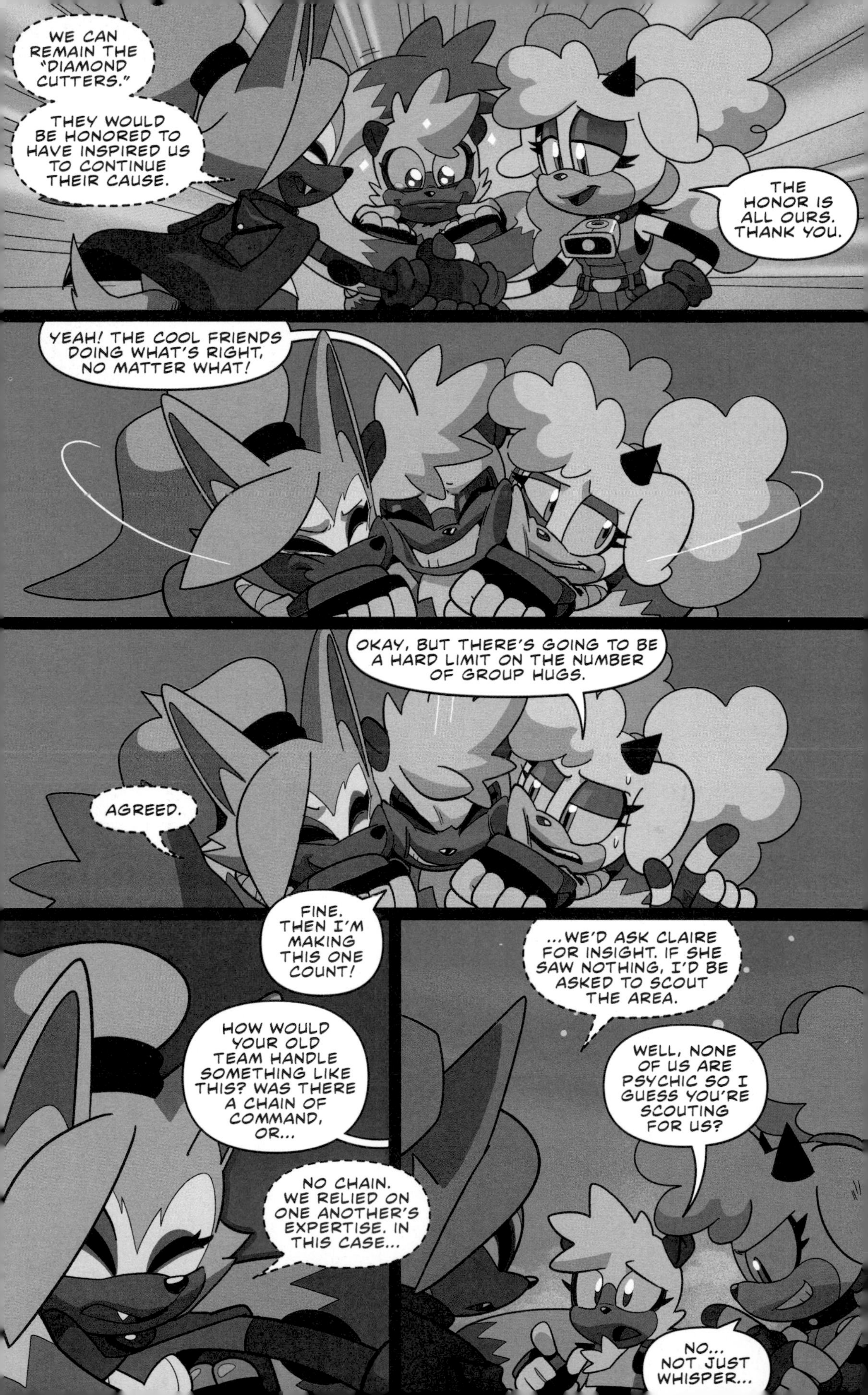
WE CAN REMAIN THE "DIAMOND CUTTERS."
THEY WOULD BE HONORED TO HAVE INSPIRED US TO CONTINUE THEIR CAUSE.
THE HONOR IS ALL OURS. THANK YOU.
YEAH! THE COOL FRIENDS DOING WHAT'S RIGHT, NO MATTER WHAT!
OKAY, BUT THERE'S GOING TO BE A HARD LIMIT ON THE NUMBER OF GROUP HUGS.
AGREED.
FINE. THEN I'M MAKING THIS ONE COUNT!
HOW WOULD YOUR OLD TEAM HANDLE SOMETHING LIKE THIS? WAS THERE A CHAIN OF COMMAND, OR...
NO CHAIN. WE RELIED ON ONE ANOTHER'S EXPERTISE. IN THIS CASE...
...WE'D ASK CLAIRE FOR INSIGHT. IF SHE SAW NOTHING, I'D BE ASKED TO SCOUT THE AREA.
WELL, NONE OF US ARE PSYCHIC SO I GUESS YOU'RE SCOUTING FOR US?
NO... NOT JUST WHISPER...

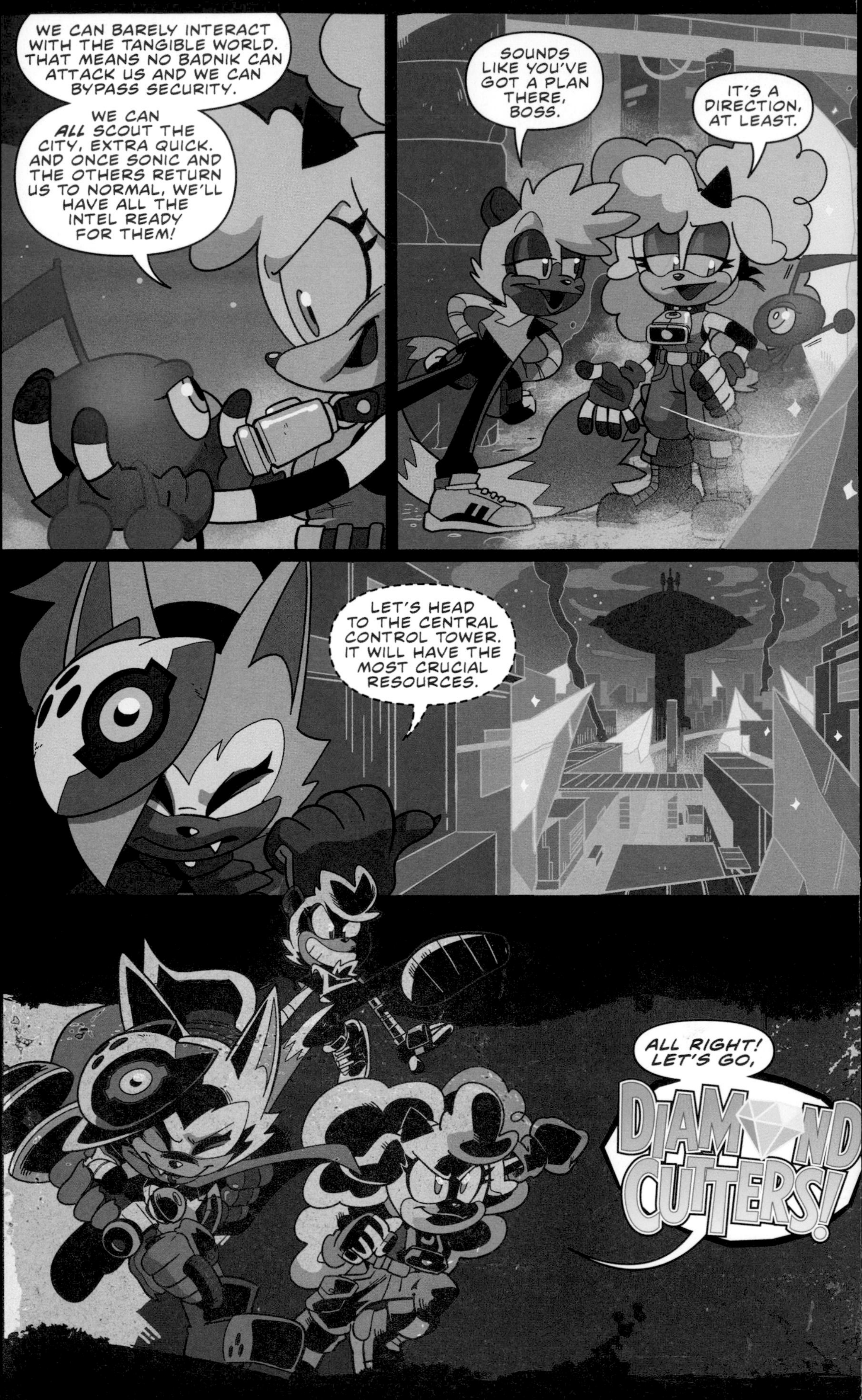
WE CAN BARELY INTERACT WITH THE TANGIBLE WORLD. THAT MEANS NO BADNIK CAN ATTACK US AND WE CAN BYPASS SECURITY.
WE CAN ALL SCOUT THE CITY, EXTRA QUICK. AND ONCE SONIC AND THE OTHERS RETURN US TO NORMAL, WE'LL HAVE ALL THE INTEL READY FOR THEM!
SOUNDS LIKE YOU'VE GOT A PLAN THERE, BOSS.
IT'S A DIRECTION, AT LEAST.
LET'S HEAD TO THE CENTRAL CONTROL TOWER. IT WILL HAVE THE MOST CRUCIAL RESOURCES.
ALL RIGHT! LET'S GO,
DIAMOND CUTTERS!

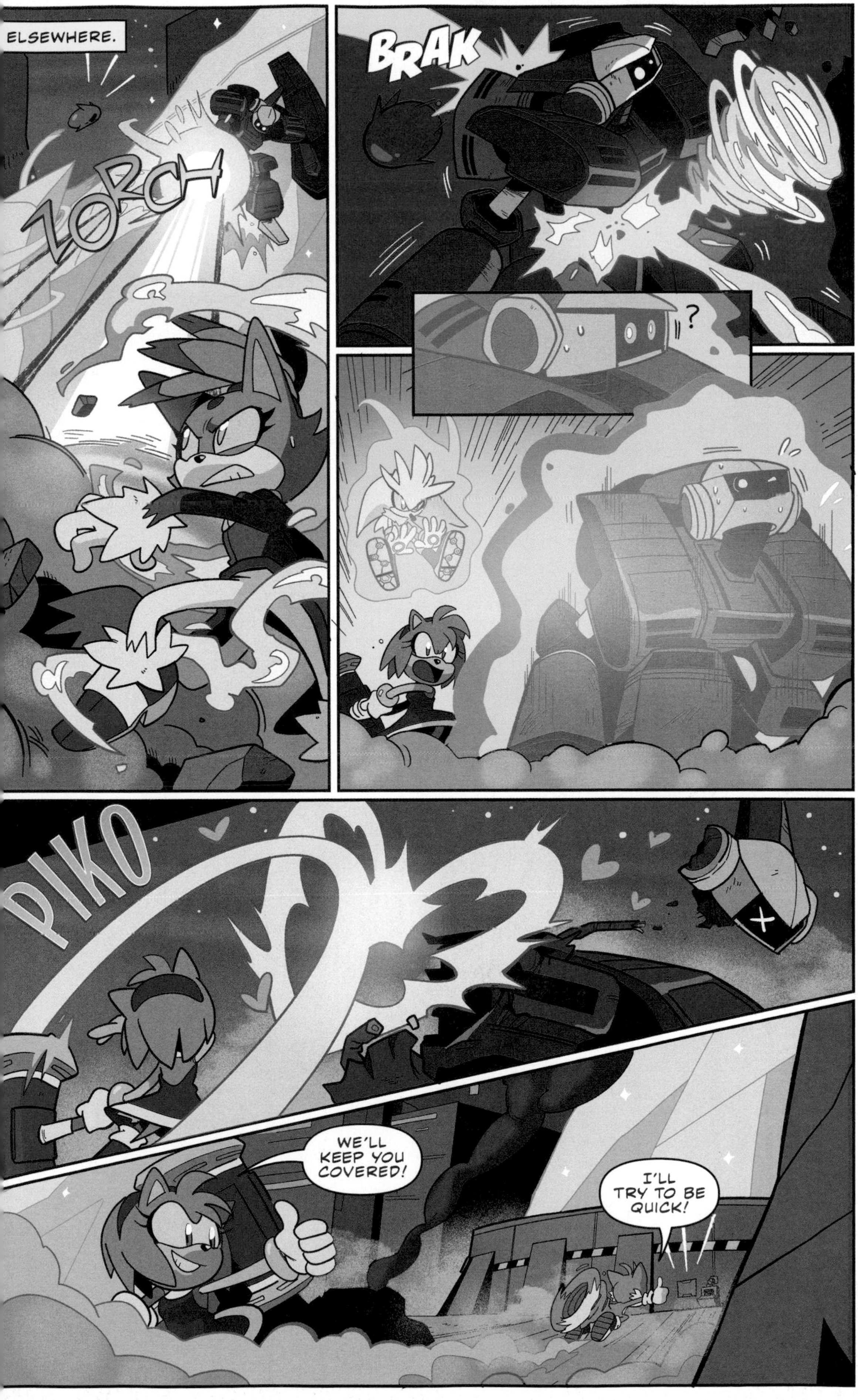
ELSEWHERE.
ZORCH
BRAK
?
PIKO
WE'LL KEEP YOU COVERED!
I'LL TRY TO BE QUICK!

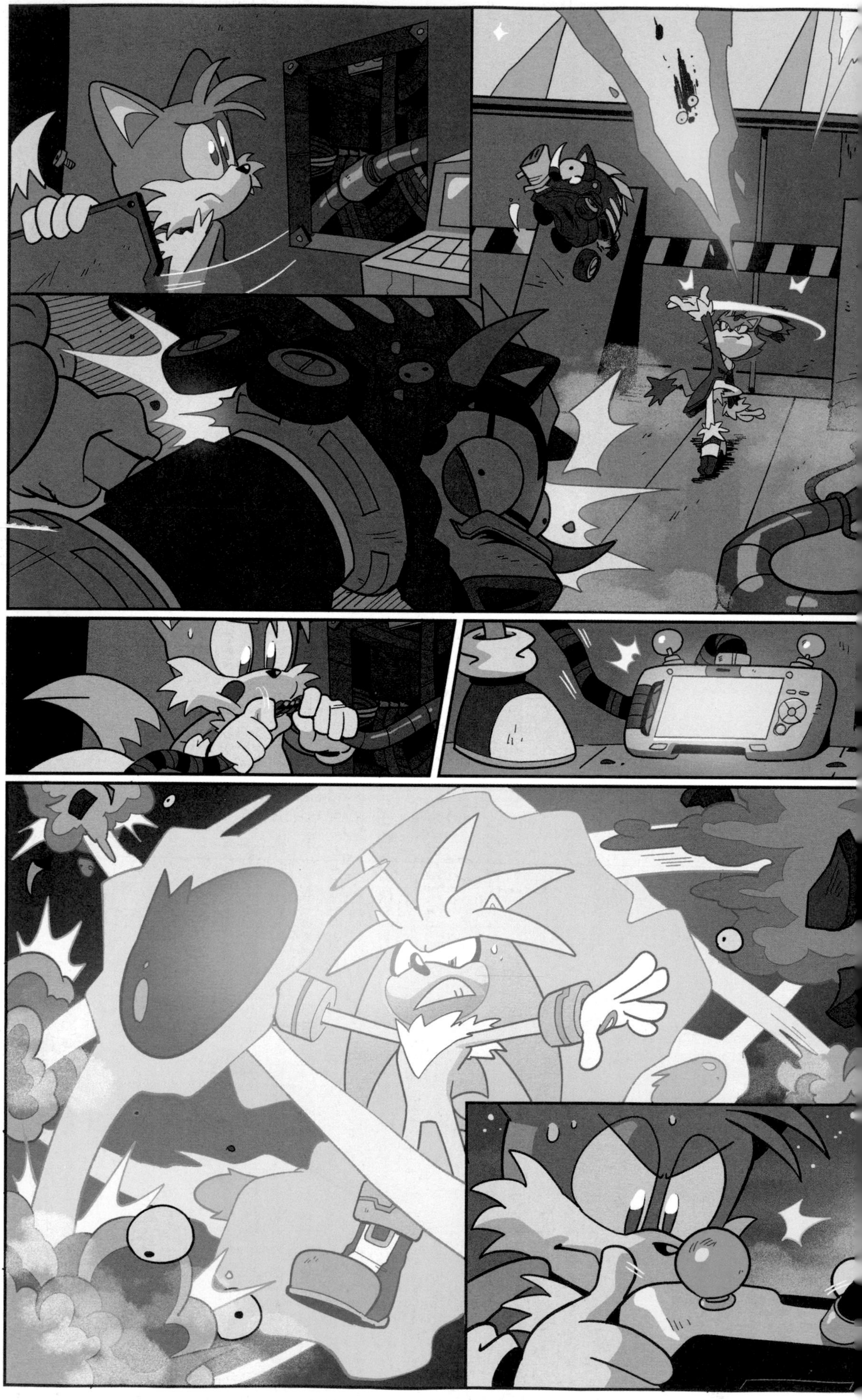

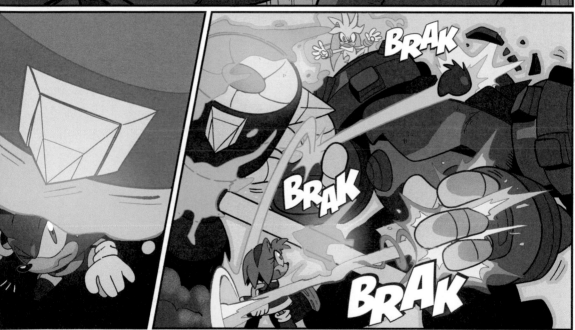

BRAK

BRAK

BRAK

SILVER! GIVE ME A BOOST!

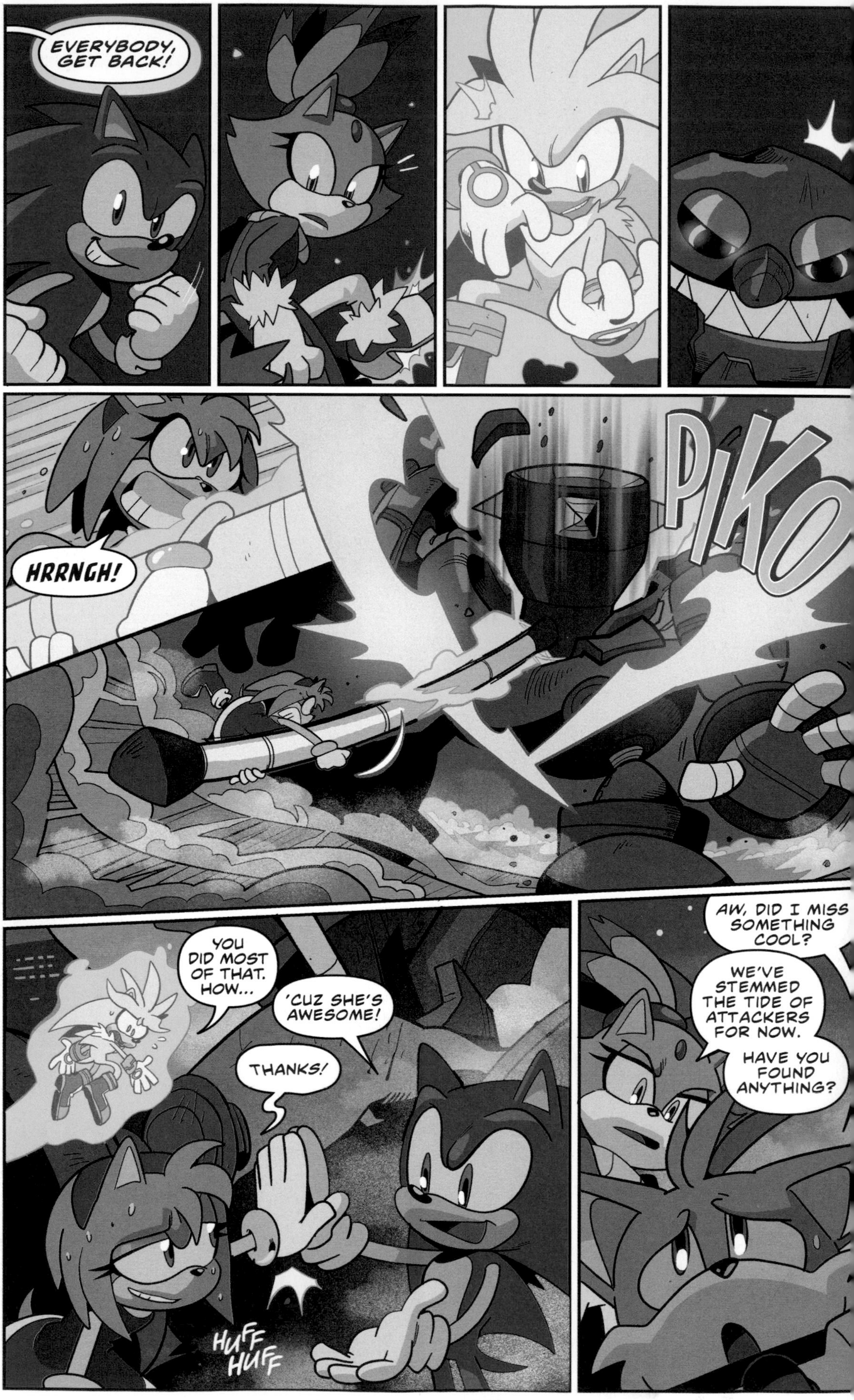
EVERYBODY, GET BACK!
PIKO
HRRNGH!
YOU DID MOST OF THAT. HOW...
'CUZ SHE'S AWESOME!
THANKS!
HUFF HUFF
AW, DID I MISS SOMETHING COOL?
WE'VE STEMMED THE TIDE OF ATTACKERS FOR NOW.
HAVE YOU FOUND ANYTHING?

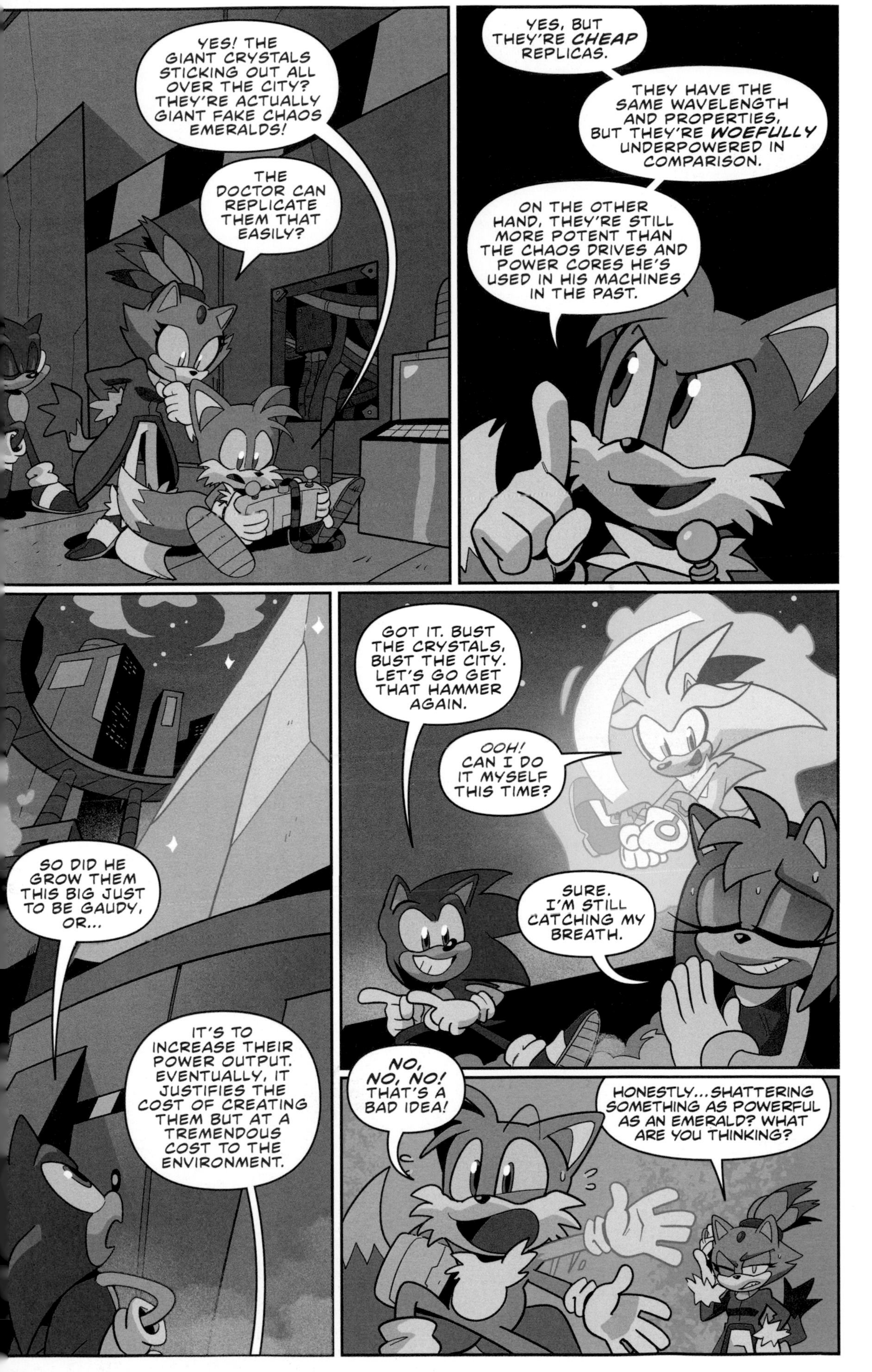
YES! THE GIANT CRYSTALS STICKING OUT ALL OVER THE CITY? THEY'RE ACTUALLY GIANT FAKE CHAOS EMERALDS!
THE DOCTOR CAN REPLICATE THEM THAT EASILY?
YES, BUT THEY'RE *CHEAP* REPLICAS.
THEY HAVE THE SAME WAVELENGTH AND PROPERTIES, BUT THEY'RE ***WOEFULLY*** UNDERPOWERED IN COMPARISON.
ON THE OTHER HAND, THEY'RE STILL MORE POTENT THAN THE CHAOS DRIVES AND POWER CORES HE'S USED IN HIS MACHINES IN THE PAST.
SO DID HE GROW THEM THIS BIG JUST TO BE GAUDY, OR...
IT'S TO INCREASE THEIR POWER OUTPUT. EVENTUALLY, IT JUSTIFIES THE COST OF CREATING THEM BUT AT A TREMENDOUS COST TO THE ENVIRONMENT.
GOT IT. BUST THE CRYSTALS, BUST THE CITY. LET'S GO GET THAT HAMMER AGAIN.
OOH! CAN I DO IT MYSELF THIS TIME?
SURE. I'M STILL CATCHING MY BREATH.
NO, NO, NO! THAT'S A BAD IDEA!
HONESTLY...SHATTERING SOMETHING AS POWERFUL AS AN EMERALD? WHAT ARE YOU THINKING?

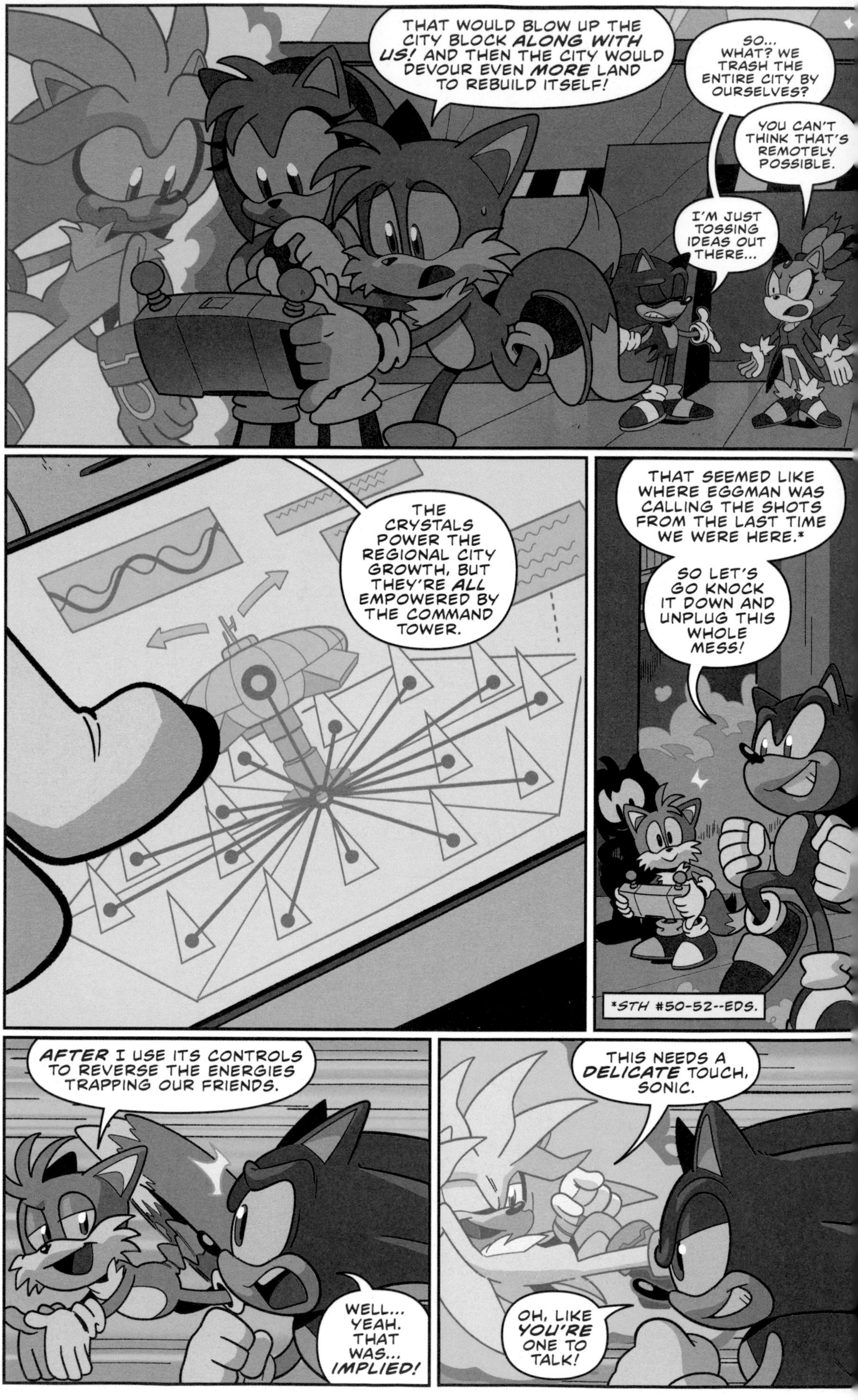
THAT WOULD BLOW UP THE CITY BLOCK ALONG WITH US! AND THEN THE CITY WOULD DEVOUR EVEN MORE LAND TO REBUILD ITSELF!
SO... WHAT? WE TRASH THE ENTIRE CITY BY OURSELVES?
YOU CAN'T THINK THAT'S REMOTELY POSSIBLE.
I'M JUST TOSSING IDEAS OUT THERE...
THE CRYSTALS POWER THE REGIONAL CITY GROWTH, BUT THEY'RE ALL EMPOWERED BY THE COMMAND TOWER.
THAT SEEMED LIKE WHERE EGGMAN WAS CALLING THE SHOTS FROM THE LAST TIME WE WERE HERE.*
SO LET'S GO KNOCK IT DOWN AND UNPLUG THIS WHOLE MESS!
*STH #50-52--EDS.
AFTER I USE ITS CONTROLS TO REVERSE THE ENERGIES TRAPPING OUR FRIENDS.
WELL... YEAH. THAT WAS... IMPLIED!
THIS NEEDS A DELICATE TOUCH, SONIC.
OH, LIKE YOU'RE ONE TO TALK!

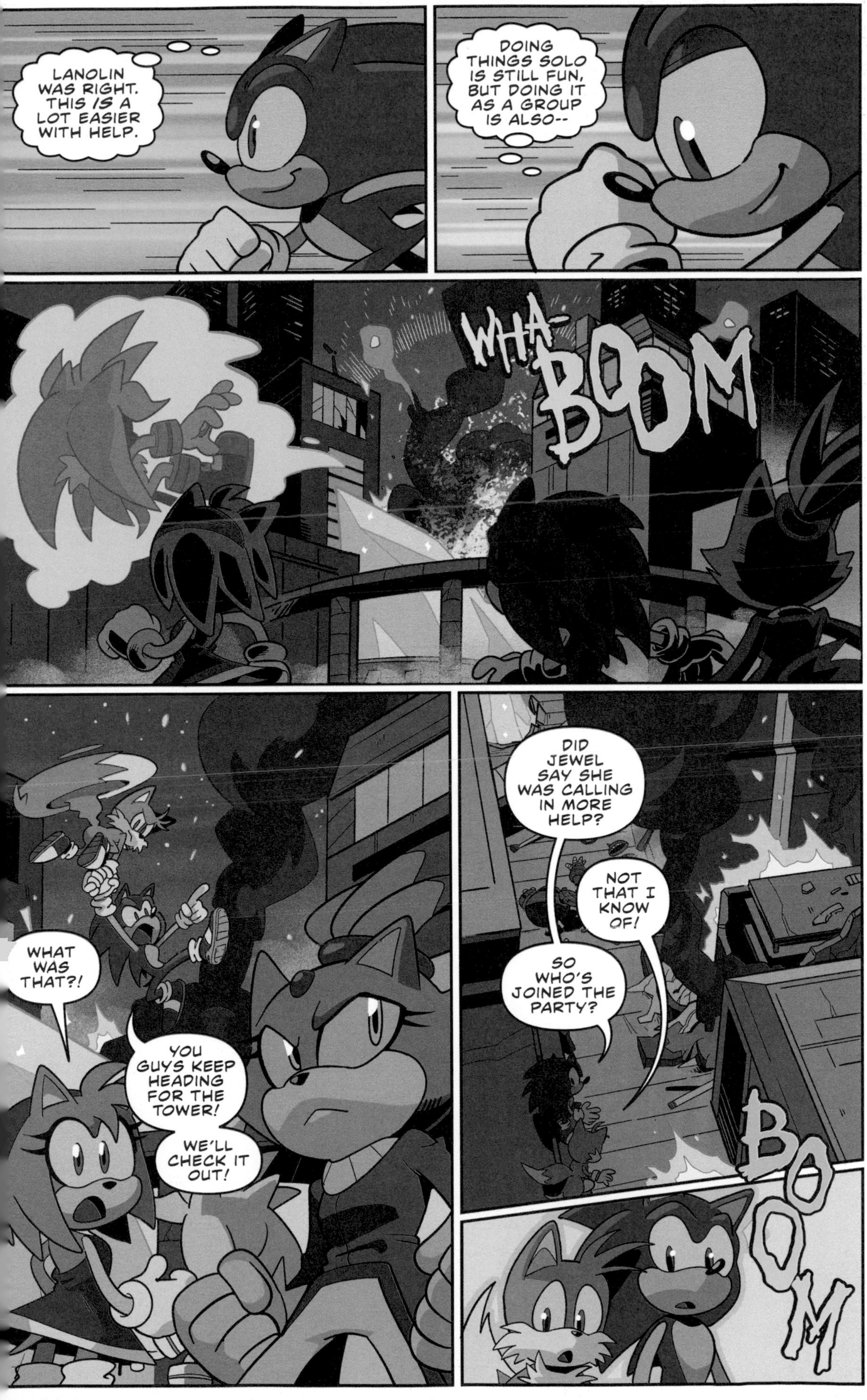
LANOLIN WAS RIGHT. THIS *IS* A LOT EASIER WITH HELP.
DOING THINGS SOLO IS STILL FUN, BUT DOING IT AS A GROUP IS ALSO--
WHA-BOOM
WHAT WAS THAT?!
YOU GUYS KEEP HEADING FOR THE TOWER!
WE'LL CHECK IT OUT!
DID JEWEL SAY SHE WAS CALLING IN MORE HELP?
NOT THAT I KNOW OF!
SO WHO'S JOINED THE PARTY?
BOOOM

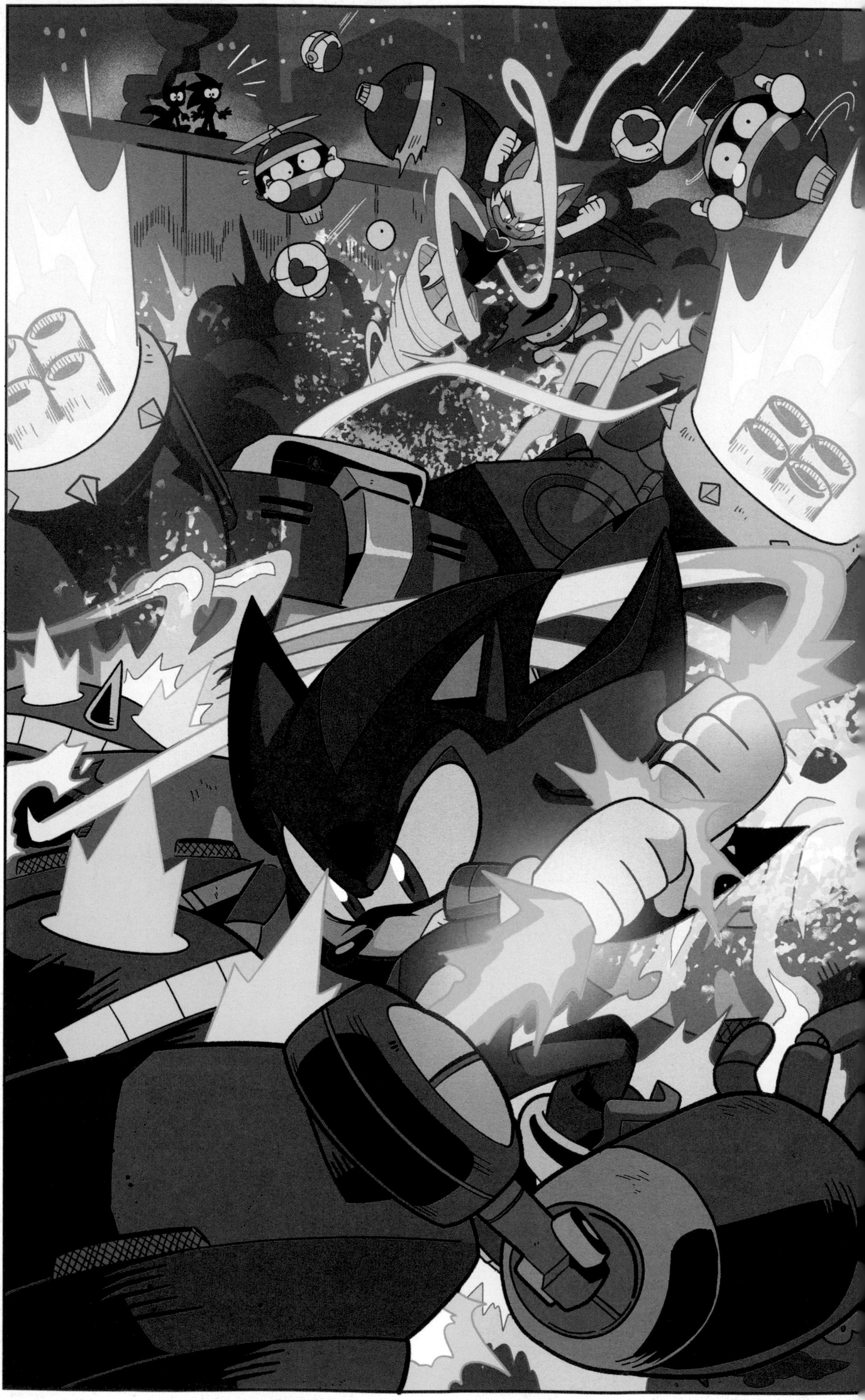

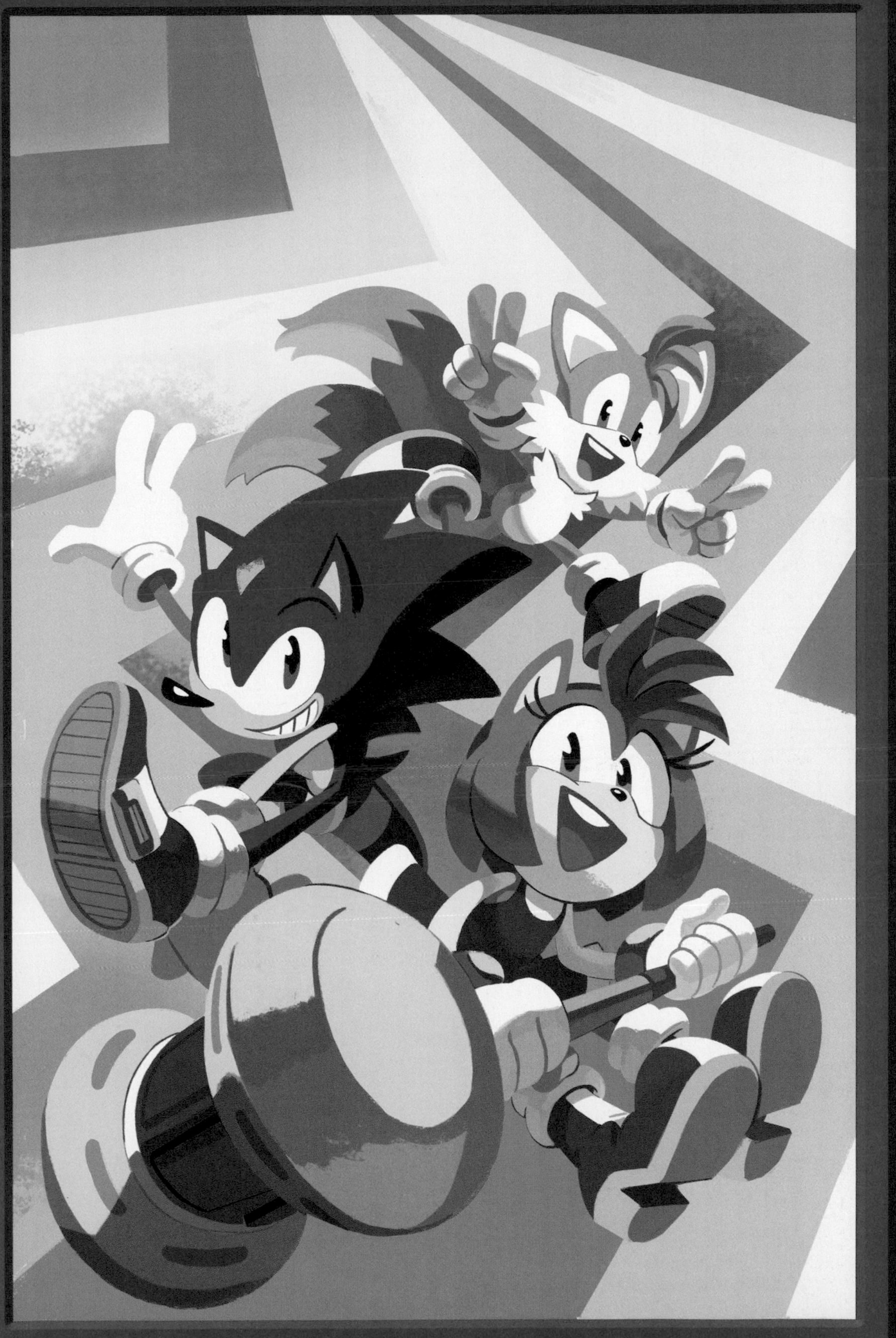

ART BY **NATHALIE FOURDRAINE**

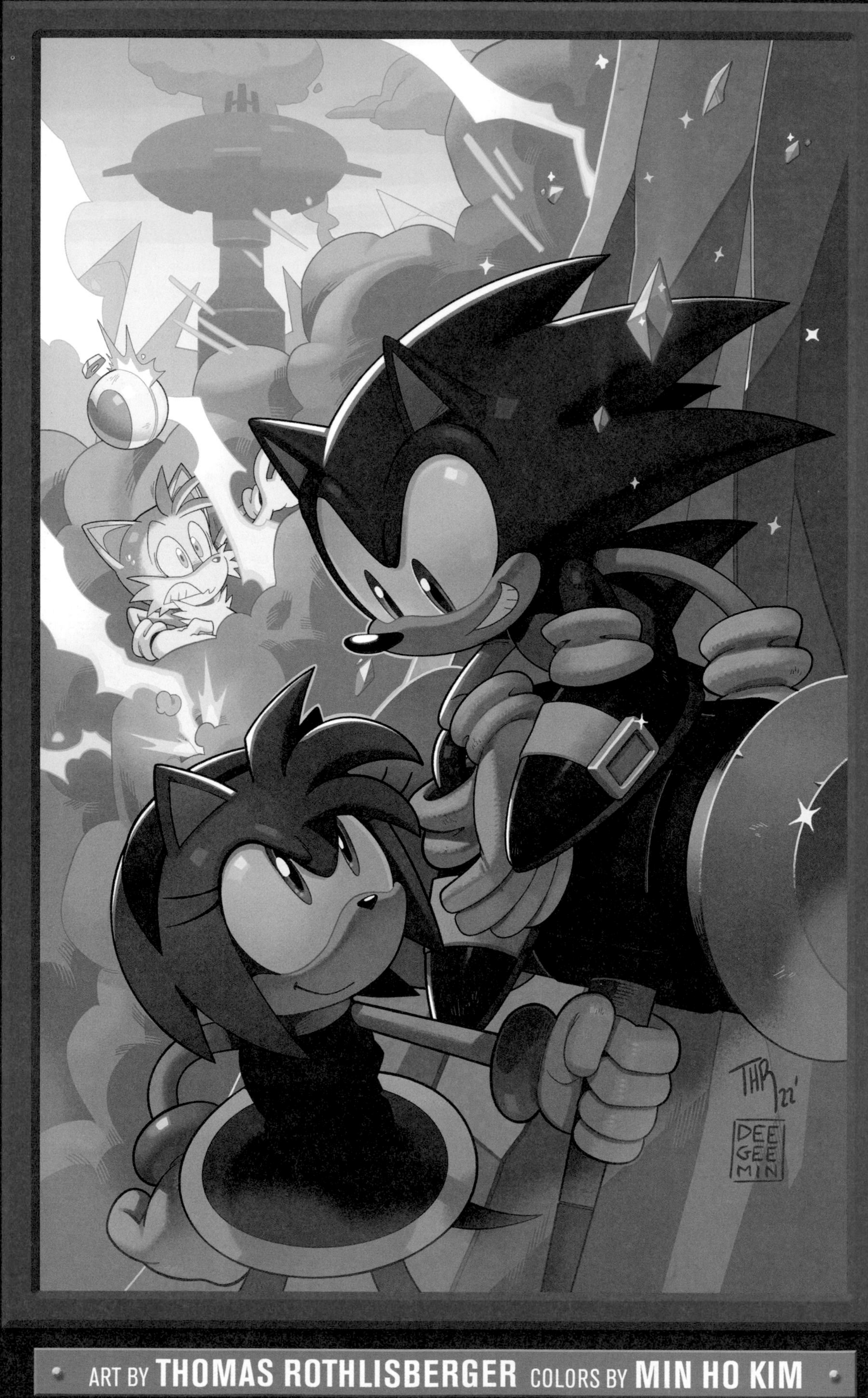
THR 22'
DEE GEE MIN

ART BY **THOMAS ROTHLISBERGER** COLORS BY **MIN HO KIM**

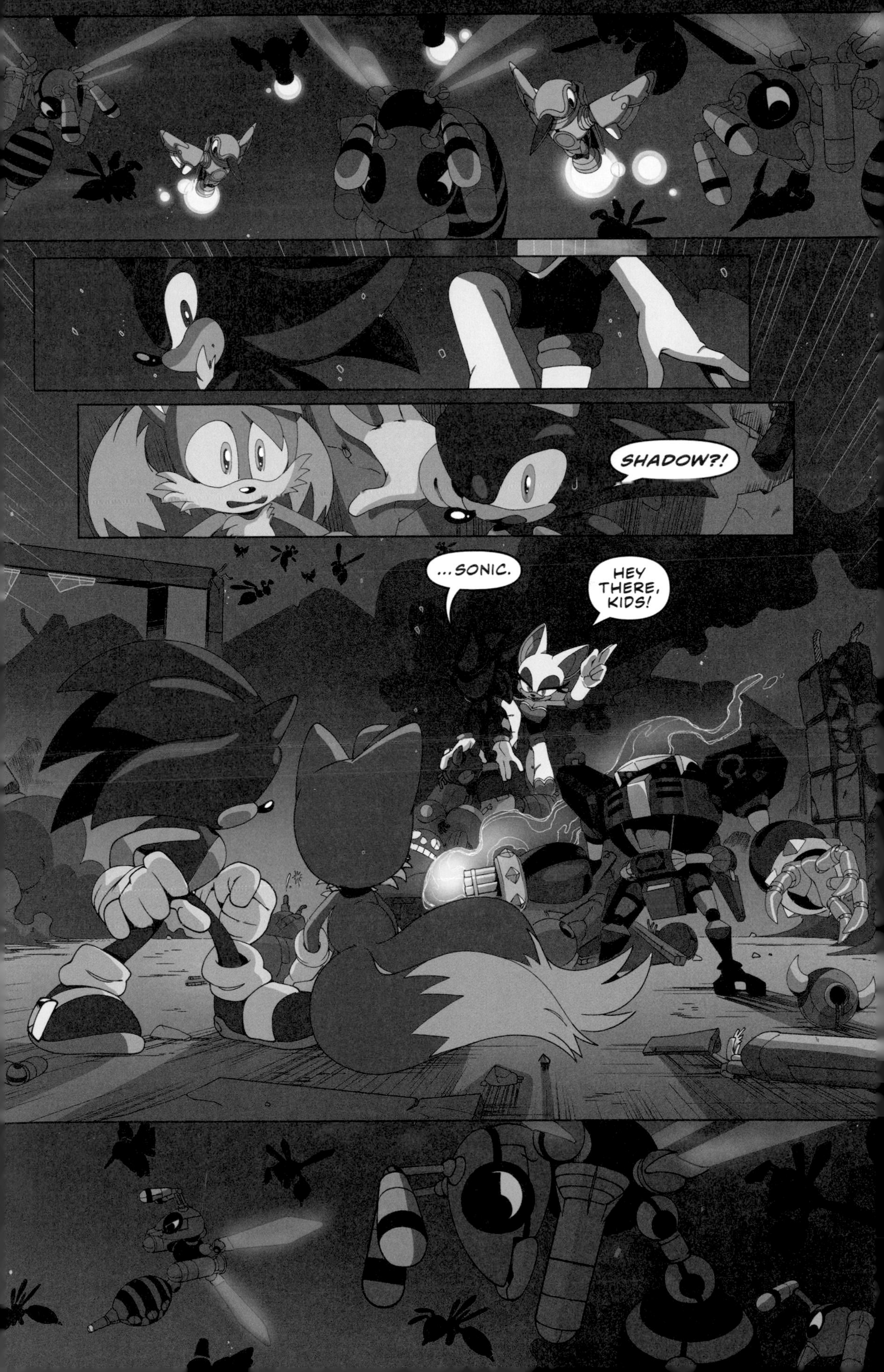
SHADOW?!
...SONIC.
HEY THERE, KIDS!

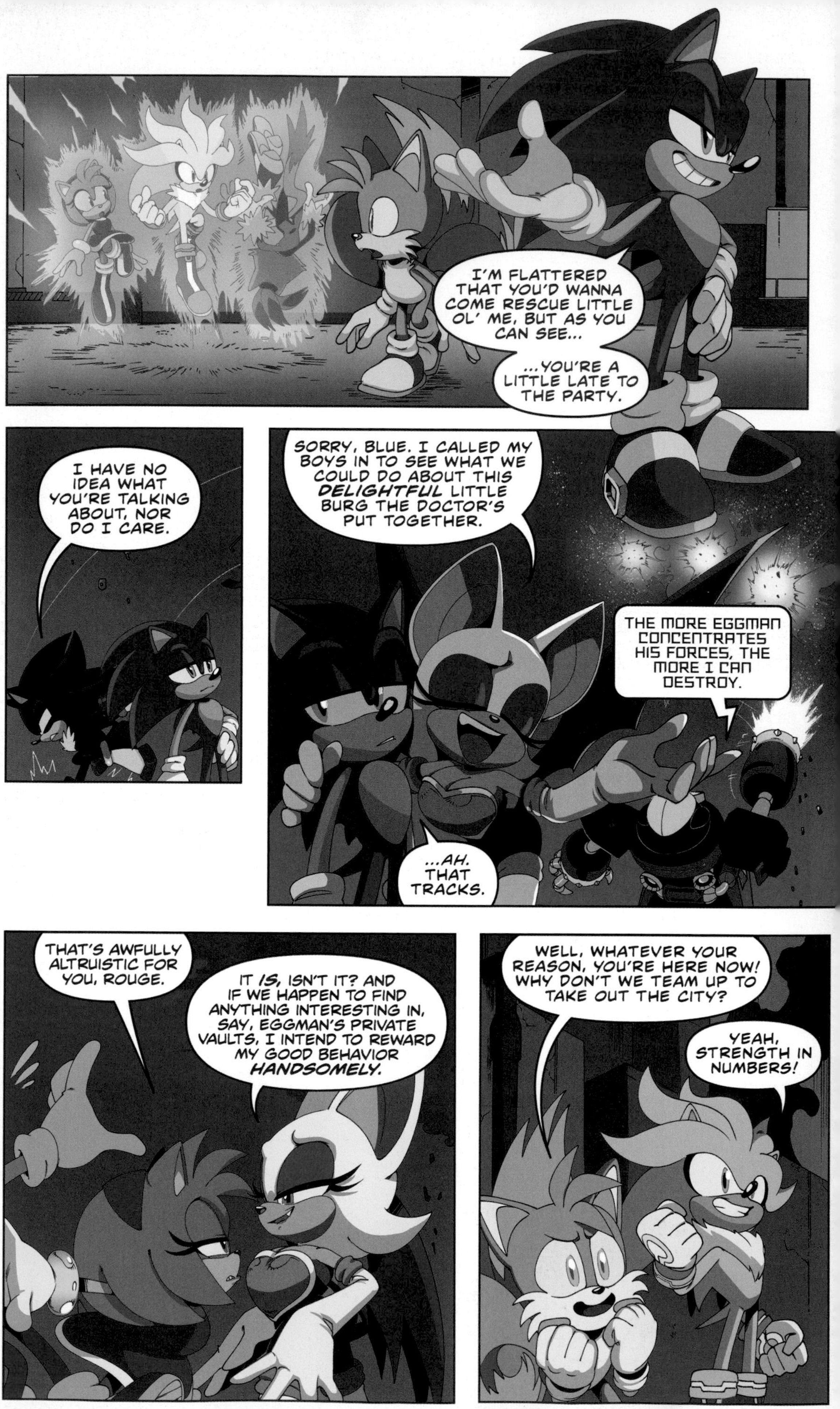
I'M FLATTERED THAT YOU'D WANNA COME RESCUE LITTLE OL' ME, BUT AS YOU CAN SEE...
...YOU'RE A LITTLE LATE TO THE PARTY.
I HAVE NO IDEA WHAT YOU'RE TALKING ABOUT, NOR DO I CARE.
SORRY, BLUE. I CALLED MY BOYS IN TO SEE WHAT WE COULD DO ABOUT THIS DELIGHTFUL LITTLE BURG THE DOCTOR'S PUT TOGETHER.
THE MORE EGGMAN CONCENTRATES HIS FORCES, THE MORE I CAN DESTROY.
...AH. THAT TRACKS.
THAT'S AWFULLY ALTRUISTIC FOR YOU, ROUGE.
IT IS, ISN'T IT? AND IF WE HAPPEN TO FIND ANYTHING INTERESTING IN, SAY, EGGMAN'S PRIVATE VAULTS, I INTEND TO REWARD MY GOOD BEHAVIOR HANDSOMELY.
WELL, WHATEVER YOUR REASON, YOU'RE HERE NOW! WHY DON'T WE TEAM UP TO TAKE OUT THE CITY?
YEAH, STRENGTH IN NUMBERS!

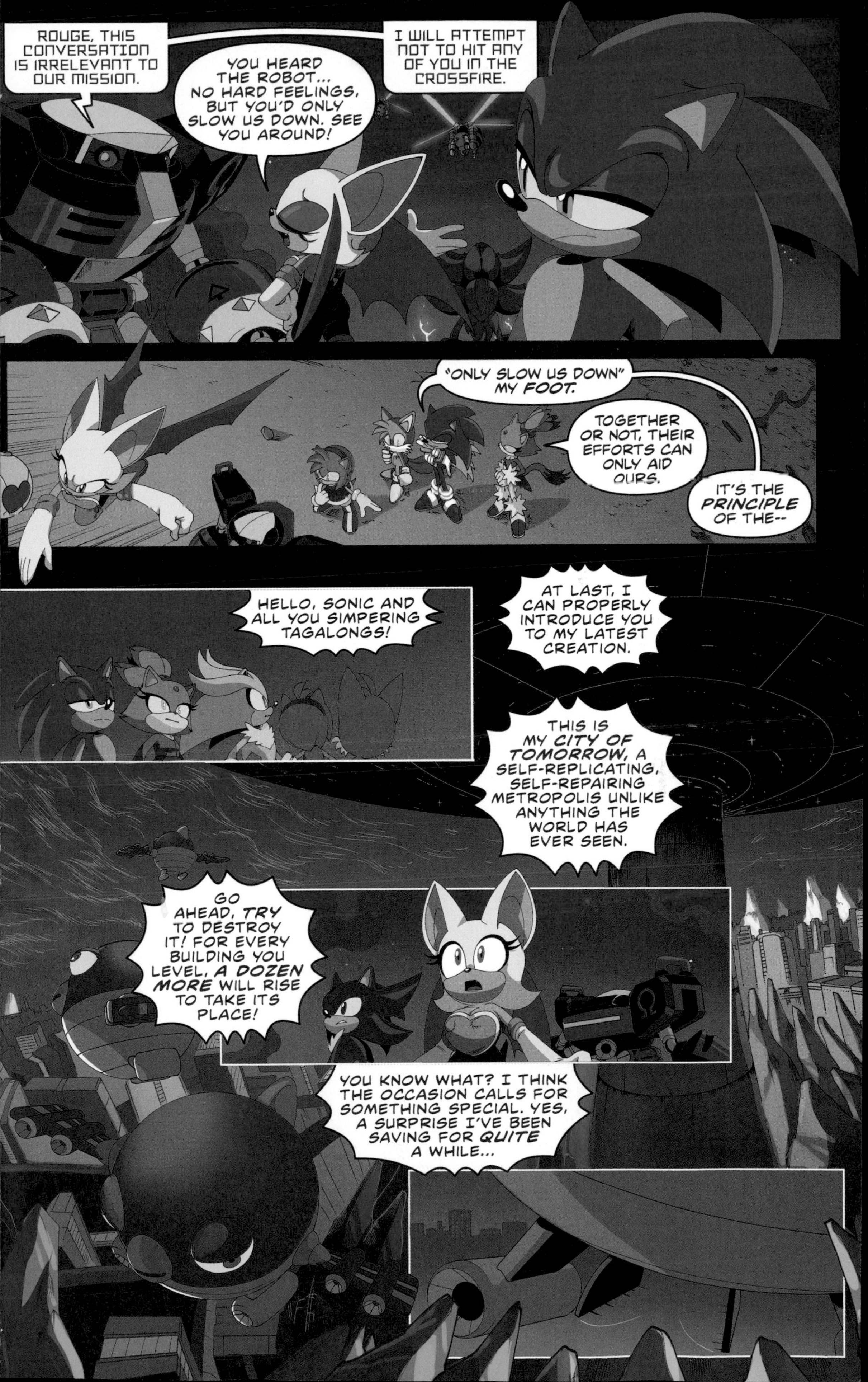
ROUGE, THIS CONVERSATION IS IRRELEVANT TO OUR MISSION.
YOU HEARD THE ROBOT... NO HARD FEELINGS, BUT YOU'D ONLY SLOW US DOWN. SEE YOU AROUND!
I WILL ATTEMPT NOT TO HIT ANY OF YOU IN THE CROSSFIRE.
"ONLY SLOW US DOWN" MY FOOT.
TOGETHER OR NOT, THEIR EFFORTS CAN ONLY AID OURS.
IT'S THE PRINCIPLE OF THE--
HELLO, SONIC AND ALL YOU SIMPERING TAGALONGS!
AT LAST, I CAN PROPERLY INTRODUCE YOU TO MY LATEST CREATION.
THIS IS MY CITY OF TOMORROW, A SELF-REPLICATING, SELF-REPAIRING METROPOLIS UNLIKE ANYTHING THE WORLD HAS EVER SEEN.
GO AHEAD, TRY TO DESTROY IT! FOR EVERY BUILDING YOU LEVEL, A DOZEN MORE WILL RISE TO TAKE ITS PLACE!
YOU KNOW WHAT? I THINK THE OCCASION CALLS FOR SOMETHING SPECIAL. YES, A SURPRISE I'VE BEEN SAVING FOR QUITE A WHILE...

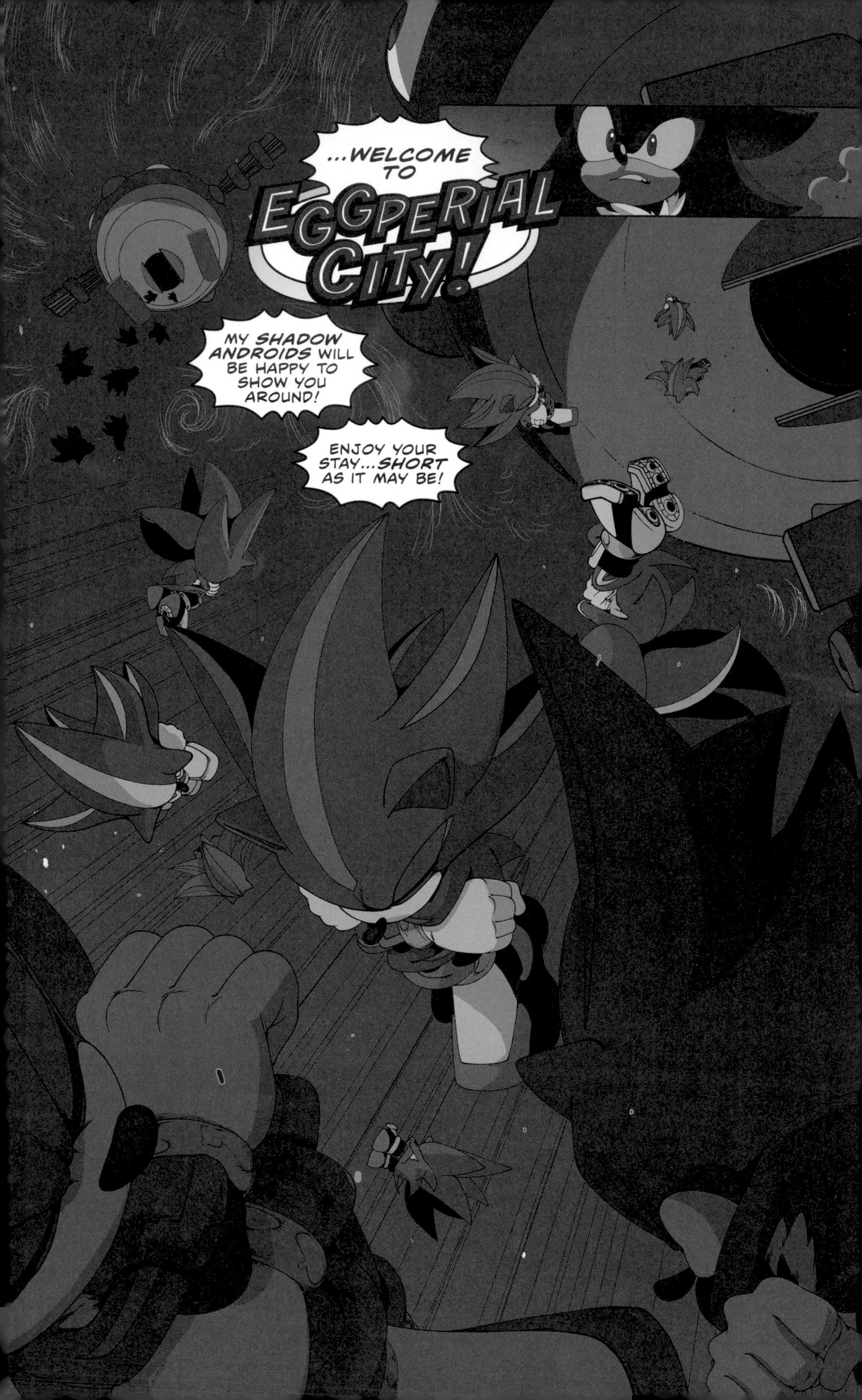
...WELCOME TO
EGGPERIAL CITY!
MY SHADOW ANDROIDS WILL BE HAPPY TO SHOW YOU AROUND!
ENJOY YOUR STAY...SHORT AS IT MAY BE!

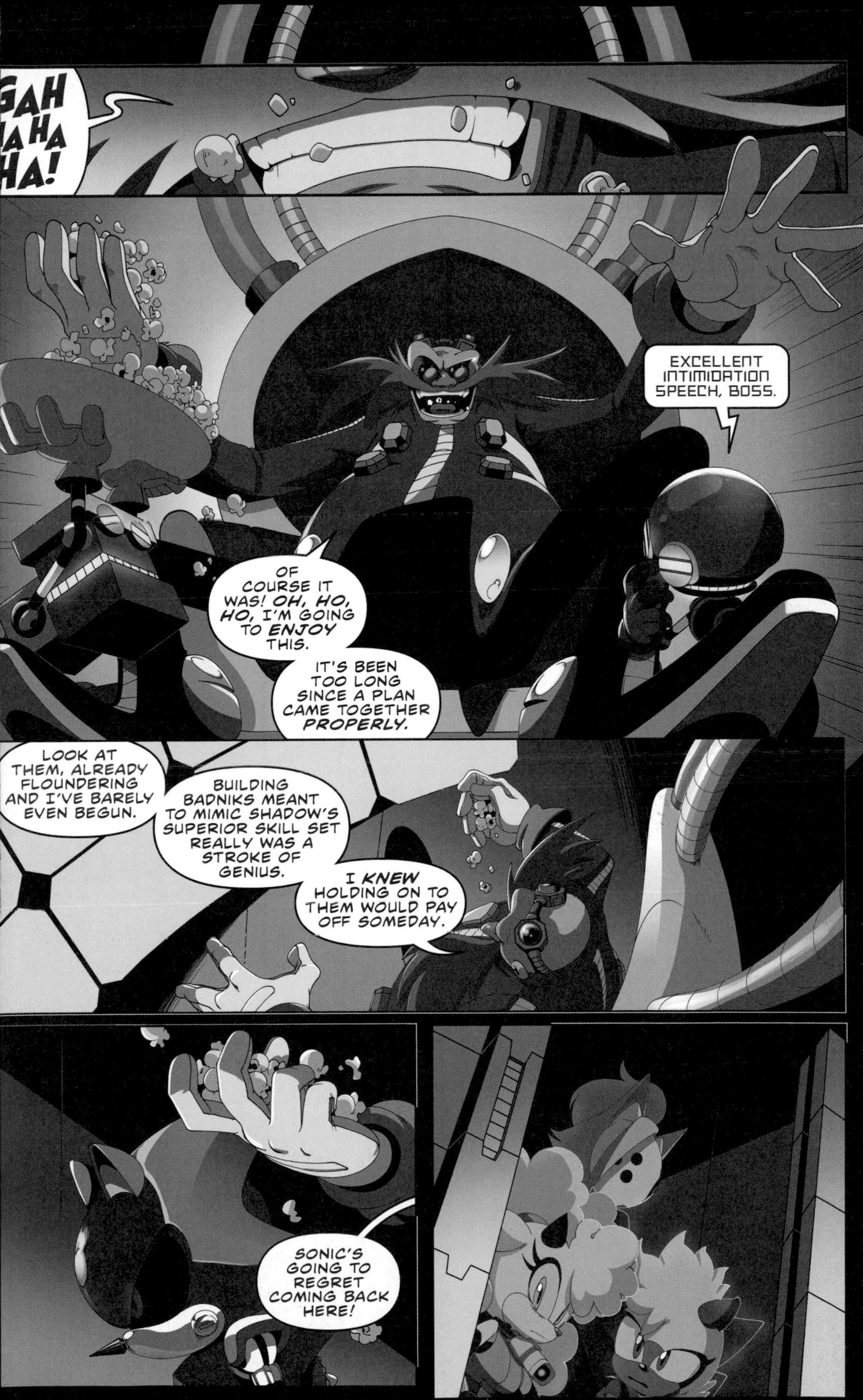
GAH HAHA HA!
EXCELLENT INTIMIDATION SPEECH, BOSS.
OF COURSE IT WAS! OH, HO, HO, I'M GOING TO ENJOY THIS.
IT'S BEEN TOO LONG SINCE A PLAN CAME TOGETHER PROPERLY.
LOOK AT THEM, ALREADY FLOUNDERING AND I'VE BARELY EVEN BEGUN.
BUILDING BADNIKS MEANT TO MIMIC SHADOW'S SUPERIOR SKILL SET REALLY WAS A STROKE OF GENIUS.
I KNEW HOLDING ON TO THEM WOULD PAY OFF SOMEDAY.
SONIC'S GOING TO REGRET COMING BACK HERE!

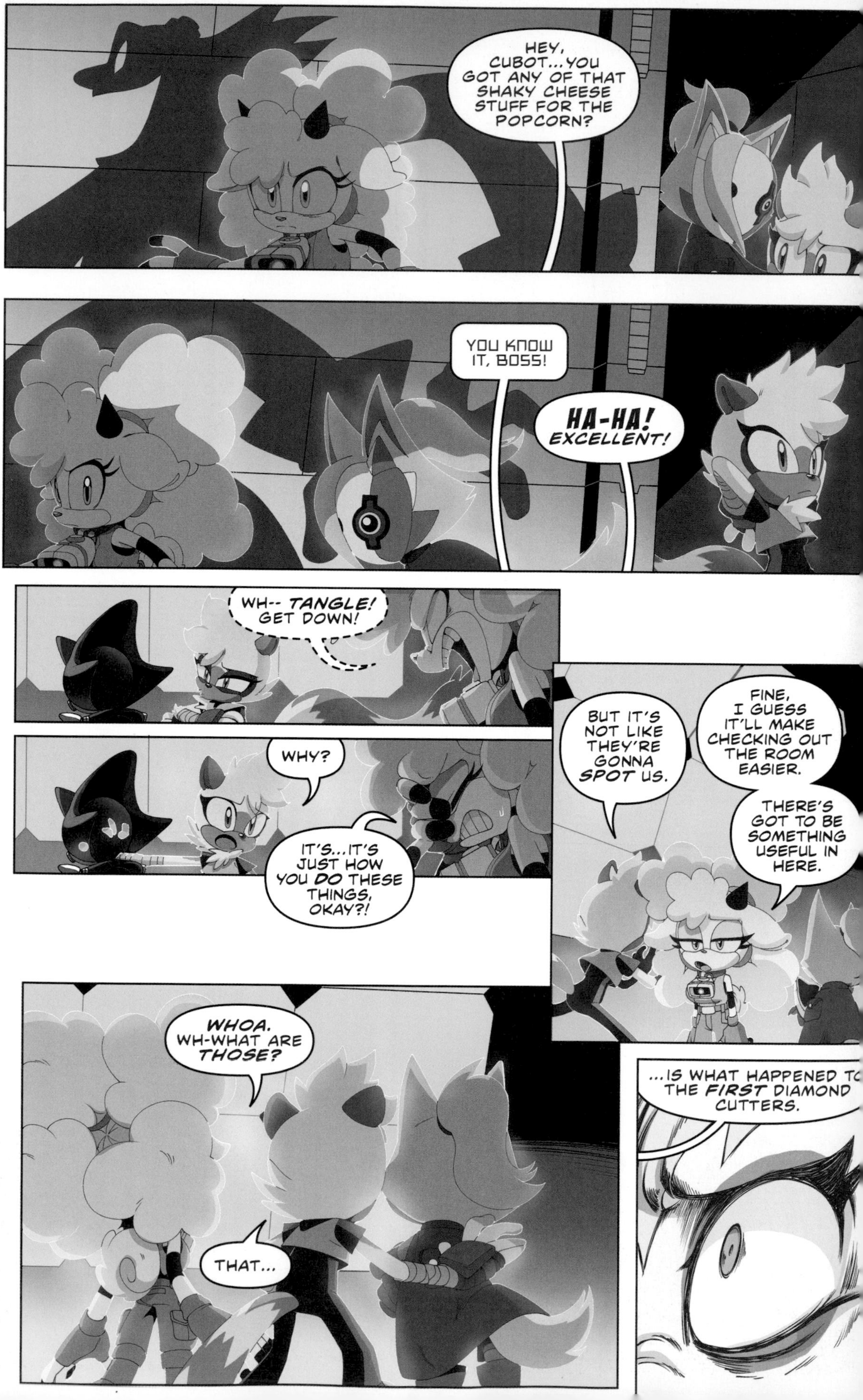
HEY, CUBOT...YOU GOT ANY OF THAT SHAKY CHEESE STUFF FOR THE POPCORN?
YOU KNOW IT, BOSS!
HA-HA! EXCELLENT!
WH-- TANGLE! GET DOWN!
WHY?
IT'S...IT'S JUST HOW YOU DO THESE THINGS, OKAY?!
BUT IT'S NOT LIKE THEY'RE GONNA SPOT US.
FINE, I GUESS IT'LL MAKE CHECKING OUT THE ROOM EASIER.
THERE'S GOT TO BE SOMETHING USEFUL IN HERE.
WHOA. WH-WHAT ARE THOSE?
THAT...
...IS WHAT HAPPENED TO THE FIRST DIAMOND CUTTERS.

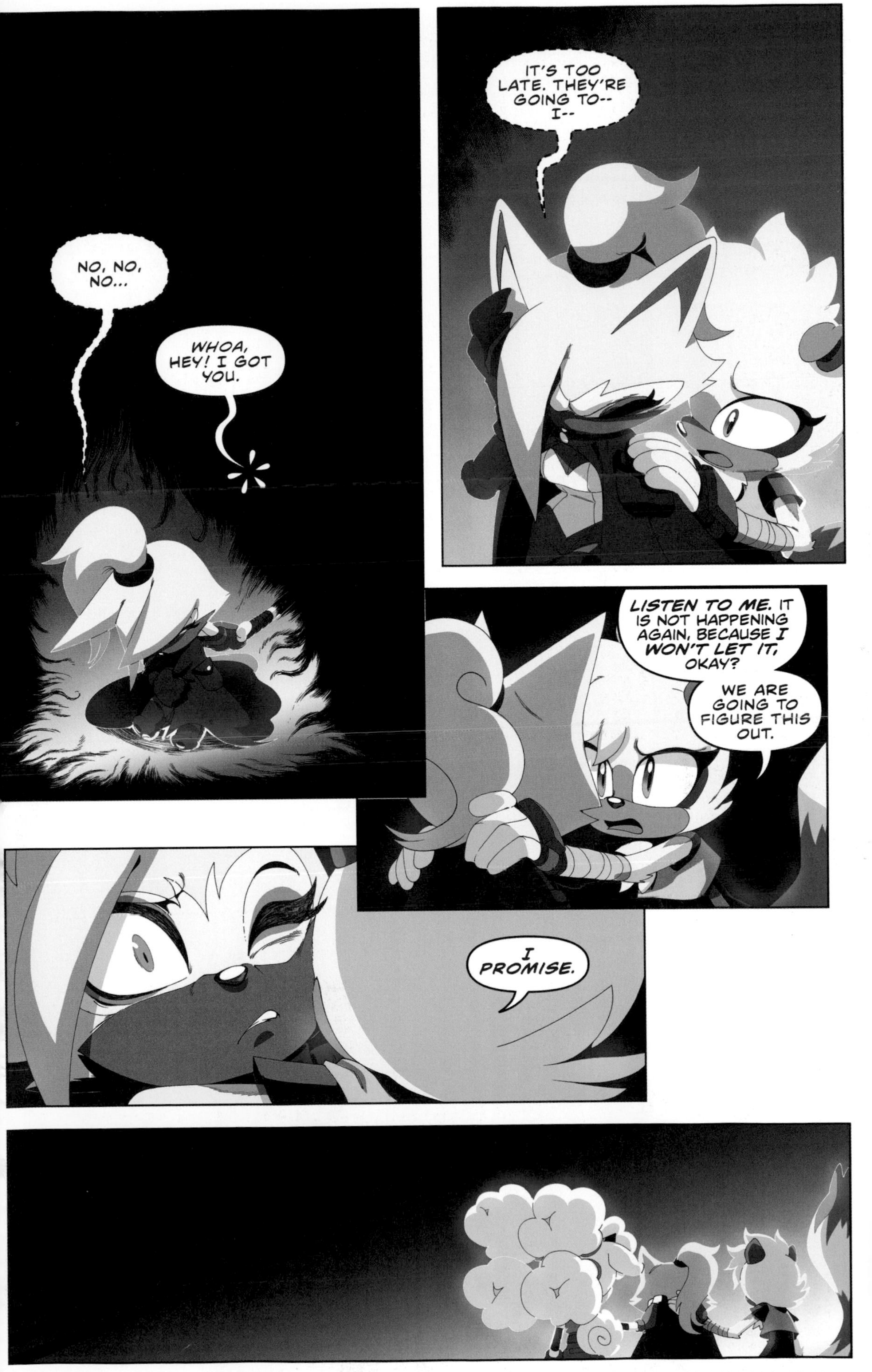
NO, NO, NO...
WHOA, HEY! I GOT YOU.
IT'S TOO LATE. THEY'RE GOING TO-- I--
LISTEN TO ME. IT IS NOT HAPPENING AGAIN, BECAUSE I WON'T LET IT, OKAY?
WE ARE GOING TO FIGURE THIS OUT.
I PROMISE.

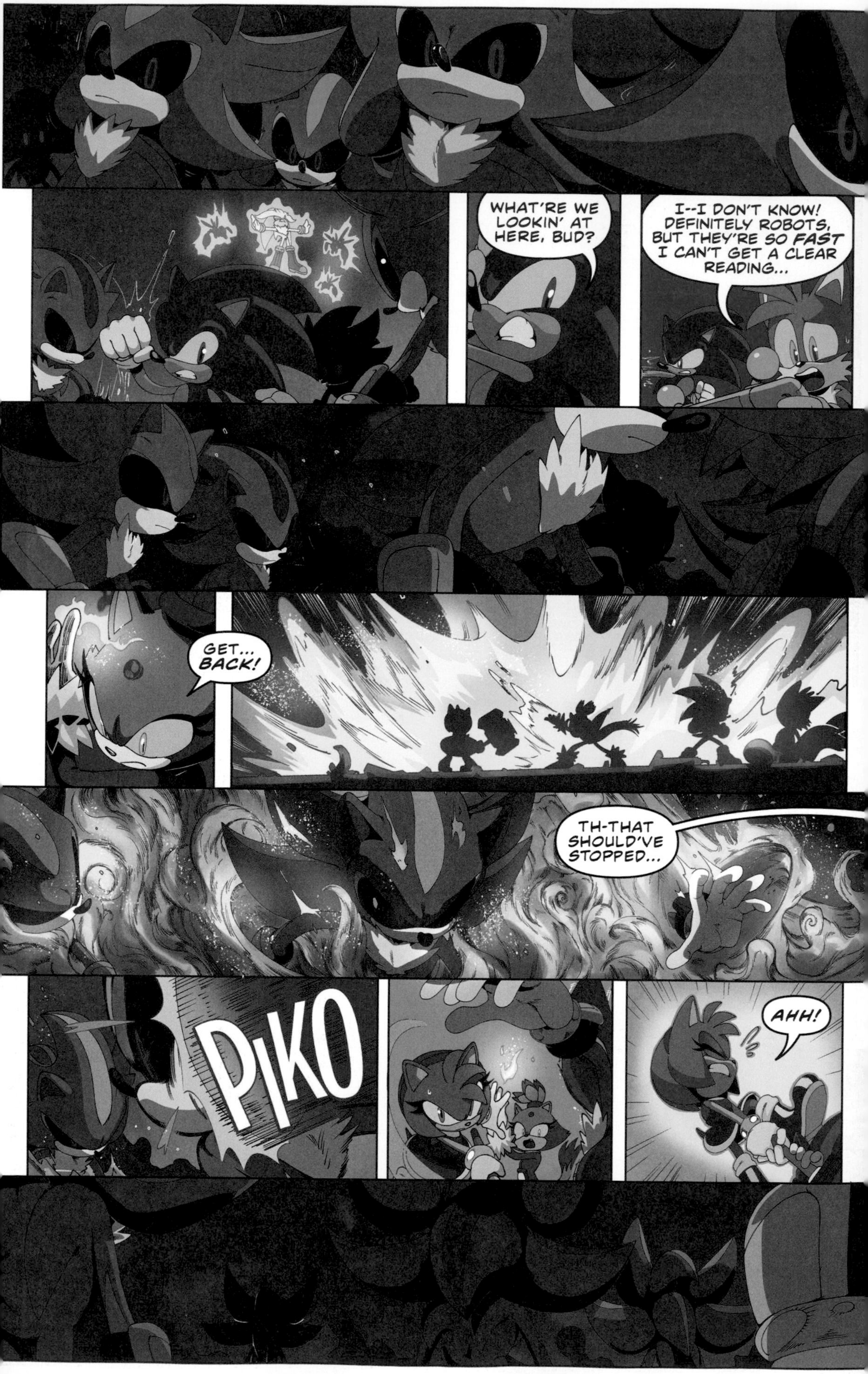
WHAT'RE WE LOOKIN' AT HERE, BUD?
I--I DON'T KNOW! DEFINITELY ROBOTS, BUT THEY'RE SO FAST I CAN'T GET A CLEAR READING...
GET... BACK!
TH-THAT SHOULD'VE STOPPED...
PIKO
AHH!

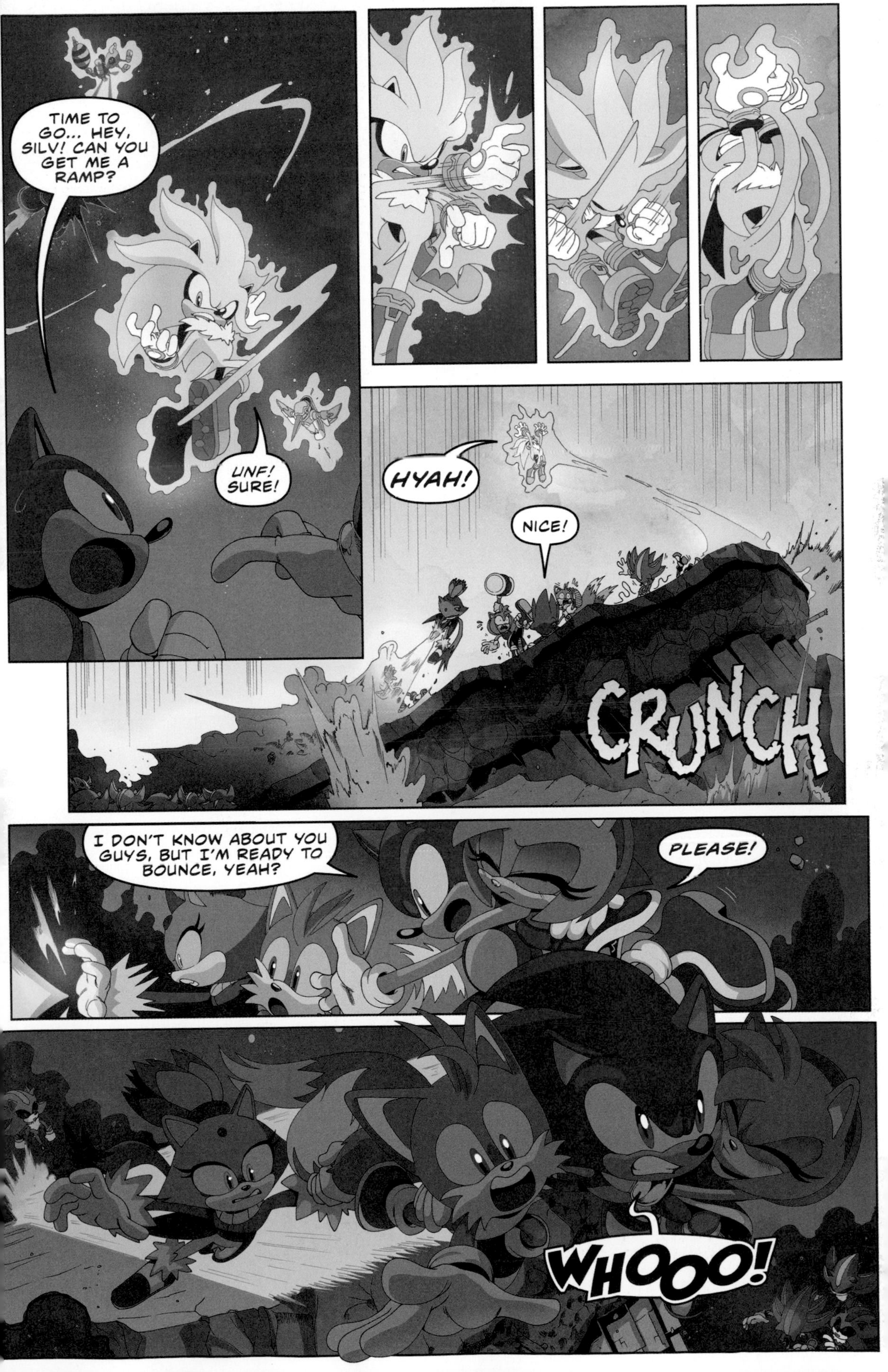
TIME TO GO... HEY, SILV! CAN YOU GET ME A RAMP?
UNF! SURE!
HYAH!
NICE!
CRUNCH
I DON'T KNOW ABOUT YOU GUYS, BUT I'M READY TO BOUNCE, YEAH?
PLEASE!
WHOOO!

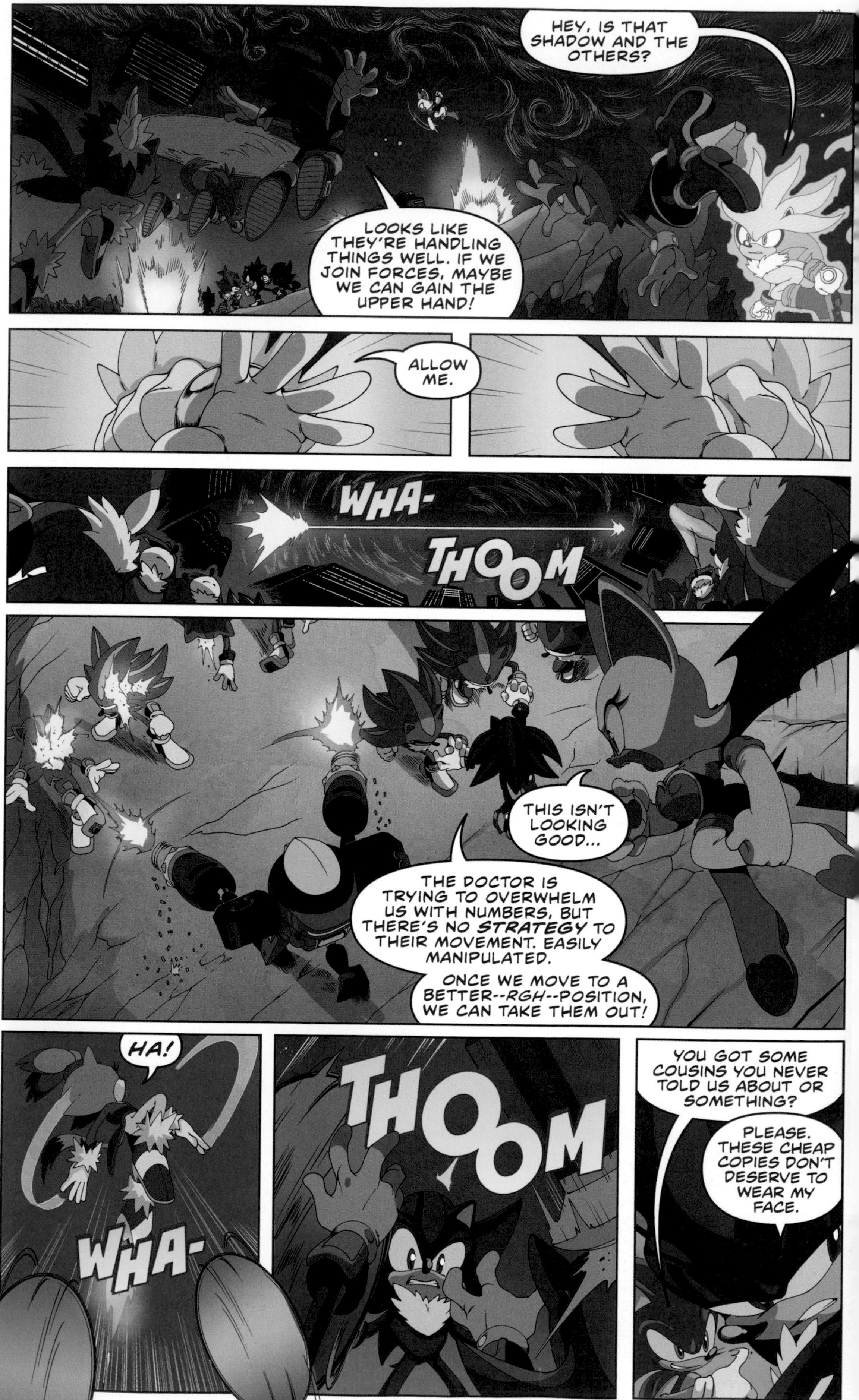
HEY, IS THAT SHADOW AND THE OTHERS?
LOOKS LIKE THEY'RE HANDLING THINGS WELL. IF WE JOIN FORCES, MAYBE WE CAN GAIN THE UPPER HAND!
ALLOW ME.
WHA-
THOOM
THIS ISN'T LOOKING GOOD...
THE DOCTOR IS TRYING TO OVERWHELM US WITH NUMBERS, BUT THERE'S NO STRATEGY TO THEIR MOVEMENT. EASILY MANIPULATED.
ONCE WE MOVE TO A BETTER--RGH--POSITION, WE CAN TAKE THEM OUT!
HA!
WHA-
THOOM
YOU GOT SOME COUSINS YOU NEVER TOLD US ABOUT OR SOMETHING?
PLEASE. THESE CHEAP COPIES DON'T DESERVE TO WEAR MY FACE.

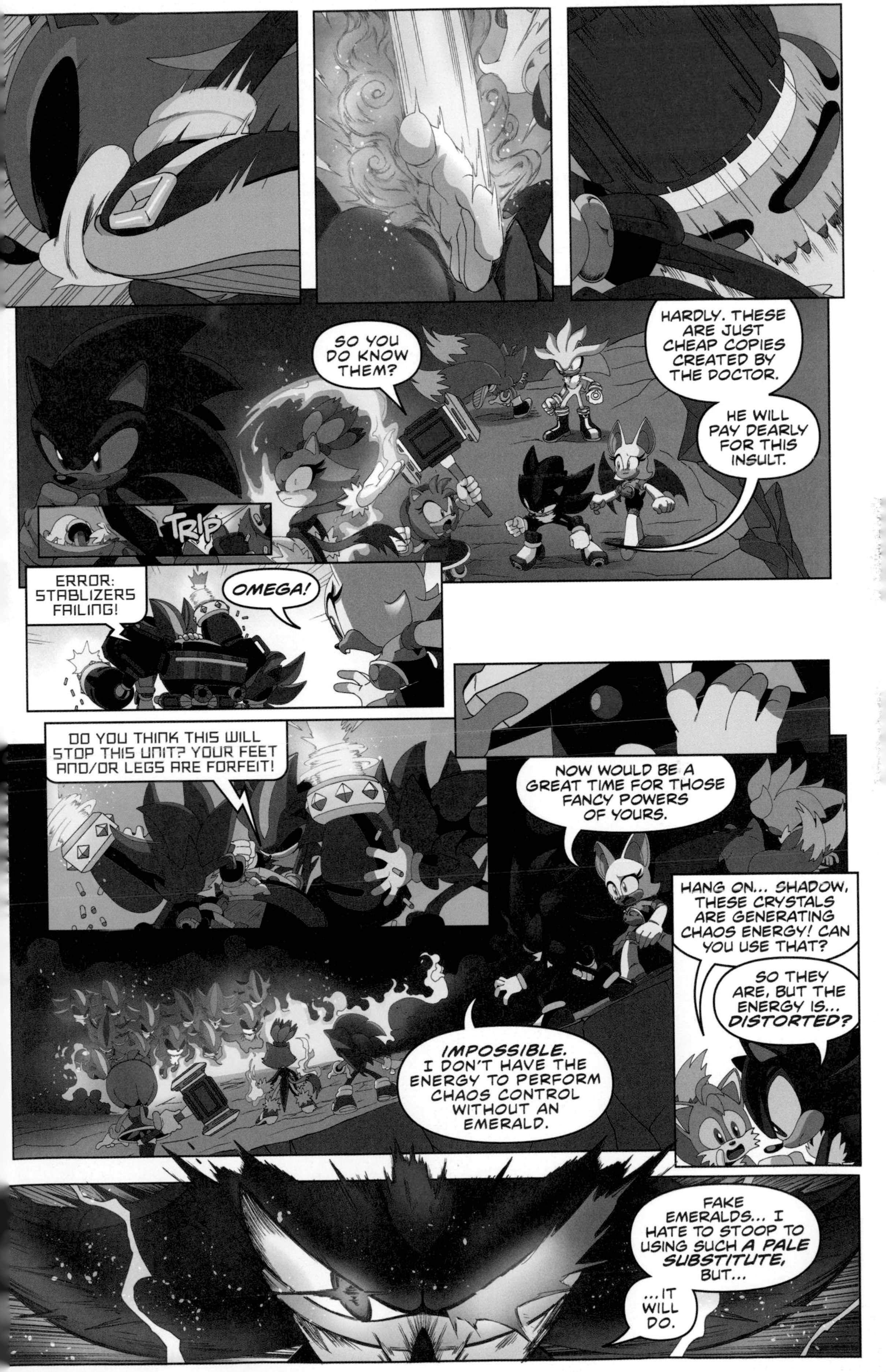
SO YOU DO KNOW THEM?
HARDLY. THESE ARE JUST CHEAP COPIES CREATED BY THE DOCTOR.
HE WILL PAY DEARLY FOR THIS INSULT.
TRIP
ERROR: STABLIZERS FAILING!
OMEGA!
DO YOU THINK THIS WILL STOP THIS UNIT? YOUR FEET AND/OR LEGS ARE FORFEIT!
NOW WOULD BE A GREAT TIME FOR THOSE FANCY POWERS OF YOURS.
IMPOSSIBLE. I DON'T HAVE THE ENERGY TO PERFORM CHAOS CONTROL WITHOUT AN EMERALD.
HANG ON... SHADOW, THESE CRYSTALS ARE GENERATING CHAOS ENERGY! CAN YOU USE THAT?
SO THEY ARE, BUT THE ENERGY IS... DISTORTED?
FAKE EMERALDS... I HATE TO STOOP TO USING SUCH A PALE SUBSTITUTE, BUT...
...IT WILL DO.

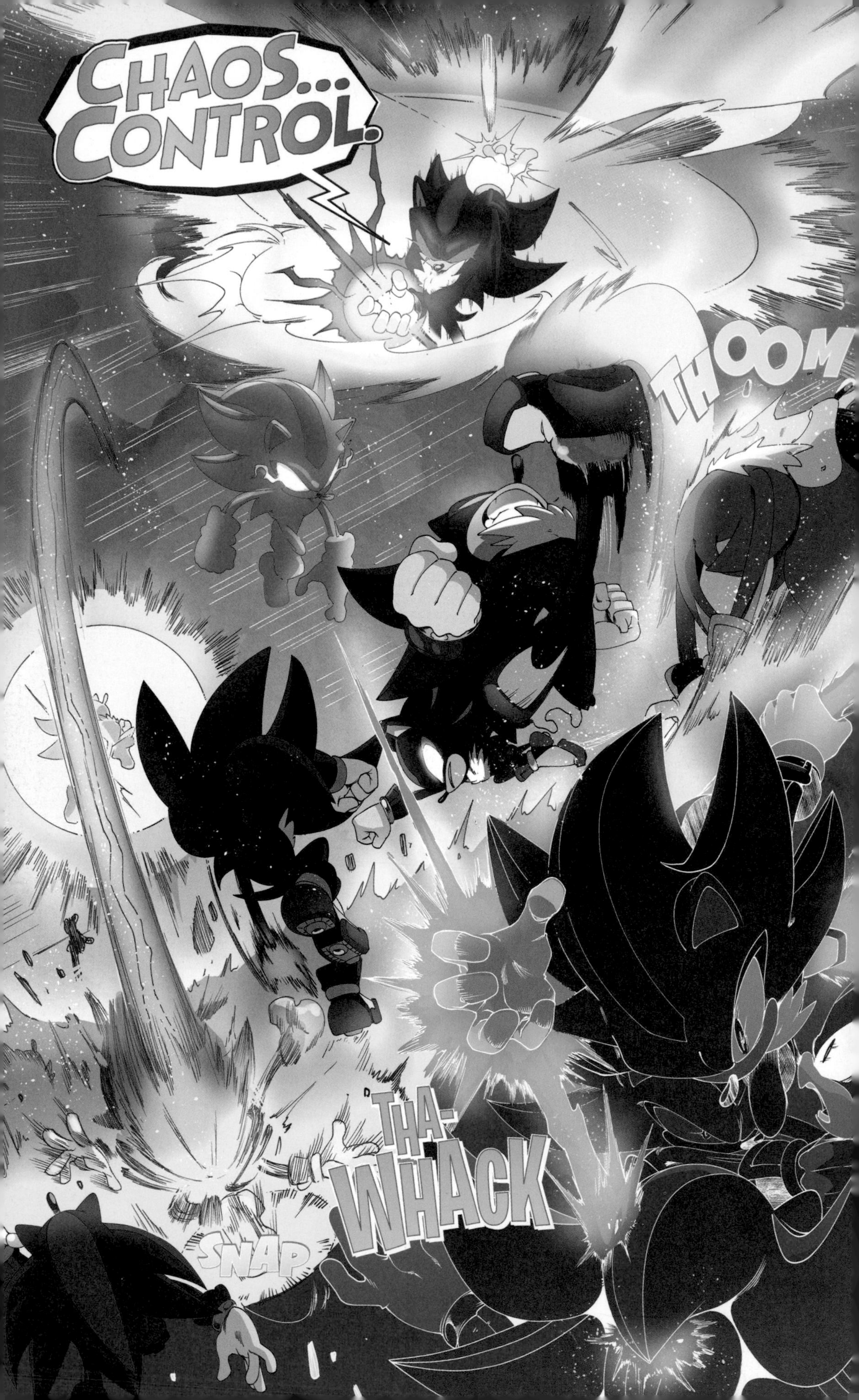
CHAOS... CONTROL.
THOOM
THA-WHACK
SNAP

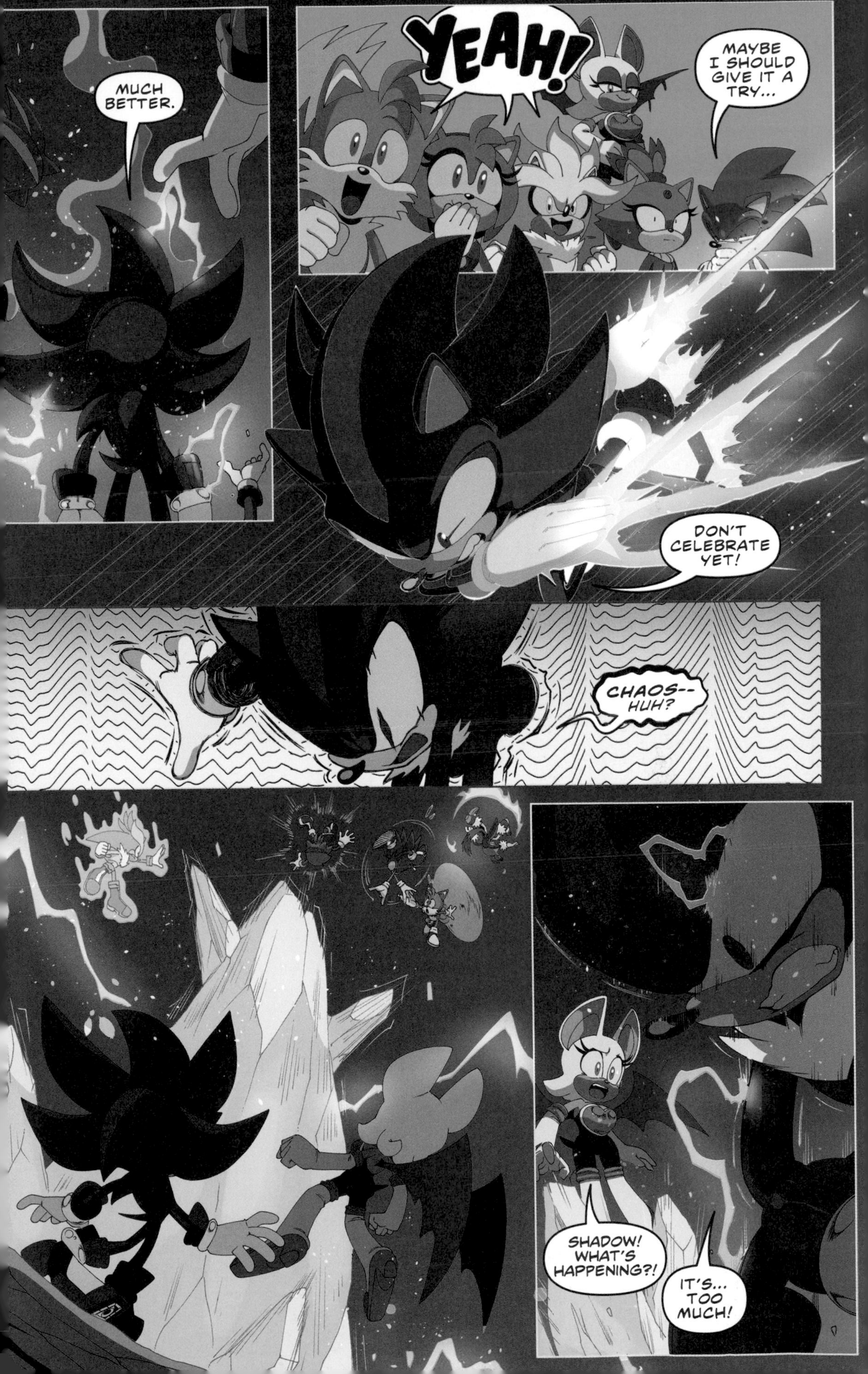
MUCH BETTER.
YEAH!
MAYBE I SHOULD GIVE IT A TRY...
DON'T CELEBRATE YET!
CHAOS-- HUH?
SHADOW! WHAT'S HAPPENING?!
IT'S... TOO MUCH!

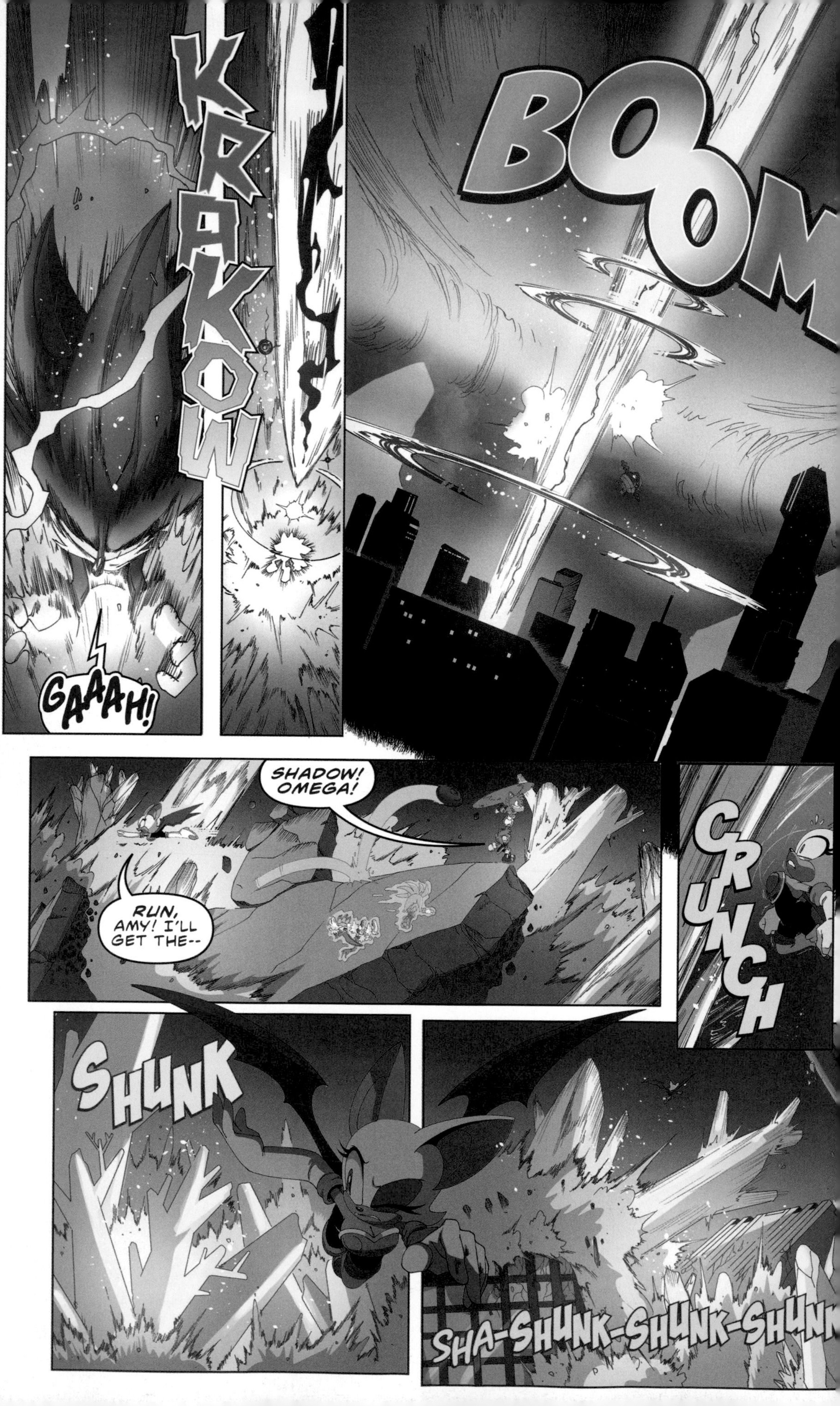
KRAKOW
GAAAH!
BOOOM
SHADOW! OMEGA!
RUN, AMY! I'LL GET THE--
CRUNCH
SHUNK
SHA-SHUNK-SHUNK-SHUNK

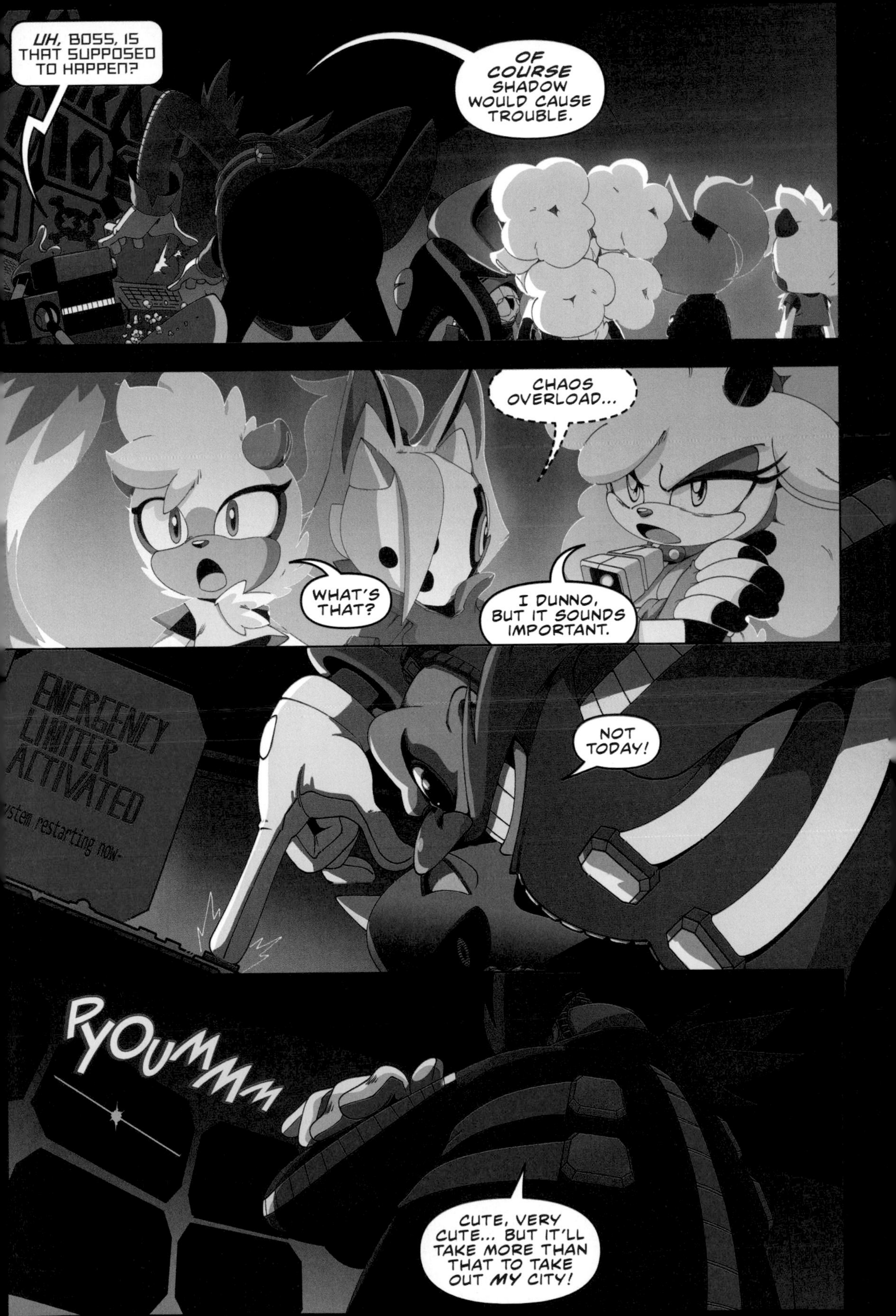
UH, BOSS, IS THAT SUPPOSED TO HAPPEN?
OF COURSE SHADOW WOULD CAUSE TROUBLE.
CHAOS OVERLOAD...
WHAT'S THAT?
I DUNNO, BUT IT SOUNDS IMPORTANT.
EMERGENCY LIMITER ACTIVATED
ystem restarting now-
NOT TODAY!
RYOUMMM
CUTE, VERY CUTE... BUT IT'LL TAKE MORE THAN THAT TO TAKE OUT MY CITY!

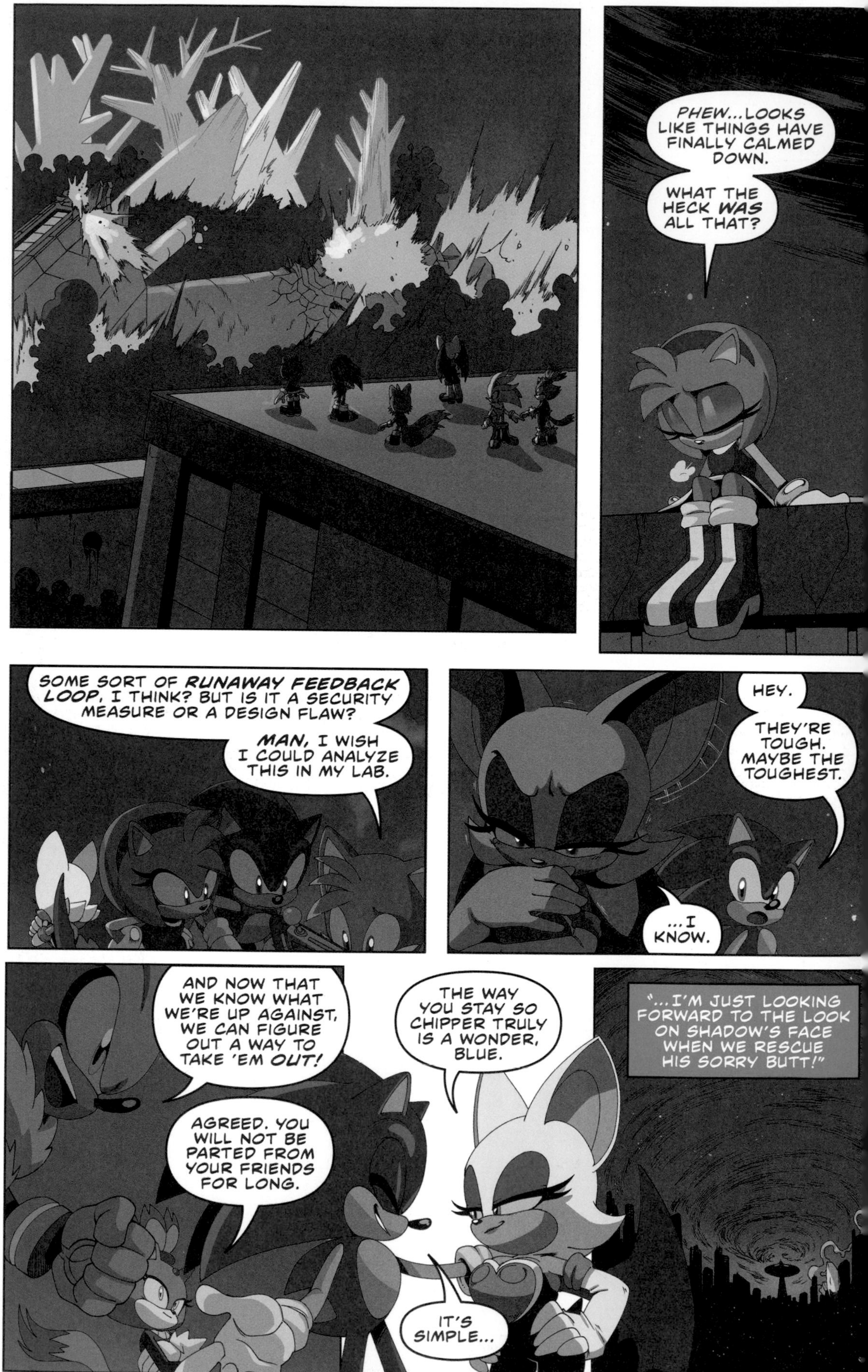
PHEW...LOOKS LIKE THINGS HAVE FINALLY CALMED DOWN.
WHAT THE HECK WAS ALL THAT?
SOME SORT OF RUNAWAY FEEDBACK LOOP, I THINK? BUT IS IT A SECURITY MEASURE OR A DESIGN FLAW?
MAN, I WISH I COULD ANALYZE THIS IN MY LAB.
HEY.
THEY'RE TOUGH. MAYBE THE TOUGHEST.
...I KNOW.
AND NOW THAT WE KNOW WHAT WE'RE UP AGAINST, WE CAN FIGURE OUT A WAY TO TAKE 'EM OUT!
AGREED. YOU WILL NOT BE PARTED FROM YOUR FRIENDS FOR LONG.
THE WAY YOU STAY SO CHIPPER TRULY IS A WONDER, BLUE.
IT'S SIMPLE...
"...I'M JUST LOOKING FORWARD TO THE LOOK ON SHADOW'S FACE WHEN WE RESCUE HIS SORRY BUTT!"

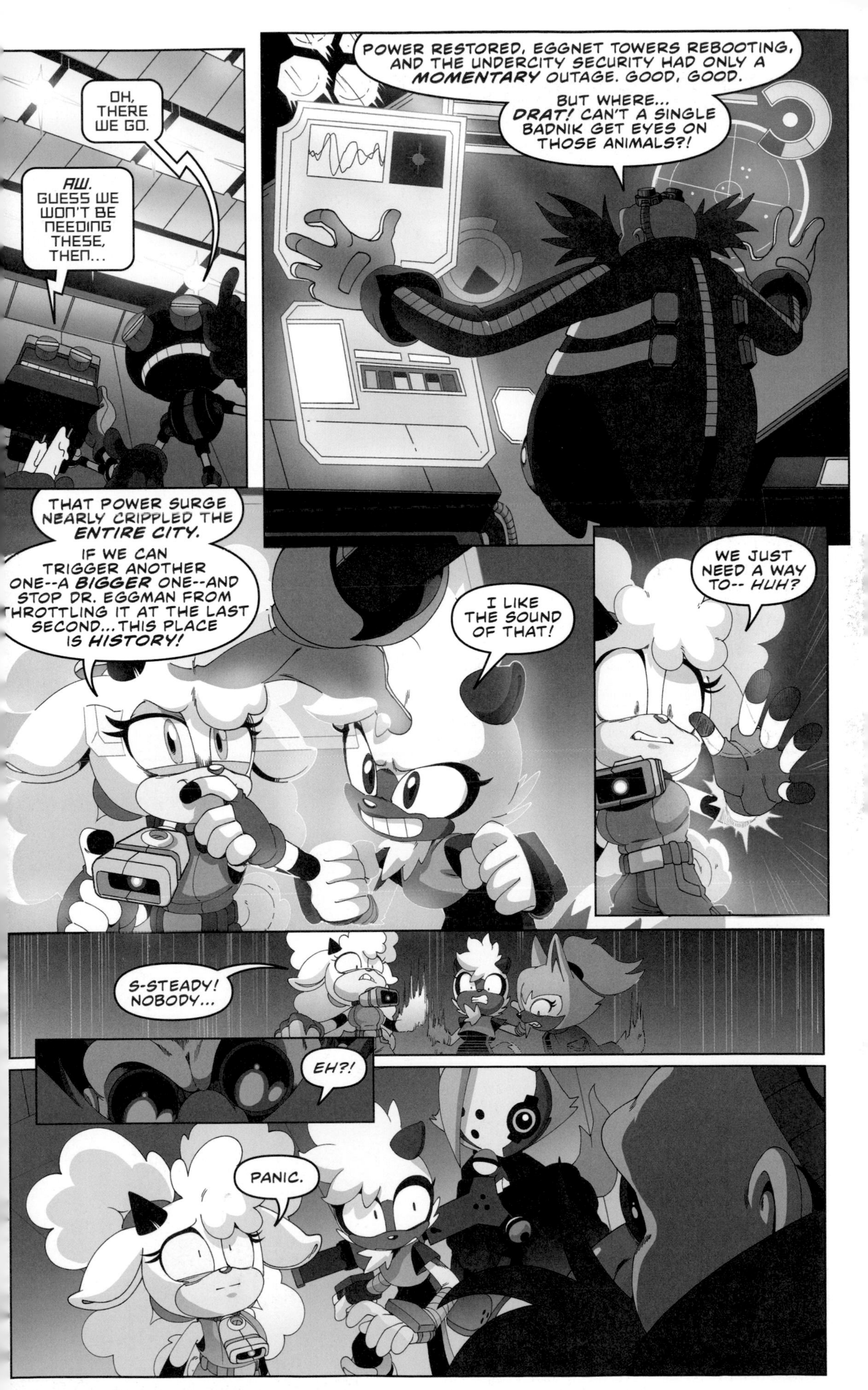
OH, THERE WE GO.
AW. GUESS WE WON'T BE NEEDING THESE, THEN...
POWER RESTORED, EGGNET TOWERS REBOOTING, AND THE UNDERCITY SECURITY HAD ONLY A MOMENTARY OUTAGE. GOOD, GOOD.
BUT WHERE... DRAT! CAN'T A SINGLE BADNIK GET EYES ON THOSE ANIMALS?!
THAT POWER SURGE NEARLY CRIPPLED THE ENTIRE CITY.
IF WE CAN TRIGGER ANOTHER ONE--A BIGGER ONE--AND STOP DR. EGGMAN FROM THROTTLING IT AT THE LAST SECOND...THIS PLACE IS HISTORY!
I LIKE THE SOUND OF THAT!
WE JUST NEED A WAY TO-- HUH?
S-STEADY! NOBODY...
EH?!
PANIC.

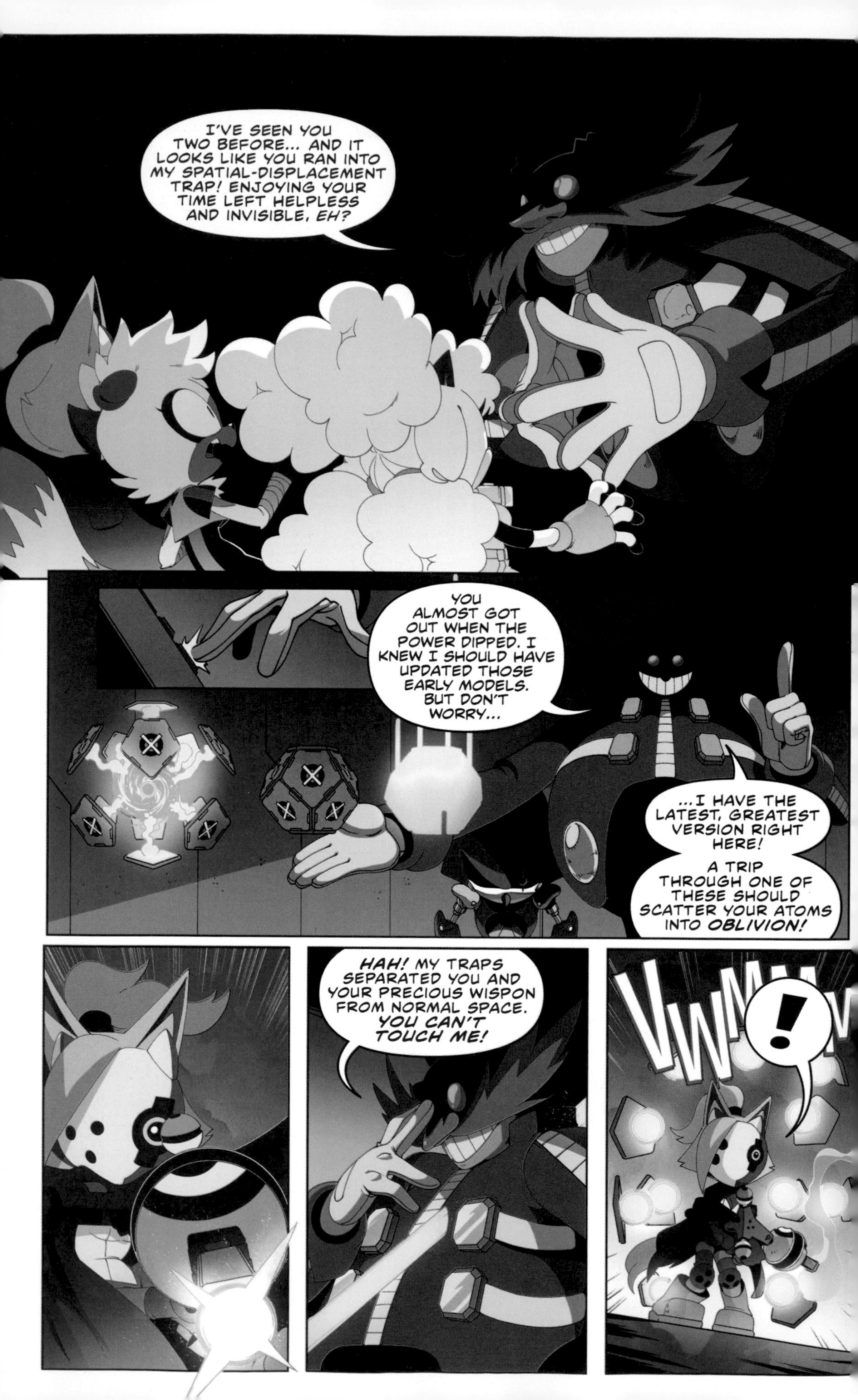
I'VE SEEN YOU TWO BEFORE... AND IT LOOKS LIKE YOU RAN INTO MY SPATIAL-DISPLACEMENT TRAP! ENJOYING YOUR TIME LEFT HELPLESS AND INVISIBLE, EH?
YOU ALMOST GOT OUT WHEN THE POWER DIPPED. I KNEW I SHOULD HAVE UPDATED THOSE EARLY MODELS. BUT DON'T WORRY...
...I HAVE THE LATEST, GREATEST VERSION RIGHT HERE!
A TRIP THROUGH ONE OF THESE SHOULD SCATTER YOUR ATOMS INTO OBLIVION!
HAH! MY TRAPS SEPARATED YOU AND YOUR PRECIOUS WISPON FROM NORMAL SPACE. YOU CAN'T TOUCH ME!
!

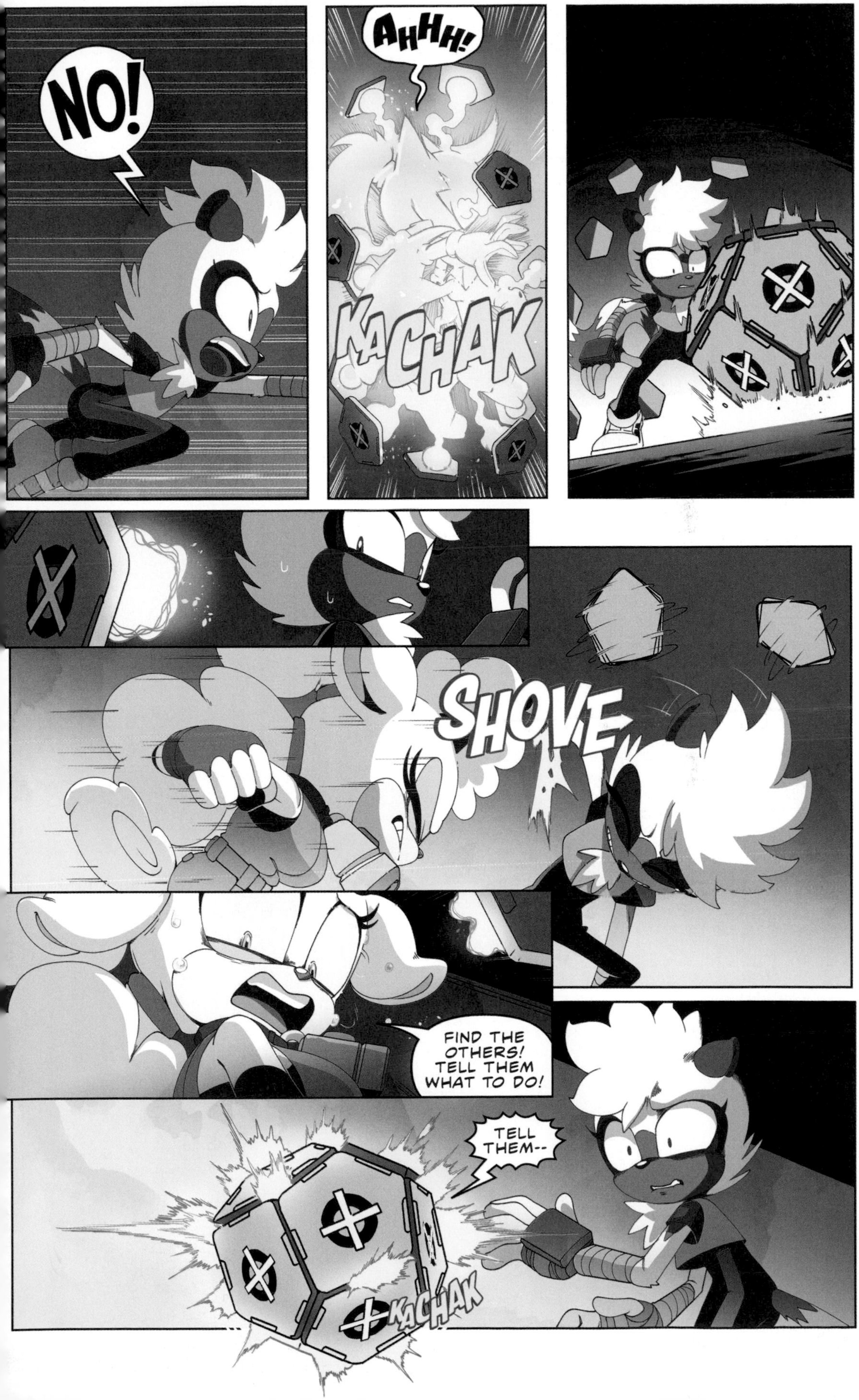
NO!
AHHH!
KACHAK
SHOVE
FIND THE OTHERS! TELL THEM WHAT TO DO!
TELL THEM--
KACHAK

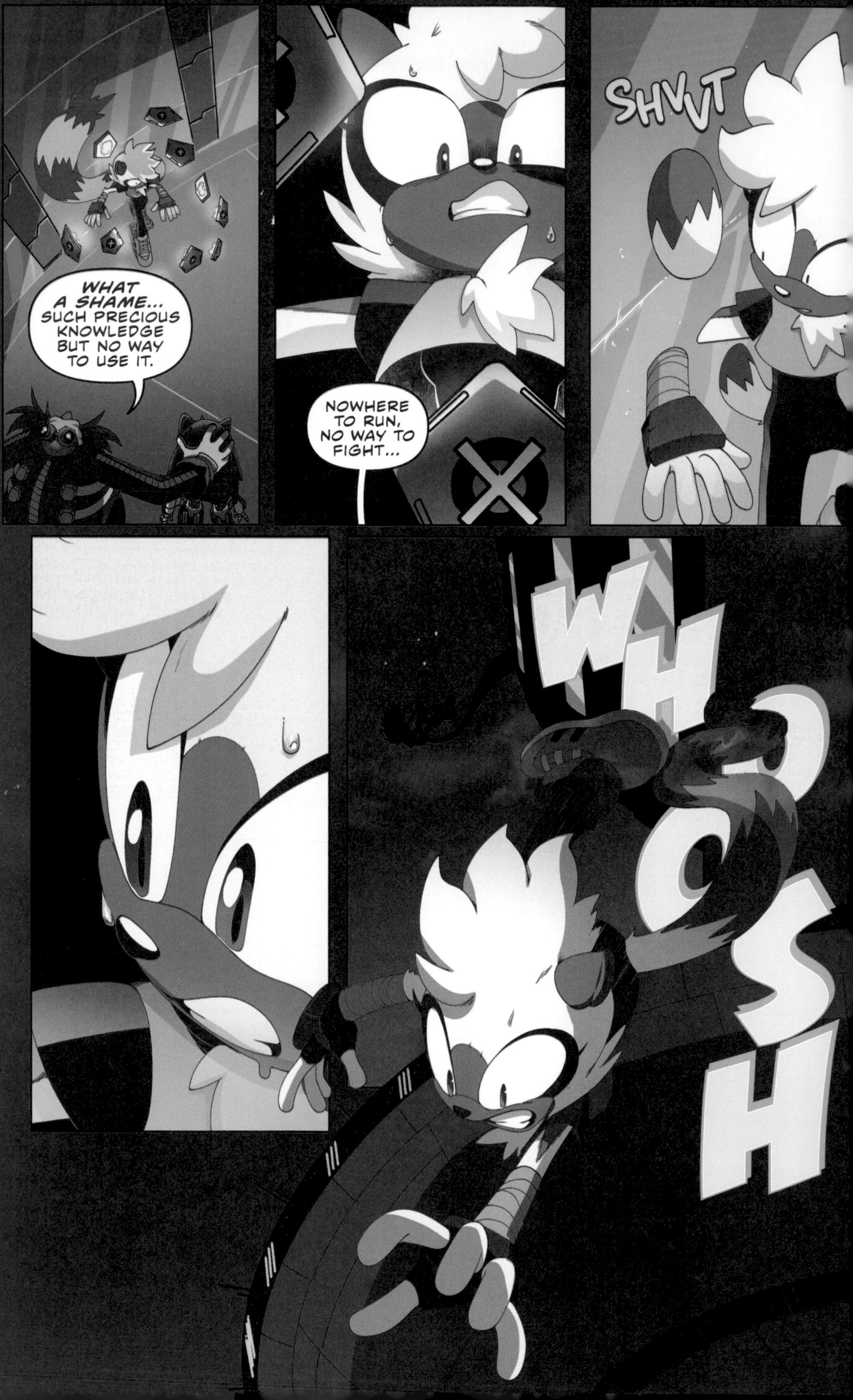
WHAT A SHAME... SUCH PRECIOUS KNOWLEDGE BUT NO WAY TO USE IT.
NOWHERE TO RUN, NO WAY TO FIGHT...
SHVVVT
WHOOSH

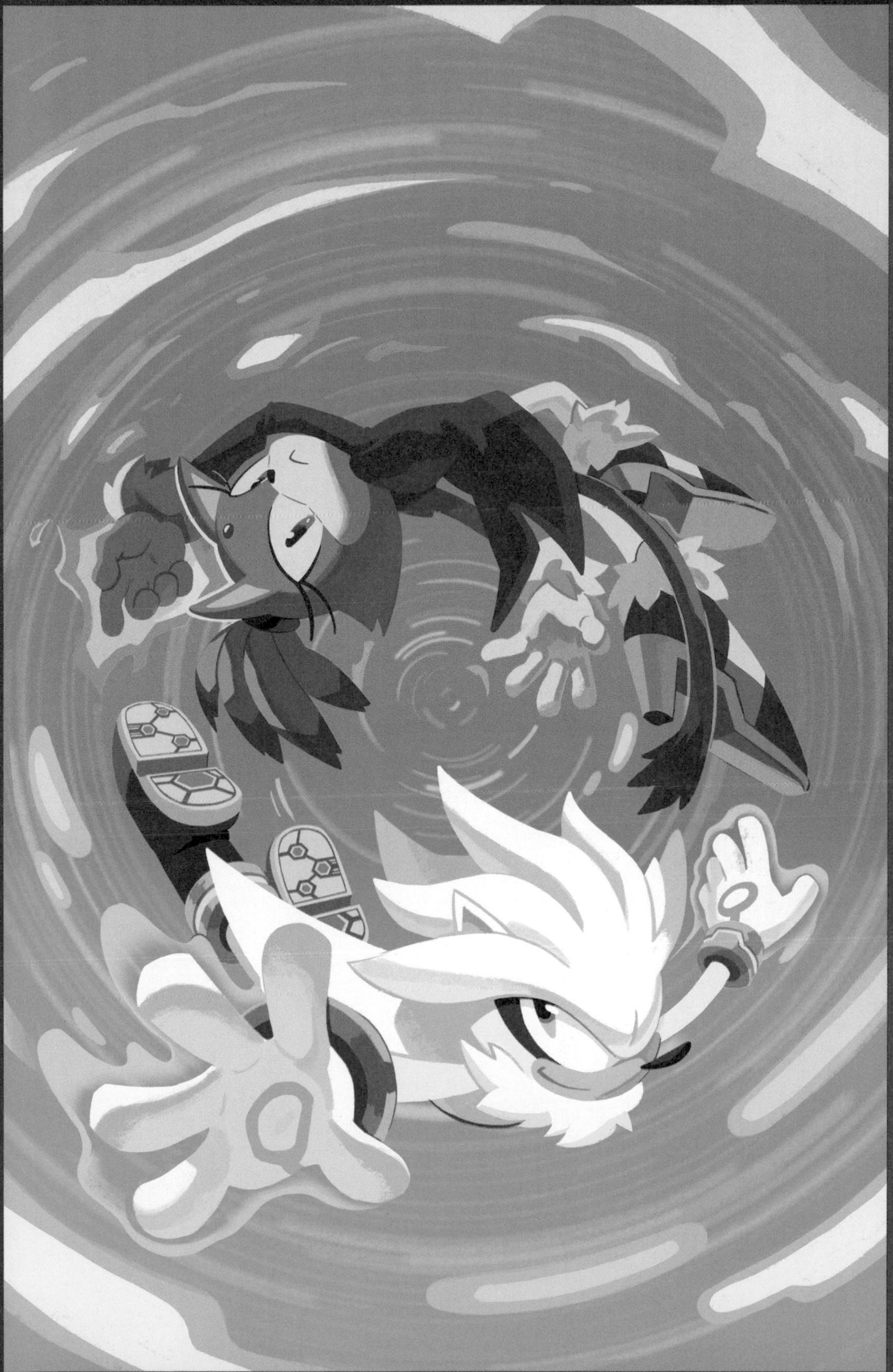

ART BY NATHALIE FOURDRAINE

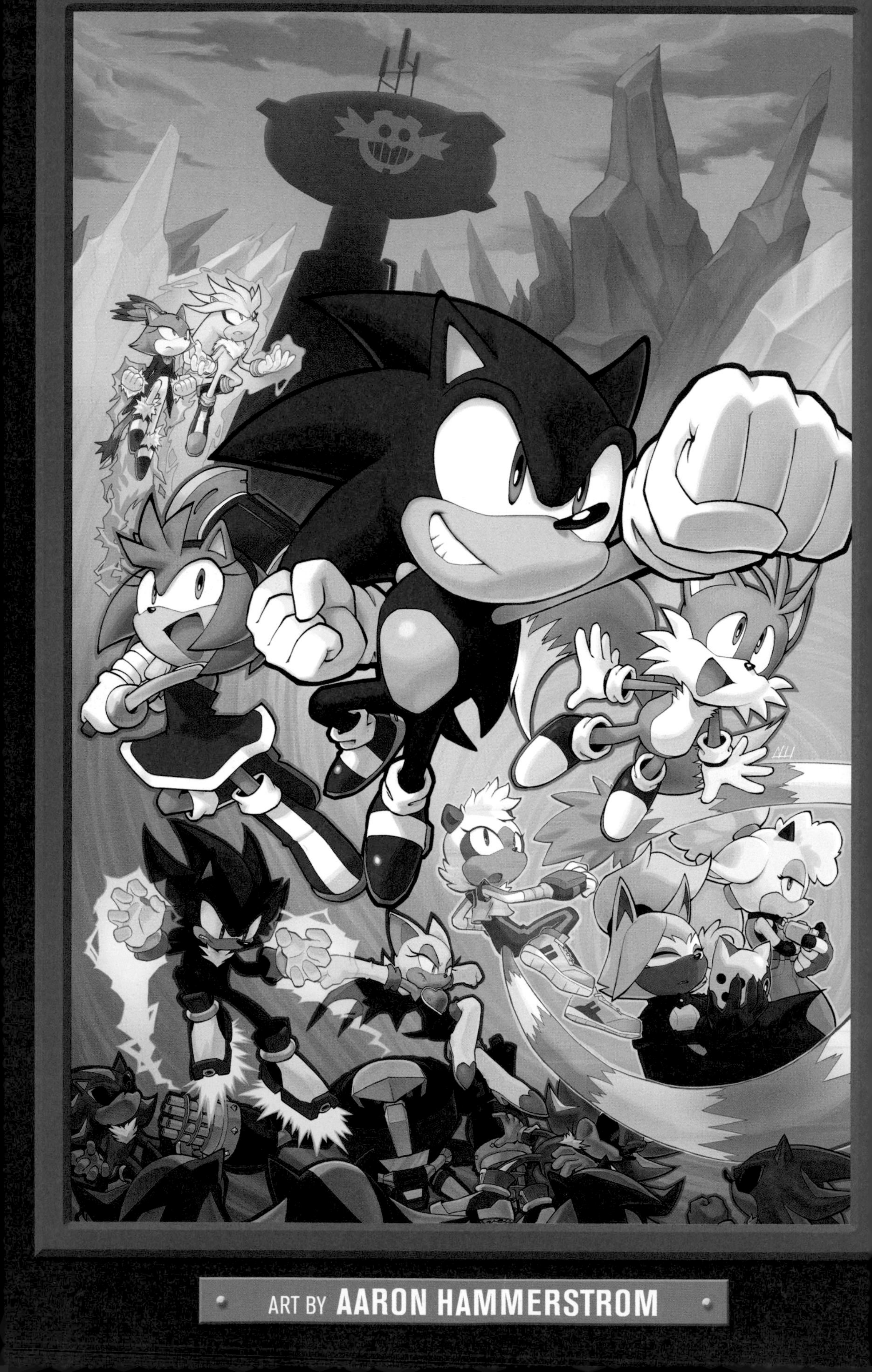

ART BY **AARON HAMMERSTROM**

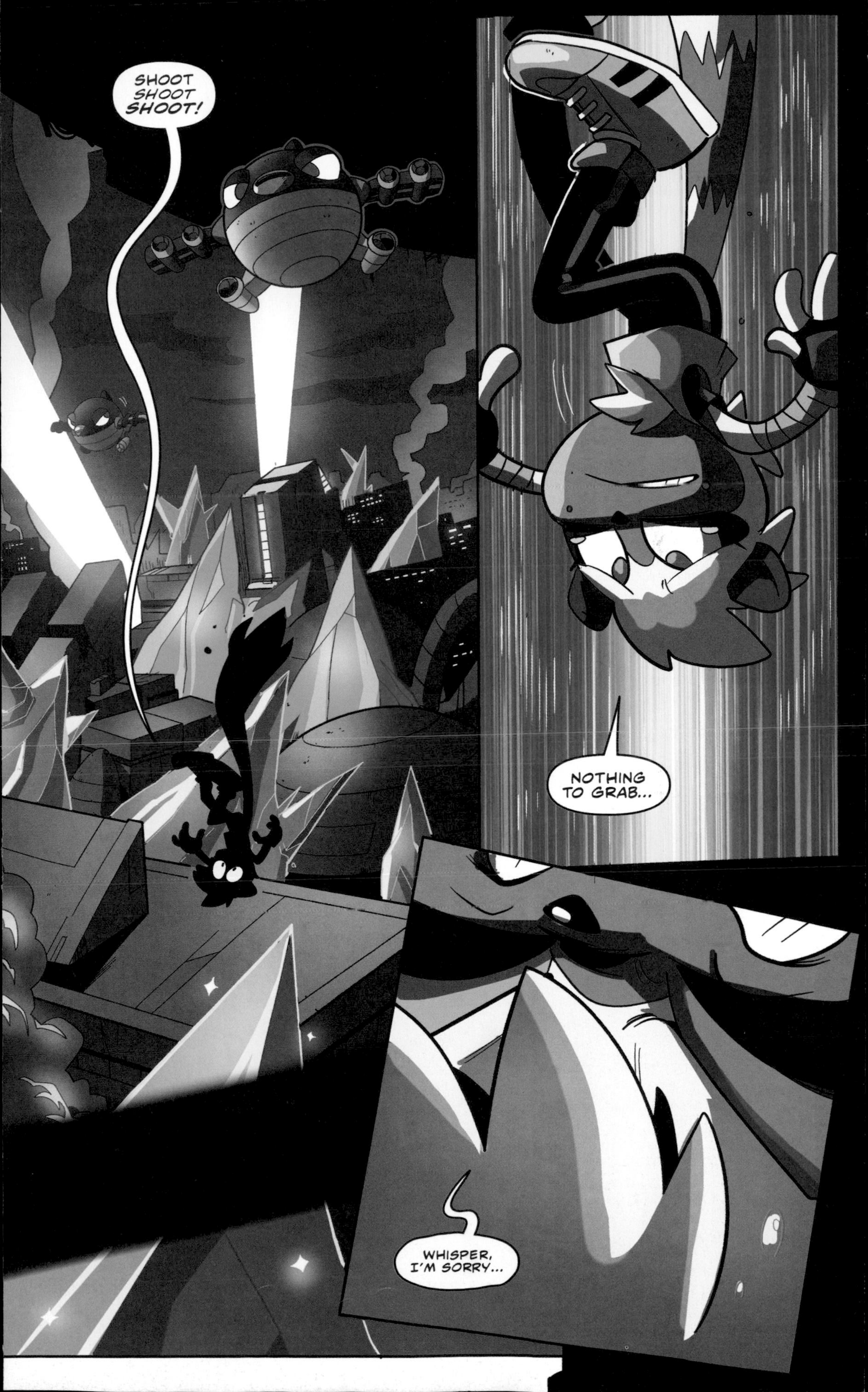
SHOOT SHOOT SHOOT!
NOTHING TO GRAB...
WHISPER, I'M SORRY...

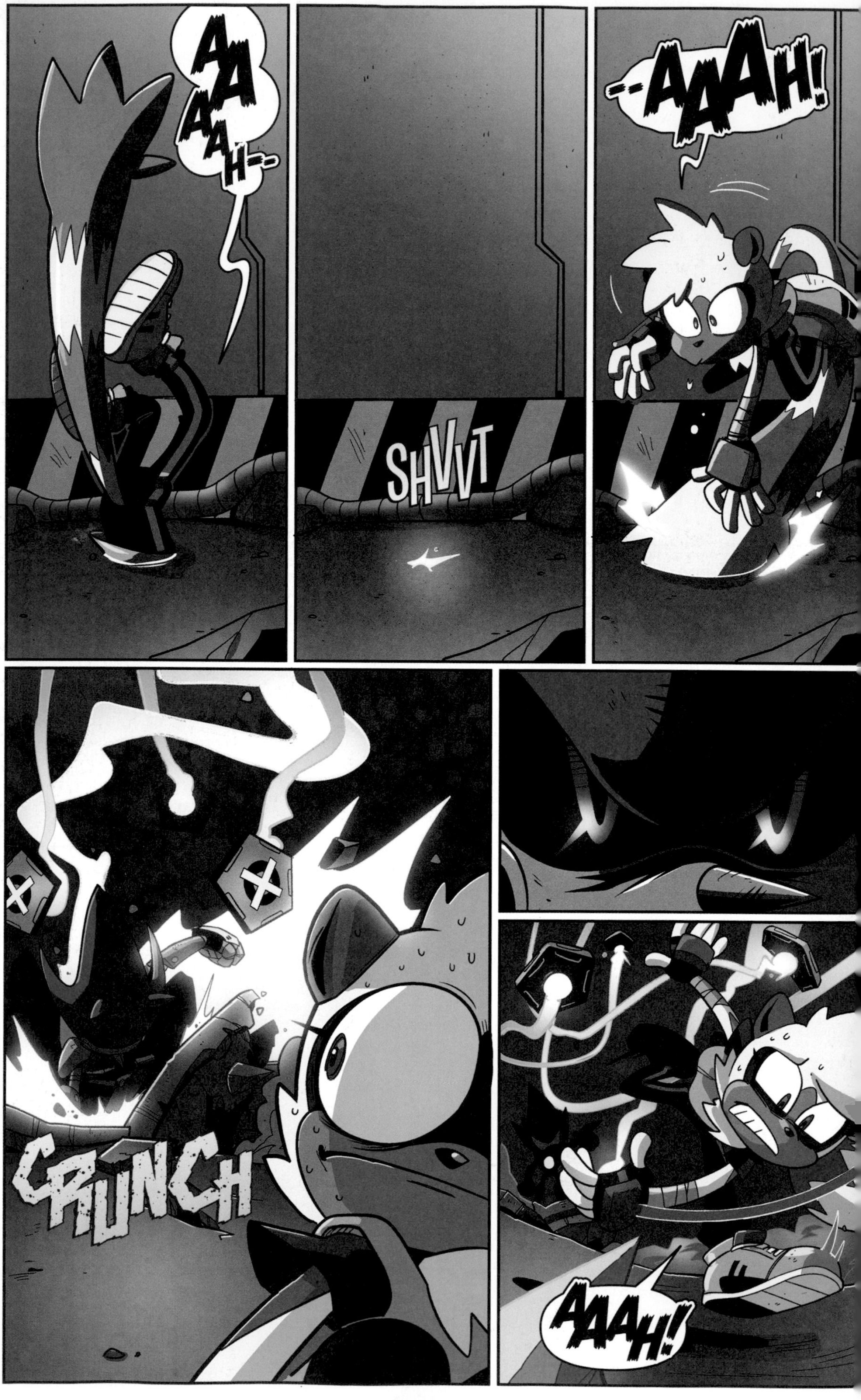
AAAAH--
SHVVVT
--AAAAH!
CRUNCH
AAAH!

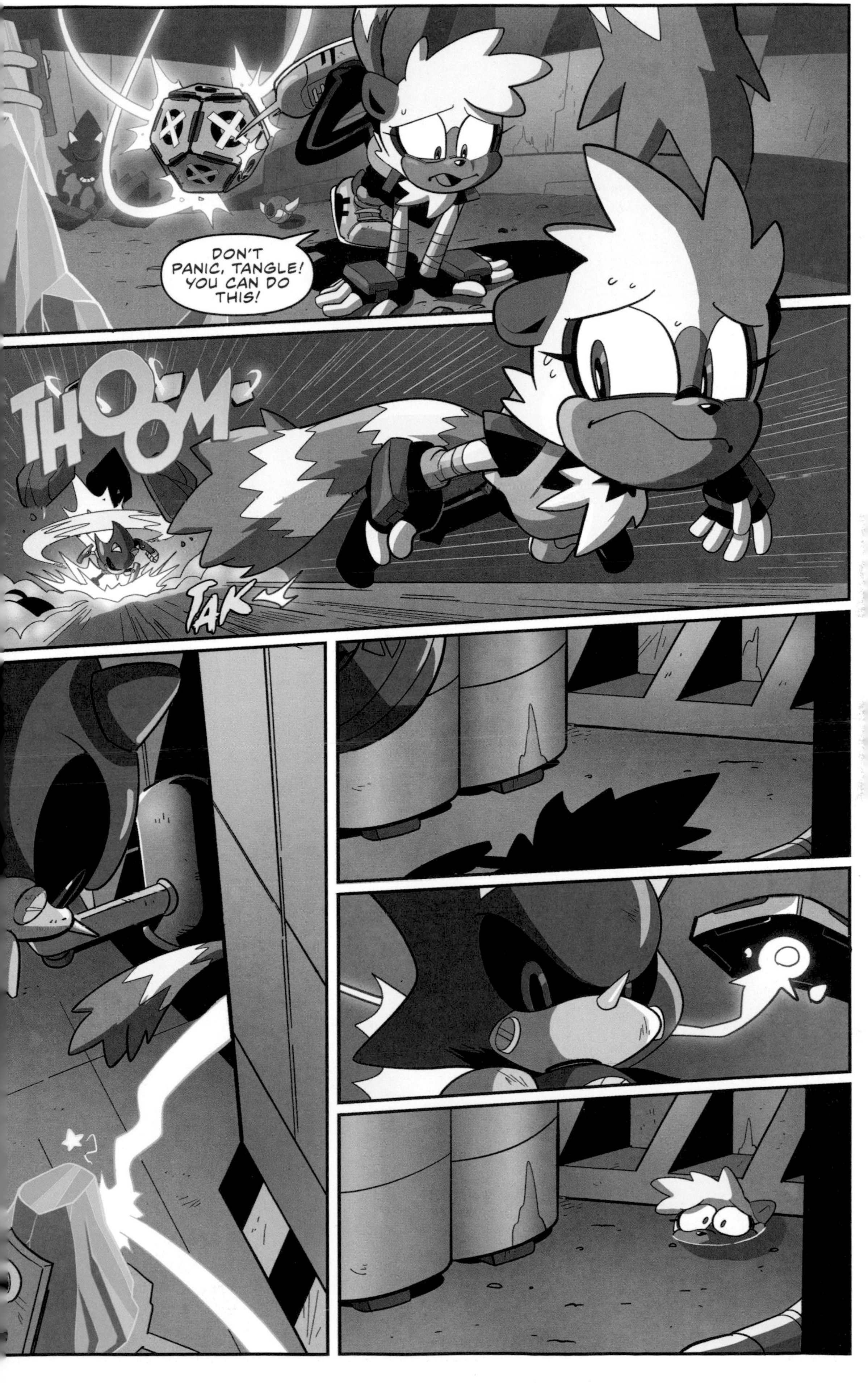
DON'T PANIC, TANGLE! YOU CAN DO THIS!
THOOM
TAK

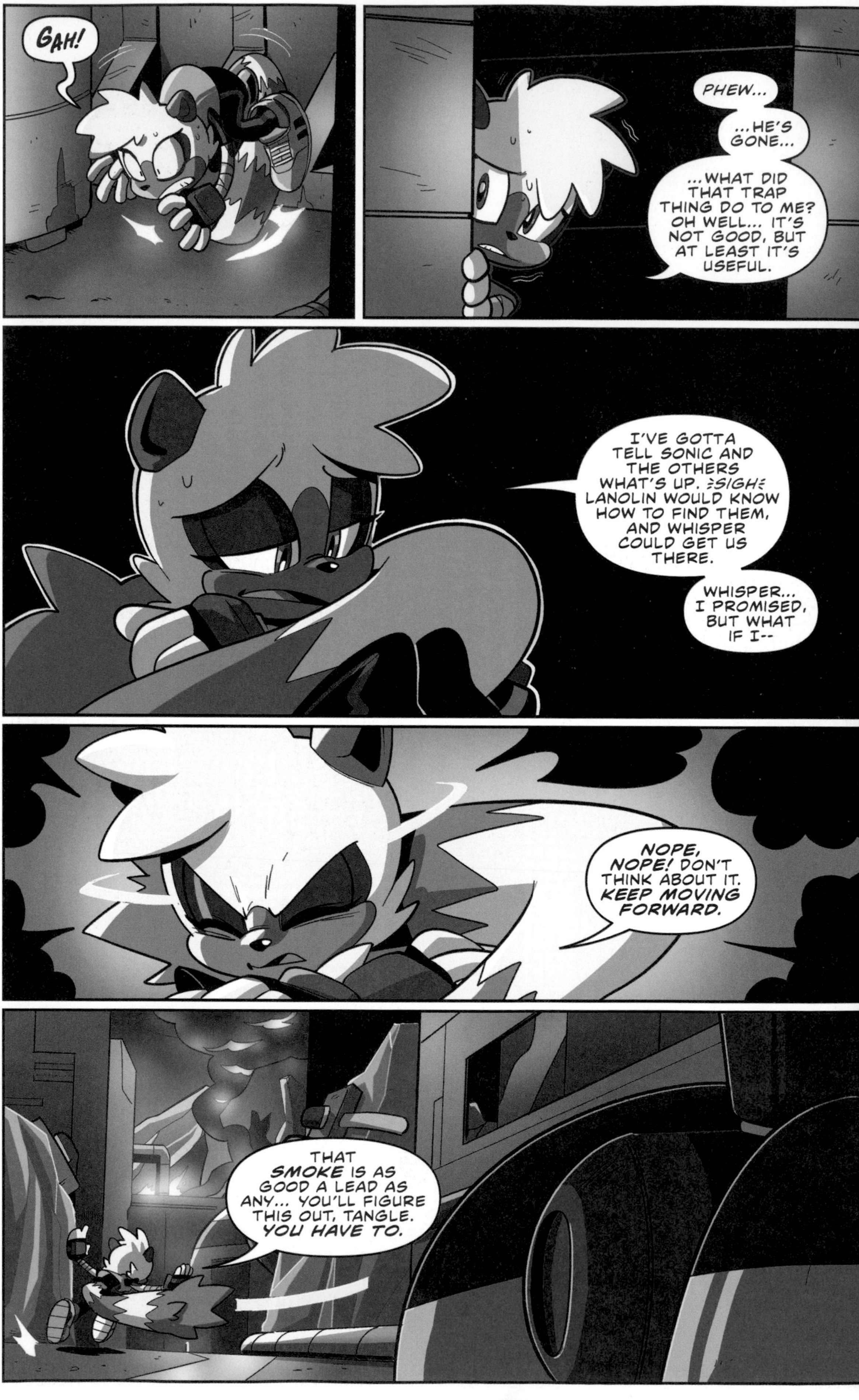
GAH!
PHEW...
...HE'S GONE...
...WHAT DID THAT TRAP THING DO TO ME? OH WELL... IT'S NOT GOOD, BUT AT LEAST IT'S USEFUL.
I'VE GOTTA TELL SONIC AND THE OTHERS WHAT'S UP. *SIGH* LANOLIN WOULD KNOW HOW TO FIND THEM, AND WHISPER COULD GET US THERE.
WHISPER... I PROMISED, BUT WHAT IF I--
NOPE, NOPE! DON'T THINK ABOUT IT. KEEP MOVING FORWARD.
THAT SMOKE IS AS GOOD A LEAD AS ANY... YOU'LL FIGURE THIS OUT, TANGLE. YOU HAVE TO.

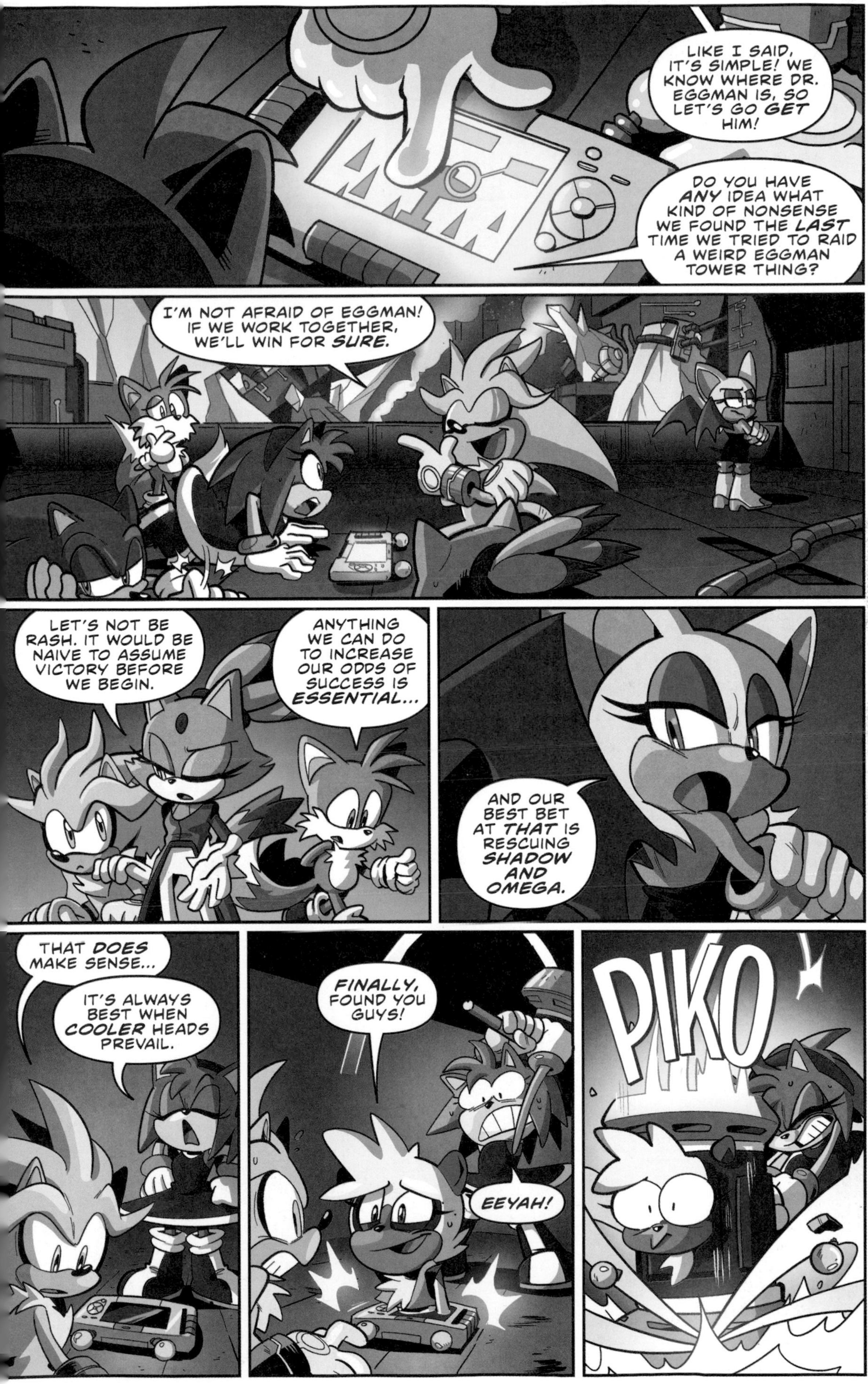
LIKE I SAID, IT'S SIMPLE! WE KNOW WHERE DR. EGGMAN IS, SO LET'S GO GET HIM!
DO YOU HAVE ANY IDEA WHAT KIND OF NONSENSE WE FOUND THE LAST TIME WE TRIED TO RAID A WEIRD EGGMAN TOWER THING?
I'M NOT AFRAID OF EGGMAN! IF WE WORK TOGETHER, WE'LL WIN FOR SURE.
LET'S NOT BE RASH. IT WOULD BE NAIVE TO ASSUME VICTORY BEFORE WE BEGIN.
ANYTHING WE CAN DO TO INCREASE OUR ODDS OF SUCCESS IS ESSENTIAL...
AND OUR BEST BET AT THAT IS RESCUING SHADOW AND OMEGA.
THAT DOES MAKE SENSE...
IT'S ALWAYS BEST WHEN COOLER HEADS PREVAIL.
FINALLY, FOUND YOU GUYS!
EEYAH!
PIKO

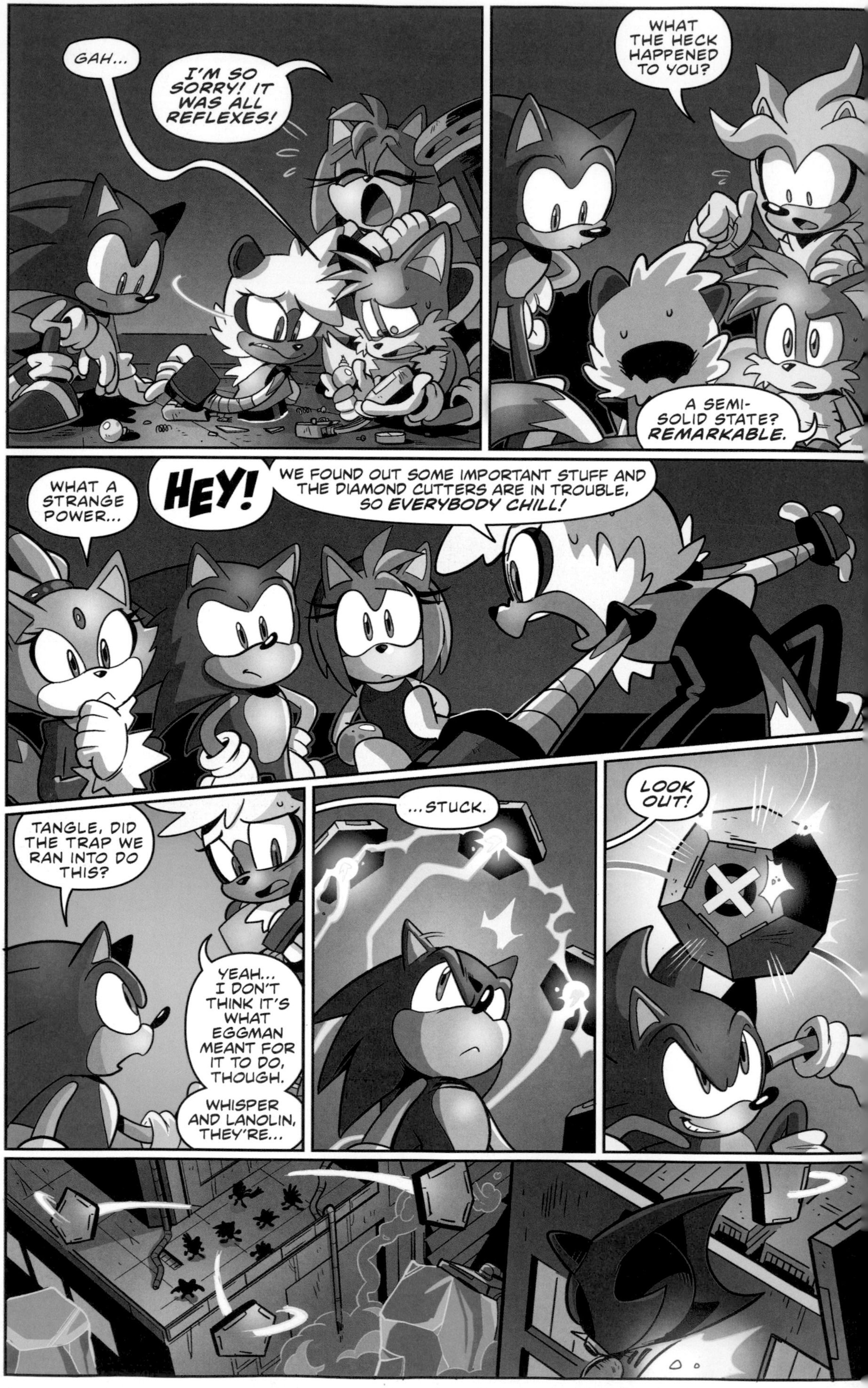
GAH...
I'M SO SORRY! IT WAS ALL REFLEXES!
WHAT THE HECK HAPPENED TO YOU?
A SEMI-SOLID STATE? REMARKABLE.
WHAT A STRANGE POWER...
HEY!
WE FOUND OUT SOME IMPORTANT STUFF AND THE DIAMOND CUTTERS ARE IN TROUBLE, SO EVERYBODY CHILL!
TANGLE, DID THE TRAP WE RAN INTO DO THIS?
YEAH... I DON'T THINK IT'S WHAT EGGMAN MEANT FOR IT TO DO, THOUGH.
WHISPER AND LANOLIN, THEY'RE...
...STUCK.
LOOK OUT!

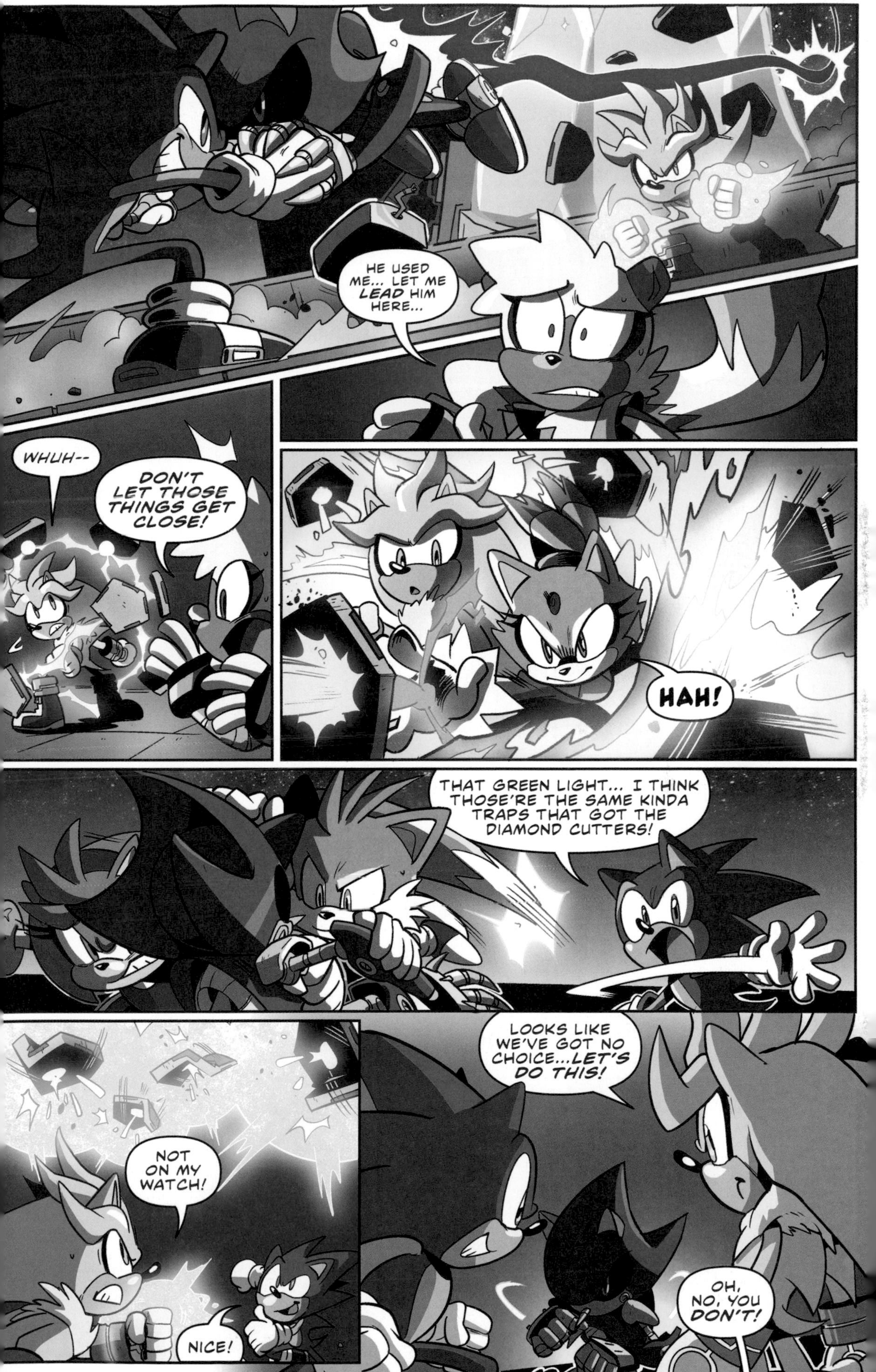
HE USED ME... LET ME LEAD HIM HERE...
WHUH--
DON'T LET THOSE THINGS GET CLOSE!
HAH!
THAT GREEN LIGHT... I THINK THOSE'RE THE SAME KINDA TRAPS THAT GOT THE DIAMOND CUTTERS!
NOT ON MY WATCH!
NICE!
LOOKS LIKE WE'VE GOT NO CHOICE...LET'S DO THIS!
OH, NO, YOU DON'T!

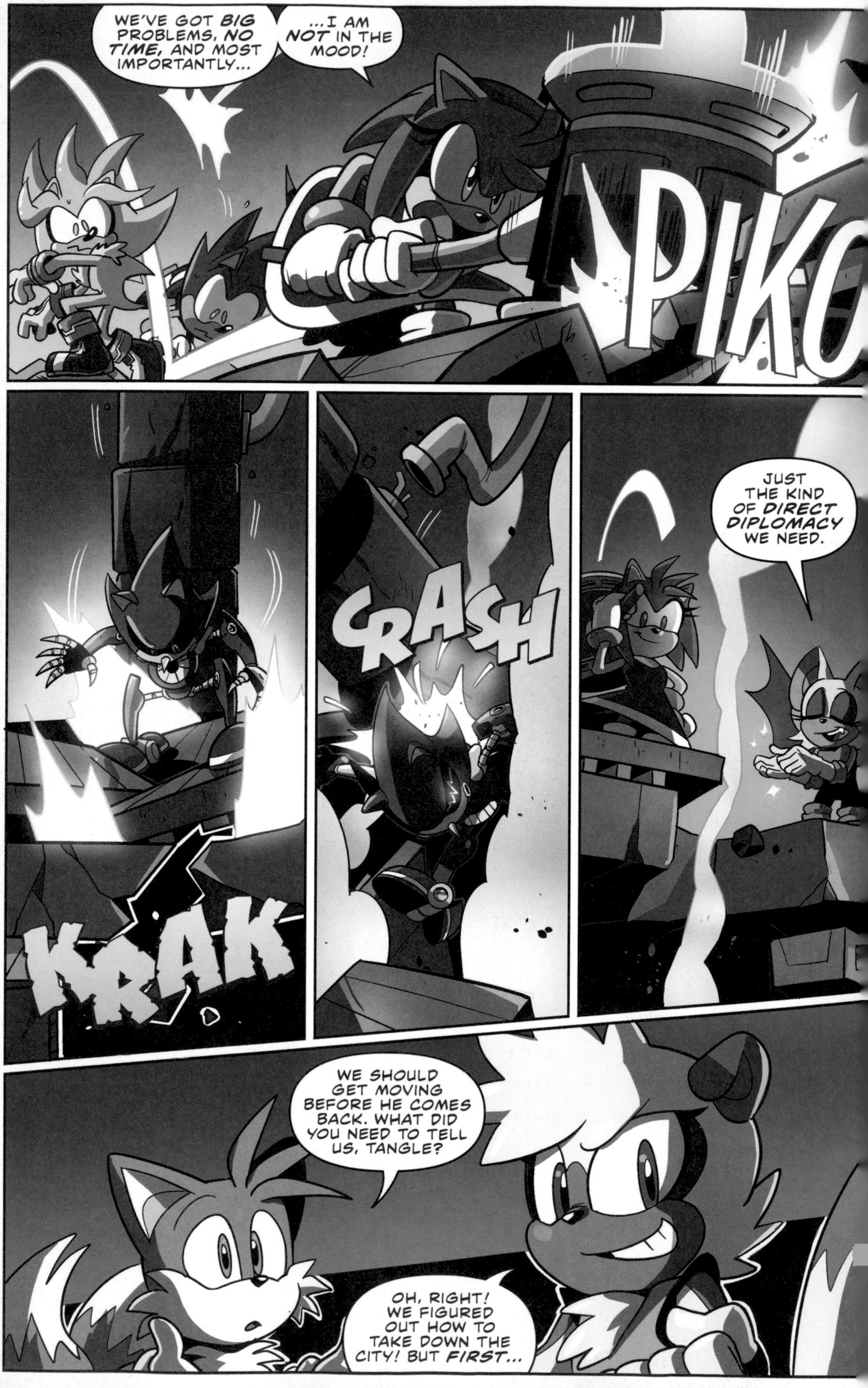
WE'VE GOT BIG PROBLEMS, NO TIME, AND MOST IMPORTANTLY...
...I AM NOT IN THE MOOD!
PIKO
KRAK
CRASH
JUST THE KIND OF DIRECT DIPLOMACY WE NEED.
WE SHOULD GET MOVING BEFORE HE COMES BACK. WHAT DID YOU NEED TO TELL US, TANGLE?
OH, RIGHT! WE FIGURED OUT HOW TO TAKE DOWN THE CITY! BUT FIRST...

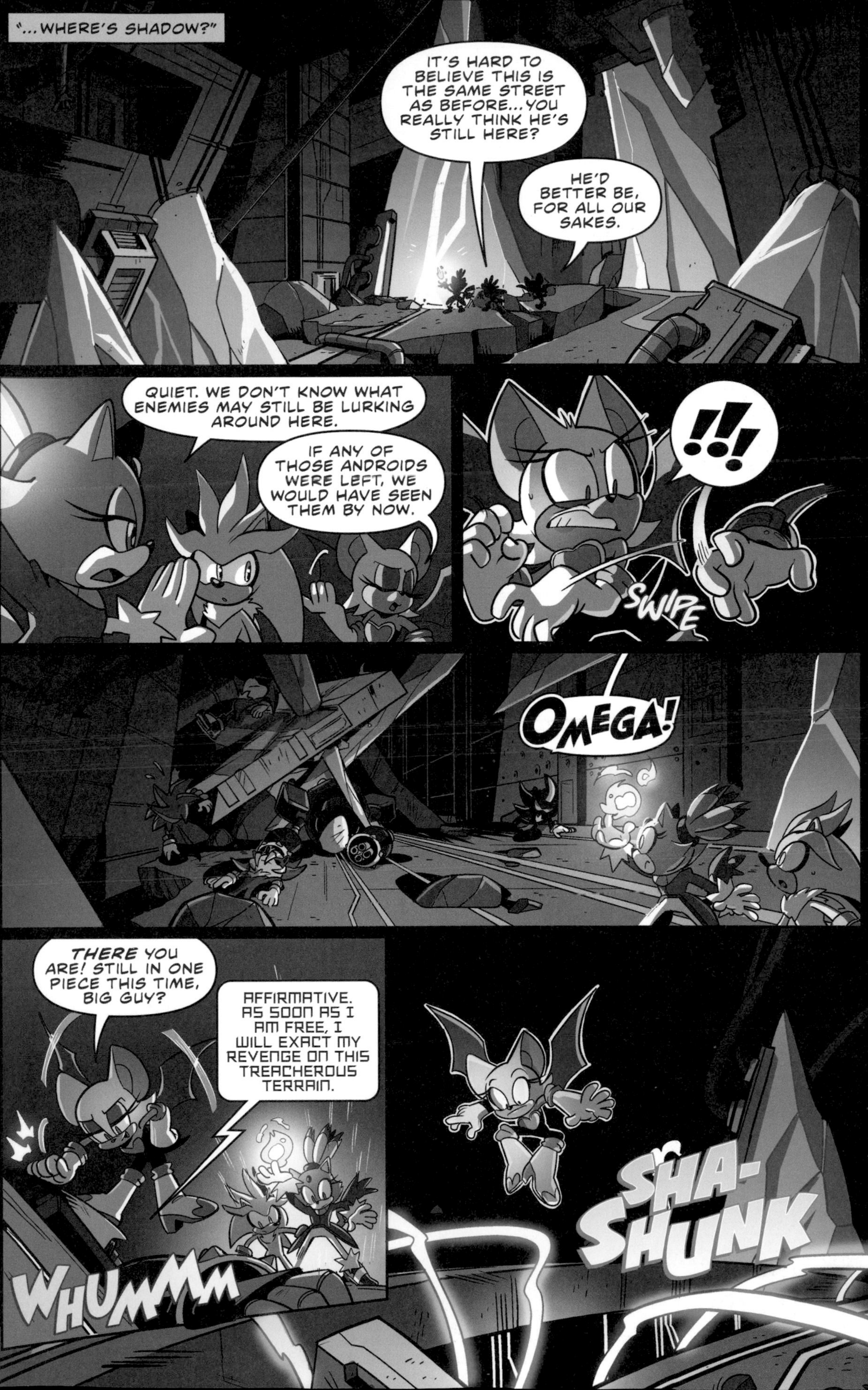
"...WHERE'S SHADOW?"
IT'S HARD TO BELIEVE THIS IS THE SAME STREET AS BEFORE...YOU REALLY THINK HE'S STILL HERE?
HE'D BETTER BE, FOR ALL OUR SAKES.
QUIET. WE DON'T KNOW WHAT ENEMIES MAY STILL BE LURKING AROUND HERE.
IF ANY OF THOSE ANDROIDS WERE LEFT, WE WOULD HAVE SEEN THEM BY NOW.
!!!
SWIPE
OMEGA!
THERE YOU ARE! STILL IN ONE PIECE THIS TIME, BIG GUY?
AFFIRMATIVE. AS SOON AS I AM FREE, I WILL EXACT MY REVENGE ON THIS TREACHEROUS TERRAIN.
WHUMMM
SHA-SHUNK

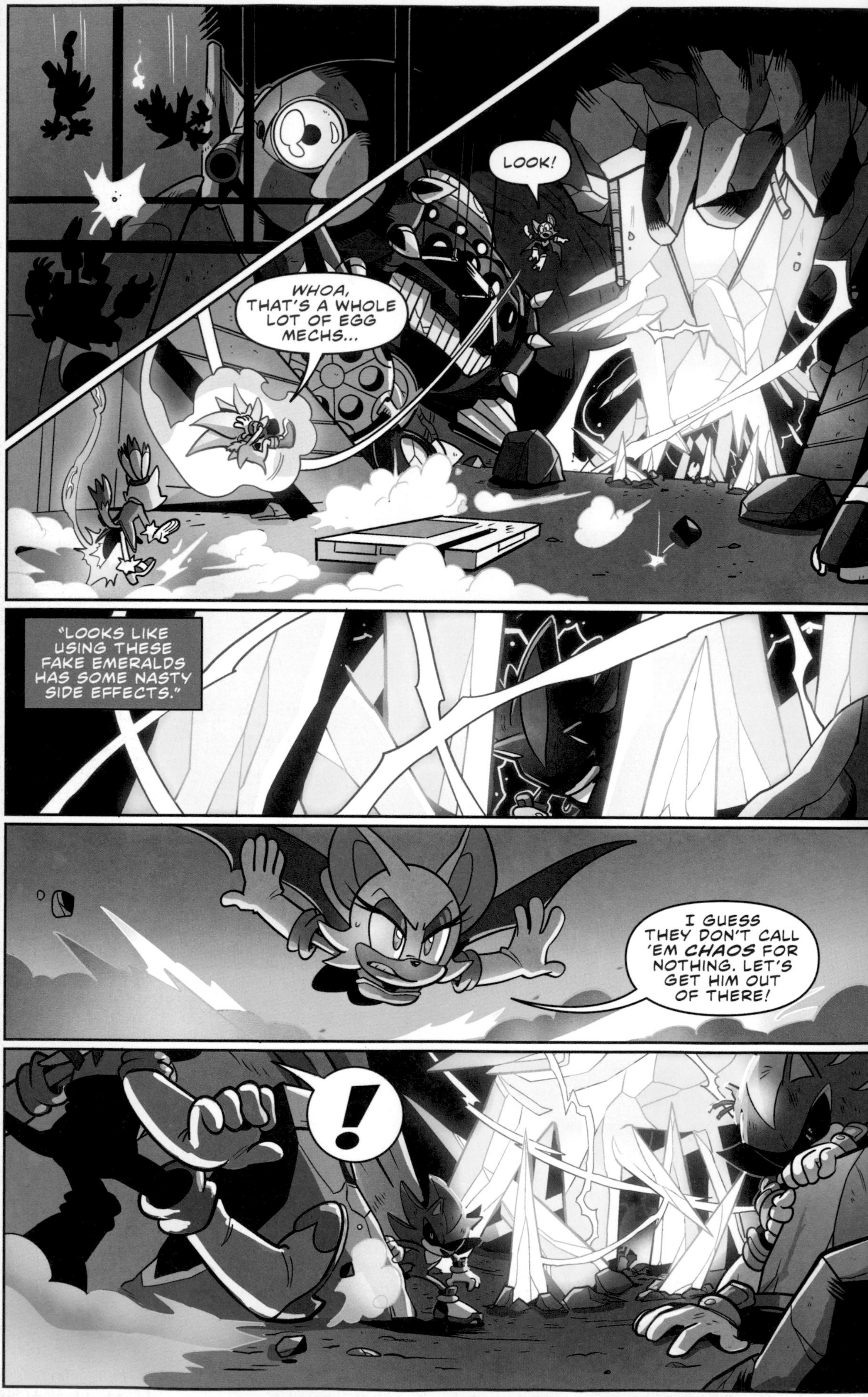
LOOK!
WHOA, THAT'S A WHOLE LOT OF EGG MECHS...
"LOOKS LIKE USING THESE FAKE EMERALDS HAS SOME NASTY SIDE EFFECTS."
I GUESS THEY DON'T CALL 'EM CHAOS FOR NOTHING. LET'S GET HIM OUT OF THERE!
!

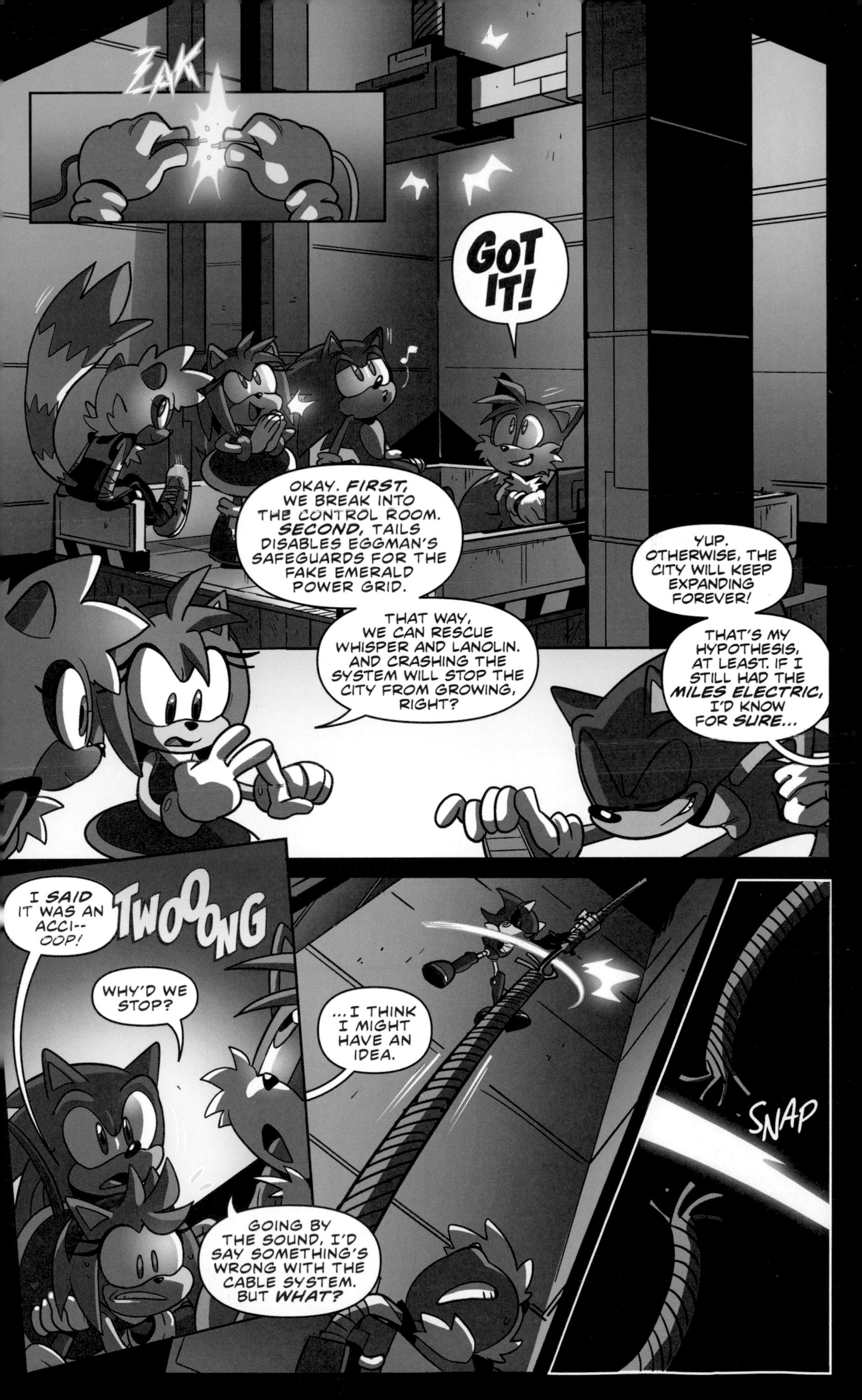
ZAK
GOT IT!
OKAY. FIRST, WE BREAK INTO THE CONTROL ROOM. SECOND, TAILS DISABLES EGGMAN'S SAFEGUARDS FOR THE FAKE EMERALD POWER GRID.
THAT WAY, WE CAN RESCUE WHISPER AND LANOLIN. AND CRASHING THE SYSTEM WILL STOP THE CITY FROM GROWING, RIGHT?
YUP. OTHERWISE, THE CITY WILL KEEP EXPANDING FOREVER!
THAT'S MY HYPOTHESIS, AT LEAST. IF I STILL HAD THE MILES ELECTRIC, I'D KNOW FOR SURE...
I SAID IT WAS AN ACCI-- OOP!
TWOOONG
WHY'D WE STOP?
...I THINK I MIGHT HAVE AN IDEA.
GOING BY THE SOUND, I'D SAY SOMETHING'S WRONG WITH THE CABLE SYSTEM. BUT WHAT?
SNAP

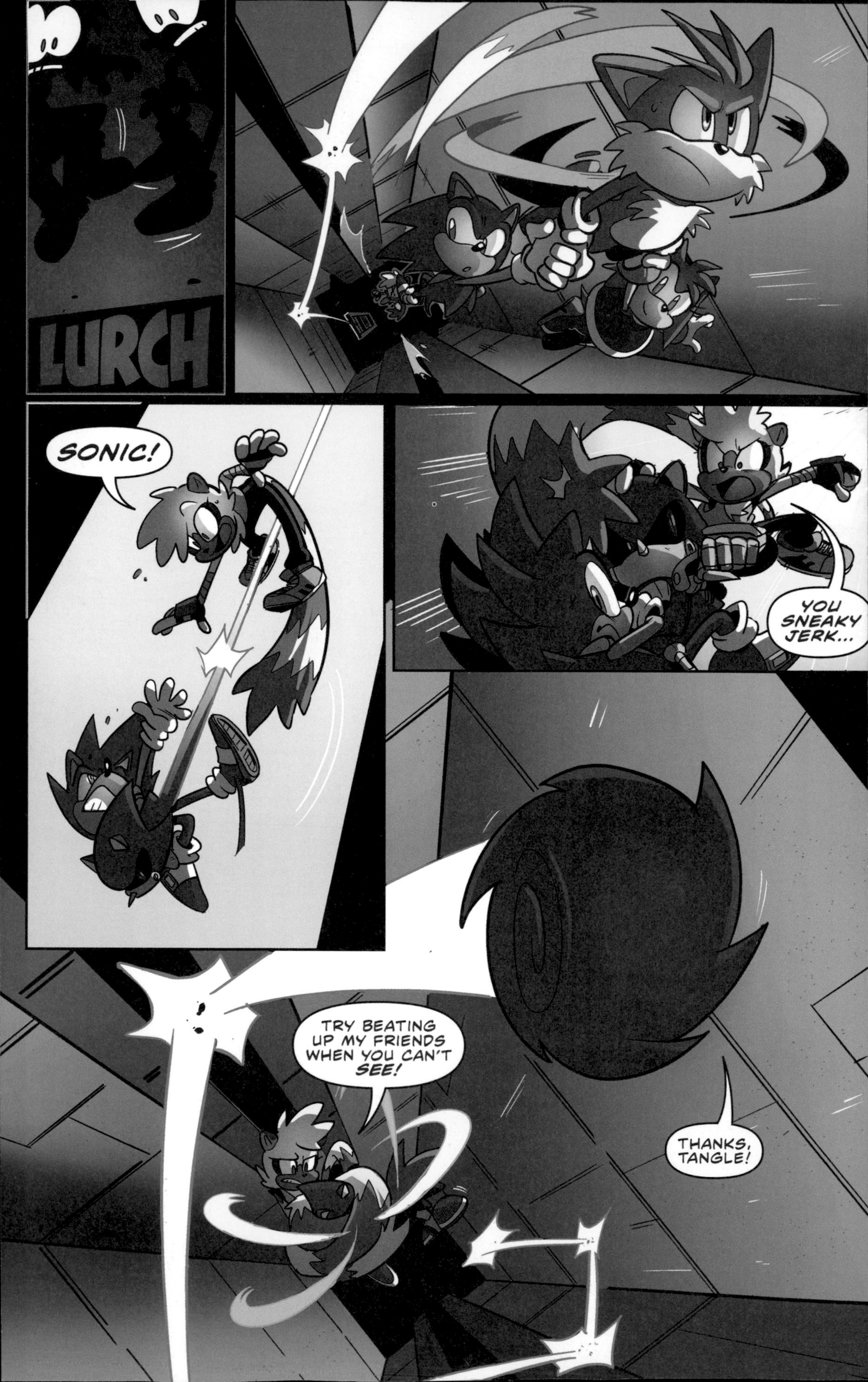
LURCH
SONIC!
YOU SNEAKY JERK...
TRY BEATING UP MY FRIENDS WHEN YOU CAN'T SEE!
THANKS, TANGLE!

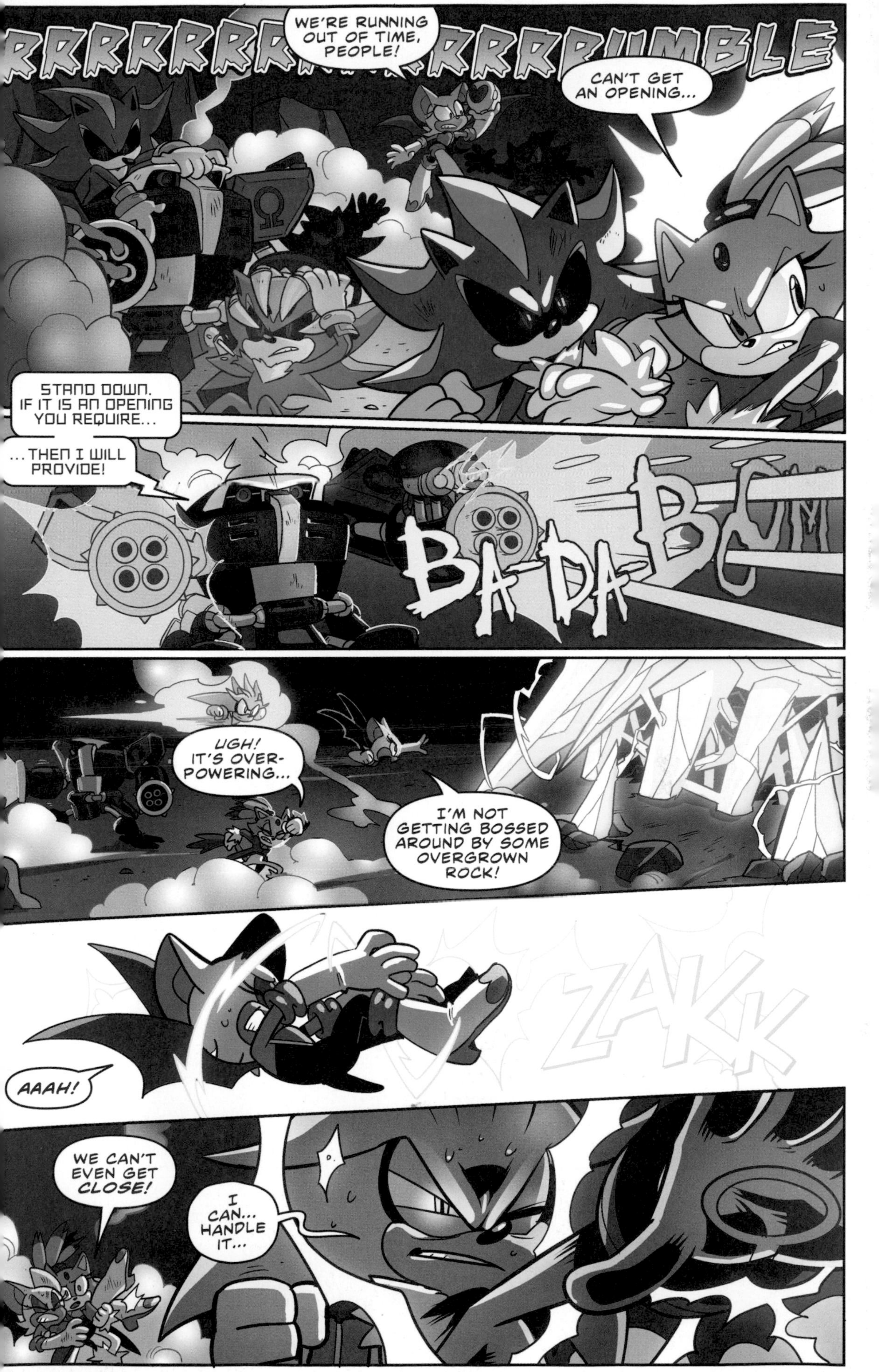
RRRRRRR...RRRRRUMBLE
WE'RE RUNNING OUT OF TIME, PEOPLE!
CAN'T GET AN OPENING...
STAND DOWN. IF IT IS AN OPENING YOU REQUIRE...
...THEN I WILL PROVIDE!
BA-DA-BOOM
UGH! IT'S OVER-POWERING...
I'M NOT GETTING BOSSED AROUND BY SOME OVERGROWN ROCK!
ZAKK
AAAH!
WE CAN'T EVEN GET CLOSE!
I CAN... HANDLE IT...

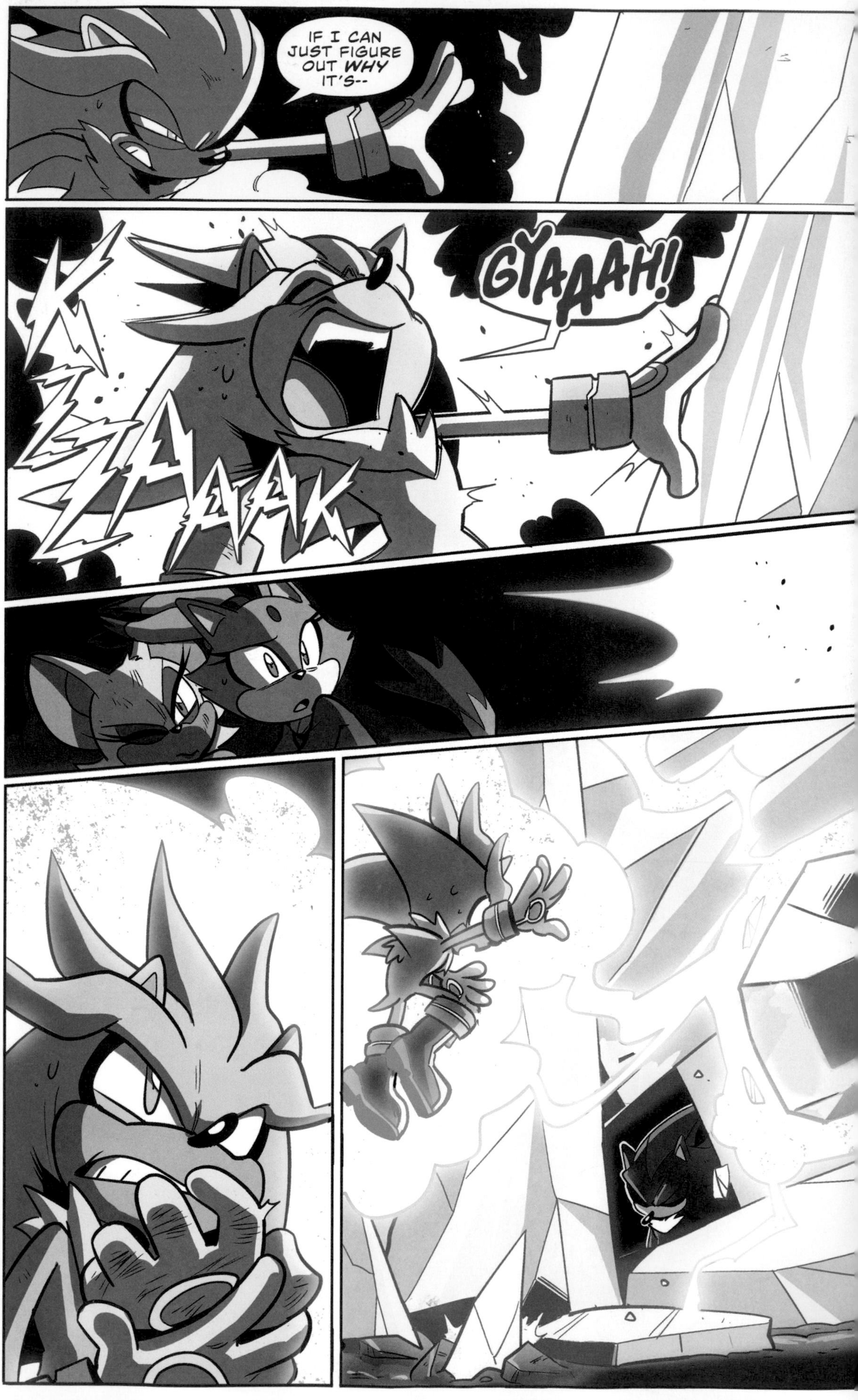
IF I CAN JUST FIGURE OUT WHY IT'S--
KZZAAK
GYAAAH!

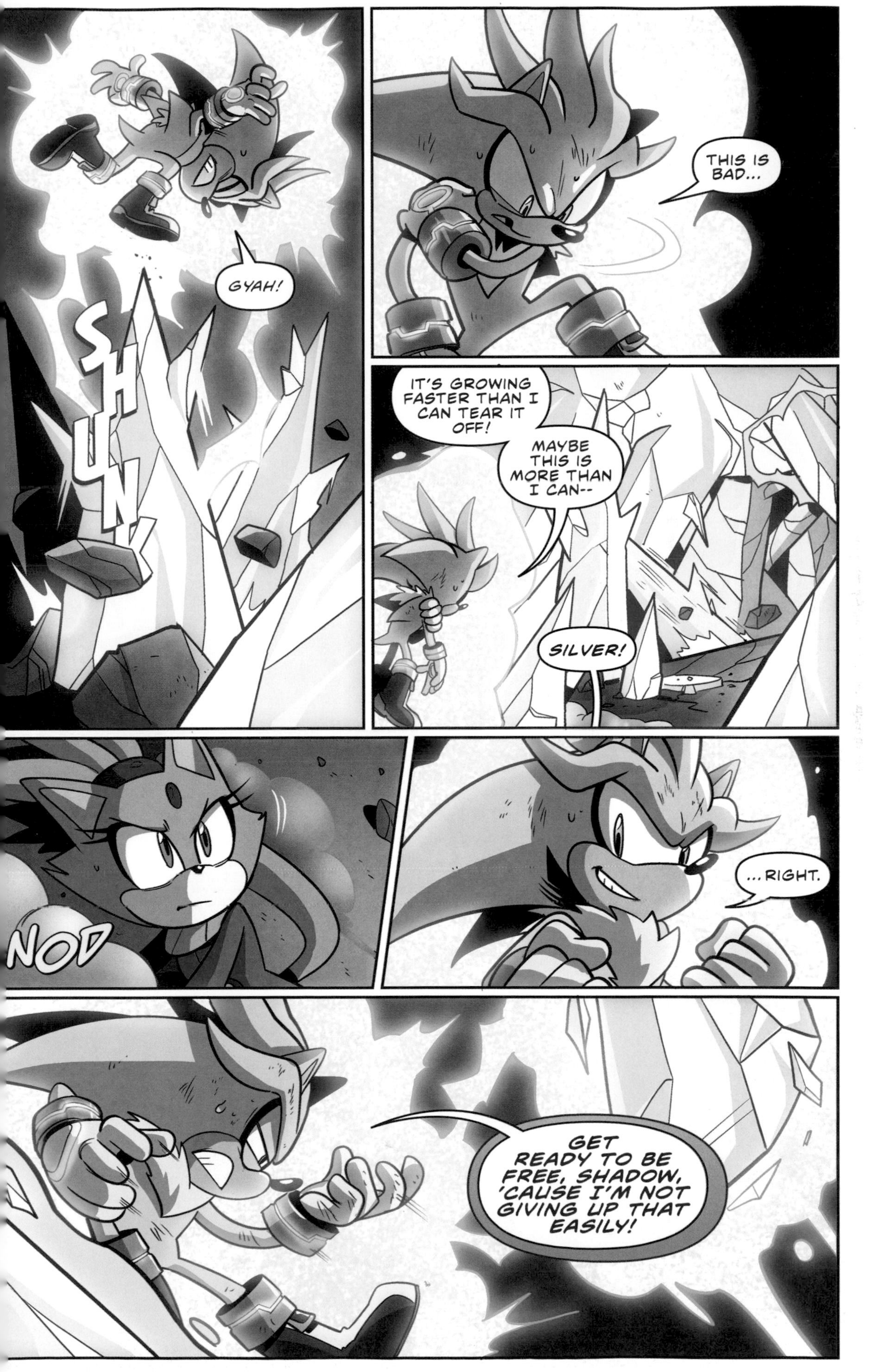
GYAH!
SHUNK
THIS IS BAD...
IT'S GROWING FASTER THAN I CAN TEAR IT OFF!
MAYBE THIS IS MORE THAN I CAN--
SILVER!
NOD
...RIGHT.
GET READY TO BE FREE, SHADOW, 'CAUSE I'M NOT GIVING UP THAT EASILY!

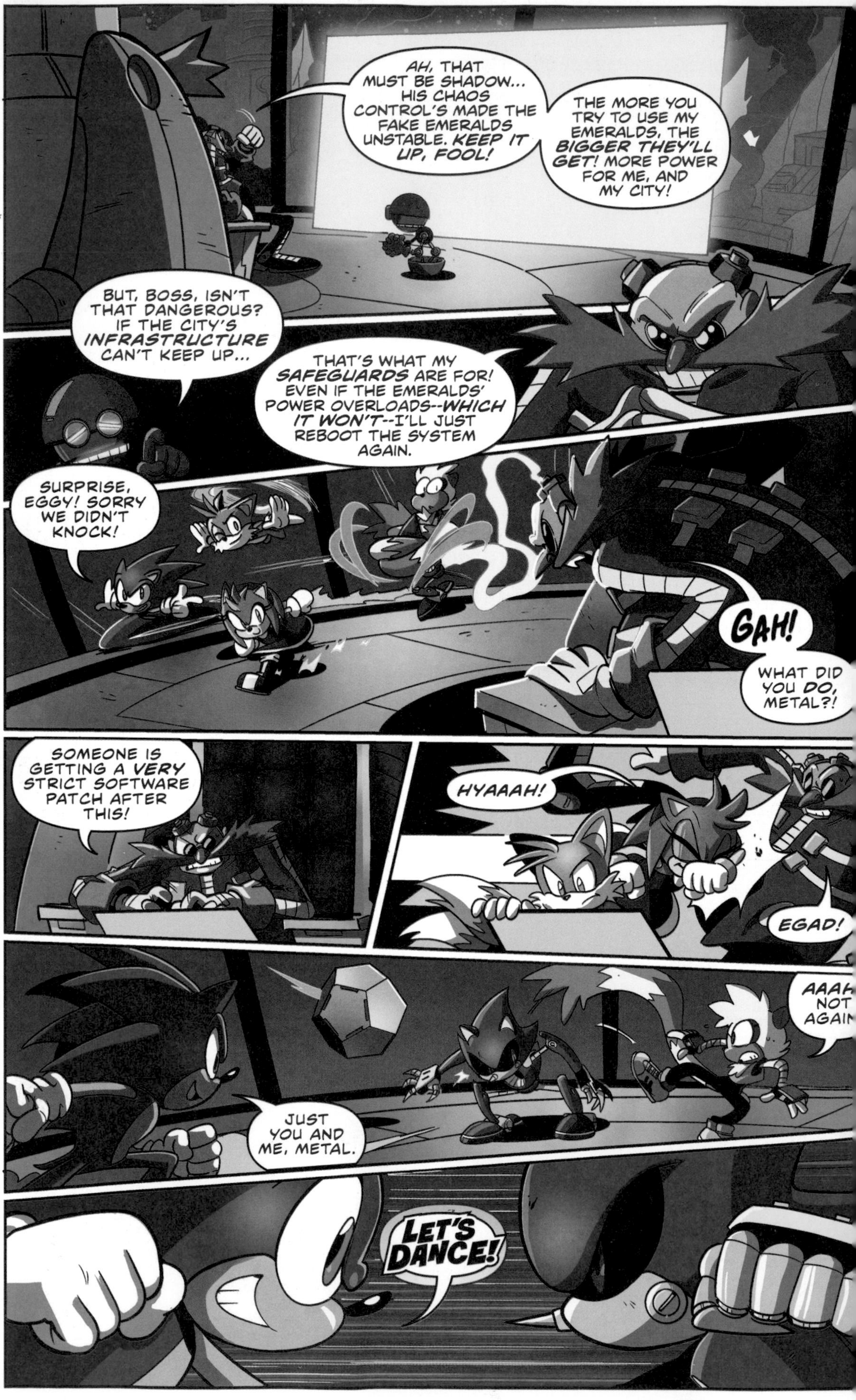
AH, THAT MUST BE SHADOW... HIS CHAOS CONTROL'S MADE THE FAKE EMERALDS UNSTABLE. KEEP IT UP, FOOL!
THE MORE YOU TRY TO USE MY EMERALDS, THE BIGGER THEY'LL GET! MORE POWER FOR ME, AND MY CITY!
BUT, BOSS, ISN'T THAT DANGEROUS? IF THE CITY'S INFRASTRUCTURE CAN'T KEEP UP...
THAT'S WHAT MY SAFEGUARDS ARE FOR! EVEN IF THE EMERALDS' POWER OVERLOADS--WHICH IT WON'T--I'LL JUST REBOOT THE SYSTEM AGAIN.
SURPRISE, EGGY! SORRY WE DIDN'T KNOCK!
GAH!
WHAT DID YOU DO, METAL?!
SOMEONE IS GETTING A VERY STRICT SOFTWARE PATCH AFTER THIS!
HYAAAH!
EGAD!
JUST YOU AND ME, METAL.
LET'S DANCE!

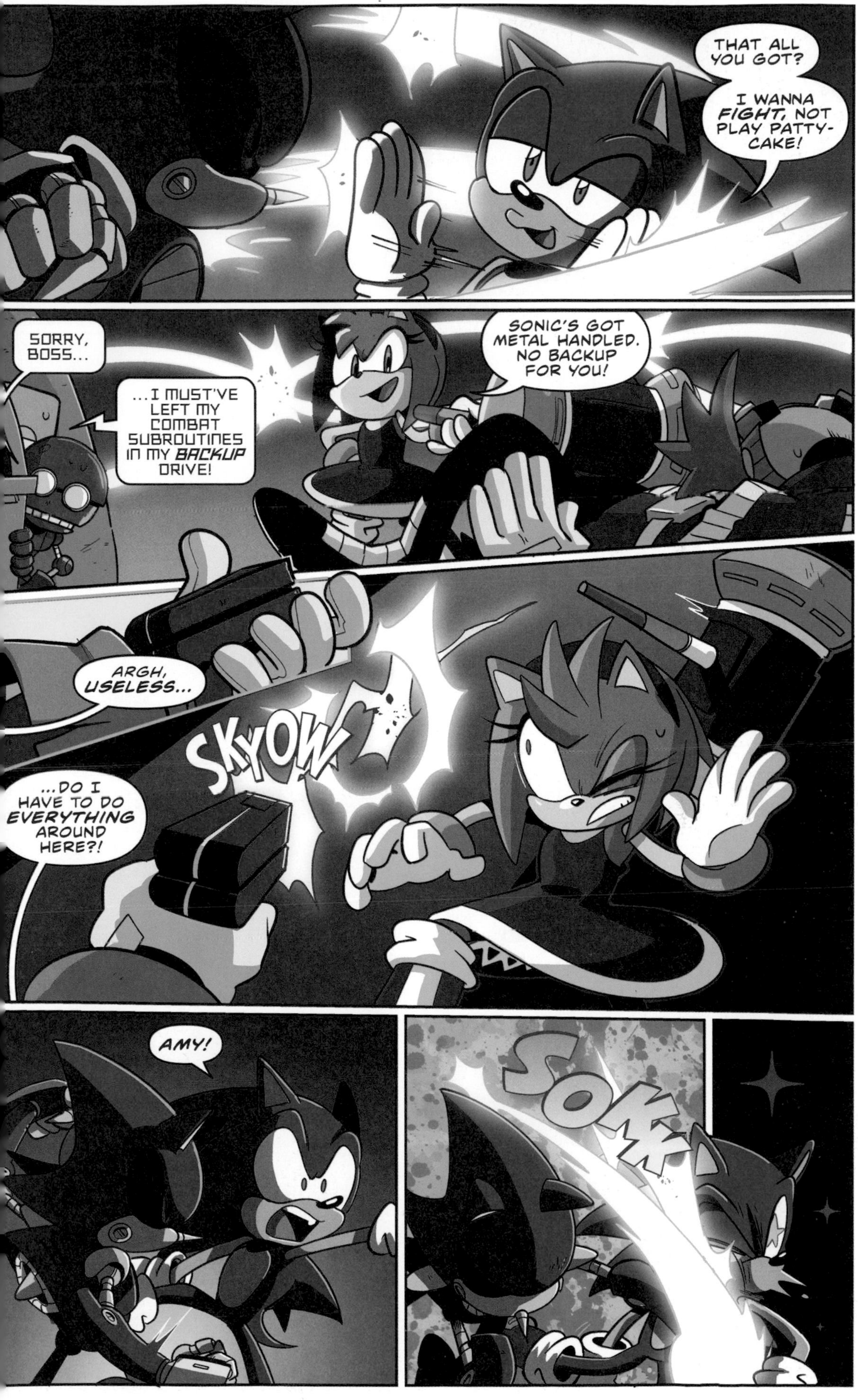
THAT ALL YOU GOT?
I WANNA *FIGHT,* NOT PLAY PATTY-CAKE!
SORRY, BOSS...
...I MUST'VE LEFT MY COMBAT SUBROUTINES IN MY *BACKUP* DRIVE!
SONIC'S GOT METAL HANDLED. NO BACKUP FOR YOU!
ARGH, *USELESS...*
...DO I HAVE TO DO *EVERYTHING* AROUND HERE?!
SKYOW!
AMY!
SOK

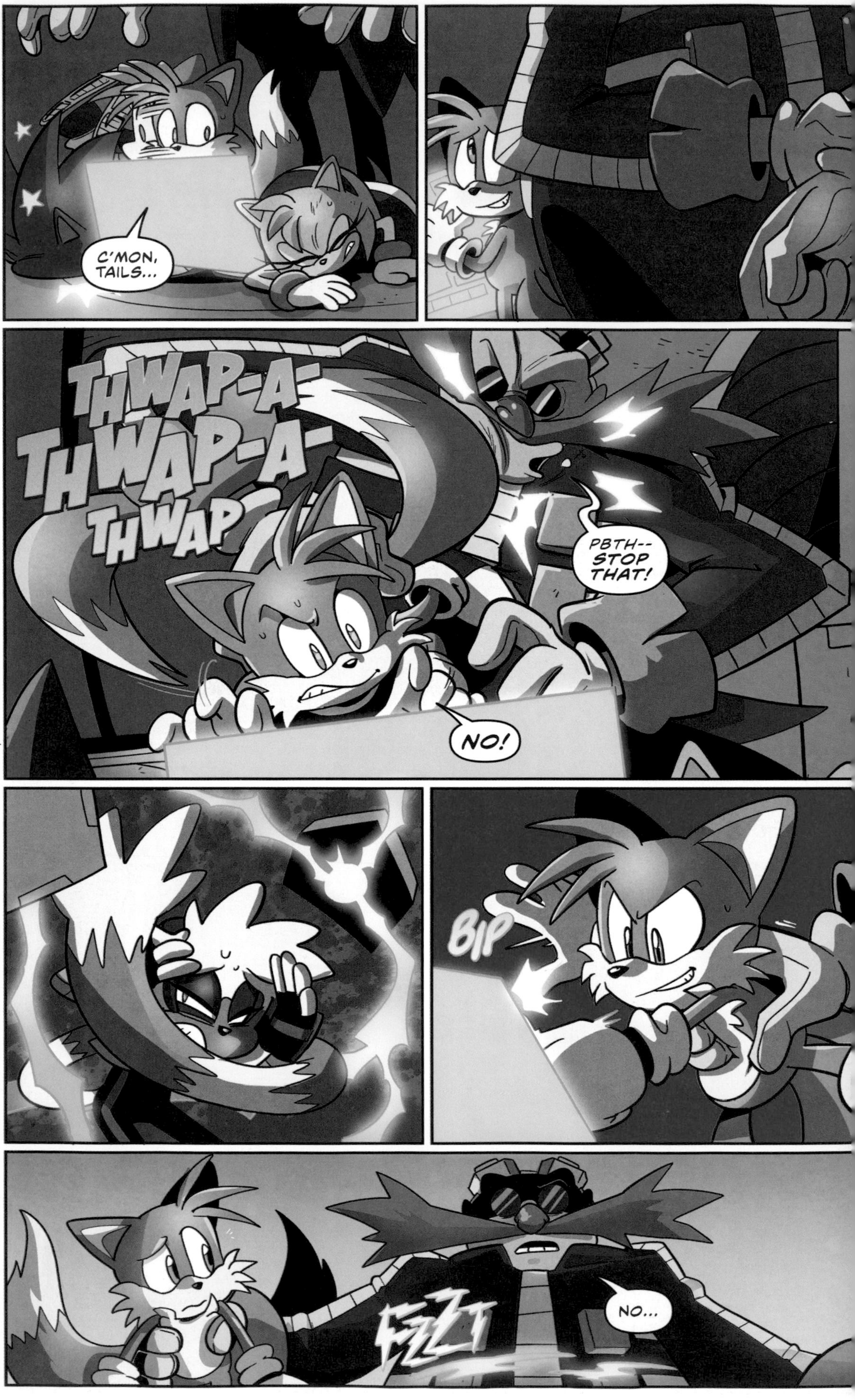
C'MON, TAILS...
THWAP-A-THWAP-A-THWAP
PBTH--STOP THAT!
NO!
BIP
FZZT
NO...

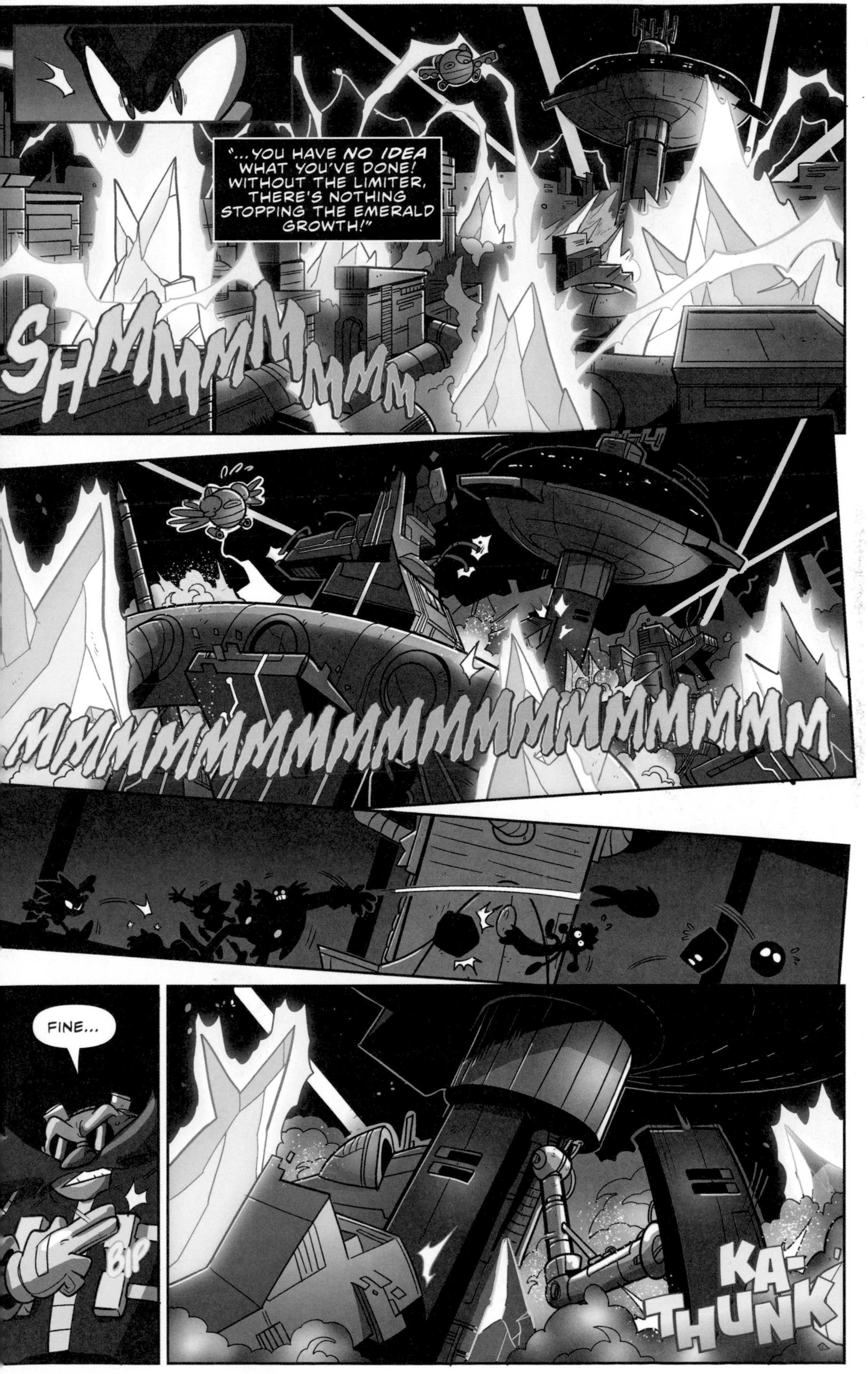
"...YOU HAVE NO IDEA WHAT YOU'VE DONE! WITHOUT THE LIMITER, THERE'S NOTHING STOPPING THE EMERALD GROWTH!"
SHMMMMMMM
MMMMMMMMMMMMMMMMMMMMM
FINE...
BIP
KA-THUNK

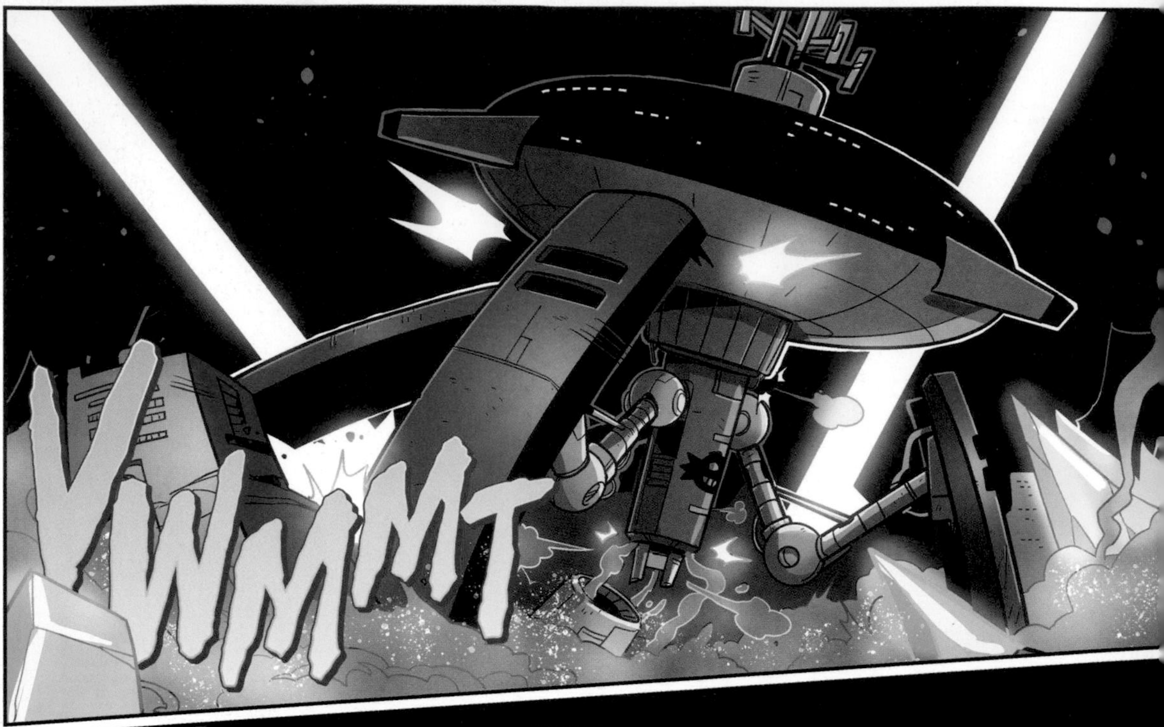
VWMMT

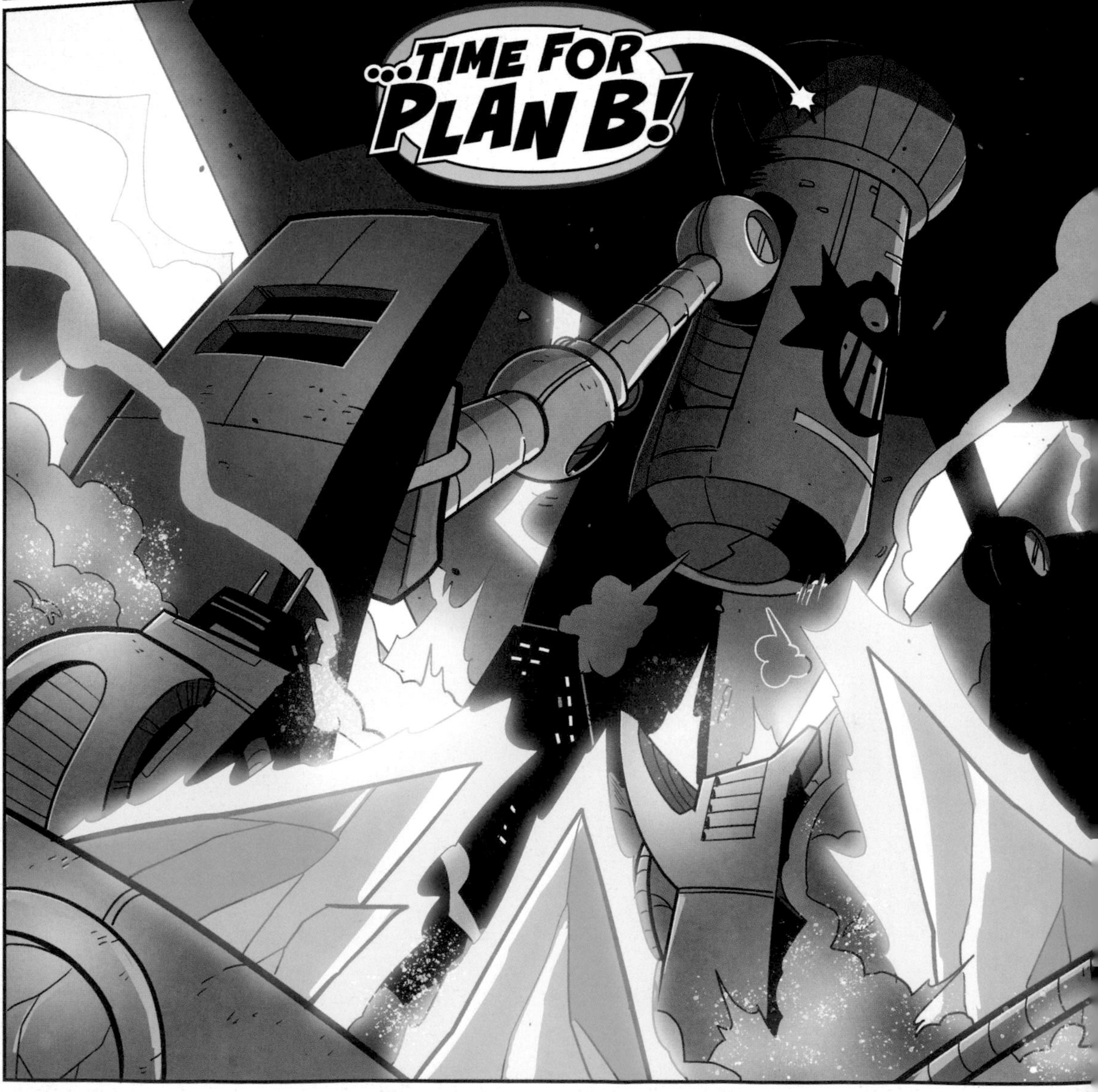
...TIME FOR PLAN B!

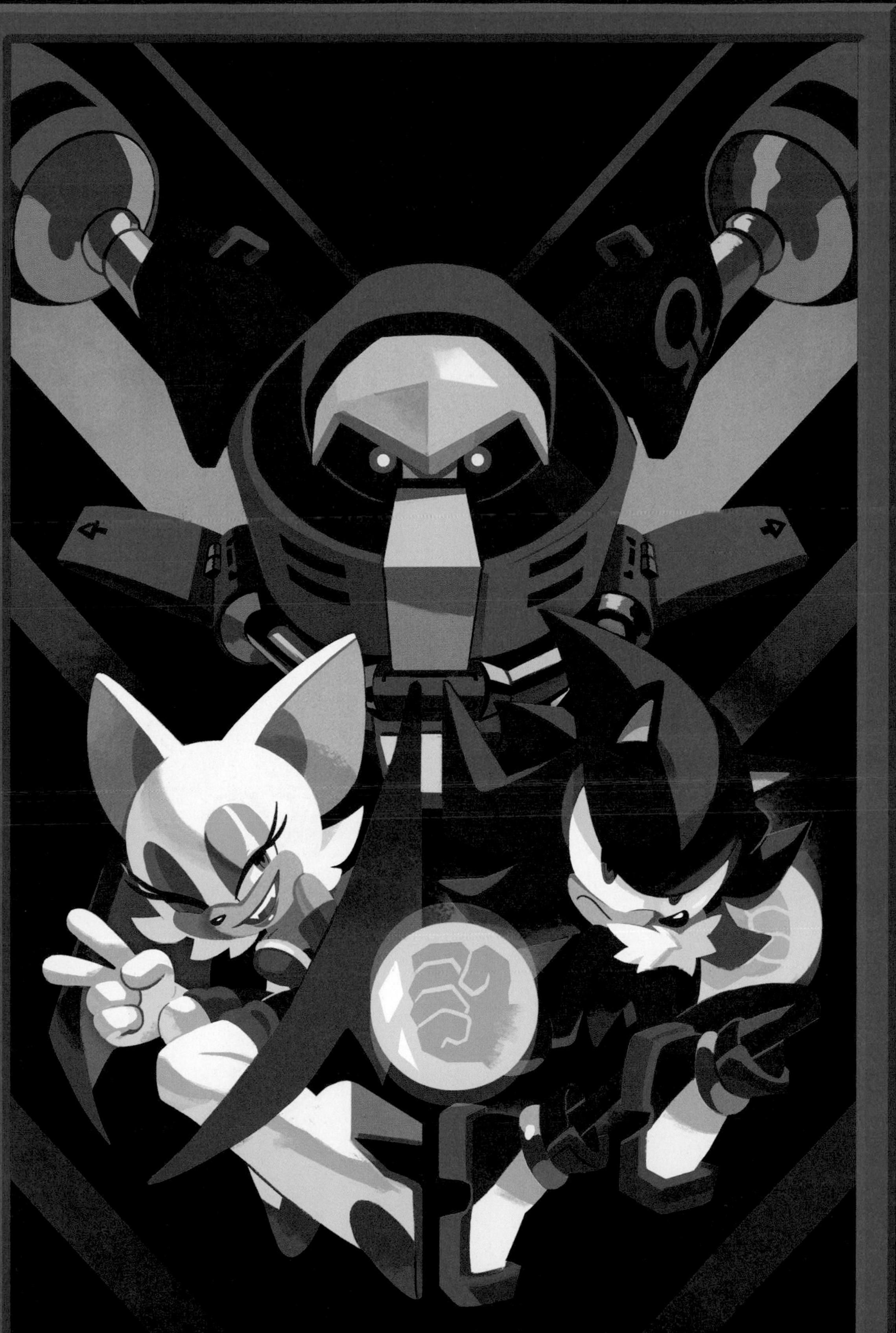

ART BY **NATHALIE FOURDRAINE**

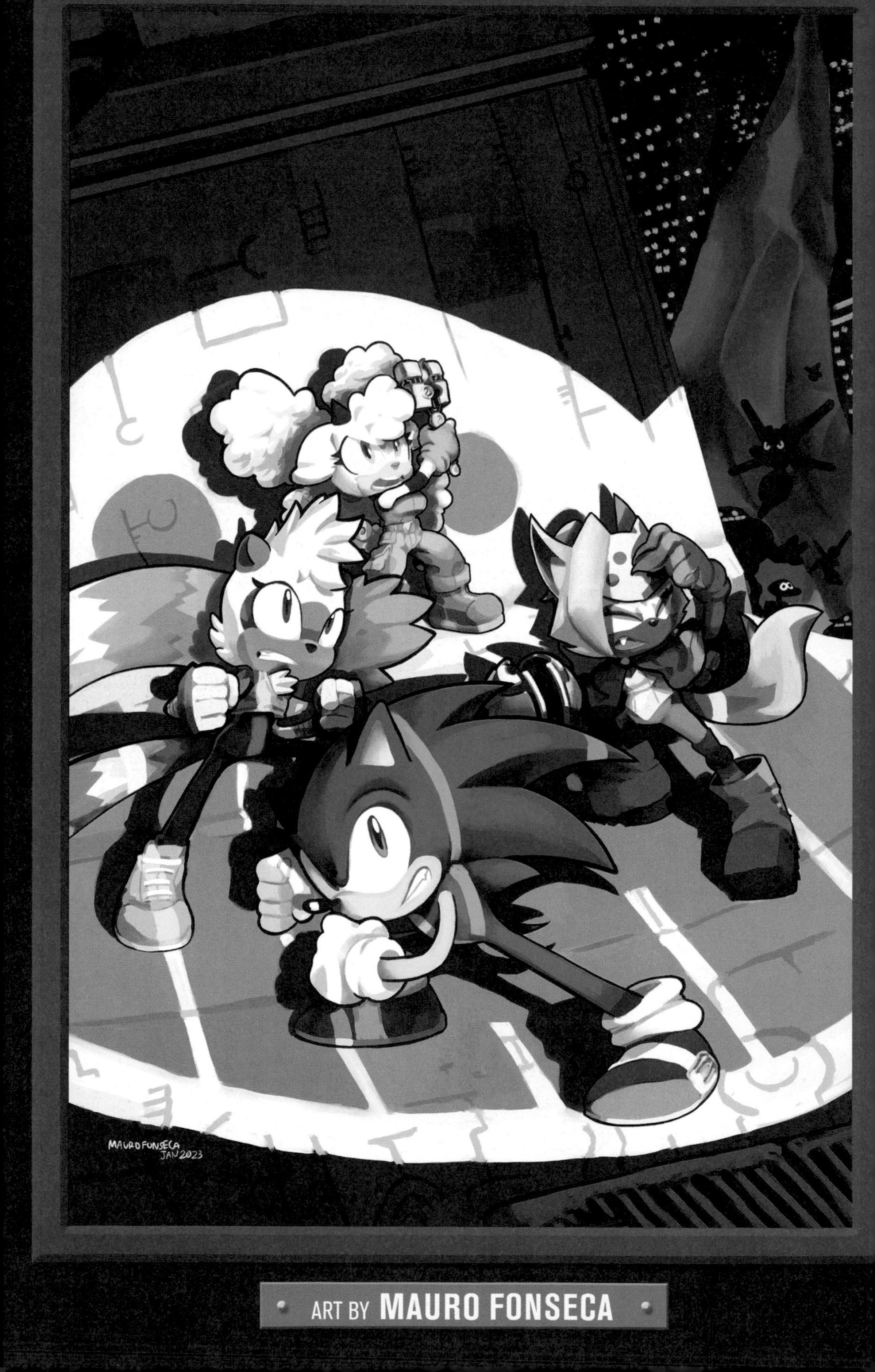
MAURO FONSECA
JAN 2023

ART BY **MAURO FONSECA**

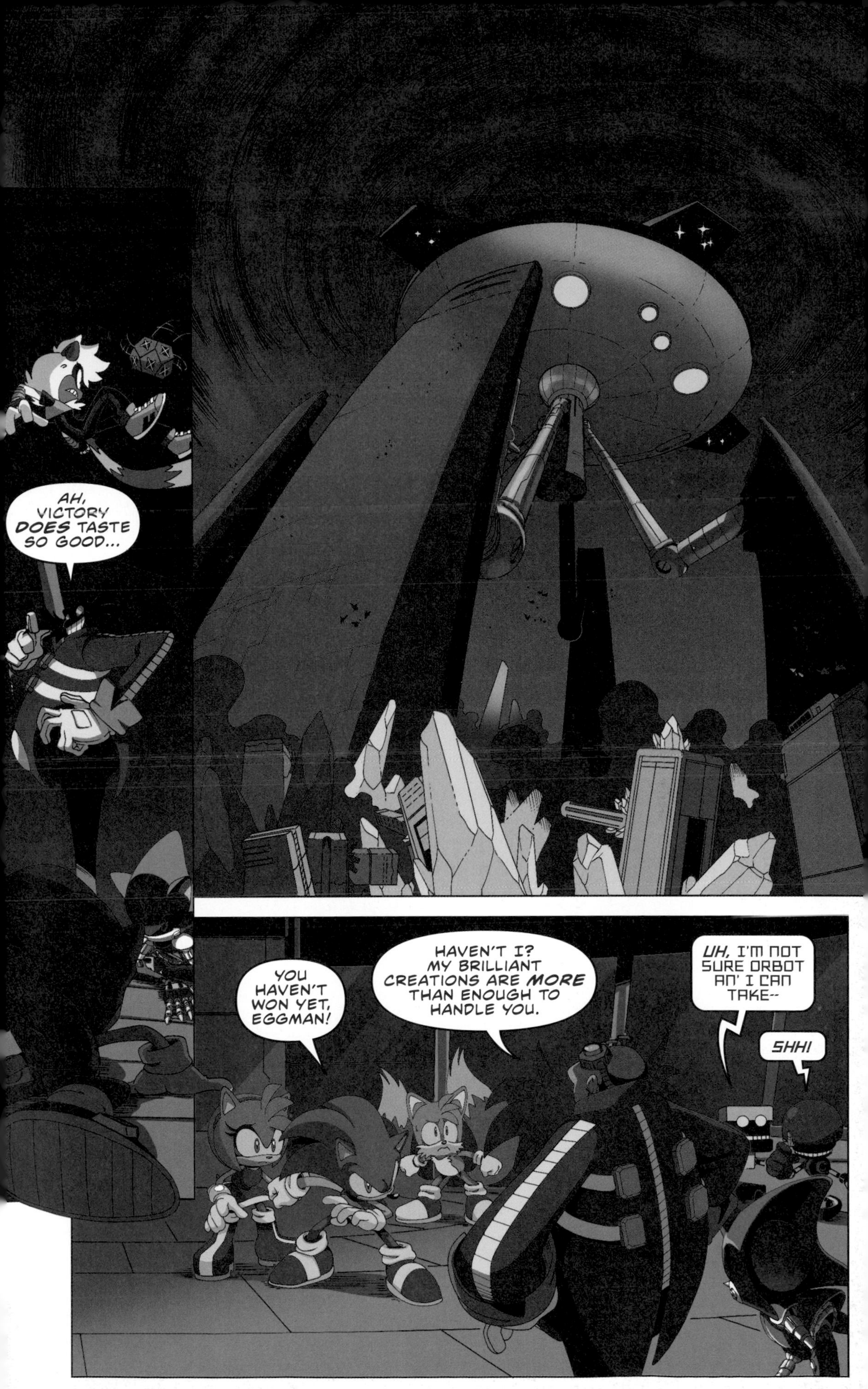
AH, VICTORY DOES TASTE SO GOOD...
YOU HAVEN'T WON YET, EGGMAN!
HAVEN'T I? MY BRILLIANT CREATIONS ARE MORE THAN ENOUGH TO HANDLE YOU.
UH, I'M NOT SURE ORBOT AN' I CAN TAKE--
SHH!

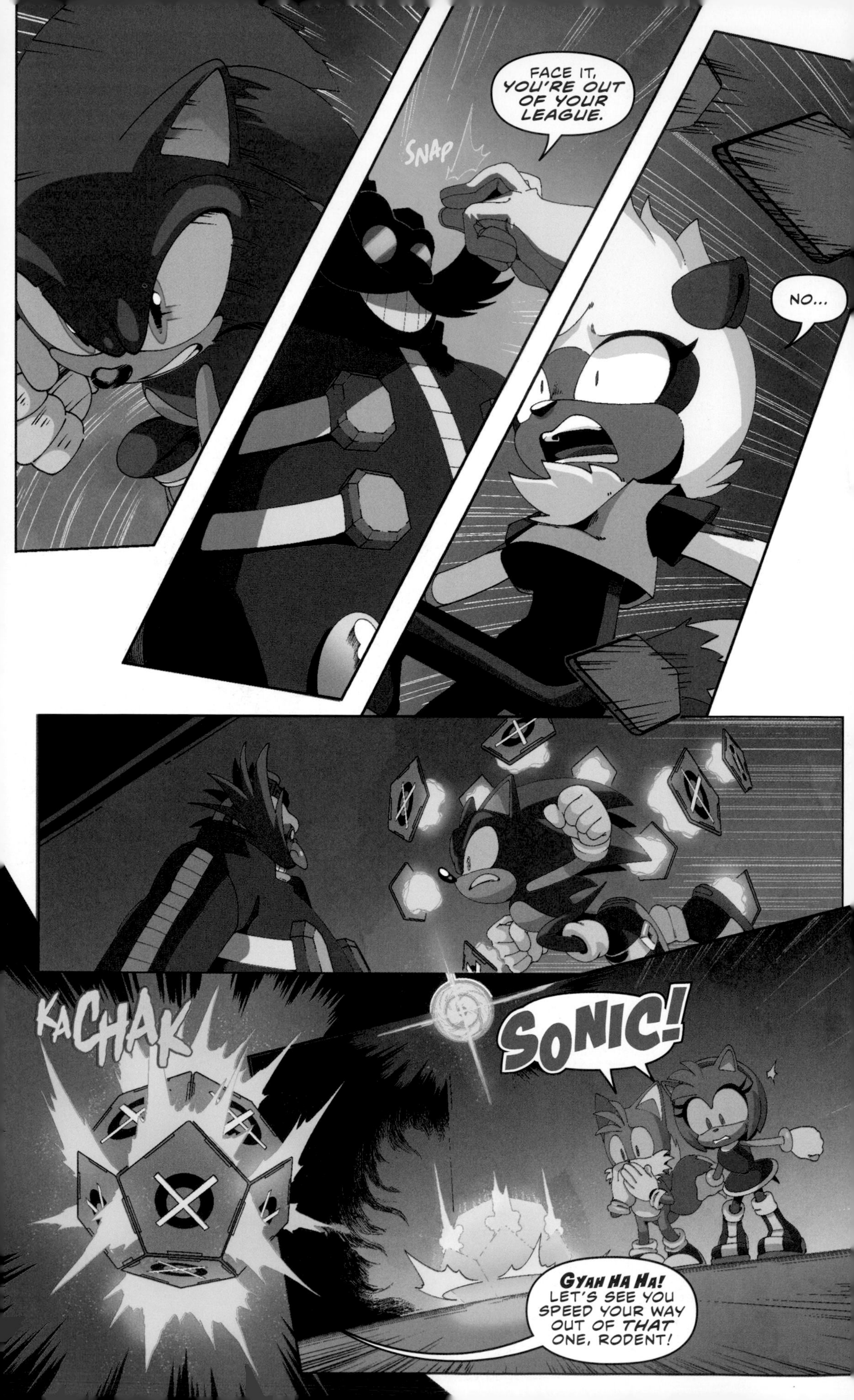
FACE IT, YOU'RE OUT OF YOUR LEAGUE.
SNAP
NO...
KACHAK
SONIC!
GYAH HA HA! LET'S SEE YOU SPEED YOUR WAY OUT OF THAT ONE, RODENT!

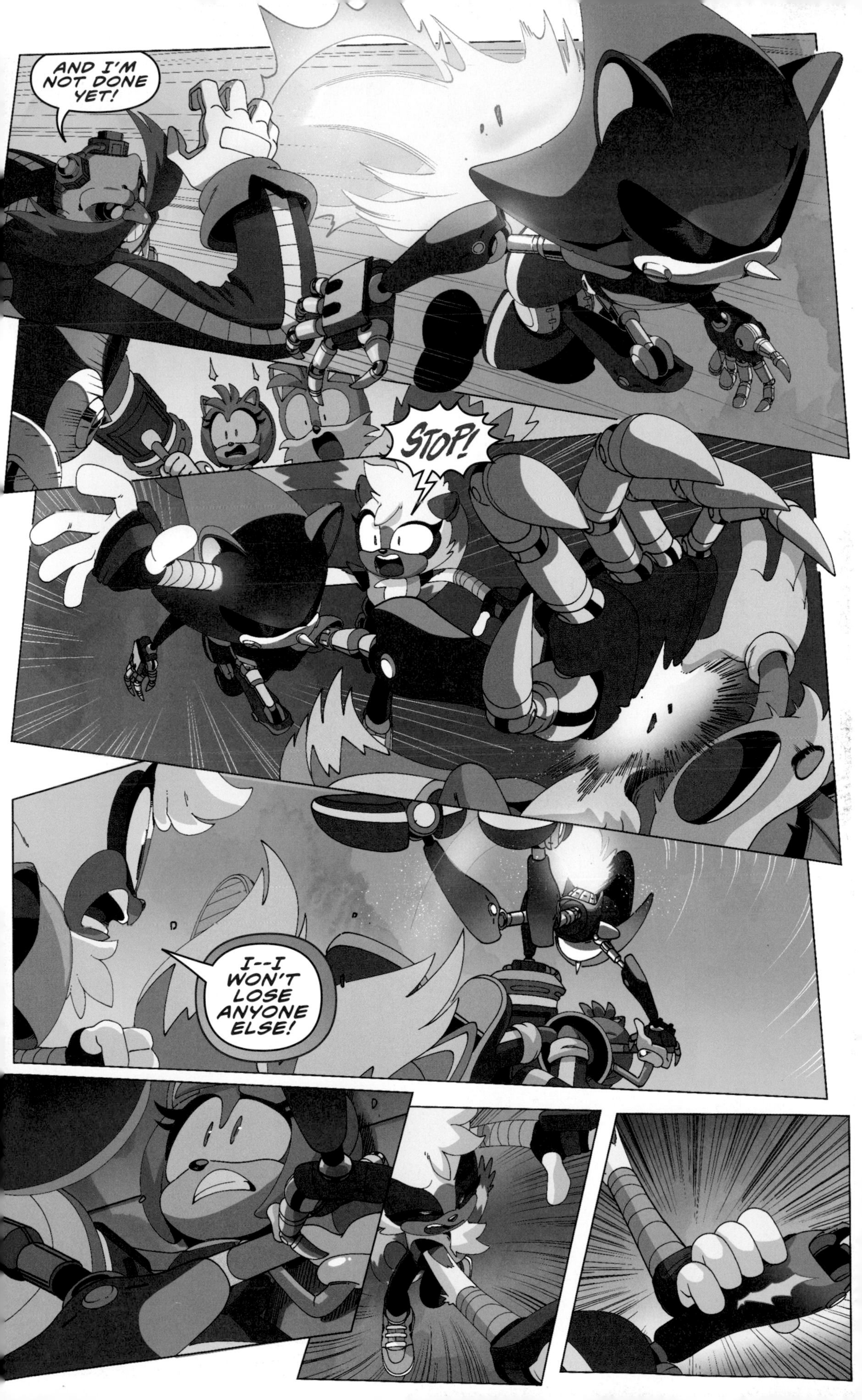
AND I'M NOT DONE YET!
STOP!
I--I WON'T LOSE ANYONE ELSE!

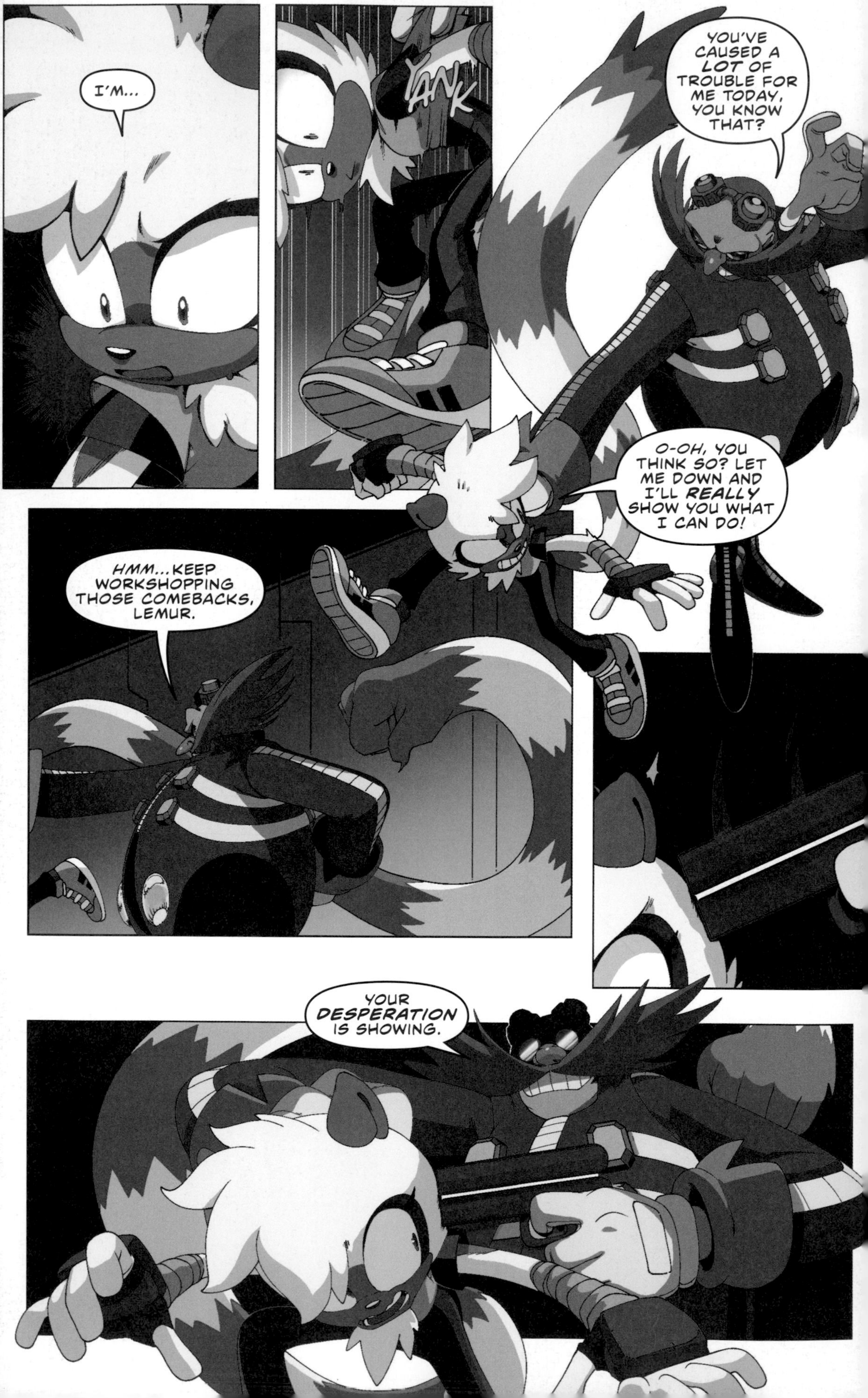
I'M...
YANK
YOU'VE CAUSED A LOT OF TROUBLE FOR ME TODAY, YOU KNOW THAT?
O-OH, YOU THINK SO? LET ME DOWN AND I'LL REALLY SHOW YOU WHAT I CAN DO!
HMM...KEEP WORKSHOPPING THOSE COMEBACKS, LEMUR.
YOUR DESPERATION IS SHOWING.

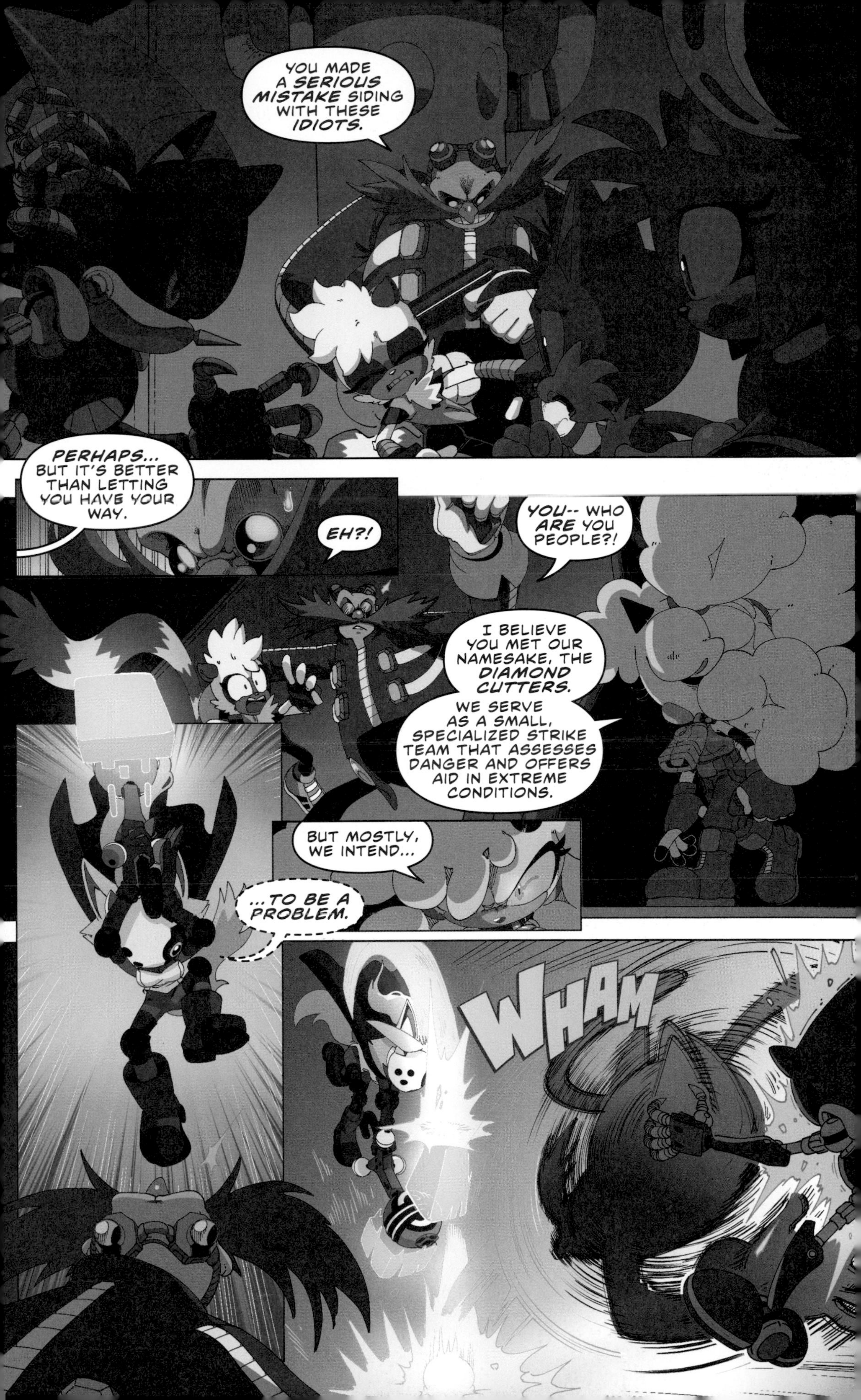

YOU MADE A SERIOUS MISTAKE SIDING WITH THESE IDIOTS.
PERHAPS... BUT IT'S BETTER THAN LETTING YOU HAVE YOUR WAY.
EH?!
YOU-- WHO ARE YOU PEOPLE?!
I BELIEVE YOU MET OUR NAMESAKE, THE DIAMOND CUTTERS.
WE SERVE AS A SMALL, SPECIALIZED STRIKE TEAM THAT ASSESSES DANGER AND OFFERS AID IN EXTREME CONDITIONS.
BUT MOSTLY, WE INTEND...
...TO BE A PROBLEM.
WHAM

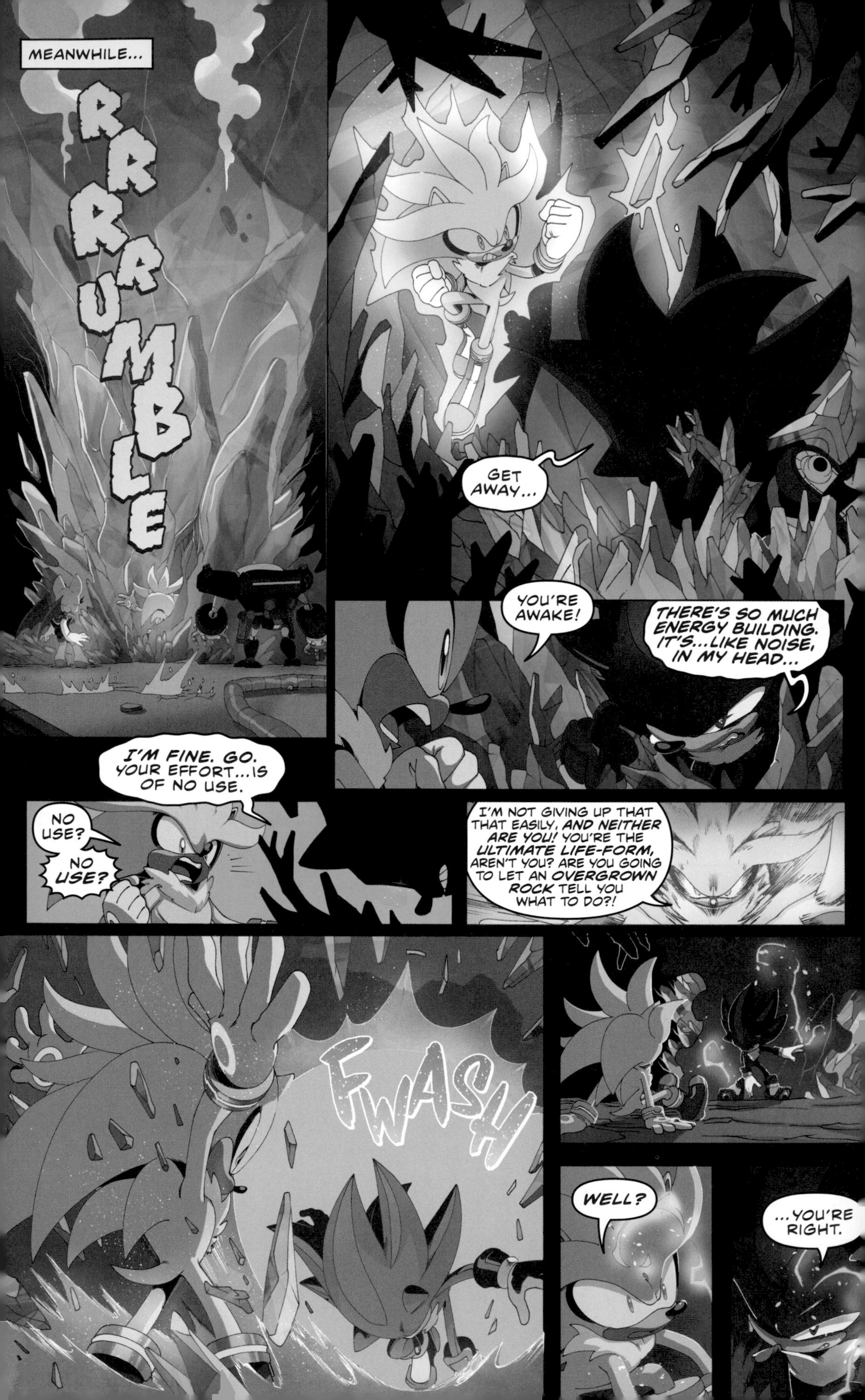
MEANWHILE...
RRRRUMBLE
GET AWAY...
YOU'RE AWAKE!
THERE'S SO MUCH ENERGY BUILDING. IT'S...LIKE NOISE, IN MY HEAD...
I'M FINE. GO. YOUR EFFORT...IS OF NO USE.
NO USE?
NO USE?
I'M NOT GIVING UP THAT THAT EASILY, AND NEITHER ARE YOU! YOU'RE THE ULTIMATE LIFE-FORM, AREN'T YOU? ARE YOU GOING TO LET AN OVERGROWN ROCK TELL YOU WHAT TO DO?!
FWASH
WELL?
...YOU'RE RIGHT.

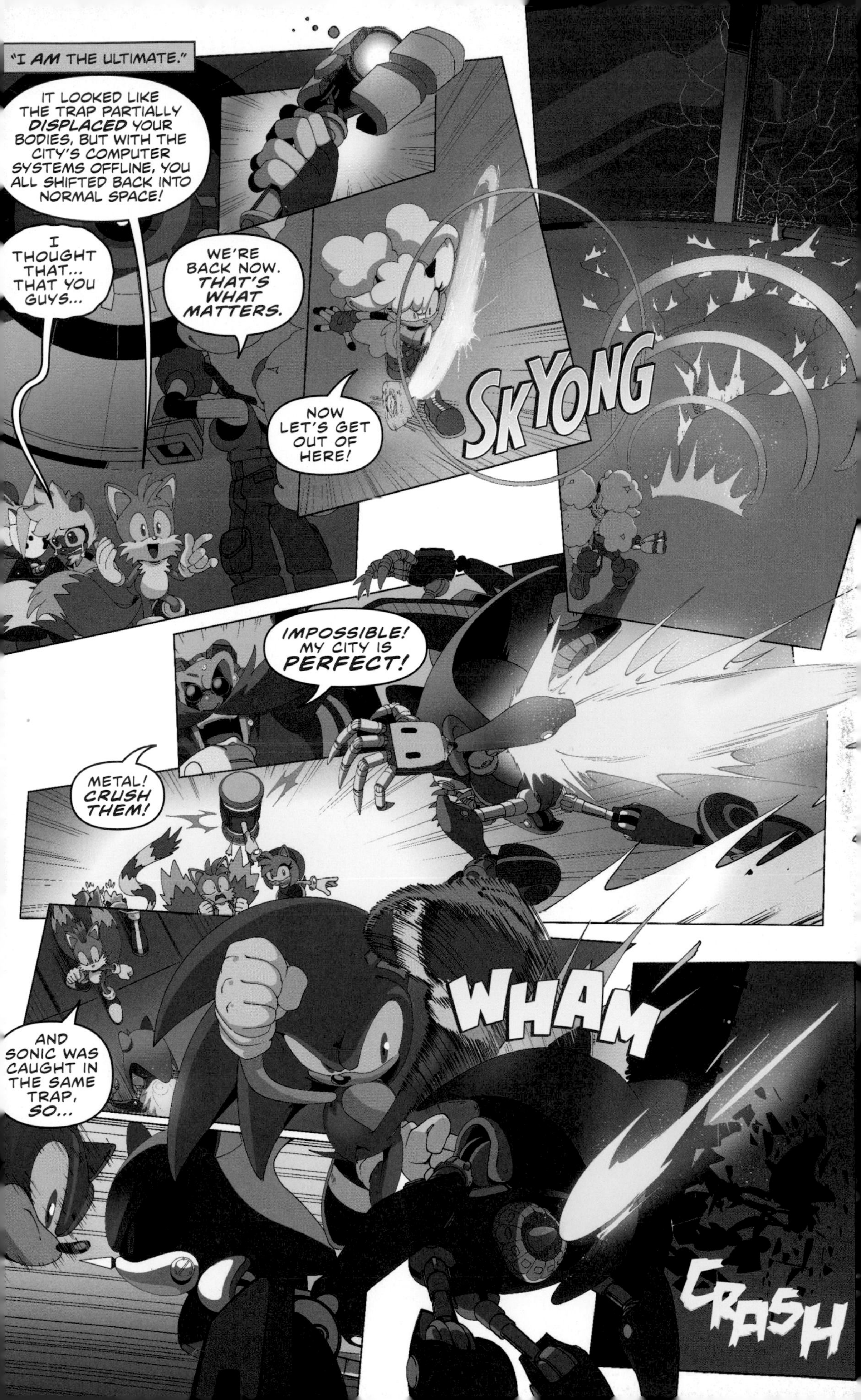
"I AM THE ULTIMATE."
IT LOOKED LIKE THE TRAP PARTIALLY DISPLACED YOUR BODIES, BUT WITH THE CITY'S COMPUTER SYSTEMS OFFLINE, YOU ALL SHIFTED BACK INTO NORMAL SPACE!
I THOUGHT THAT... THAT YOU GUYS...
WE'RE BACK NOW. THAT'S WHAT MATTERS.
NOW LET'S GET OUT OF HERE!
SKYONG
IMPOSSIBLE! MY CITY IS PERFECT!
METAL! CRUSH THEM!
WHAM
AND SONIC WAS CAUGHT IN THE SAME TRAP, SO...
CRASH

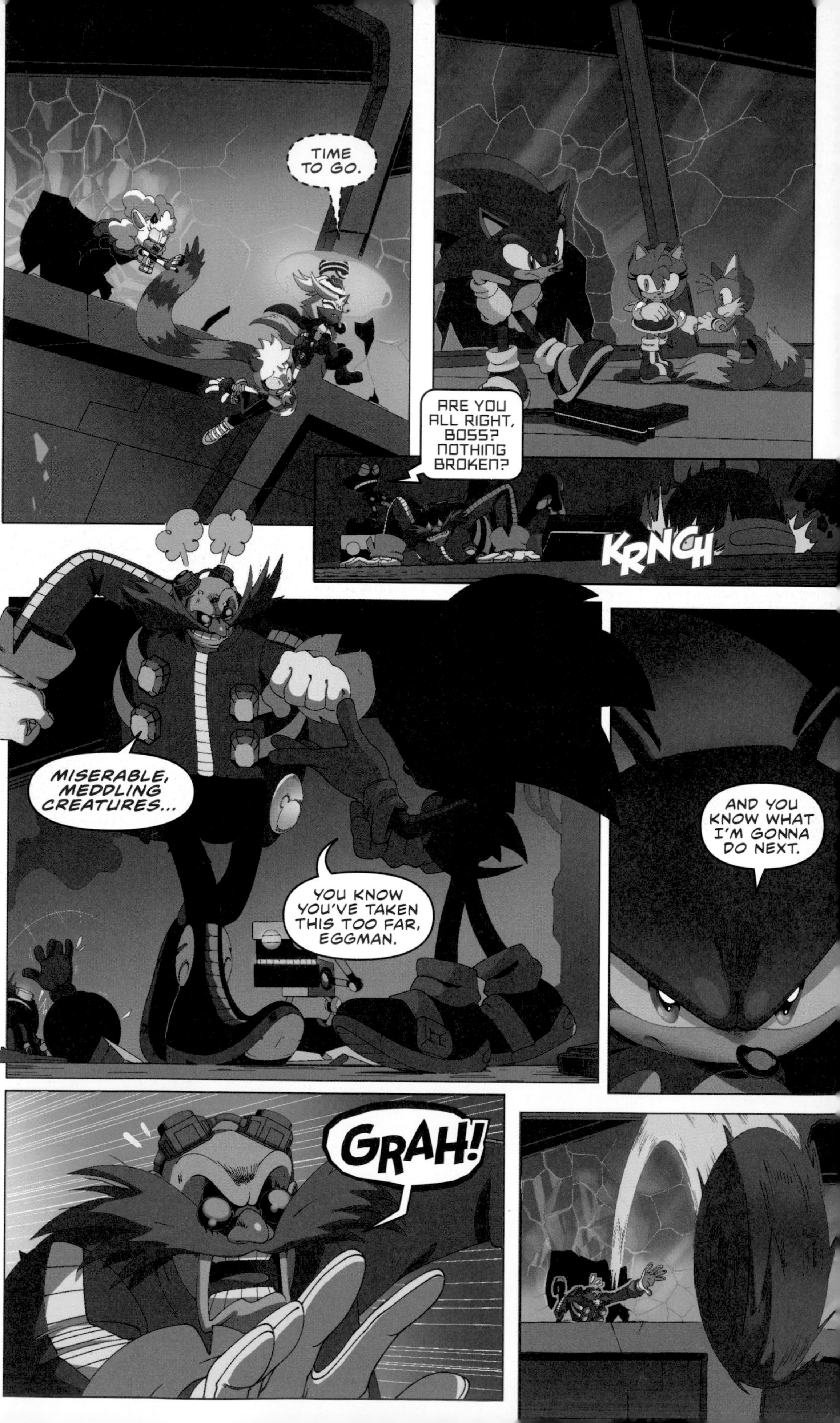
TIME TO GO.
ARE YOU ALL RIGHT, BOSS? NOTHING BROKEN?
KRNCH
MISERABLE, MEDDLING CREATURES...
YOU KNOW YOU'VE TAKEN THIS TOO FAR, EGGMAN.
AND YOU KNOW WHAT I'M GONNA DO NEXT.
GRAH!

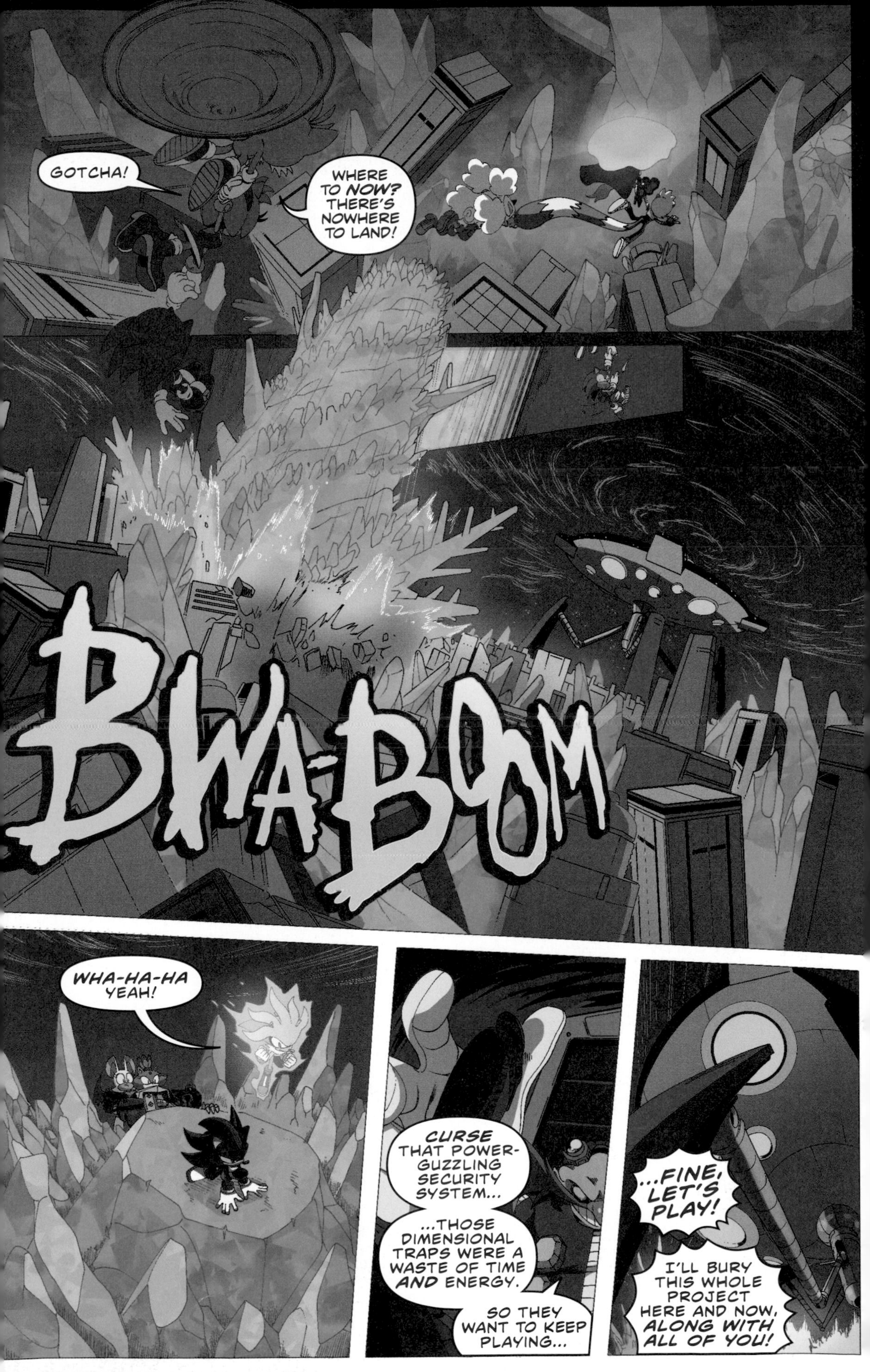

GOTCHA!
WHERE TO NOW? THERE'S NOWHERE TO LAND!
BWA-BOOM
WHA-HA-HA YEAH!
CURSE THAT POWER-GUZZLING SECURITY SYSTEM...
...THOSE DIMENSIONAL TRAPS WERE A WASTE OF TIME AND ENERGY.
SO THEY WANT TO KEEP PLAYING...
...FINE, LET'S PLAY!
I'LL BURY THIS WHOLE PROJECT HERE AND NOW, ALONG WITH ALL OF YOU!

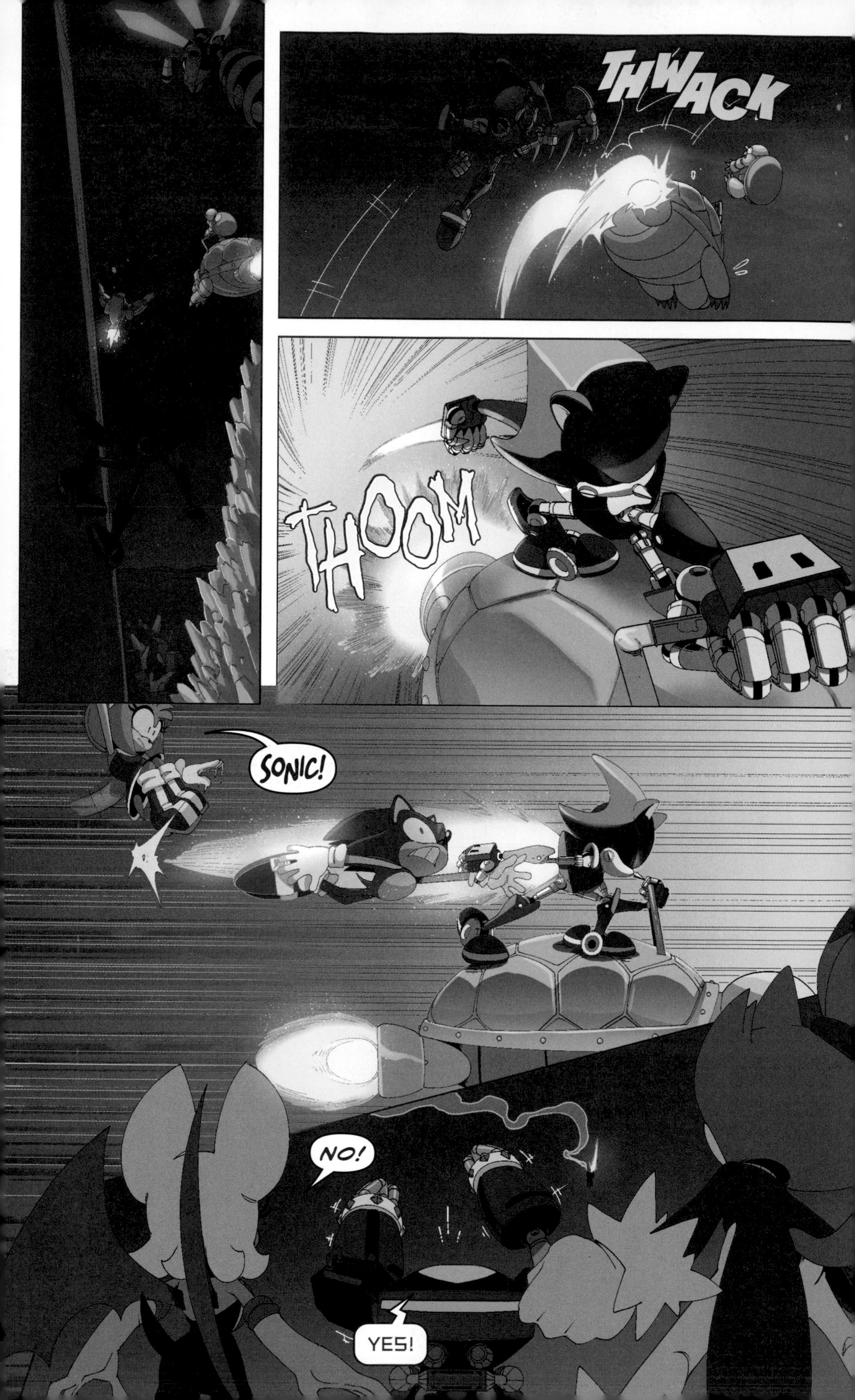
THWACK
THOOM
SONIC!
NO!
YES!

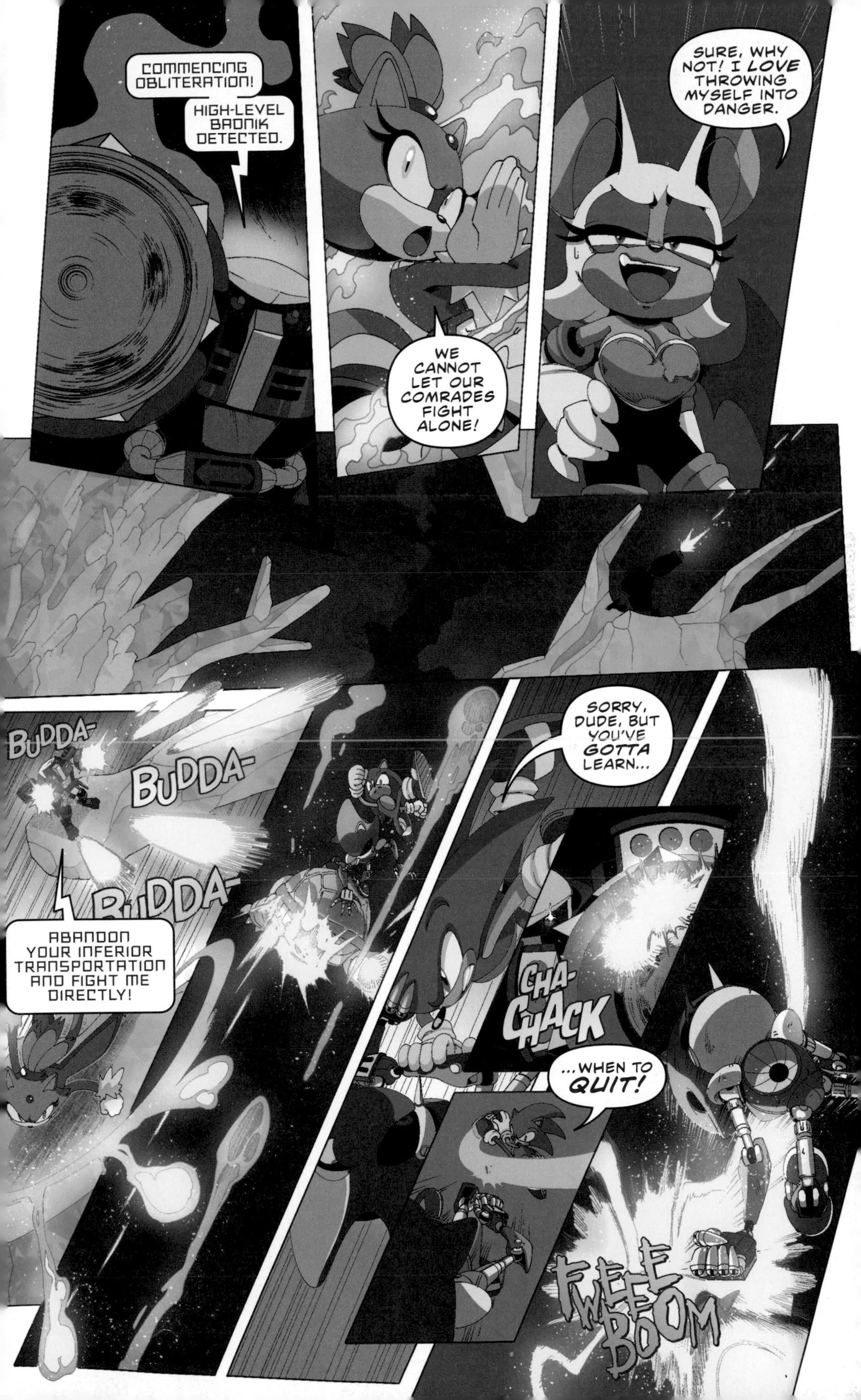
COMMENCING OBLITERATION!
HIGH-LEVEL BADNIK DETECTED.
WE CANNOT LET OUR COMRADES FIGHT ALONE!
SURE, WHY NOT! I LOVE THROWING MYSELF INTO DANGER.
BUDDA-
BUDDA-
BUDDA-
ABANDON YOUR INFERIOR TRANSPORTATION AND FIGHT ME DIRECTLY!
SORRY, DUDE, BUT YOU'VE GOTTA LEARN...
CHA-CHACK
...WHEN TO QUIT!
FWEEE BOOM

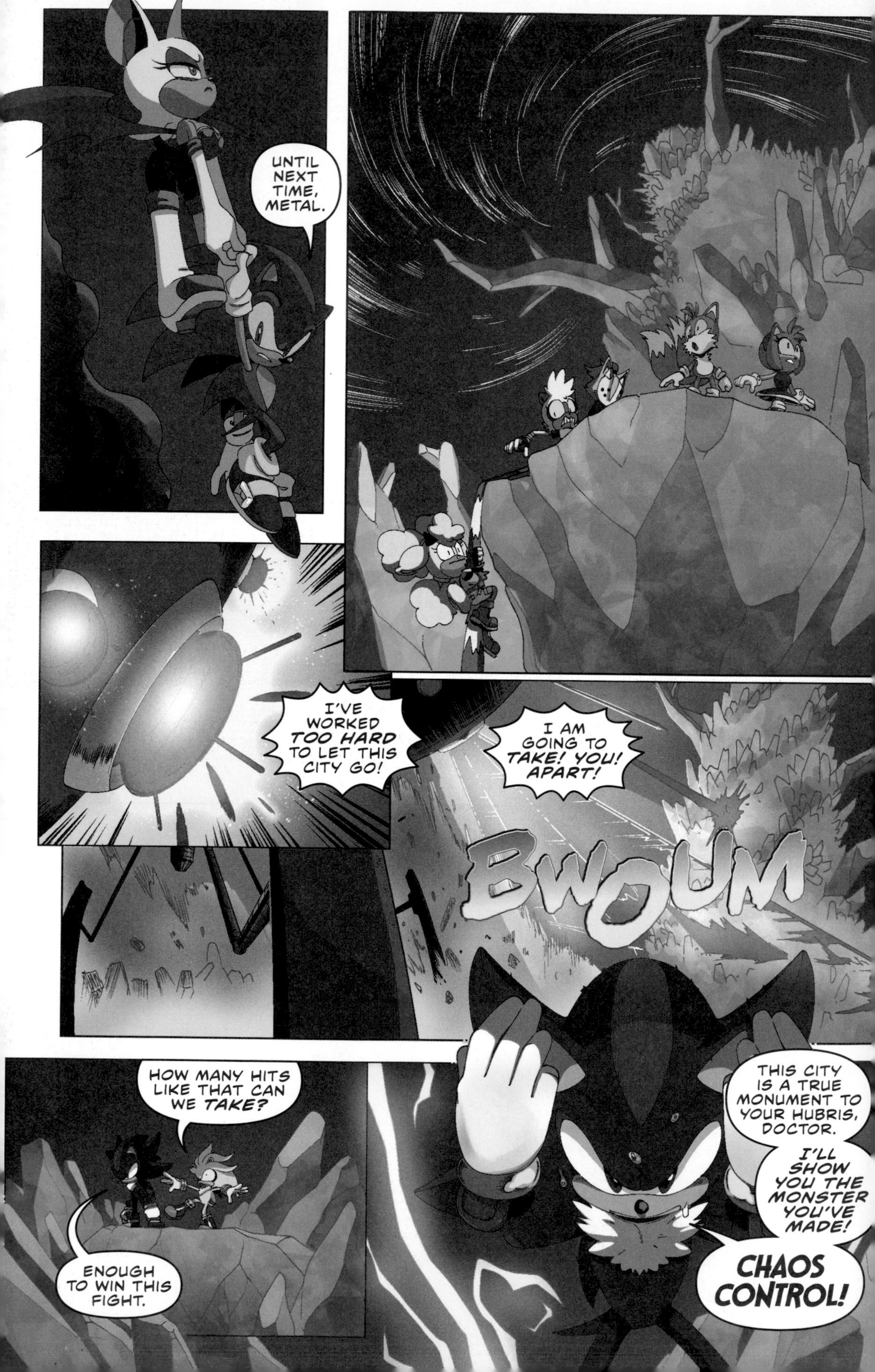
UNTIL NEXT TIME, METAL.
I'VE WORKED TOO HARD TO LET THIS CITY GO!
I AM GOING TO TAKE! YOU! APART!
BWOUM
HOW MANY HITS LIKE THAT CAN WE TAKE?
ENOUGH TO WIN THIS FIGHT.
THIS CITY IS A TRUE MONUMENT TO YOUR HUBRIS, DOCTOR.
I'LL SHOW YOU THE MONSTER YOU'VE MADE!
CHAOS CONTROL!

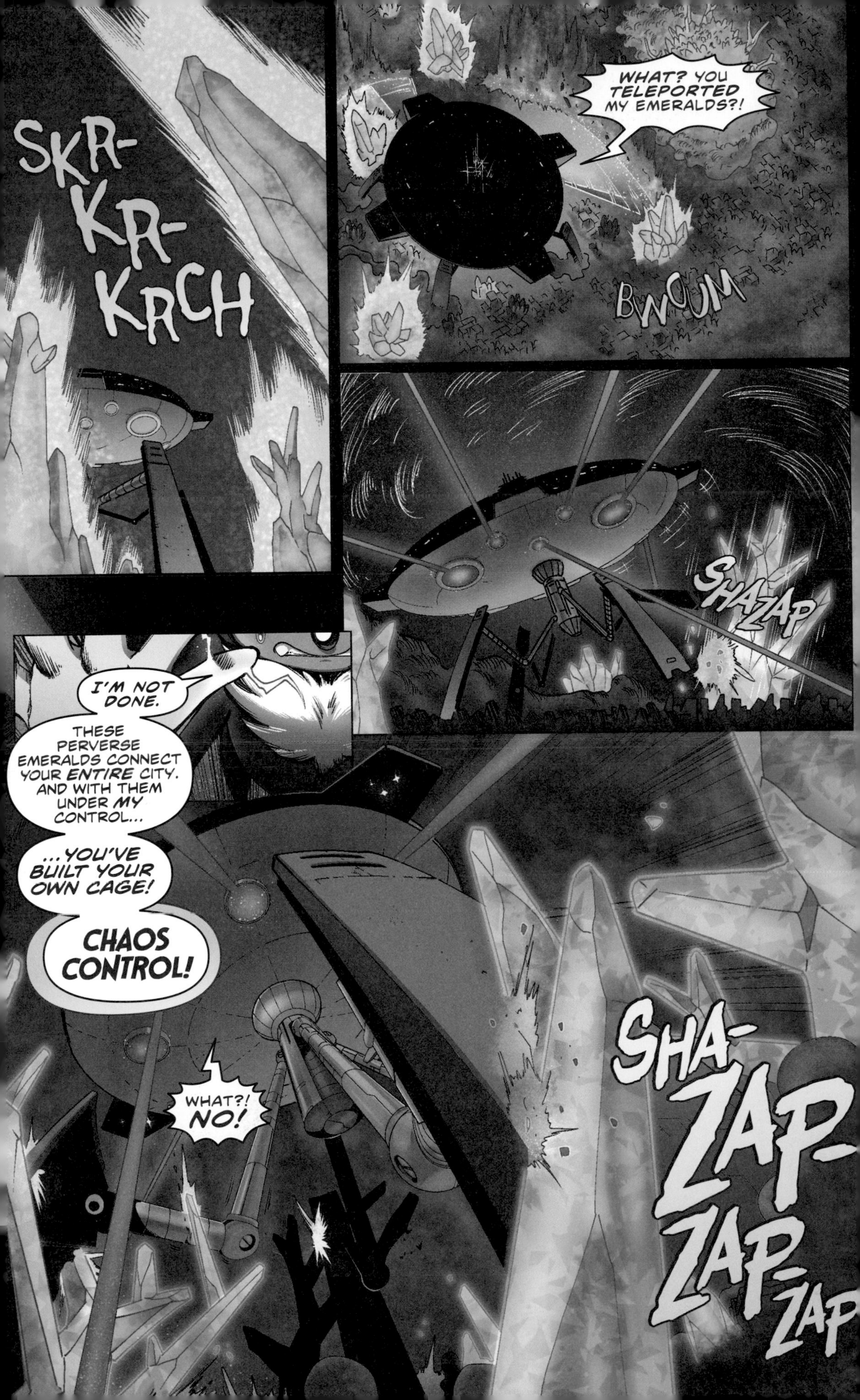
SKR-
KR-
KRCH
WHAT? YOU TELEPORTED MY EMERALDS?!
BWOUM
SHAZAP
I'M NOT DONE.
THESE PERVERSE EMERALDS CONNECT YOUR ENTIRE CITY. AND WITH THEM UNDER MY CONTROL...
...YOU'VE BUILT YOUR OWN CAGE!
CHAOS CONTROL!
WHAT?! NO!
SHA-
ZAP-
ZAP-
ZAP

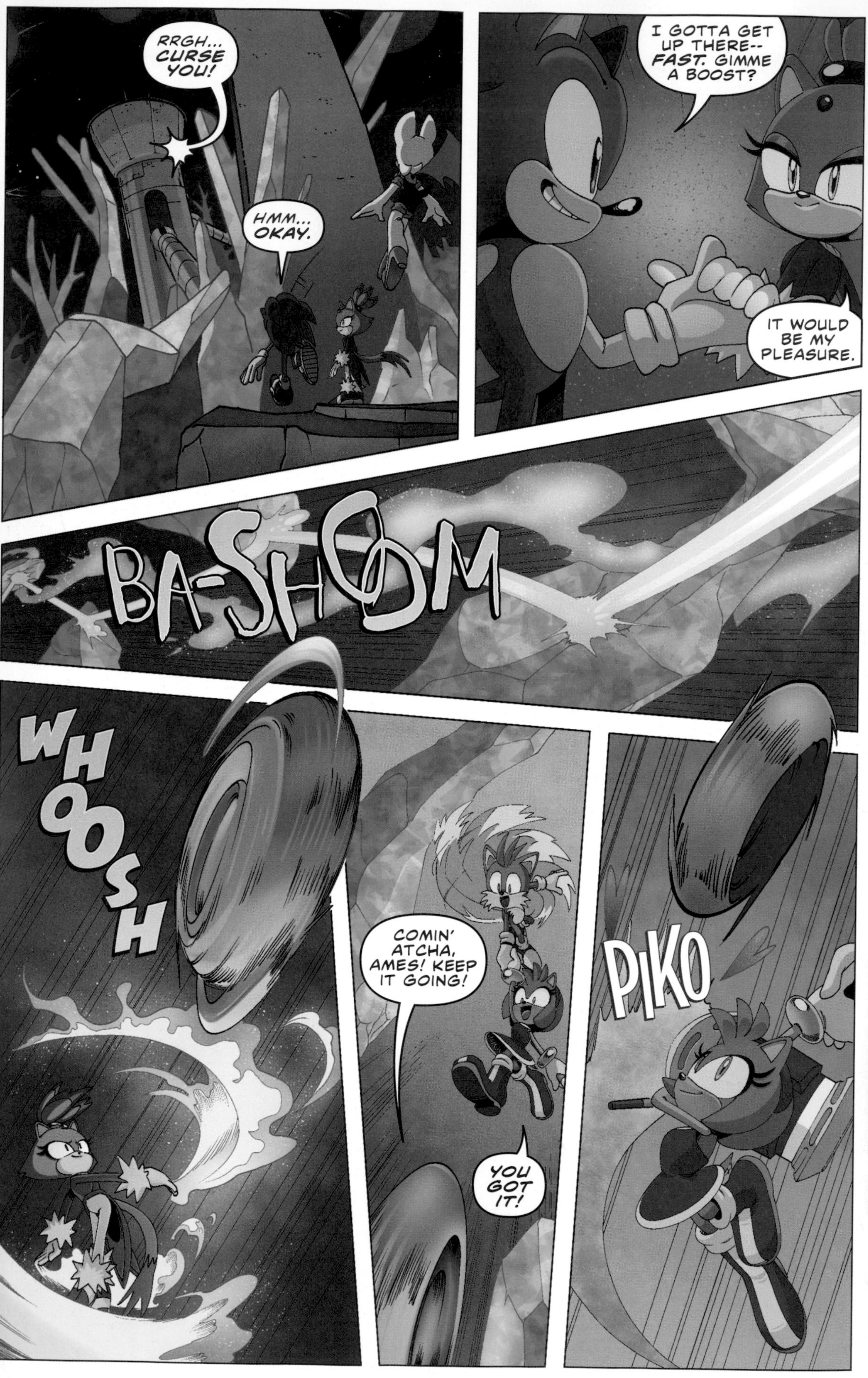
RRGH... CURSE YOU!
HMM... OKAY.
I GOTTA GET UP THERE-- FAST. GIMME A BOOST?
IT WOULD BE MY PLEASURE.
BA-SHOOM
WHOOSH
COMIN' ATCHA, AMES! KEEP IT GOING!
YOU GOT IT!
PIKO

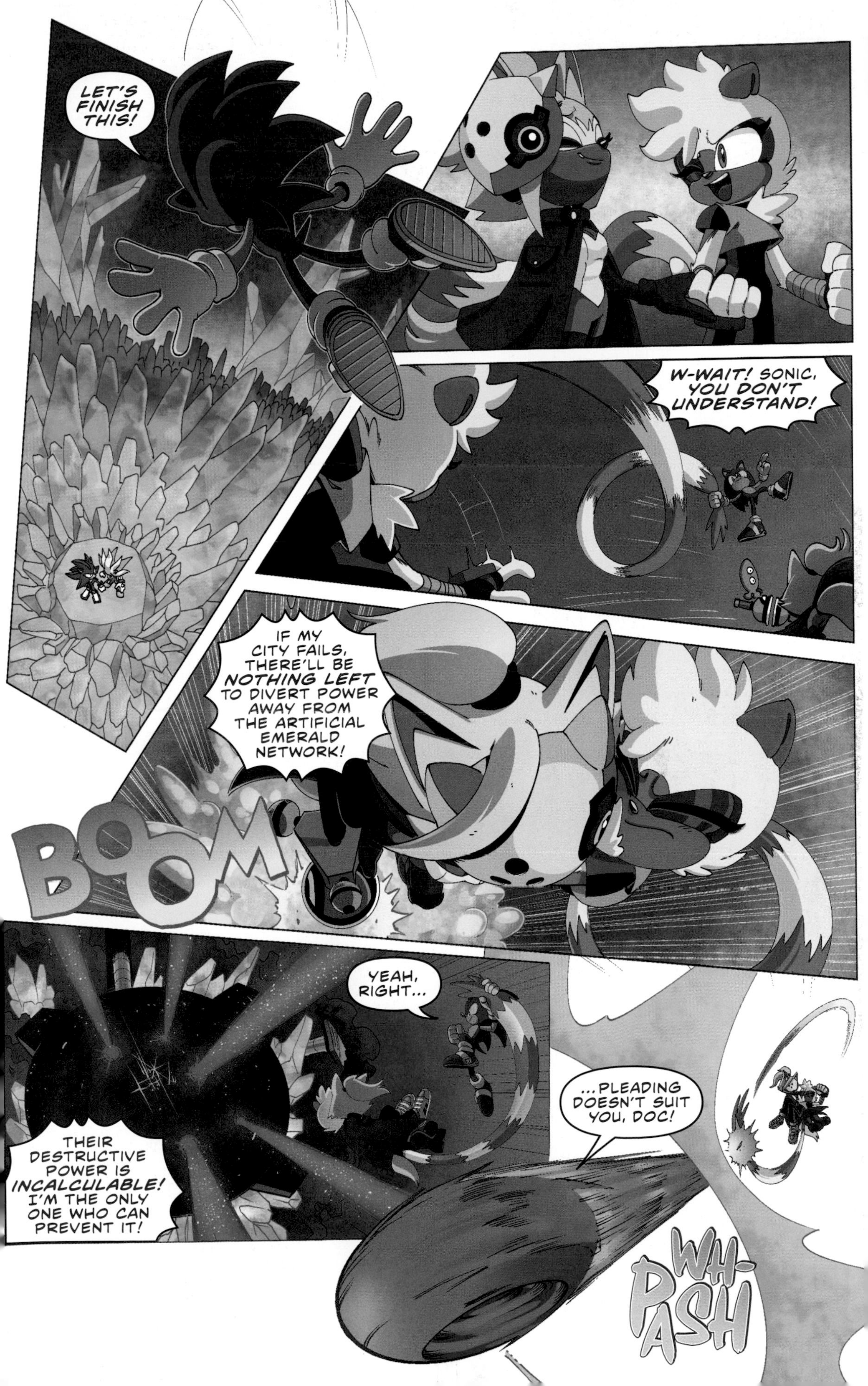
LET'S FINISH THIS!
W-WAIT! SONIC, YOU DON'T UNDERSTAND!
IF MY CITY FAILS, THERE'LL BE NOTHING LEFT TO DIVERT POWER AWAY FROM THE ARTIFICIAL EMERALD NETWORK!
BOOM
THEIR DESTRUCTIVE POWER IS INCALCULABLE! I'M THE ONLY ONE WHO CAN PREVENT IT!
YEAH, RIGHT...
...PLEADING DOESN'T SUIT YOU, DOC!
WH-PASH

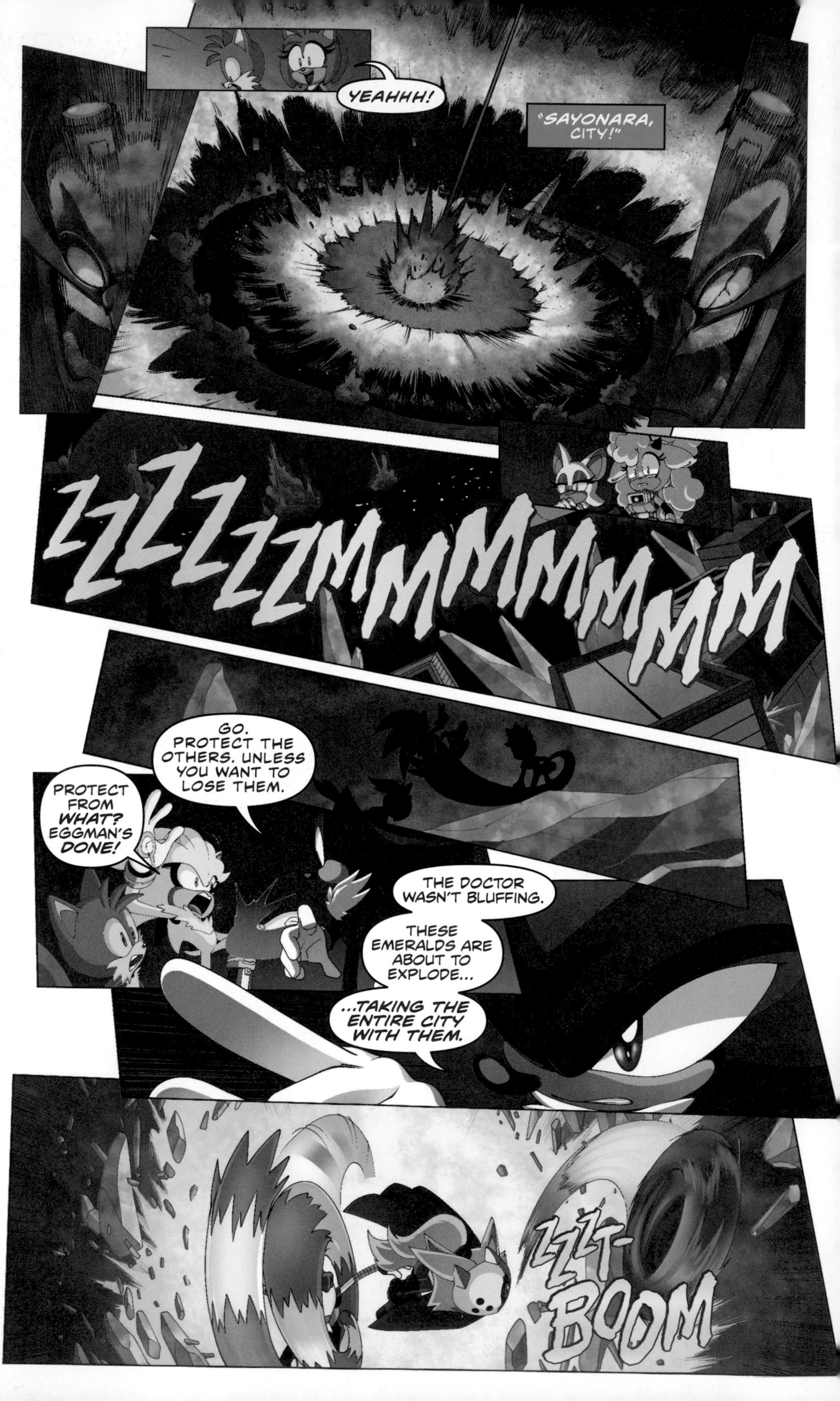
YEAHHH!
"SAYONARA, CITY!"
ZZZZZZMMMMMMMMM
GO. PROTECT THE OTHERS. UNLESS YOU WANT TO LOSE THEM.
PROTECT FROM WHAT? EGGMAN'S DONE!
THE DOCTOR WASN'T BLUFFING.
THESE EMERALDS ARE ABOUT TO EXPLODE...
...TAKING THE ENTIRE CITY WITH THEM.
ZZZT-BOOM

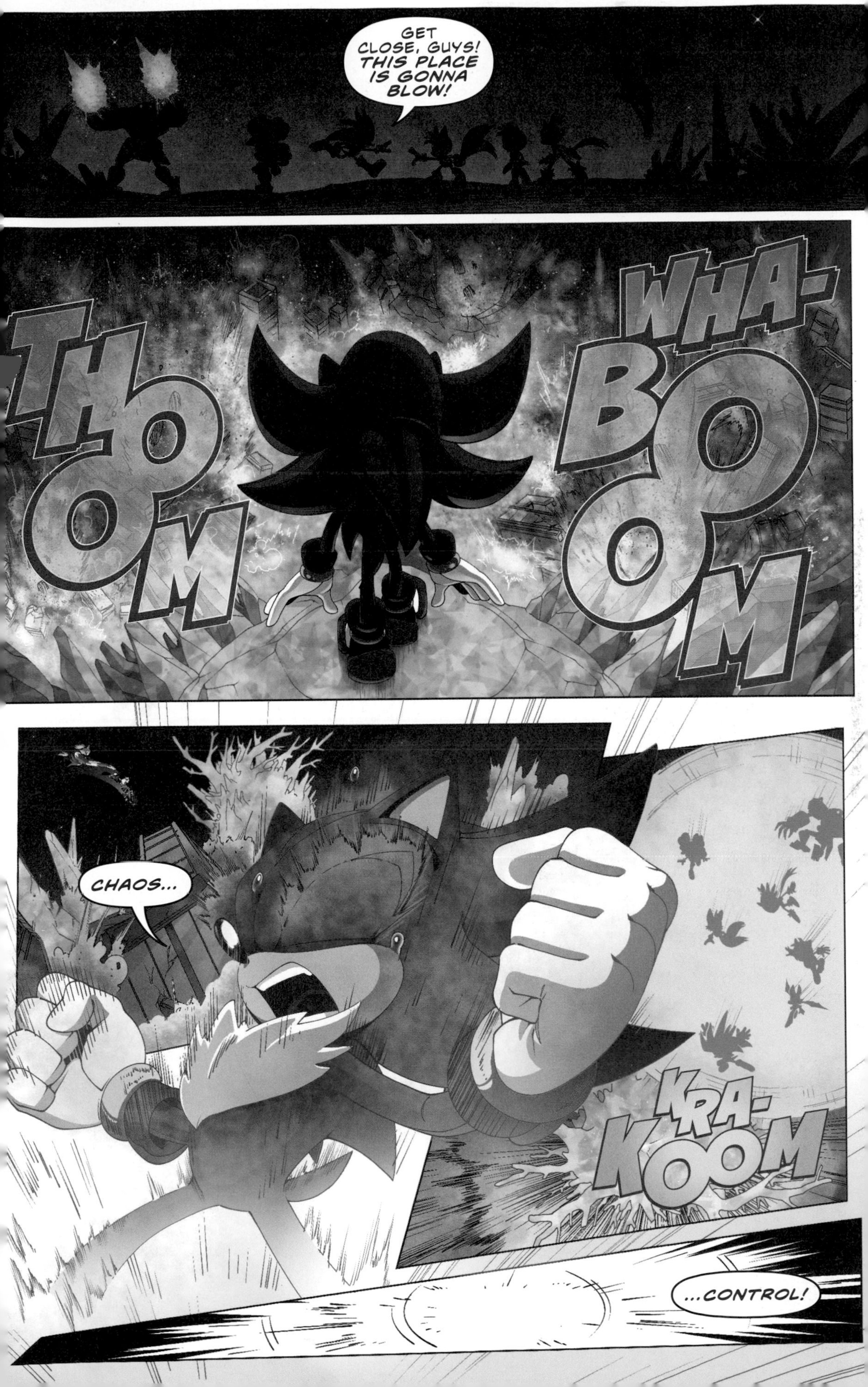
GET CLOSE, GUYS! THIS PLACE IS GONNA BLOW!
THOOM
WHA-BOOM
CHAOS...
KRA-KOOM
...CONTROL!

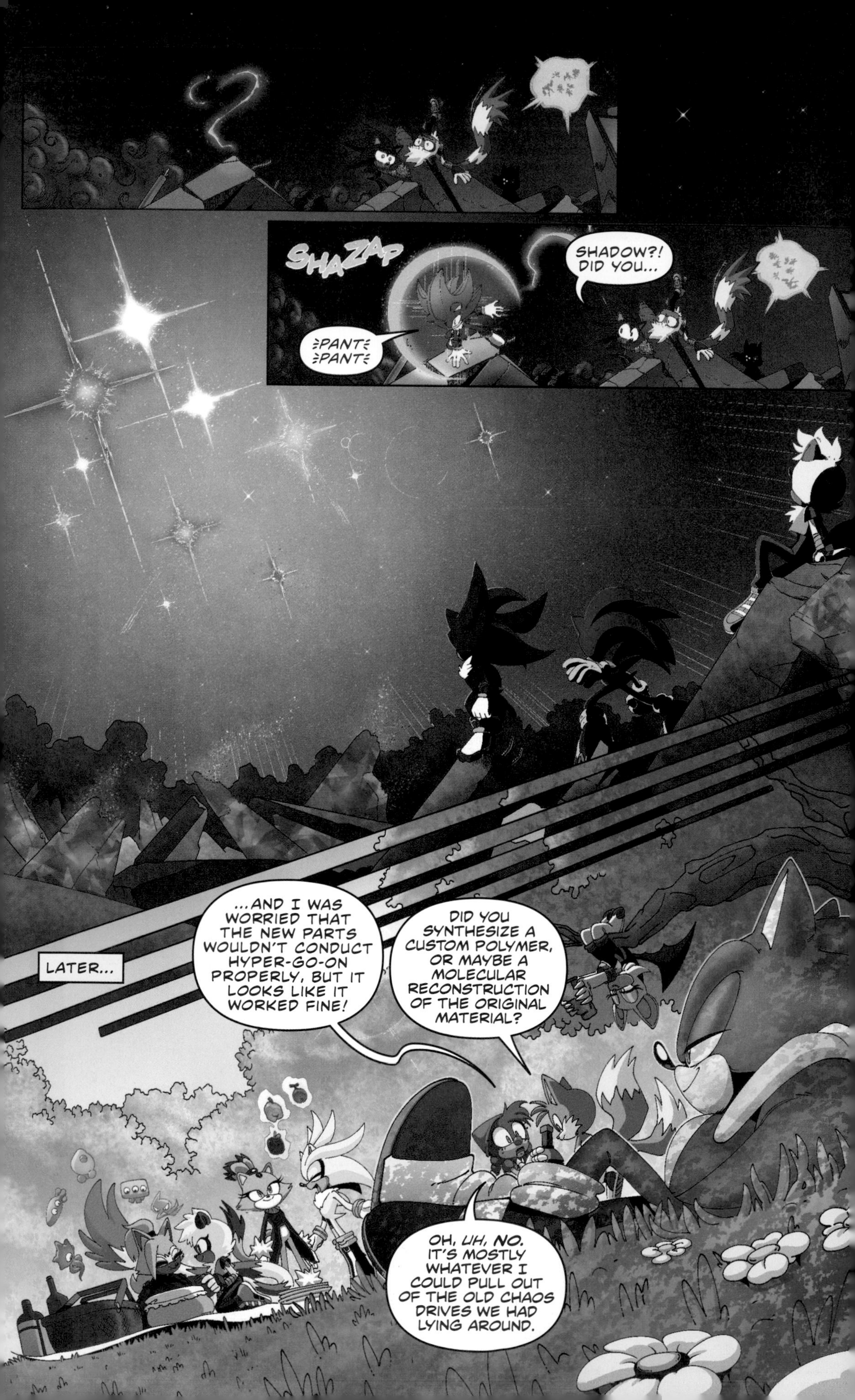
SHAZAP
SHADOW?! DID YOU...
PANT PANT
LATER...
...AND I WAS WORRIED THAT THE NEW PARTS WOULDN'T CONDUCT HYPER-GO-ON PROPERLY, BUT IT LOOKS LIKE IT WORKED FINE!
DID YOU SYNTHESIZE A CUSTOM POLYMER, OR MAYBE A MOLECULAR RECONSTRUCTION OF THE ORIGINAL MATERIAL?
OH, *UH*, **NO.** IT'S MOSTLY WHATEVER I COULD PULL OUT OF THE OLD CHAOS DRIVES WE HAD LYING AROUND.

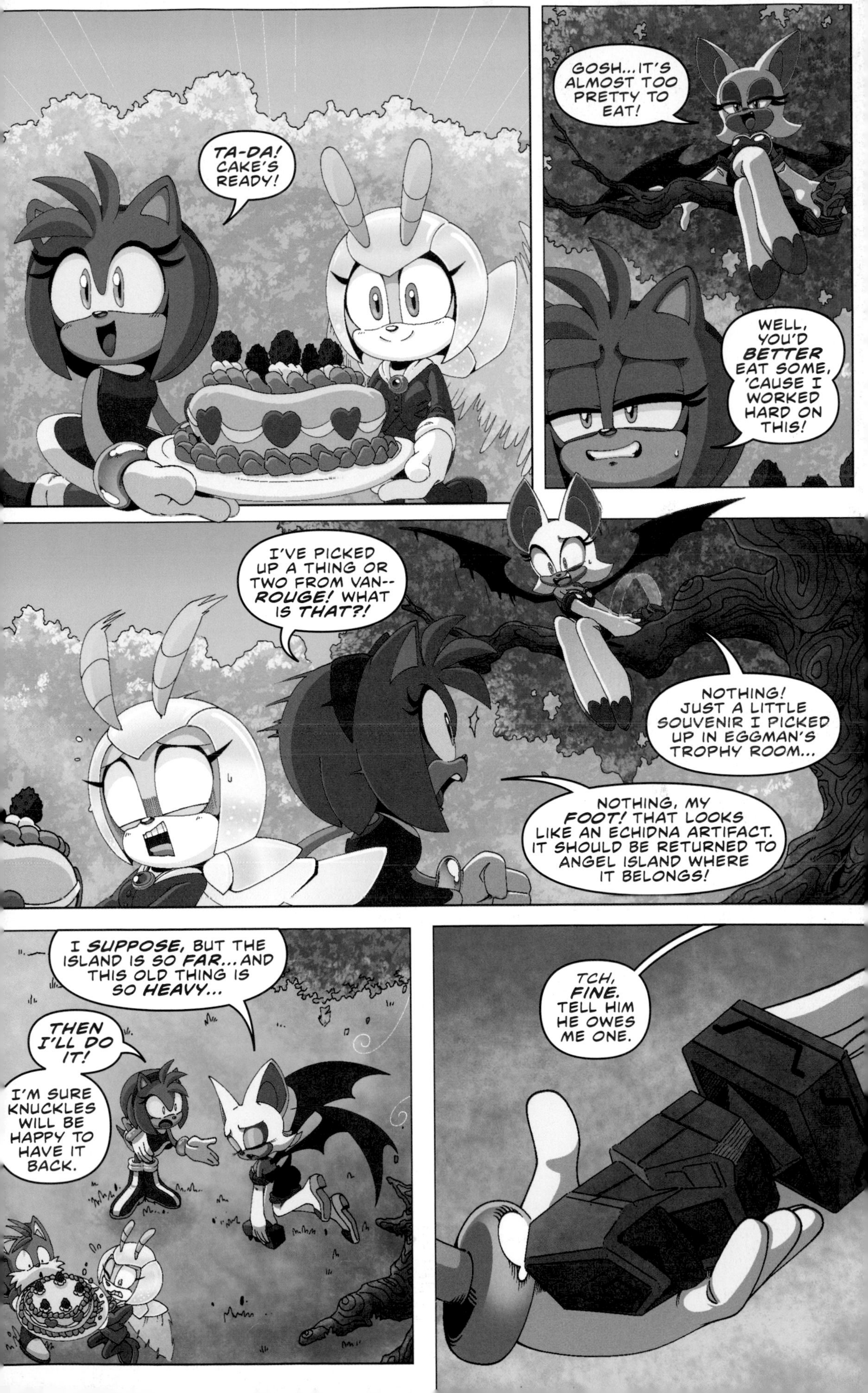
TA-DA! CAKE'S READY!
GOSH...IT'S ALMOST TOO PRETTY TO EAT!
WELL, YOU'D BETTER EAT SOME, 'CAUSE I WORKED HARD ON THIS!
I'VE PICKED UP A THING OR TWO FROM VAN-- ROUGE! WHAT IS THAT?!
NOTHING! JUST A LITTLE SOUVENIR I PICKED UP IN EGGMAN'S TROPHY ROOM...
NOTHING, MY FOOT! THAT LOOKS LIKE AN ECHIDNA ARTIFACT. IT SHOULD BE RETURNED TO ANGEL ISLAND WHERE IT BELONGS!
I SUPPOSE, BUT THE ISLAND IS SO FAR...AND THIS OLD THING IS SO HEAVY...
THEN I'LL DO IT!
I'M SURE KNUCKLES WILL BE HAPPY TO HAVE IT BACK.
TCH, FINE. TELL HIM HE OWES ME ONE.

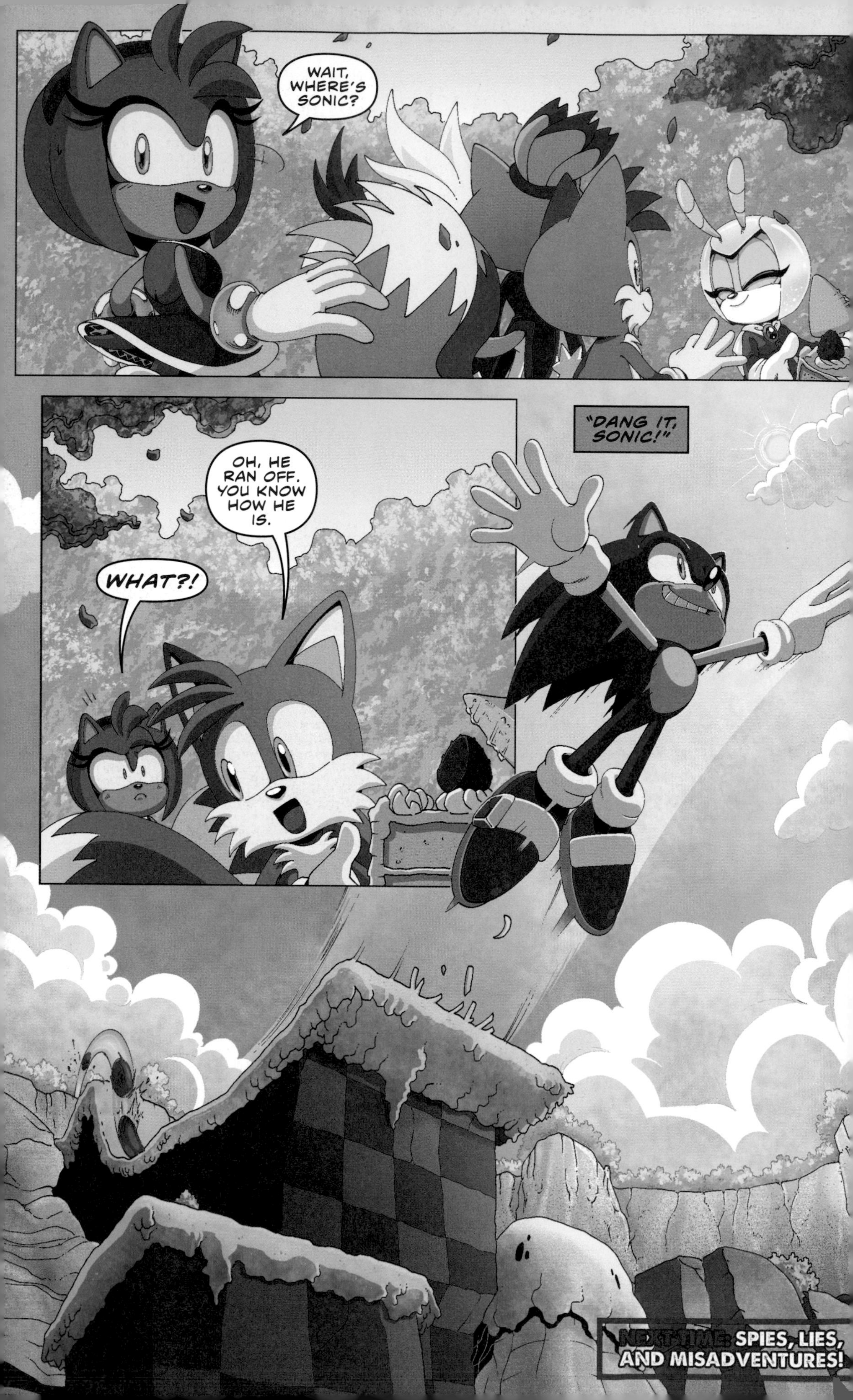
WAIT, WHERE'S SONIC?
OH, HE RAN OFF. YOU KNOW HOW HE IS.
WHAT?!
"DANG IT, SONIC!"
NEXT TIME: SPIES, LIES, AND MISADVENTURES!

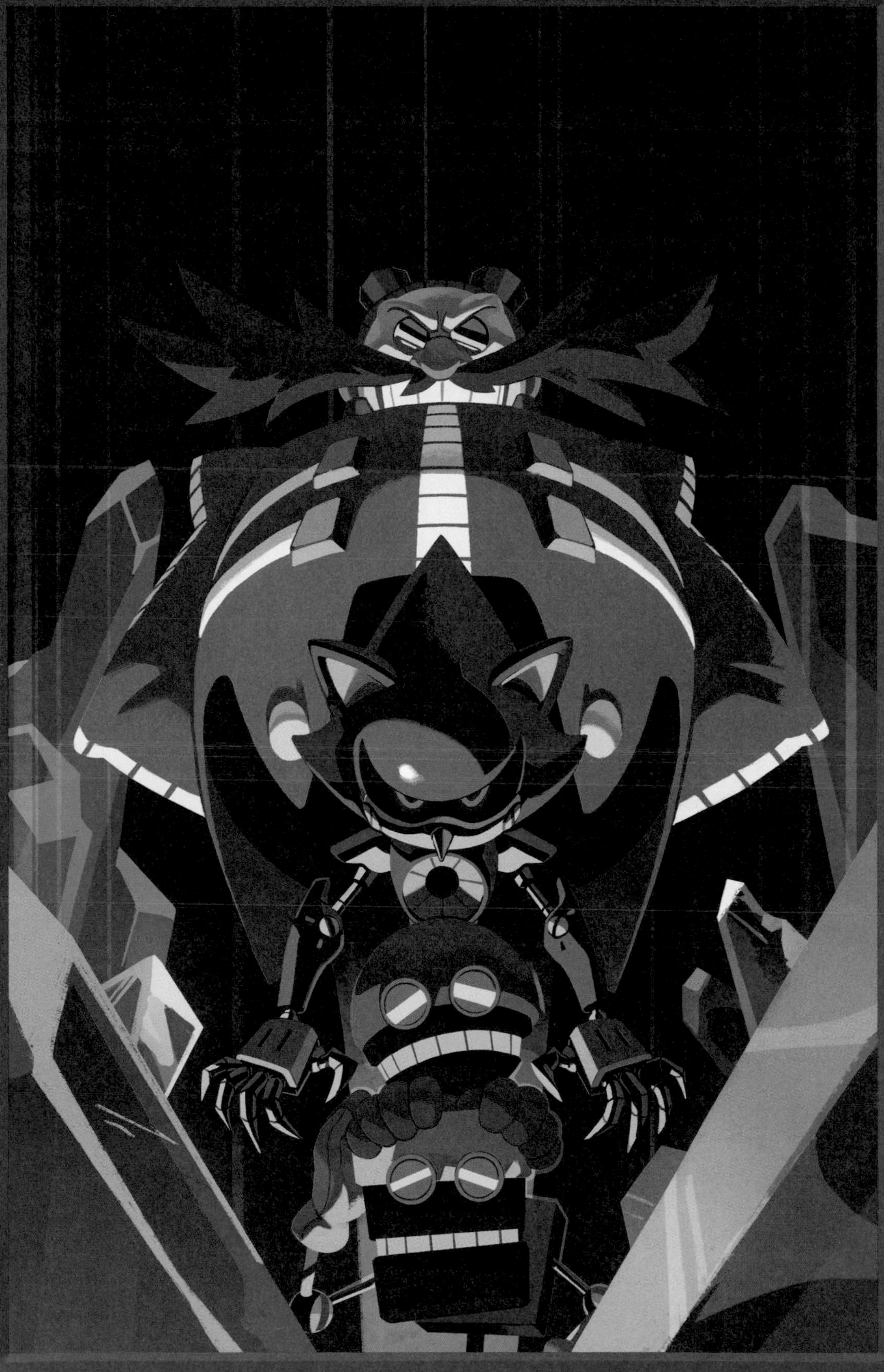

ART BY **NATHALIE FOURDRAINE**

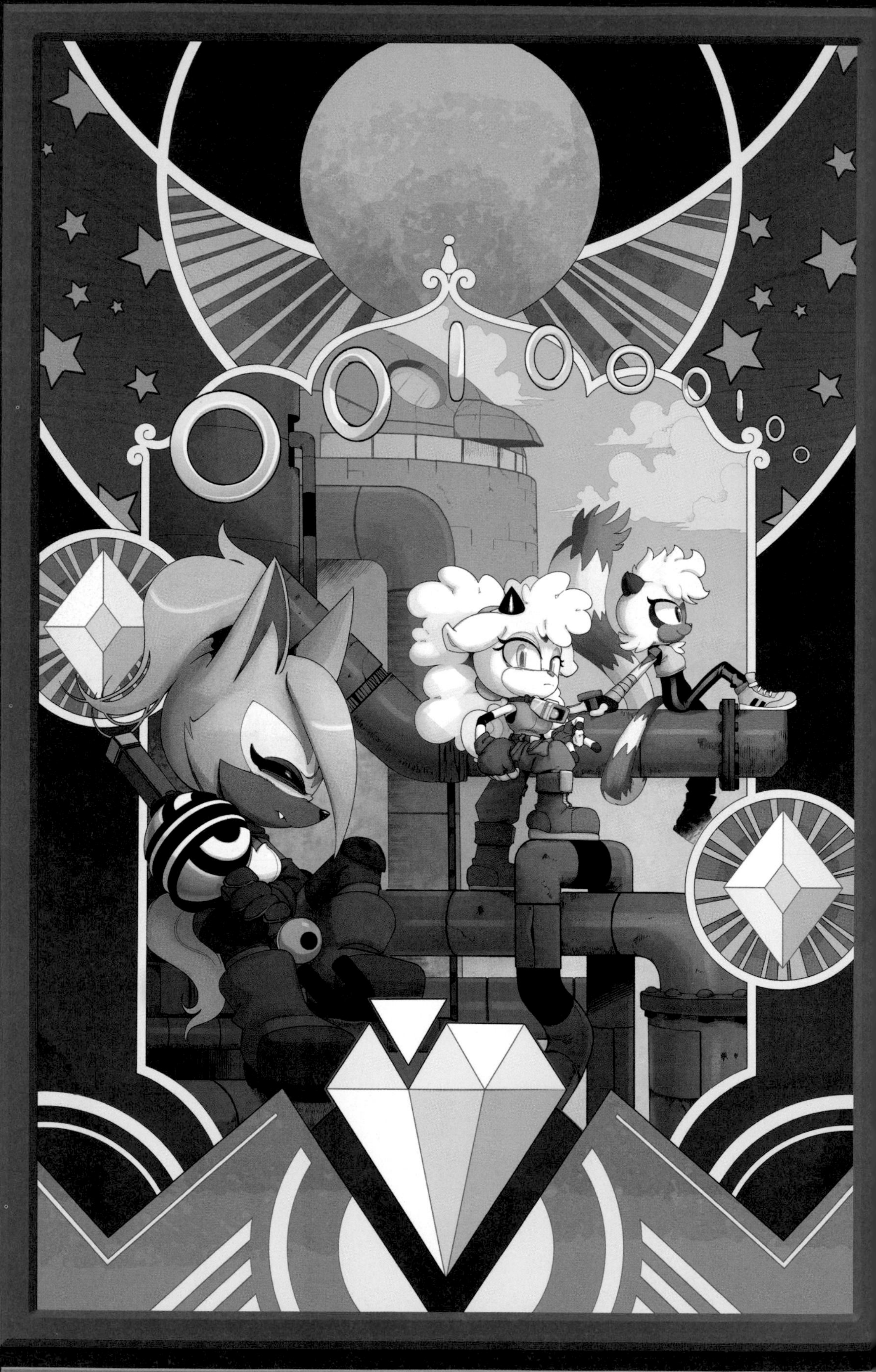

ART BY **ADAM BRYCE THOMAS** COLORS BY **REGGIE GRAHAM**

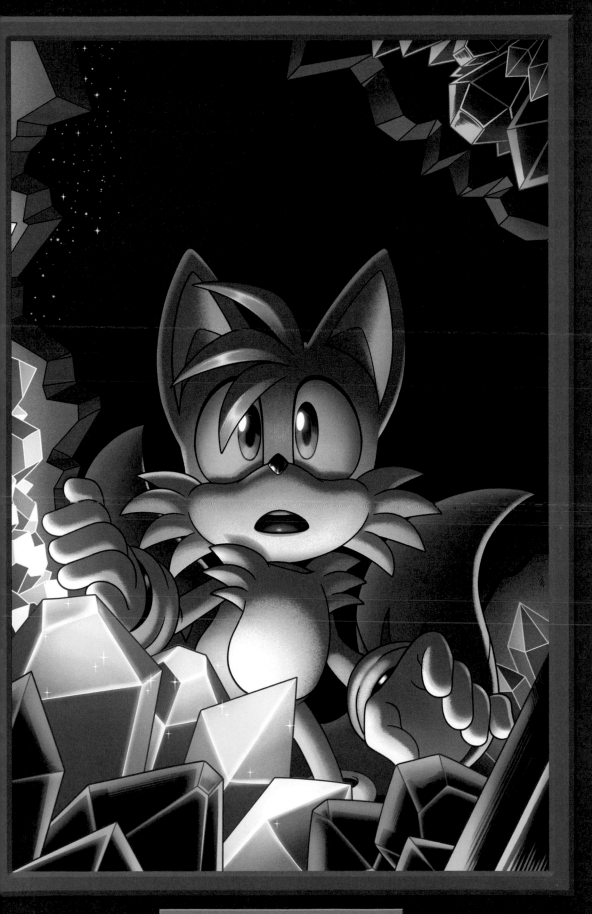

ART BY **ABIGAIL OZ**

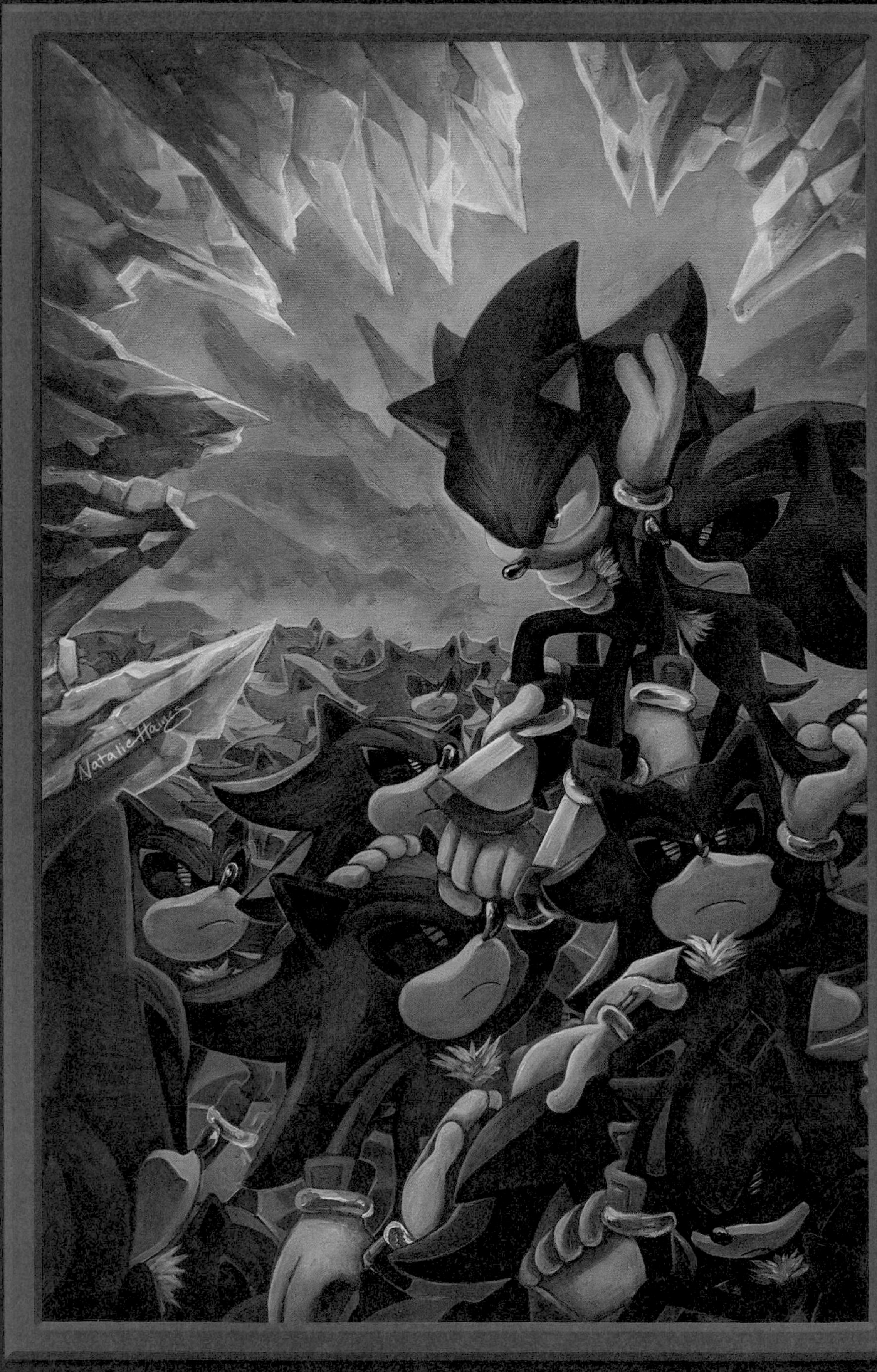
NatalieHaines

ART BY **NATALIE HAINES**

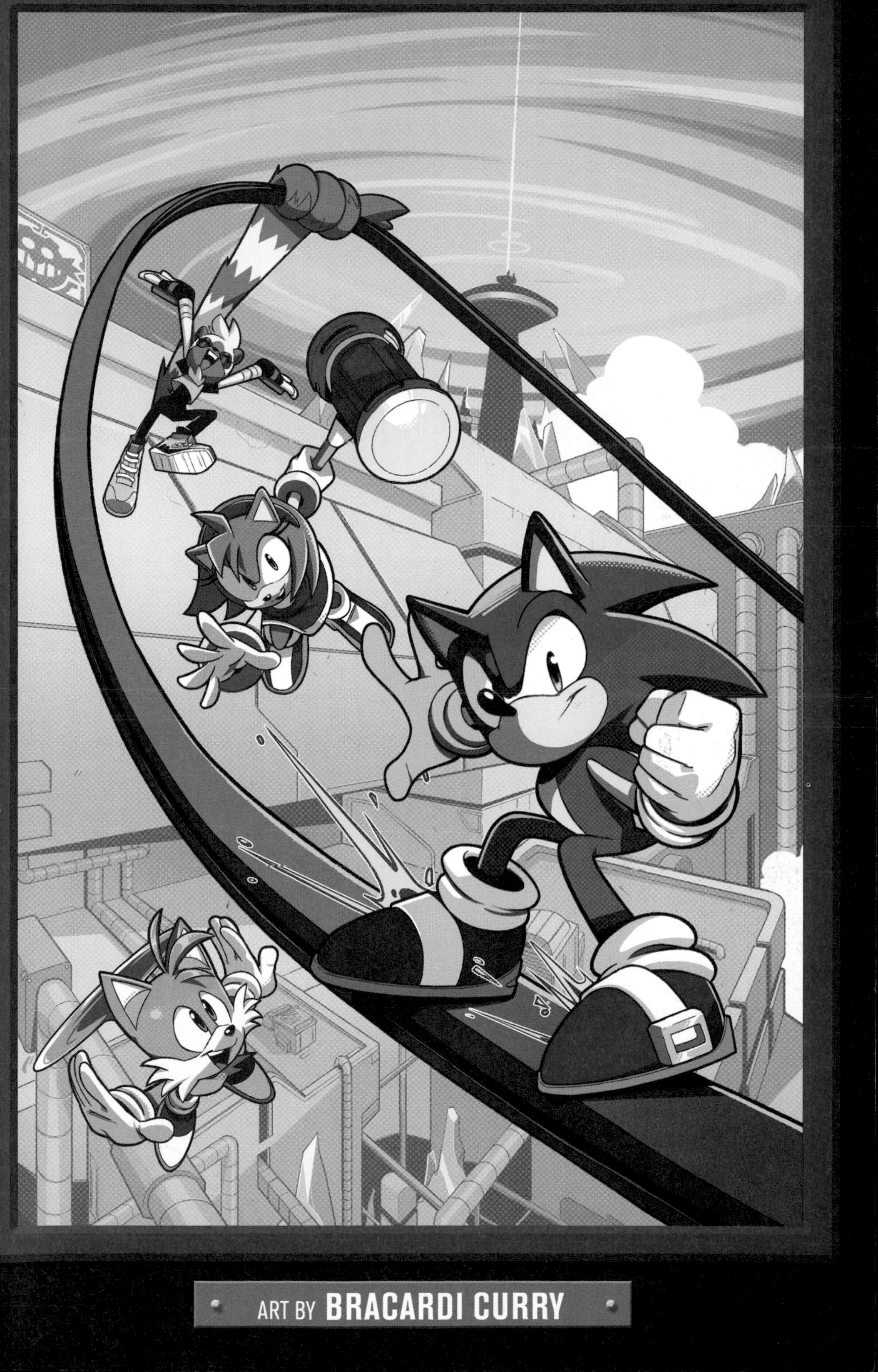

ART BY **BRACARDI CURRY**

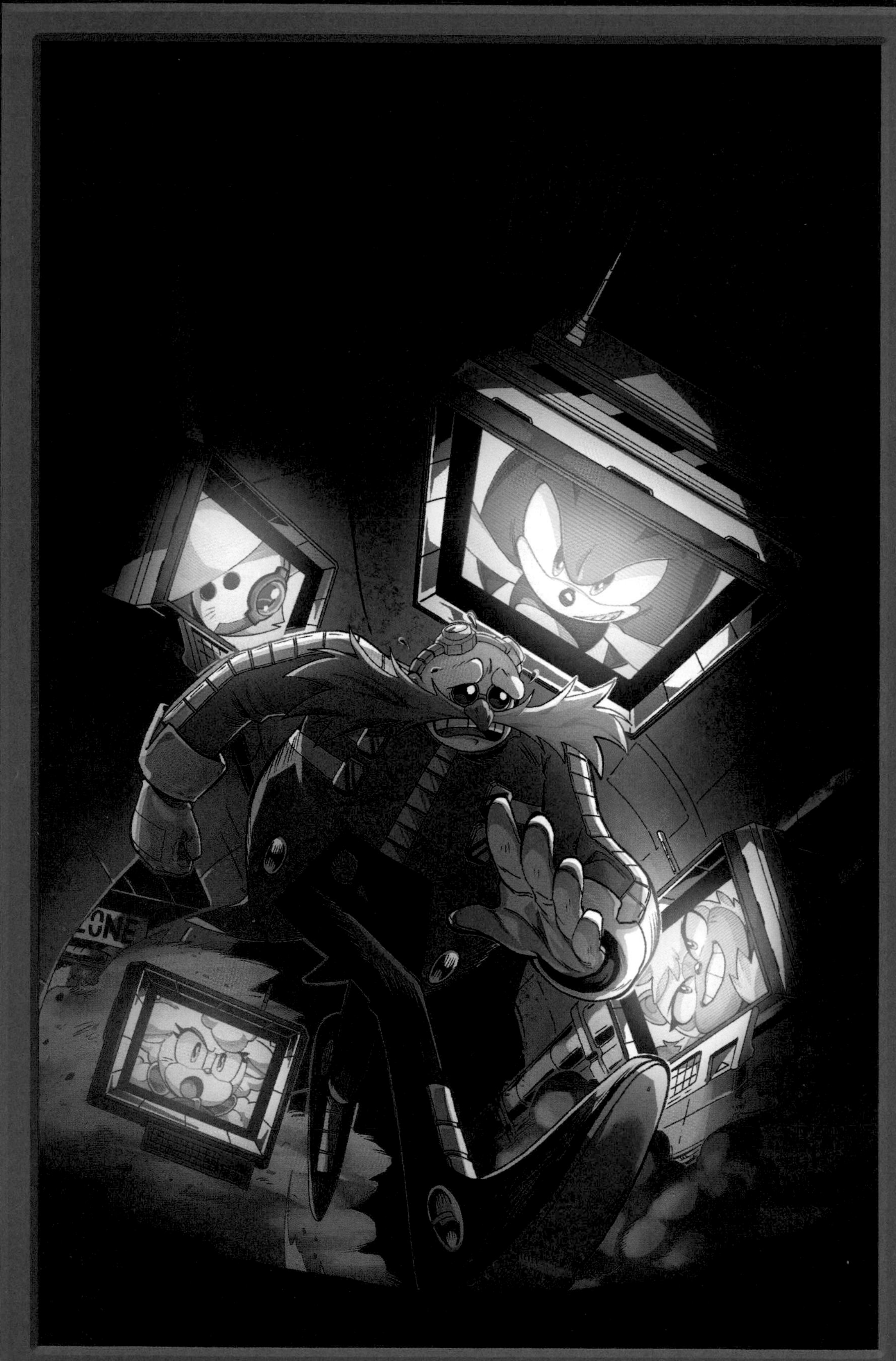

ART BY **MILES ARQ**

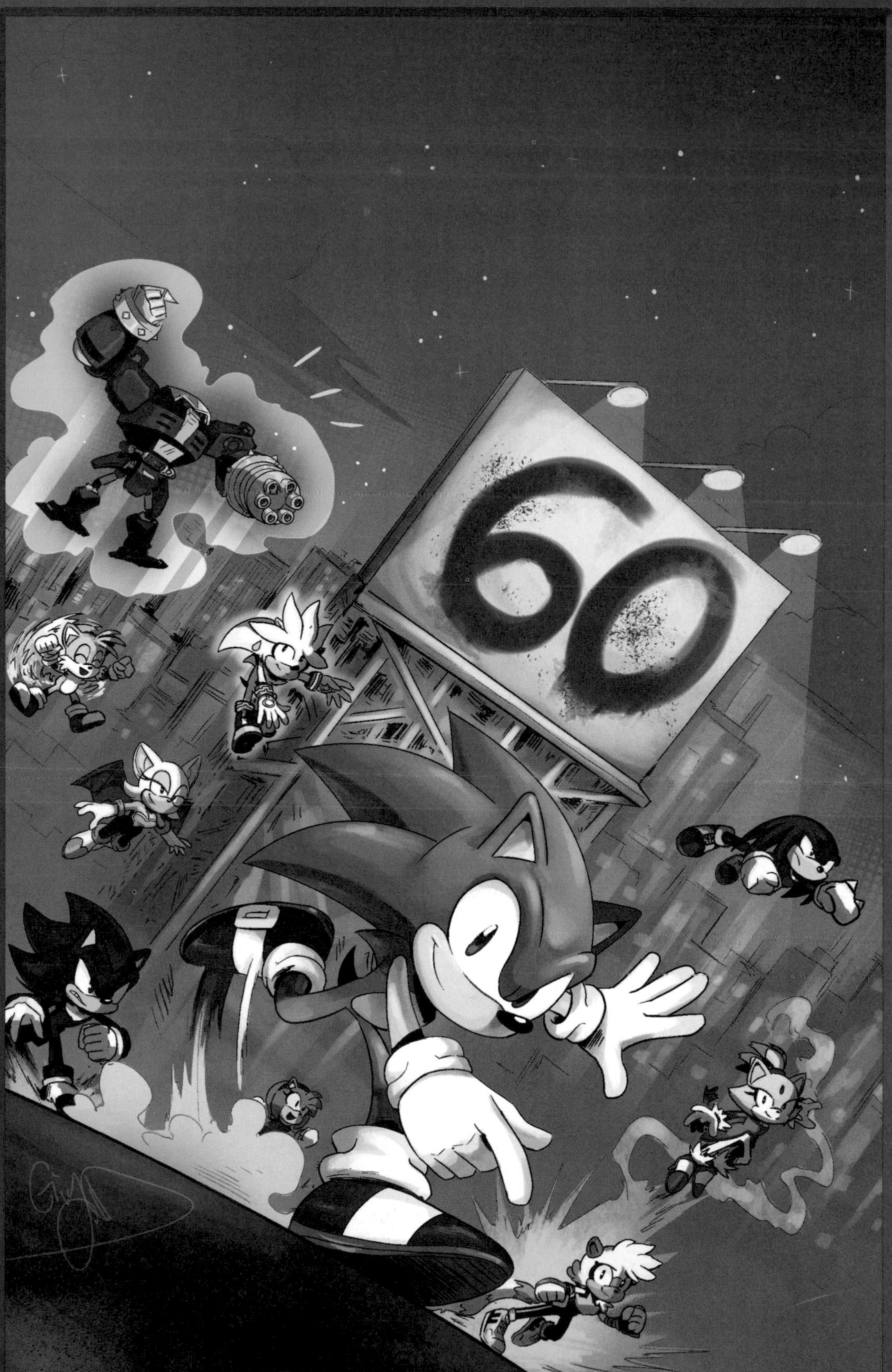
60

ART BY **GIGI DUTREIX**

SONIC™
THE HEDGEHOG

URBAN WARFARE

SEGA®

3 1901 10092 5116